Hollywood Bodies

J.R. Waterbear

Published by J.R. Waterbear, Burbank, California, 2024.

This is a work of fiction. Similarities to real people, places, or events are entirely coincidental.

HOLLYWOOD BODIES

First edition. September 1, 2024.

Copyright © 2024 J.R. Waterbear.

ISBN: 978-1964094038

Written by J.R. Waterbear.

To fine friends and musicians:

Stephen Hines

Albert Moreno

CHAPTER ONE

Hollywood, California 1987

Glenda Birdsong dragged herself home and pried off her high heels. She gratefully shucked off her clothing— Spandex leggings, a big belt and her favorite fifty-dollar Donna Karin blouse with great shoulder pads. The night wasn't entirely a disaster, she thought, but that was only because the night wasn't over. She knew she was an overachiever when it came to calamity. Her first date in a year had ended with Harold the hornbug accidentally lighting his chest hair on fire with a table candle at Miceli's. He'd been leaning over to tell her what the rabbi, the Irishman and the kangaroo were doing in a bar. Harold was lucky he hadn't died from polyester burns when his shirt began to smolder.

When they parted, Glenda had escaped Harold's octopus advances only to hit a nightclub on Sunset Boulevard, where she'd managed to have both feet stomped on within ten minutes. She had limped four blocks to her home with her wounded toes bulging from her high heels like overcooked sausages.

And then to top it off, Glenda had spent an hour on the phone ranting in futility at the answering machine of her producer, Bernie Sherman, who'd stolen her best song.

On the other hand, she consoled herself, it was less than two weeks until Halloween— her favorite holiday —and three until her probation officially ended. Then she would be free. She'd return to her passion and really work on restoring her rock career. Hell, she thought gleefully, maybe she'd become a total outlaw. She might even *jaywalk*.

So at least she was going to bed with a bright future, she thought to herself.

Then the phone rang.

"Glenda?" said a whiny voice. "We're in trouble. You gotta help me. You gotta get my dick."

"Who is this?"

"Larry," the voice said.

"Oh, no," Glenda said. "I can't talk to you. I'm still on probation."

"Don't hang up," he said, an edge of panic in his voice. "I heard you threaten him. The cops wouldn't like that."

"Threaten who?" Glenda asked.

"You know who," Larry replied snappishly. "The dead guy in the bathtub."

CHAPTER TWO

Glenda was taking a bubble bath, trying to wash away the stench of eau-de-Harold and burning chest hair while MTV's "Headbanger's Ball" pounded from the TV in her living room.

She wore a shower cap to protect her hair, a chestnut pile of curls that had led her dad to nickname her "Baby Buffalo." Glenda couldn't decide if her 'do was a heritage of his African ancestors or her mother's kinky Jewish red locks. Either way, she was proud of her Jewfro.

Her weight, not so much. Glenda didn't think of herself as fat. At five-nine, she could carry a few extra pounds. Or twenty. It just seemed to have snuck up on her. Of course, she'd have to lose a few pounds when her career restarted. It was rock, after all, and rock had never been kind to overweight singers— except Mealoaf. But then Glenda recalled the diet pills that had helped destroy her three years earlier. She shuddered despite the warmth of the bath.

She blew out a breath, expelling the ghosts, and sank, gratefully, deeper into the comforting broth of Clairol Herbal Essence.

Her belly crested the waterline. Glenda idly contemplated the pool in her navel. It was so deep, she reflected glumly, you could fish in it or do a remake of "Blue Lagoon"— although, Brooke Shields would probably drown.

She reached for the sponge, breathed the scented air and let out a sigh of perfect bliss— which ended with her gulping a mouthful of soapy water.

MTV had cut to a commercial, and Glenda suddenly heard her own song— the one she'd been working on for over a year— being played on a *xylophone!*

Coughing and spitting, she scrambled from the tub and stomped to the living room. She still wasn't finished with "In the Flow" and yet here it was, being used as a jingle in a diarrhea commercial.

A jingle in a diarrhea commercial!

She stared aghast at the TV screen. It showed skinny bitches playing tennis, petting dogs and jogging.

"Immo-Scorbate'" a kind, concerned voice intoned. "All you need to know to stop the flow. When you can't wait to wait."

"You bastard!" Glenda shrieked at the screen. She stood, naked and furious, dripping water and suds.

She swore at the TV until the tennis players flounced back to the court and joyfully swatted a tennis ball.

Suddenly, Glenda knew whose balls she wanted to smack. She grabbed for the phone. In as many words – and there were a lot of them – she told Bernie Sherman that she was going to murder him.

LARRY THE COKE DEALER burst out laughing as the crazy woman phoned again.

"Pick up the phone, Bernie, you sack of shit..."

The two men lying in the gold-painted emperor bed had a fit of the giggles until the tape machine finally cut off the rant.

Bernie Sherman thumbed tears from his eyes.

"Wow. Six times in, what, thirty minutes?" Larry said. "She always was persistent. Is she gonna call all night?"

"Who knows?" Bernie said. "Last week she did eighteen takes of a single lyric in one of her songs because she wanted the reverb just *so*. That's why she'll never finish her album. I swear to God, once she gets her jaws in something..."

"She's like a hyena on crack," Larry finished. "I mean, if hyenas did crack." He scratched his tousled surfer hair. "When I was a roadie and pharmacist for her band, she never asked for crack. I wouldn't sell it anyway; coke and pot only. Crack is a gateway drug. People need to watch what they put in their bodies."

He gave Bernie a sideways glance of disapproval. The man had always been lean, but now he had a hollowed-out look. A baroque dressing gown failed to conceal his sunken chest.

Bernie snorted. "Pass me the mirror." He snorted another line. "Anyways," he continued, "she's got no reason to bitch. I have the legal right to give her songs to anybody I want. She's burning up studio time and she hasn't produced squat. And I've got expenses." He rubbed his nose with the back of his hand.

The telephone rang.

"Here she goes again," Larry said. The answering machine gave its greeting and beeped. But the caller wasn't Glenda.

"Bernie," said a soft male voice. "What have you done?"

Bernie lunged for the handset on the nightstand and jammed it to his ear. He listened silently for a full minute before protesting: "No, no. It's not like that." Larry recognized the tone. Bernie was in sneaky-bastard mode. But Bernie looked worried.

"It's nothing like that!" Bernie said vehemently. "I don't know where you heard... listen, hold on a second, okay?" Bernie put a hand over the mouthpiece and looked at Larry, who was pretending hard not to be listening— and failing.

"Hey, time for you to hit the road. I'm gonna be busy here."

"I'll wait downstairs," Larry said.

Bernie waved a hand dismissively.

"Nope. I gotta concentrate. Just take off."

Larry began to protest again, but Bernie cut him short.

"Fuck off, Larry. Right now," he said sharply, and his face darkened. "Grab your shit and go. I'll see you later."

Larry bolted off the bed, grabbed his pants and left the room, slamming the door. He stomped down the staircase and dressed on the Persian rug in the living room under the gaze of a dozen Buddhas displayed on the mantel. Bernie had apparently told his decorator to recreate a Burmese junk shop. The room was cluttered with Oriental artifacts, wall-mounted daggers and masks of dark wood. The floor was a minefield of potted palms, carpets and black teak furniture smothered by embroidered silk pillows. However, Larry saw bare spots on the walls. Bernie had been selling artwork to feed his coke habit. Larry felt a twinge of guilt that some of Bernie's money had gone to fund his merchandise. But, Larry reasoned, at least his stuff was clean.

Larry suddenly remembered that Bernie had yet to pay him. There was at least a gram left up there. *Screw this,* he decided. He turned around abruptly and was about to stride purposefully to the staircase when he tripped over an ottoman and went sprawling into a pot-bellied statue of Ganesha. The big, gaudy piece toppled with a thump. The elephant's big eyes glared at him.

"Sorry, man," Larry said, staggering to his feet. He tried to lug the statue upright but it seemed to weigh a hundred pounds.

Larry patted the tusked head and gave up. He was ruining his exit. Best now, maybe, to let it go. Bernie was in one of his moods, after all. Besides, Larry had his pride. If Bernie kicked him out, then forget him; Mr. Sherman could just be deprived of his glorious company. The more he thought about it, Larry reckoned he was damned if he would go back up there.

Besides, if he pissed Bernie off, Larry might not see him for a week. He might even find somebody else to fill his prescriptions. And then Bernie's repeated promise to put Larry in a band would disappear as fast as a toot up Bernie's nose.

But it was mainly pride that propelled Larry out the door, down the driveway and into his car.

It took almost a half-hour before he changed his mind.

CHAPTER THREE

Glenda's heart hammered as she squelched up the steps to Bernie's front door. Being here was creepy. Thanks to the drizzle, her hair was a rat's nest. She didn't want to do this. She didn't want to sneak around the house. She was breaking all kinds of laws, not to mention shredding her probation. But what she'd yelled on the phone to Bernie might not sound, well, innocent to the cops. Or even rational.

Most of all, though, Glenda didn't want to be at Bernie's house because she didn't want to see Bernie. It had been horrible enough when Larry had described what was waiting there.

She slogged up the driveway to the front door. Larry had warned her that there was water gushing from the house. Now she saw it was spilling eerily from under the front door and down the steps.

Glenda nerved herself as she pulled a pair of yellow dishwashing gloves from her raincoat and tugged them on. They went to her elbows but they were the only gloves she owned, and she didn't want to leave fingerprints. Larry had said the door was unlocked, which also seemed odd.

Like everything else tonight, she thought.

Cautiously, Glenda grabbed the handle and opened the front door. The living room was a palatial bog. The floor was covered by a sheen of water glistening in the porch light.

The air was clammy; the heating must be off.

Glenda navigated around water-logged furnishings that bulked ominously. A toppled elephant statue had a trunk like a water snake arching above the flood. She noticed empty spaces on the cluttered walls and a gap in a row of Buddha statues on the mantel. The Buddhas— Glenda nervously counted eleven —seemed to leer disapprovingly at her with their enlightened eyes as if to say: *Girl, you are messing with your karma.*

David Bowie should write a song about this place, Glenda decided. "Scary Monsters" indeed.

Water coursed down the stairs from the second floor. Glenda looked up; it was pitch black at the top. She gripped the banister tightly and went up. As she ascended, she heard two things: Madonna on a TV and the sound of splashing water.

At the landing, Glenda paused. To her left, a dozen feet away, a bar of light escaped from beneath a closed door and shone on the carpet. Water oozed from under the door.

Glenda *really* didn't want to go there.

Like I have a choice? she reminded herself.

Madonna was through singing about the pretty island by the time Glenda steeled herself to move. She inched forward. The narrow, shadowed darkness made her think of *The Shining*. But if what Larry had said was right, Bernie was in no shape to attack her with an ax.

Glenda shook her head. She had a tendency to babble when she was nervous, yet here she was with nobody around, babbling in her own skull. She shook her head to clear it of bullshit. She was supposed to get in and out, not linger. In and out, before somebody called the cops.

For an instant, Glenda imagined trying to explain what she was doing in a drenched house, wearing rubber gloves. Especially given what the police would find up here...

A jolt of adrenalin pushed her forward. She made it to the door, took a breath, and opened it.

Bernie's bedroom. A big color TV sat in a corner. Whatever music video program had been on was over. Now there was a guy demonstrating some kind of magic potato peeler.

The room contained an enormous bed, painted gold and about as tasteless as Glenda would have expected from Bernie. The midnight-blue silk sheets were rumpled and dusted with white powder. She wondered if it was dandruff or baby powder or coke. Given the quantity, all three choices troubled her. Water gushed from an en suite bathroom. The bathroom door stood slightly open.

Through it, Glenda saw a scalloped sink set into a pink-and-grey marble countertop below a gold-framed oval mirror. On the counter, two fleecy towels were neatly folded. Next to them a tidy row of colognes and oils stood in expensive ranks next to a gold-handled razor and a cheap black comb.

All very normal. Which Glenda knew this was not.

Larry had warned her not to look in the bathroom. Glenda told herself she didn't *want* to look in the bathroom. But what Larry had described was so bizarre, she had to explore. She edged over hesitantly, the way people do when they know they shouldn't be doing what they're doing— and so taking twice as long to do the thing and doing it clumsily.

She closed her eyes, took a breath and pushed the door wide. She counted to three, then to five, and at ten forced herself to open her eyes.

Bernie was mooning her.

Glenda caught a glimpse of his dead white buttocks protruding from a claw-footed bathtub. Water cascaded over the lip of the tub onto the marble floor.

Water poured from the gold-plated tap. The sound echoed loudly in the tiled room.

Folded over the edge of the tub, Bernie lay with his head in the water. He'd clearly been dead for some time, judging by the amount of water flowing through the house. Glenda took another step into the bathroom but then stopped. She had no desire to see Bernie's face. She imagined something like the expression on a dead and bloated goldfish. Her stomach lurched. She swallowed hard. There was no blood in the overflowing tub, but streaks and spatters of blood decorated the tiles above it.

Glenda thought Bernie must have slipped, thumped his head on the tiling and tumbled over into the filling tub. He'd probably been knocked goofy and drowned. She instinctively wanted to turn off the faucet but realized that would seem odd to the police, so she backed carefully out of the bathroom, panting as if she'd just run a race.

She turned and looked around the bedroom. The room was high-ceilinged and decorated like a cut-rate Versailles. The wallpaper was gold and white, so was the furniture, and the lighting came from a crystal chandelier that would have made Liberace gag. The TV was ensconced in a Louis Quatorze-style wardrobe.

On the ceiling over the bed— of course —a large mirror had been secured.

Glenda spotted the answering machine on a bedside table. In this wedding-cake room, its functional black shape made it seem like an alien artifact.

Her stomach churned.

She went to the table. On it were the answering machine, the TV remote control, a white Princess phone and a square, gilt-framed mirror on which lay a razor blade. A large empty plastic baggie had fallen on the soggy carpet.

Glenda thought about playing the answering machine tape to check whether her threatening calls were still on it. She could just erase them. But she couldn't afford to waste time fiddling with the unfamiliar machine. She already felt as if she'd been in this house for a century, and she didn't want to remain another second. In her imagination, Glenda could already hear the scream of a police siren.

She decided simply to snatch the cassette. She opened the lid of the answering machine and removed the tape, stuffing it quickly into her raincoat pocket. Then it occurred to her that she probably should replace it. A blank tape would be less suspicious than no tape. Glenda opened the drawer of the nightstand and found a couple of fresh cassettes. She grabbed one, unwrapped it and stuck it into the machine, then turned to go before catching herself.

She cursed. She'd nearly forgotten Larry's dick.

She rummaged through the drawers of both nightstands as neatly as she could, but found nothing. The same was true of the TV cabinet, the dresser and the liquor cabinet. She even got down on the floor to peer under the bed. All she got for her trouble were cold, soggy knees.

Minutes were flying by, Glenda thought anxiously, and here she was playing burglar. She turned at last to the walk-in closet and flicked on the light. The closet was nearly the size of her apartment and stuffed with suits. The shelves held dozens of hats and shoes. She rummaged among the shelves, sliding out the built-in drawers to display neat rows of socks, underwear and silk handkerchiefs.

This was all taking too much time.

Screw Larry, Glenda thought. She was through playing find-the-salami, no matter what she'd promised him.

At the rear of the closet was a full-length mirror. Glenda saw her own hefty figure, hands absurdly clad in yellow gloves. She approached the mirror and saw smudges on one side of the panel. She put her gloved palm on the spot and pressed. A click sounded, and the side of the mirror moved outward. Glenda pulled, and the panel swung smoothly forward on hidden hinges. Lights automatically went on, revealing shelves.

Arranged neatly on two shelves, like trophies, were at least two dozen penises.

Glenda gave a start. It took her a moment before she realized what they were, which was the largest collection of dildos she had ever seen.

The dildos were in an amazing range of colors, from flesh tones to spring green to a painful plum. Some were gold or silver. Several were made of some clear material swimming with golden flecks, like wealthy sperm. Aside from that, the objects looked disturbingly realistic.

Glenda finally recovered herself and got down to business.

Which one belonged to Larry?

Each dildo stood to attention on the shelf. Glenda wished Bernie had labeled them or put up brass plaques underneath each one, like in a museum.

Time was ticking away. She decided to just grab them all and sort them out later— which would certainly make for an interesting evening.

She grabbed one at random, then turned it over. There *was* a label, affixed to the bottom of the shaft. It read "Axl."

Glenda ran through "Freddie," "Duke," "Javier" and "Dasheel" before she finally found Larry's dong. Only then did she realize the faux penises were arranged in order of ascending size. For a small man, Larry was impressive, Glenda thought. From the looks of it, he was hung somewhere between a buffalo and a killer whale.

Glenda grabbed the dildo. It was surprisingly soft and rubbery and wobbled a bit as she stashed it in her raincoat pocket. She swung the mirror back in place and scuttled from the room. She barely avoided tumbling down the slippery stairs and sloshed to the front door, her feet making little sucking sounds on the inundated carpet.

On the way home, Glenda tried to blot out the image of the bathtub and of Bernie's sodden and undignified final salute.

CHAPTER FOUR

A half-hour after leaving Bernie's house, Larry changed his mind and turned his car around. He was rehearsing a confrontation with Bernie in his head when he almost collided with a car coming down the hill.

The Cadillac screeched around a blind corner, swerved just in time, and missed Larry's 1971 powder-blue Thunderbird by inches. The driver leaned on the horn. Larry gave him the finger.

He reached a turnout at the top of the grade. He glanced for a second at the panoramic view of downtown that was now blurred by patches of moving mist. The Hollywood Hills were definitely the place to be if you wanted to look down on people, Larry thought. And if they tried to look back, your average rich guy could retreat back inside for privacy, surrounded by gates and security cameras while still feeling close to nature— that is, imported Italian pines and canyons full of poodle-eating coyotes.

Larry rolled his big boat of a car to a halt in the curving driveway.

He got out and walked to the house, wishing he'd brought a jacket. It was cold and cloudy. Last year at this time, two weeks before Halloween, there had been Santa Ana winds. The temperature had hit ninety degrees, and the air was so dry it made his skin crack.

The driveway was a loop. The top end connected to a brick walkway, so slippery Larry almost tumbled. That was odd, he thought, because it hadn't rained yet. When he reached the steps, he saw a sheet of water cascading from beneath the heavy oak front door.

He got an uncomfortable feeling, like somebody putting an ice cube down his back. He climbed the steps to the porch, trying hard to keep his sneakers from getting soaked. He pressed the intercom button.

"Bernie? It's Larry. You awake?"

No answer.

"Bernie?" Larry waited. "Okay," he said at last.

He gave a tentative knock on the door, barely a tap, then grabbed the wrought-iron handle.

The door was unlocked.

Cautiously, Larry opened it.

"Bernie?" he asked.

Three minutes later, as the mist turned to a heavy drizzle, Larry zoomed toward Hollywood Boulevard. Wrapped around his wrist was a gleaming gold Rolex.

The Thunderbird was doing fifty when Larry heard a siren whoop. Glancing in the rear-view mirror, he saw flashing blue and red lights.

He swore, hit the brakes, and the car slewed on the road. Larry straightened it out and pulled to the curb under a streetlight across from the Capitol Records building, its spire haloed with fog.

He heard the squawk of the police radio and the slam of the patrol car doors. His palms were damp as he clutched the steering wheel. He rolled the window down as two cops came up, one on either side of the T-bird. They were big and crew-cut and kept their hands on their holsters. Their breath plumed.

"Hello, Larry," said one, leaning down to peer in the window. "What a surprise to see you out and about on this lovely night. Where you headed?"

"Just home," Larry mumbled.

"Well, that's a good idea. This chilly weather. You want to be home, snuggled up with a good book and a cup of cocoa..."

"And a line of coke," his partner finished.

"No, no, not Larry," said the first cop, whose nametag read Moon. "Larry doesn't do lines. Buckets, maybe."

The other cop, whose tag said Moreno, laughed.

"Look, guys, it's been a long night. Just give me the ticket, okay?"

Moon looked at Moreno. They both made exaggerated faces of puzzlement.

"What for, Lare? D'jya do somethin' wrong?"

"Naw," Moreno said, walking over to join his partner. "Larry's a good citizen."

"Hollywood's finest," Moon agreed.

"Finest something, for sure," Moreno said.

"Look, guys, I don't have to take this," Larry said, his leg jumping nervously. "Just give me the ticket and make your quota, okay?"

Moon sighed. "Okay, Larry. Here's the deal. We saw you blasting that heap down Vine Street. You almost bottomed at the end of the hill, and then you blew through the light at Franklin. You're just lucky the weather kept a lot of folks indoors. Now why were you in such a hurry?"

"Maybe he's making a delivery?" Moreno suggested.

"I'm clean," Larry protested.

"Yeah. Like last time," Moon said. "So you wouldn't mind if we searched your trunk, then?"

Larry hunched his shoulders and held the steering wheel in a death grip.

"Do you what you gotta do," he said in a near-whisper. Larry waited as the two policemen rifled the trunk.

"Hey," Moon called. "Didn't I see these socks in here last time?"

"Sure smells like it," Moreno said.

Finally, the officers slammed the trunk lid. Moon strolled over to Larry.

"Told you I was clean," Larry said.

"Well, I wouldn't go that far," Moon said. "Do you ever do your laundry?"

"The Boy Scout uniform looked clean," Moreno said.

"Yeah, I don't really want to know about that," Moon said.

"It's for Halloween," Larry said. "Are you guys done?"

"Guess so. Just wish I knew what was making you so jumpy." Moon produced his flashlight, a foot of black metal, and held it in his fist as if he were going to stab Larry with it. The cop clicked it on and Larry flinched away from the glare.

"Let's see your eyes," Moon said. He played the light over Larry's face, then snapped it off and shook his head at his partner. Moon leaned over again. Larry nervously tapped his fingers on the steering wheel. He felt Moon's eyes on him like chips of blue marble.

At last, Moon straightened up.

"Well, Larry, it's cold and I need a donut. So we'll let you go home. But try to drive safe, okay? This rain might get heavy."

Larry puffed out his cheeks in relief.

"Thanks, guys." He turned the key and the V8 rumbled to life.

Moon turned his back and took a couple of steps. Then he stopped, turned around and walked back to the car. He leaned down and looked at Larry.

"There's just one more thing, Larry," Moon said. He pointed at Larry's wrist. "Where'd you get the watch?"

"The watch?" Larry asked. His nose gave a rabbity twitch.

"That thing on your wrist that goes tick-tick," Moon said. "You didn't have it last time we ran into each other."

"I didn't have to be anywhere," Larry said.

"What?"

"I didn't have an appointment. So I didn't need to know what time it was."

"But you needed to know tonight?"

"Well, I did. Earlier. Not now." Larry glanced at the watch. "You know what *time* it is?"

"What I mean, Larry," Moon pressed, "is what appointment *did* you have tonight?"

Larry swallowed hard, as if dislodging a chunk of objectionable food. "I ... met a friend. We played bongos."

"Bongos?" Moreno called out in disbelief. "Did he just say *bongos*?"

"We drummed," Larry said defensively. "I'm a percussionist."

"Oh, so you percussed with a guy," Moreno said. "Is he a Boy Scout?"

"I told you..." Larry began, but Moon stuck out his hand.

"May I see the watch, please?" he asked.

"My watch?"

"Please."

"It's not for sale," Larry said.

"I'm not interested in buying it..." Moon began.

"Besides, you already have a watch," Larry pointed out.

Moon straightened again, raising his hands in exasperation. Then he bent back to Larry.

"I just want to jot down the serial number, Larry. You know, in case you lose it. Or somebody else lost it. I'll give it right back."

Cautiously, Larry unfastened the clasp and handed over the Rolex. It gleamed in the streetlight.

Moon took out his notebook, turned the watch over and began writing. Then he handed it back.

"You know, Larry, this reminds me of a joke," Moon said.

"I like jokes," Larry said nervously.

"It goes like this," Moon said. "This yuppie is in a car crash. Totals his car. He's lying on the ground, groaning, when the ambulance arrives. He asks the ambulance guy: 'What happened?'

"'You've been in a car accident,' the guy says. The yuppie looks over at his car, and moans: 'My Mercedes! My Mercedes!'

"'My God, man, forget about your car,' the ambulance guy says. 'You've been hurt. Your whole left arm's been ripped off.' The yuppie looks over at where his arm should be, his eyes go wide and he says: 'My Rolex! My Rolex!'"

Larry looked at Moon blankly.

"It's a *joke*, Larry," Moon said.

Larry still appeared puzzled. Moon and Moreno eyed each other. They shook their heads and went back to their patrol car.

When they finally let him go, Larry drove straight home. He didn't understand cops. Why would anybody laugh about a serious auto accident where somebody lost their *arm*?

The thought made him queasy. To settle his stomach, he made himself an instant hot cocoa with mini-marshmallows. He looked at the watch.

Larry had panicked when he'd seen Bernie's body. Instinctively, he'd taken the watch on the bathroom counter— well, Bernie owed him, after all —and then scuttled the hell out of there. Now, as Larry's probing lips snared a mini-marshmallow, he suddenly realized the police probably were going to find Bernie's body soon. Bernie had a housekeeper who came in every couple of days. She'd find Bernie and call the cops. Well, he thought, first she'd probably scream or faint. *Then* she'd call the cops.

Larry wasn't sure the cleaning lady knew anything about his relationship with Bernie. He'd never seen her. Which was just as well, because Larry wasn't sure the officers of the law would be understanding about things like that.

After all, they told jokes about maimed accident victims...

He was licking a chocolate mustache from his upper lip when a horrible thought hit him.

He'd left behind a damning piece of evidence. It would prove he'd had a— *close* —relationship with the dead man.

Larry froze with a gooey marshmallow stuck in his teeth. He felt a sudden icy grip around his heart.

He had to get the— what was the word, incriminating? —item out of Bernie's house.

But he couldn't go back to Bernie's place. Too risky. The police already had stopped him once tonight, and not too far from Bernie's house.

Somebody else would have to go. But who?

It took another three cups of cocoa for him to figure it out. He had an idea. And he had some leverage to use. Larry called information. The number he needed was listed.

He hung up and dialed again.

"Glenda?" Larry said in a whiny voice. "We're in trouble. You gotta help me. You gotta get my dick."

CHAPTER FIVE

Dawn was only a couple of hours off as Glenda drove up to her apartment building on Formosa Avenue. The overcast sky was gray and pink, like undercooked meat.

Glenda owned the four-unit stucco building. That and a tired Porsche were the only things she had managed to salvage from her once high-flying musical career.

The lobby of the Casa Grande smelled of greasy soup and age. The building had probably been classy back in the days when gents with Brylcreemed hair escorted women with seamed stockings to some hoped-for rendezvous. But these were the eighties, and now the grand lady was a dowager, her entry tiles shoe-worn, and her walls yellowed to the color of old lace no matter how many coats of paint had been slapped on her. No chrome and black leather for this lady but there was a backyard with a square of grass just big enough for a table and lawn chairs. Glenda charged her tenants a couple hundred dollars a month and usually cleared enough to buy cigarettes.

Her tenants were a Polish plumber who pronounced his name Sarack but spelled it only with consonants; a sweet, half-blind retired manicurist named, naturally, Blanche; and the Potreros. Mrs. Potrero made the best menudo in the neighborhood. Mr. Potrero kept a rooster in the backyard. The rooster thought midnight was sunrise. Sometimes it crowed at random— but never at sunrise. Glenda had complained and warned him to get rid of the bird, but Mr. Potrero had pleaded that El Guapo had saved his wife's life, crowing to alert him that she was being swept away when they'd crossed the Rio Grande. Every so often Mr. Potrero vanished with the bird, and it was a slightly different color when it returned. Mr. Potrero swore he took it to be groomed. Anyway, he always paid the rent on time, in cash, in small bills.

Trudging up the narrow stairs to her second-floor apartment, Glenda grunted with fatigue, trying to be as quiet as she could. She unlocked her door, stepped inside and closed it. She took the rubber gloves and Larry's dick from her pockets and tossed them onto the little table by the door where she kept her mail.

She shrugged out of her raincoat, letting it drop on the floor and staggered to her bedroom, barely taking time to kick off her boots before flopping face down onto the bed.

Letting the tension of the night drop from her like a stone, she relaxed. Her shoulders eased. The dreamless, delicious dark welcomed her.

She was jolted awake by a squawking metallic shriek. It sounded like a tour bus sideswiping a freeway guardrail. It came again and again. Outside her window, El Guapo was welcoming the new day. Glenda cursed. For the first time ever, the lousy, chronologically challenged bird was on time.

CHAPTER SIX

Glenda, living on two hours of sleep, walked east on Hollywood Boulevard to her job. Between El Guapo and her nightmares, she'd had a rough night. Every time she had tried to sleep, she'd dreamed of Bernie flopping out of the tub and gasping on the marble floor. Then it was Harold the hornbug in the tub, face up in his polyester shirt, his chest hair smoldering. In the dream, Harold gave off a charcoal smell like a grilled halibut.

Glenda's office was on north Sycamore Avenue, just off Hollywood Boulevard and only six blocks from home. She didn't use her car for work, which in L.A. made her not just a freak, but a pedestrian. She had refused to give up her precious vehicle, a signal red 1964 Porsche 356— the same model as Janis Joplin's. But Glenda also couldn't afford to get a ticket— red sports cars were like red flags to cops— and she couldn't pay for repairs if something happened to it. So the car mostly lived in her carport.

As usual, Glenda stopped off for breakfast at the Vietnamese donut shop. She collected a dozen for the office and, as usual, Mister Pham threw in an extra jelly donut Glenda knew would never make it to the office door.

She licked her fingers guiltily as she shouldered open the bronze-and-glass door into the lobby of the Gillespie Building. It had once been Gillespie Savings and Trust, but the marble walls were dingy. A directory board listing a half-dozen talent agencies, some would-be casting agents and a lone dentist covered one side.

Gould & Troutman Talent Agency occupied space on the second floor. Flaking gold on a wooden door announced its presence. Gould was deceased. Troutman had hired Glenda because he thought she might get him some music industry clients. So far, she'd not met his expectations in that regard, but she did have a certain genius for office work, bringing sanity to Troutman's chaotic accounting system. Glenda also had a knack for dealing with the agency's bread-and-butter clients: clowns, magicians, balloon artists and pony wranglers for children's parties.

She tried the knob and found the door was unlocked. It usually was. Saul Troutman was always first in and last out of the agency. Glenda suspected he slept there.

Troutman was paunchy and pushing sixty from the wrong side. He wore a suit so old and creased, it looked like someone had been buried in it. But his eyes twinkled behind silver-rimmed spectacles. He was annoyingly chipper.

"Ah hah! The donut queen arrives!" Troutman said. Troutman said it every morning.

"Morning, Max."

Glenda set the donuts on Troutman's desk and made a beeline for the coffee pot. The only plus side to her boss's morning energy was that he usually made the coffee. Glenda picked up a chipped mug, filled it and carried to her desk, which was about ten feet from Troutman's.

A third desk was empty. Trina, the part-timer, was off today.

Troutman tried to look busy until Glenda settled herself, then asked: "So, Glenda, how are you this morning?"

"Good," Glenda said.

"You look a little tired. Late night?"

"Something like that." Glenda sipped the coffee gratefully. It was black and strong.

Troutman gave her a knowing look.

"When did you get in?"

Glenda looked up. "Why do you want to know?"

Troutman put up his hands. "You're right, you're right. It's none of my business." Then he gave her a sly smile. "How's my nephew Harold?"

Glenda gritted her teeth. "I don't know."

"Okay, okay."

"We didn't sleep together," Glenda said. "We had dinner, I went home, I stayed up late, I went to bed very late and then I got woken up too early by a rooster."

Troutman nodded. "A rooster," he said.

"Yes."

He beamed. "Got it."

"Can we get to work now, Max?"

"Of course. Of course." Troutman shuffled papers on his desk for a moment.

"So," he said, still looking busy. "When are you and the rooster getting together again?"

"Oh, for God's sake!" Glenda said.

"Okay, okay already. Not my business. I got it!"

"And stop smirking!"

"Sorry." Troutman reached for a chocolate éclair, examined it with a connoisseur's eye, then stuffed half of it into his mouth.

"So," he mumbled. "First thing, we need more clowns. I got a call from a Hollywood guy, Sal somebody, did some shark movies. He's got a Halloween party."

"Let me guess," Glenda said. "He wants killer clowns." Stephen King's novel *It* had come out a year earlier and since then, everybody wanted to hire Pennywise at Halloween.

"How many does he want?" Glenda asked.

"Baker's dozen."

"Thirteen?" Glenda said. "A week before Halloween?"

"He's paying four thousand dollars," Troutman said.

"I don't care if he pays a million," Glenda said. "It's not possible. Every single regular has a killer clown gig that night already. You know that, Max."

Troutman made a soothing gesture. "They don't have to be performers. He just wants waiters. Call around, get some costumes, find some people..."

"I can just about guarantee that every costume shop from here to Bakersfield has sold out of clown costumes. Max, come on!" Glenda felt a headache coming on, and it was only nine in the morning.

"I know you can do it," Troutman said. "You got magic." He gulped down the last bite of éclair, wiped filling from his chin and got to his feet. He picked up a battered briefcase and shuffled to the door.

"Where are you going?" Glenda asked. "You're not going to help me?"

"Oh, didn't I tell you?" Troutman said. "I got a plane to catch. My niece, Carol, is getting married in Toronto. I ask you, who's gonna go to a wedding in Canada in October? She'll have polar bears for bridesmaids." Troutman grabbed his hat from a stand near the door.

"You can't leave!" Glenda said.

Troutman gave her a kindly look. "You're in charge, kid," he said. "I trust you. I'll be checking in, and I'll be back next week."

He winked and went out.

"Schmuck!" Glenda cursed under her breath. She got up, went over to Troutman's desk, picked up the box of donuts in a death grip, brought them back to her own desk, slammed them down, grabbed the telephone receiver and got to work.

She managed to find six clowns before calling it a day. It was four o'clock. She was exhausted, frazzled and blitzed on sugar and coffee. The empty donut box stared at her accusingly.

She locked up and walked home.

GLENDA DROPPED HER purse on the floor and kicked off her shoes. She was overtired and her nerves jangled. She crossed the living room, giving a rueful glance at Banshee in the corner. Her beloved guitar was shark-tailed and blood red. Even just sitting there on its stand, the instrument seemed to be sneering. She felt a twinge of guilt. That guitar reminded her of a neglected lover. But at the moment, Glenda's brain and limbs refused to do any work. Instead, she flopped down in front of the TV, which was permanently tuned to MTV. She stared at the screen without really watching, occasionally dozing. The day was moving on into evening before Glenda actually got around to playing Bernie's answering machine tape. She did it out of curiosity, to see how crazy she had sounded.

Besides, she could come up with some good lines when she was pissed; maybe there were lyrics somewhere in her ranting. She remembered calling Bernie a "Vinyl Vampire." That would make a great title for a song— maybe even an album. Glenda might feel a bit guilty about trashing Bernie, given that he was dead.

On the other hand, so was Stalin.

Glenda picked up the cassette from the little table and put it into her Phone-Mate.

She hit the button.

She heard *nothing*.

"What the hell?" Glenda said to herself. She took out the tape, turned it over, reinserted it, hit the button.

Nothing except an empty hiss.

Glenda pulled the tape and looked at it closely. Had Bernie erased it? Why would he? Larry? No reason for him to erase it, either.

Turning the cassette upside down, she looked closely at the thin strip of magnetic tape. She got a pencil, inserted it into one of the little gear-toothed sprockets and wound the tape back and forth.

There were no tiny scratches, and the shiny gloss hadn't been rubbed off.

The tape, Glenda realized, was new and unused.

Somebody had done what she'd just done: removed the cassette from Bernie's machine and inserted a fresh one from the drawer.

That meant someone had been in the house *after* Larry left and *before* Glenda arrived; Someone who didn't want something on the tape to be heard.

Glenda shook her head. It was ridiculous. She was no Columbo. Her detective skills began and ended with clown-wrangling.

And yet...

Somebody had wanted to hide *something*. Otherwise, why mess with the tape?

It might have been the mysterious caller Larry had mentioned. Glenda made a mental note to ask Larry what the caller had sounded like.

Okay, Glenda mused, *what was that person hiding?*

Then a worse thought hit her.

What had he *done*?

Ridiculous. Bernie had slipped and fallen and drowned. This wasn't a cheap murder mystery.

A voice in her head chimed in: *Wasn't it?*

Suddenly Glenda needed a cigarette, even though she'd promised herself she was going to quit. She fished a half-empty pack out of her jacket pocket, hoping for Camels. They were Silva Thins. Glenda couldn't remember buying them; maybe she had snagged them off someone's desk somewhere. The Silva Thins ad boasted: "Cigarettes are like women. The best ones are thin and rich." Glenda was neither. She wondered what cigarette was the equivalent of a hefty, broke girl.

She took a couple of puffs, tasting menthol and not much else. She crushed it out. Coming on top of her jittery exhaustion, the cigarette nauseated her. She was mixing nicotine with fatigue poisons. Deciding she should eat something, she rummaged in the fridge and found leftover Chinese in a little white carry-out box. That would make it three days old. It smelled like garlic and old shoes. Glenda didn't care. She wrenched the plastic spork from the carton and dug in, chewing cold meat coated in gluey brown sauce.

What should she do now? Whatever suspicions she had about Bernie's death were probably bullshit fantasies. She sure wasn't going to call the police, at least until she knew what had happened to her phone messages. The other visitor could have erased them. But then again, what if that *someone* had Glenda's angry, murderous rants sitting in his pocket?

In effect, he'd be carrying around the key to her prison cell.

Glenda finished the food and came to a decision. Although the thought almost made her sick with anxiety, she would have to go back and search Bernie's house before someone called the cops— if they hadn't already. She broke out in a cold sweat. If she got caught, she would be charged with violating her probation. She could wind up spending the next three years of her life in a room tastefully outfitted in concrete and metal bars. The thought made her stomach churn. She needed to make sure, if she could, that her tape wasn't at Bernie's place.

But she wasn't going to go alone this time.

Glenda glanced at the table by the door, piled high with bills and junk mail. Jutting from it, like the prow of a ship, was Larry's dong.

CHAPTER SEVEN

"These gloves don't fit," Larry said in a stage whisper.

"They're all I had," Glenda hissed back.

"This is kidnapping *and* blackmail," Larry complained. He tugged fretfully at the yellow dish gloves as they slunk under the police tape and into Bernie Sherman's house. Glenda held the flashlight and led the way. The carpeting still squished underfoot and smelled dank.

"I didn't kidnap you," Glenda said.

"You're holding my crotch cannon hostage."

"I told you, you'll get it back as soon as we're done."

"It's one of a kind."

"I sure hope so."

They stumbled through the cluttered living room.

"What was he doing with all this stuff?" Glenda asked as she barked a knee on a carved footstool.

"He was into that Eastern stuff," Larry said. "He got his religion from George Harrison and his coke habit from Keith Richards."

"And his decorating taste from Elton John," Glenda said.

They went up the stairs and stood before Bernie's bedroom. The door was ajar. Glenda pushed it open and swept the room with the flashlight beam. Heavy brocade drapes covered the windows. Satisfied the glow from their flashlights wouldn't be seen from outside, Glenda fumbled for the switch.

The crystal chandelier blazed to life. The room looked much the same as Glenda remembered it, but police investigators had evidently been at work. The cocaine-dusted bed sheets were gone along with the drug paraphernalia from the bedside table. Glenda glanced through the open door of the bathroom. The tub was empty, but merely looking at it made her spine crawl. She turned away quickly and walked over to the answering machine beside the bed. She pressed the playback button. The room filled with the noise of tape hiss. Glenda was satisfied it was the same new tape she'd swapped into the machine. But she had to make sure the original cassette wasn't still in the room somewhere.

She hadn't seen a used tape during her first visit, but then, she hadn't been looking for one.

She turned to Larry.

"I'll check the drawers for the tape. Check the closet."

"Why would it be in the closet?" Larry asked.

"I don't know, Larry. Why would there be a dick collection in the closet?"

"Well," Larry said thoughtfully, "where else would you keep it?"

"Just check, will you?"

Glenda grunted as she bent and looked under the bed, once again wetting her knees.

Behind her she heard clumping and thumping in the walk-in closet. She looked up as Larry stomped out.

"Nothing in there," Larry said.

Glenda eyed him up and down.

"Larry," she said. "What are those?"

Larry had come in with sneakers. Now he sported zebra-skin cowboy boots.

"You like?" he asked.

"Jesus," Glenda said. She shook her head and was about to reply when she heard something.

She held up a hand and said, "Shut up." She listened intently. She caught a faint rumbling sound. After a moment, the noise resolved itself into a car engine.

And it was getting louder.

Someone was coming up the drive.

"Oh, shit," Glenda said.

The engine stopped. After a moment, Glenda heard a car door close.

"Somebody's coming," she told Larry. "Let's get out of here! Where's the back door?"

"Follow me," Larry said. He dashed out of the bedroom. Glenda snapped off the light and followed.

They had made it to the bottom of the stairs when they heard the front door lock click. The solid wooden slab swung open. Dimly silhouetted by the porch light, a black figure stood. It held something in its hand. Glenda and Larry stopped dead in the darkness at the foot of the stairs.

A click sounded, and a flashlight beam splashed onto the stranger's feet. It swung across the carpet, widening as it went. Glenda held her breath.

The beam swept methodically back and forth across the room. Glenda shrank back against the stairs and waited. There was nowhere to run. The light lapped against the bottom stair, swept past, and then veered back. It stopped and became a white circle. In the center of the circle was a pair of zebra-skin cowboy boots.

The beam hung there for a moment. Then it flashed upward and caught Glenda and Larry full in their faces, blinding Glenda. She turned her head away and put up a hand to shield her eyes. Larry shouted something incomprehensible and backed into her. A boot heel scraped her shin.

"Owwww!" Glenda shrieked, hopping on one foot.

"Glenda?" the stranger asked in a wheezy whisper.

"Who is that?" she replied.

"I'm Kirby Fink. Bernie's accountant," the man said and then was interrupted by a fit of coughing. "Sorry. Lousy cold."

A spate of silence followed, and then Fink and Glenda asked at the same time: "What are you doing here?"

"He's accounting?" Larry suggested.

"Ah, you must be Larry," Fink said. "Bernie talked a lot about you."

"Did he mention my record deal?"

"Hold on a minute," Fink said. "I need to make my way through all this junk." The flashlight beam veered around potted palms and furniture, then fixed on the big picture window. Fink's hand reached up and tugged the drapes closed.

The beam maneuvered back to the front door. There was a click and a small lamp on a table next to the door flicked on, casting a weak light.

"There we go," Fink said. "I don't want to disturb the neighbors."

Glenda saw a thin, stooped man in a wrinkled raincoat and a big-brimmed hat. He was wearing dark blue glasses, for some reason, above a hawk nose. Fink's eyebrows quirked as he noticed the bright yellow dish gloves on Glenda's and Larry's hands.

"So," Fink said slowly, eyeing them.

"So," Glenda replied cautiously.

There was an uncomfortable pause. Fink gave another cough and covered his mouth.

"We were just leaving," Larry chimed.

"Okay," Fink said.

"And nobody saw anything," Larry added in a confidential tone, shaking his head.

"What?" Fink asked.

Larry apparently thought he should take charge. "Whatever you're into, it's okay," Larry said. "And if you're looking for it, it's in the closet."

"What? Mold?" Fink asked.

"There's a mold?" Larry asked. "You think he made copies? Son of a…"

Fink looked confused.

"No. Mold like fungus," Glenda cut in with a flash of comprehension.

Fink nodded nervously and looked at Larry with distrust. "Yes," he said quickly. "I'm worried about mold. All this water, you know? Some of these furnishings are valuable."

"So," Glenda said with sudden comprehension. "You're taking them."

"That's my job," Fink said a bit defensively and coughed again. "I am executor of Bernie's estate."

Glenda glanced at her watch. It was well after midnight. She looked curiously at Fink.

He sighed.

"Look," Fink said. "Bernie owed everybody, including me, and he was years in arrears on his taxes, so you know there won't be anything left. So I'm just trying to take what's mine. A couple of those paintings. I've already got buyers."

Fink looked at Glenda and Larry as if daring them to say something.

Glenda said carefully, "Looks like everybody had the same idea."

Fink relaxed. "Actually, I'm kind of glad you're here." He pointed to a large painting in a heavy gilded frame. "I don't suppose you'd give a guy a hand?"

They toted out the big painting, which Fink said was a nineteenth-century Chinese ancestor portrait, along with a small de Kooning, a Hokusai print and a sketch by De La Roma. All of them sported

Eastern or jungle themes. Fink also needed help with a final piece, a large painting of a tiger— well, *maybe* it was a tiger. Its stripes were pink and green, and it bore a human face with a mustache. It looked like the artist had troweled on the paint while high on LSD.

Fink saw Glenda's look of distaste and laughed, which turned into a cough.

"Yeah, I hate it, too. But it's the only oil John Lennon ever did. Bernie got it as a gift from Yoko. Too bad John didn't sign it. Altogether, though, I'll clear close to seventy thousand for the lot."

He shook his head ruefully and sighed. "So now I'm an art thief."

"Yeah. Bernie brought out the best in everybody," Glenda said.

Fink seemed to bristle. "Well, to be fair," he said, "he had to work with egos and assholes. You try to be a nice guy with everybody jerking you around."

Glenda looked at him speculatively and Fink quickly appended: "Not you, of course."

"Of course," Glenda said in a clipped tone.

"Hey, guys," Larry called from the living room. "Little help here?"

It took all three of them to lug the statue of Ganesha into the back of Larry's Thunderbird. Fink insisted on helping despite fits of coughing whenever someone glanced at him. Glenda hoped she was out of his spatter range.

Larry was beaming as he snapped a seat belt around the elephant's ample belly.

"It's a karmic thing," Larry said, and gave the statue an affectionate pat.

Fink turned to Glenda. Both were panting.

"I hope you don't want one, too," Fink said.

Glenda laughed and shook her head.

"What *did* you want?" Fink asked. Glenda blew out her cheeks. She needed a believable lie.

"I wanted Bernie's copy of my contract," she improvised, then realized she did indeed need to take a look at the paperwork. Otherwise, she would have no idea where her career stood. "I didn't find any papers, and I'm not sure I have copies of everything." Glenda shook her head. "In fact, I don't even know what I don't know. I think Bernie screwed me over."

Fink gave her a piercing look, then smiled.

"He was under a lot of pressure," Fink said.

"He screwed you, too," Glenda said. "I wouldn't be so forgiving."

Fink looked uncomfortable. "Water under the bridge," he muttered. "The poor guy's dead, you know?"

"Yeah," Glenda said. "But I still need to deal with this. Hey! You've got to have copies, right?"

"I should," Fink replied slowly. "Let me look around. I'll get back to you."

"Maybe I could come by your office?" Glenda prodded.

"I'll be busy for a few days," Fink said. "Probate and all..." He caught Glenda's glare and relented. "All right, sure. Call me. You have the number?"

"Probably somewhere."

"Well, I'm in the directory."

"How about tomorrow?" Glenda asked.

The accountant coughed.

"Tomorrow?"

"Yeah. I'll call you before I come. Unless you want to set a time."

"I'm not sure I *have* the time..."

"This is important to me," Glenda said with mock reasonableness. "Whatever you can do will be great." She added, "No pressure."

"Of course, of course," Fink said quickly. He seemed to want to hurry the conversation to a close. He patted his pockets. "I don't have any cards. But I'm in the Creque Building, Hollywood and Cahuenga."

"Okay, thanks," Glenda said. They nodded at each other. Glenda was glad Fink didn't offer his hand, which he'd been using to wipe his mouth between coughing fits.

She watched his van disappear.

CHAPTER EIGHT

On Friday, it was clowns and more clowns all day for Glenda. She'd had minimal success. Short of a circus fire, Glenda wasn't sure she'd be able to find so many unemployed clowns on short notice.

In addition, her back hurt. She'd helped Larry haul that damned statue up to his second-floor apartment.

So when five o'clock rolled around, Glenda left the office with the intention of spending a quiet evening at home. She picked up Chinese from the Formosa Cafe on the corner, finally got around to doing her laundry— which had piled up like Everest —and even managed to noodle a bit on Banshee before her nocturnal exertions and lack of sleep from two broken nights finally caught up with her.

She let herself collapse on the couch.

She woke at around ten-thirty. She felt sluggish and cranky from the unplanned nap. The couch had done nothing to help her back. Yawning, she got up and, out of habit, turned on the TV.

"In the Flow" greeted her with chipper xylophone tones.

"Oh for..." Glenda said, and added a colorful string of profanity. Much of it was directed at Bernie Sherman, despite his demise. That made Glenda remember she'd forgotten to drop by the office of Sherman's accountant, Fink, to look into her contract. Well, she thought, it was way too late now.

That didn't help her mood.

Damn Bernie, Glenda thought. *Damn everything.*

Now she was so angry, she couldn't get back to sleep. She paced around the room but pacing did nothing to deflate the fury-filled balloon in her brain.

At last she stopped dead in the middle of the tiny living room, clenched her fists and forced herself to stillness. It was way too late at night to scream. El Guapo might want to do a duet.

For the same reason, Glenda couldn't release her emotions by singing and playing Banshee. But she had another remedy. Instead of sitting around fuming, she'd go find someplace to stomp out her anger. Her motto was: *When in doubt, kick it out.*

The dance floor was waiting.

Glenda tugged on black Spandex tights. She pulled on a T-shirt with a picture of Tinkerbell spewing sparkles from a tiny wand, then added her old studded black leather jacket.

Her toes were still sore from her high-heeled debacle, so she went for her favorite pair of witchy black leather ankle boots.

She went into the bathroom and attacked her hair with a brush. The brush lost. She thumbed eye shadow and lip gloss on the appropriate places.

"Okay," Glenda said, eyeing herself in the mirror. "Moping time is officially over."

As she walked north four blocks to Sunset Boulevard, twice cars rolled up and men leaned out, offering money.

"Hey baby, I got a snake in my pants. Can you tame it?" one yelled. Glenda almost laughed as she flipped him off.

Sunset Boulevard was brightly lit, and so were the people. Knots of them staggered along, laughing and full of booze and pot. Women and men both tottered on high heels. Shuffling old stoners tried to cadge quarters or joints. Cops cruised slowly down the street but allowed the carnival to continue. Skinny white kids with haystacks of hair ran around stapling gig posters to telephone poles, trailing a funk of hairspray.

When dawn rose, the rockers and the night owls would slink off to their tombs like vampires, leaving the streets to old ladies, hobos and the odd Midwestern tourist.

But for the moment, music ruled. Every coffee shop, restaurant and hole-in-the-wall cafe burst with musicians.

As Glenda moved west toward the Strip, the crowds got thicker. In the past few years, glam and metal had taken over but even so, there was plenty of everything to go around. Every flavor of rock and pop hustled Hollywood. It was like a scene from *The Warriors*. New Romantics and Madonna wannabees flounced along; Rockabilly boys pounded on the doors of the Capital Records building; hip-hoppers thrashed out rhymes in murky dance joints and up-and-coming has-beens filled cramped clubs, sweating in front of amplifier stacks better suited to Olympic stadiums.

Glenda liked to dance but chose her venues carefully. In most of them there was so much coke flying around, inhaling could make you OD. She'd done that, thank you, and never wanted to risk it again. Let the jerks with razor blades on chains around their necks get their ecstatic nosebleeds.

Glenda walked by Barney's Beanery. She wondered if Emilio Estevez or Bette Midler were inside, eating chili, drinking Scotch, imbibing the trendy, sleazy roadhouse vibe and pretending to be real working stiffs. Glenda had never been there.

She reached her favorite club, the Cripple Cafe, in the brand new city of West Hollywood, a rebel rental community full of angry old people, Russians and queers. A blast of guitars and smoke hit her. In the daylight the cafe served ranch breakfasts and the smell of eggs and toast still lingered, making Glenda's stomach rumble. But the kitchen was closed. The red leatherette booths were filled with kids in ripped T-shirts and safety pins through their faces, drinking something from cheap plastic cups and eating boxed pizza.

Oh, Christ, Glenda thought. *It's punk night.* Still, she pushed on and descended the stairs to the nightclub area, which had been cleared of its daytime tables. A bouncer the size of a refrigerator ignored her ID and waved her inside a long, narrow room with a low ceiling. An old crutch, which gave the cafe its name, hung on the wall. The crutch belonged to the owner, Claude Papillon, who had broken a leg during the Altamont riot. To Glenda's left, a band screamed obscenities over a three-chord progression while the audience yelled back. To her right a bar was doing good business in bad booze. Every so often a bottle would go sailing across the room to crash against the windows, which had been boarded up with stained and dripping plywood. The air, slashed by stage lights, swirled with cigarette smoke like a London fog and tasted like something that had leaked from the Stringfellow Acid Pits. Dimly glimpsed through the haze was a fire marshal's sign that said "Maximum Occupancy: 50." At least one hundred people in the room yelled, bounced around and slammed into each other in spastic eruptions of dance.

Punk night, Glenda thought sourly. Oh well, she was there to blow off steam. That's what punk was all about, wasn't it?

She lasted almost fifteen minutes. Every time she found a space on the dance floor, somebody slammed into her or stomped her wounded toes with their Doc Martens. Limping to the bar, Glenda ordered a vodka and tonic. Had she ever considered dance a contact sport? She didn't think so. In her day, dance was about sex, not combat. *In her day,* Glenda thought ruefully; it was only three years ago. When had she become so damned old?

The drink arrived, but it was so watered down, it might have come from an aquarium. Glenda imagined a goldfish goggling at her through the plastic cup. She put the drink down on the bar where a bristly-headed girl snatched it after miming a request to Glenda.

Glenda made her way out of the smoky cave and limped upstairs to the restaurant area. At the rear, French doors led to a balcony overlooking the city. There, she was alone except for a few sad ficus trees drooping in their pots like exhausted sentries. Muffled music came up from below, and the pounding bass made the balcony deck tremble. The damp air smelled like the sea, which lay a few miles west. High clouds overhead were garish with reflected city light, but the view under the clouds was like a sparkling carpet.

Glenda's feet hurt. She plopped herself down at a table. Her right ankle throbbed where a steel-toed boot had kicked her. She crossed her right leg onto her lap and felt for bruises. The leg was tender, but nothing seemed broken. After taking off the boot, she began massaging her foot.

A skinny youth in a leather jacket, shredded jeans and Docs— the uniform of the anarchist —clumped through the French doors onto the balcony. The boy had spiked hair and no ass. Glenda guessed he got carded at bars. The punk went to the wrought-iron railing at the edge of the balcony and lit a cigarette, blowing smoke over the city. Glenda, intent on her toes, ignored him until he coughed loudly. Twice.

Glancing up, she saw that the kid was leaning against the railing, half-turned to show her his silhouette. His chin was up. He held the cigarette like a movie prop. It was cliché cool, Glenda thought; part Marlon Brando and part Sid Vicious. She wondered how long he could hold the pose without actually taking another puff on the cigarette.

With calculated coolness, the kid turned his head slightly, caught her eye and dipped his chin to acknowledge her presence.

She rolled her eyes.

"Forget it," Glenda called out. "It's not two o'clock. I'm not that pretty yet."

The boy dropped his cigarette. Sid Vicious left the building. "No! No!" he stuttered. "It's not like that. I'm not trying to pick you up. I'm a fan!"

Glenda abandoned her toes and looked him up and down: Stud earring, skull tattoo, spiked wristband.

"You like *my* music?" Glenda said doubtfully.

"Oh, yeah," the kid said. "I loved 'Wheels.' It's hooky, but it's deep. And that octave rise in the final chorus... unbelievably badass!" He held up his hands, as if illustrating something, then seemed uncertain what to do with them and stuffed them in his pockets. He looked shy and eager at the same time.

Glenda almost wanted to pat him on the head. Instead, she dropped her toes and invited him to sit.

The kid dropped into the chair across from her. He was gangly but hard-muscled, she noticed. He smelled of sweaty leather and cigarettes.

"Thanks, Miss Birdsong."

He was *so* young.

"Just Glenda," Glenda said. "Excuse the feet." She put her foot down. "I got stomped."

"Sorry."

"My problem," Glenda said. "I didn't know it was punk night. I would have put on my steel-toed work boots instead of these." She held up her ankle boot. "Like bringing a knife to a gunfight. What's your name?"

"Nelson," the kid said. "Onstage, I'm Hurl."

"Good name," Glenda said. "Do you?"

He laughed. "All the time. Especially when I've had a bad burrito."

Glenda smiled. "What's your band?"

"Dead Rabbits. We played first."

"Thought I recognized you," Glenda lied. In fact, she'd come in late. Anyway, she'd not paid much attention to the bands. The music was pretty much interchangeable, and the performers had little to distinguish them from each other except for the number of safety pins in their faces and whether they wore Mohawks, liberty spikes or crew cuts.

"I only caught the last song," Glenda added.

Nelson seemed pleased, though. If he had a tail, Glenda thought, he'd be wagging it.

"You like punk?" Nelson asked her.

"I like what it stands for," Glenda equivocated.

Nelson nodded vigorously. "That's why I like it," he said. "Even though it's old-fashioned and simplistic."

"Don't you mean honest and primal?"

"Yeah," Nelson agreed. "That, too."

"So I take it, then, you're really into what? Hardcore, or maybe alt?"

"None of the above," Nelson said, shaking his head. "Dead Rabbits is really retro. *Ghetto* retro. We love to scream and spit onstage and play the same three chords with the feedback squealing. But really, it's more ironic than anything. That stuff they were doing a few years ago had energy but not much musicianship."

Now Glenda laughed. "But you like the Glitter Lizards? That's even older and dumber."

Nelson appeared shocked.

"You don't like your own music?" he asked, as if such a thing had never occurred to him.

"It wasn't all my music," Glenda said. "Sometimes artists have to eat."

"But 'Wheels...'" Nelson said.

"Okay, that one I loved," Glenda admitted. "There's blood on it, though. We did forty-one takes. It's the one time I put my foot down. It just *had* to be right."

"It is," Nelson agreed vigorously. "I listened to it over and over again when I was a kid."

You *are* a kid, Glenda wanted to say but didn't.

"Thanks," she said. "The band wasn't too happy with me. The final chorus was the problem. I was trying to do Janis Joplin, but her voice isn't my natural range. By the time we got it, my throat felt like I'd gargled with battery acid."

"When I was first learning guitar, I played 'Free Bird' until my fingers bled," Nelson said, shaking his head. "I know, I know, cliché. Anyway, my folks got sick of hearing it, so they put me in the barn. I plugged in next to the cows. Instead of a garage band, I was in a barn band. Or maybe a herd?"

Glenda laughed again. She saw the boy take her amusement as a compliment. Nelson leaned forward. She heard his mind working. He was thinking: *first base*. She was amused.

"So you're from sweet home Alabama?" Glenda joked.

"No," Nelson said with a grin. "Nebraska."

"And here you are, punked out in L.A."

Nelson shrugged. "For now. I got here a few months ago, saw a wanted poster for a guitarist and took the gig." Another shrug. "What about you? What are you working on?"

Glenda thought it charming that he assumed she was working.

"Well, you know, I went solo for a while. That didn't work..." Glenda trailed off, but Nelson either didn't know about her disaster of three years ago— a lifetime for him —or he was too polite to mention it.

"But I still owe an album to my producer," Glenda finished. "I'm doing that."

"At least you have a producer," Nelson said.

Glenda wanted to say: *No, I don't. He's dead.* Instead, she made a joke. "Producers are like Rottweilers," she said. "They stink but you need one to watch your back."

"He's a dick."

"I haven't told you who he is."

Nelson paused, and for an instant his expression became unreadable. Then he threw up his hands and laughed. "They're *all* dicks," he said airily. "I just assumed it's the same guy who did 'Wheels?'"

Glenda nodded. "That's right. Bernie Sherman."

"So, is this gonna be your music or his music?"

Now she laughed. "You catch on fast." She took a breath, remembering suddenly how badly Bernie had polluted at least one of her songs. She wondered if he'd stolen any others. Fink might know. Glenda reminded herself again that she had to meet with the art-cadging business manager.

"All mine," she finally said with determination. "Whether anybody likes it or not."

Nelson slapped his palm on the table dramatically.

"No retreat, no surrender!" he said.

Glenda slapped a palm on the table, too. "Amen, Springsteen!"

They both smiled.

"Did you know?" Glenda said. "It took Bruce six months to finish 'Born to Run,' and he did four full versions. One of them had *streetcar noises* on it."

"That's psycho," Nelson said. "But righteous psycho." He paused and looked at Glenda frankly. "How long are you gonna take?"

"As long as I need."

"Man, I would love to see you in action," Nelson said.

Oh, Glenda thought. *The kid made me laugh, and now he thinks he's heading to second base.* Glenda had no intention of flirting, but she had to admit Nelson was cute and smart, and he was good for her bruised ego.

"It's not glamorous," She warned. "It's just take after take. After take. Like hammering nails, then deciding you don't like 'em, pulling 'em all out and putting in screws."

"So, like really bad carpentry."

"Exactly."

"Sounds great," Nelson said. "I've never been to a studio. You can educate me." He grinned.

Glenda suppressed a wince. When it came to pickup lines, the kid could give Harold a run for his money. Even if Nelson was a fan, he was presuming a lot. He was moving too hot and fast. On the other hand, maybe Glenda had just forgotten what it was like to be young and star-struck. She decided to give him the benefit of the doubt. "Okay," she said. "Tuesday night. Bronson Studios. Prepare to be bored."

"I won't be bored," Nelson told her seriously.

"Hey! There you are!"

Glenda looked up as a girl in a black miniskirt, ripped nylons and raccoon makeup tottered through the French doors. The girl came up behind Nelson and put her hands on his shoulders.

Nelson gave a twitch of irritation. He kept his hands flat on the table.

"I'm starving!" the girl said. "Let's go eat!" She ignored Glenda.

Glenda looked at the girl's bony hips. She could probably inhale cheeseburgers and not put on a pound.

Nelson looked faintly uncomfortable.

"Just give me a second." His eyes apologized to Glenda.

Glenda swore she saw the girl's black-painted harpy fingers dig into Nelson's shoulders proprietarily. The girl leaned in and put her lips to Nelson's ear.

"*Starving!*" the girl shouted.

Nelson lurched forward and clapped his hand to his ear.

"Jesus!" he said. "I'm not deaf!"

Glenda didn't want the night to end with an argument, and Nelson seemed ready to start one. He clearly wanted to stay and he clearly was embarrassed Glenda had seen his girlfriend— or whatever she was.

"Well, I'm hitting the road," she said loudly and reached for her boot. She put one leg on a chair, zipped up the boot and smiled at the boy. "Nelson, it was a pleasure talking music with you." She got up.

"Yeah," Nelson said. He looked as if he wanted to say more but nodded instead.

Glenda gave him one more smile as the harpy, using her eyes like claws, dragged Nelson to the door.

As the pair left, she heard the girl say: "I couldn't find you. It's been, like, an hour. What were you doing with that old lady?"

"You don't even know who she is," Nelson said.

"She better not be your sugar momma," the girl said and laughed.

Glenda swore at their retreating backs. She wasn't an "old lady" and she'd only talked to Nelson for ten minutes. That bony bimbo didn't know how to tell time. The only thing between her ears was her nose ring.

CHAPTER NINE

There is the dream, and there is the nightmare.

In the dream, Glenda is on stage at the Palladium, spotlights clothing her in silver and flame. She is singing her heart out while Banshee wails.

But tonight the nightmare visits her.

Glenda is in the middle of her first— and as it turns out, only —solo tour. She is backstage at the Greek Theatre. She is dehydrated, high, barely able to hold Banshee as stagehands strap her into a harness. Glenda stumbles onstage into blinding light. She is nauseated. Glenda misses the opening beat of the song but recovers quickly and slams into "Days of Lightning" as the crowd roars. Her voice and her fingers are doing their thing while her brain watches as if from a tethered balloon. Then here comes the highlight: A huge pounding of drums, then she screams a note and rises high into the air. She hovers, then soars over the audience. The lights swoop like drunken stars, the people shriek and raise their arms to her, paying homage. Glenda feels their devotion.

And then, mid-chord, she collapses. She feels dizzy, then sick, then... *nothing*.

Glenda has blacked out. She dangles from the harness, thirty feet above the crowd like a puppet with its strings cut, until she is reeled back in.

In the nightmare, Glenda knows she is dangling there, even though during the real event, she was unconscious. She also knows, somehow, that she will spend three days in the hospital and two months in rehab, and that will signal the end of her career.

Sometimes she relives it all again but instead of a harness, she is suspended by meat hooks, and the faces below her belong to slavering wolves.

CHAPTER TEN

The telephone woke her. The incessant ringing merged with the retreating fragments of Glenda's nightmare. At last she fumbled the receiver to her ear.

"Uh," Glenda said groggily.

"Oh, good, you haven't left yet," her mother said.

Glenda knuckled her forehead.

"I just woke up, Mom."

There was frosty silence. "It's noon," her mother said.

"I had a long night," Glenda said. "What's up?"

"What's up?" her mother said. "Did you forget about the party?"

"The party?" Glenda asked fuzzily. "Isn't that Sunday?"

"Saturday, Glenda. Today." Her mother had adopted the exasperation-tinged tone Glenda remembered vividly from her childhood. It was the same tone her mother used when talking about Ronald Reagan.

"Oh, shit!" Glenda exclaimed, wrestling free of the sheets with the phone to her ear. "Are you sure?"

"Oh, no, dear. I could be wrong. Your father must just be out there cooking an entire cow by mistake. And everybody coming over in two hours? I guess they're all going to be a day early. Sorry to disturb your beauty sleep."

Glenda sighed and rubbed grit from her eyes. "Sorry, Mom, sorry, sorry. I'll get ready right now. I'll be there. Was there something else?"

"There was," her mother said huffily. "I was going to ask if you like kiwi."

"I like kiwi, Mom."

"Well, I was going to make a fruit salad, but our market's out. I was hoping you could pick some up on your way through Pasadena but if you're running late, we can live without kiwi."

Glenda swore she could see her mother's put-upon expression. Nobody did guilt like her mother. She had a Ph.D. in guilting. She could teach Guiltology 101.

"I'll pick some up," Glenda promised. "See you soon, Mom."

"And some canned mandarin slices, too, if they have them."

"Okay, Mom."

"And be careful driving. The streets are still wet, and you know L.A. drivers can't drive in the rain. Plus, how much sleep have you had?"

Glenda heard the unspoken questions: Were you out all night at some club? Did you take anything? And the deeper fear: *Are you slipping back?*

"I'm fine, Mom. Really." Glenda meant every word.

"Good. Well, I'll let you go, then. Oh, and don't forget the present."

"It's all wrapped, Mom."

"Which reminds me," her mother said. "When you get here, we need to talk about your *sister*." Her mother spat the word like a curse.

"Mom..." Glenda said guardedly. "What now?"

"She's mad at me," her mother said.

"Why?"

"I won't let her go to the zoo. In Illinois."

"What?"

Glenda's mother sighed. "She wants to drive to Peoria with her little girlfriend and an eighteen-year-old boy to see dead leopards."

Glenda wondered if she'd heard correctly. Then the pieces clicked into place.

"No, Mom. Not dead leopards. Def Leppard. It's a band."

"I know," her mother said firmly. "We have a record store, dear, remember? The point is, that boy is eighteen years old, and he's going to drive them two thousand miles. I said no."

"Good call, Mom."

"Your father said he would drive them." Her mother did not sound happy. "Anyway, your sister said that would be embarrassing. So she's not talking to me."

"Oh, Mom, I don't need to get involved in this..."

"I just want your moral support if it comes up."

"It's her birthday. It's not going to come up. Unless *you* mention it."

"I won't cause a scene. I'm just saying."

"I've got to get ready, Mom. Traffic is gonna be bad."

"All right. Be careful."

"I will, Mom. Bye."

"Bye."

Glenda hung up, wondering why her mother seemed to think of her as a child or a charity case. But she was being unfair, she knew. Only three years ago she *had* been a charity case.

But I'm a grownup now, she thought. She felt like stamping her feet.

GLENDA PUT FIVE DOLLARS of gas in the Porsche and pointed it toward Altadena. She drove with the top down despite the cold. Not from choice; the top refused to go up. It lay on the back of the car with its accordion folds partly raised. It looked like an exhausted bat had flopped there. Glenda had no money to fix it.

The sky looked like dirty cottage cheese. Glenda prayed it wouldn't rain. Again.

She took I-5 to the 134 to the Foothill Freeway, and at each transition, somebody nearly skated into her. At the Lake Avenue off-ramp, a semi nearly sideswiped the Porsche, forcing Glenda to swerve and jam on the brakes before she was pancaked. She swore briskly. L.A. drivers didn't know how to handle rain. Her mother had been right.

That irritated Glenda even more.

She reached her parents' home and pulled up under their pepper tree, hoping it would provide some shelter for the car if the rain restarted.

The short driveway led to a 1950s ranch home. It was white with brick trim under the windows, which were flanked by fake shutters. The front door was overhung by a scrap of porch supported by scrollwork posts. The roof sported a triangular peak with three holes in it: a faux birdhouse. Glenda had no idea why the builder had done that. She wondered if there were fake birds inside. A side gate led to the backyard.

Glenda found her father in the back, roofing the patio with a tarpaulin. He was so tall, he didn't need a ladder.

Her father bore the stoop common to tall men, but Glenda thought his shoulders were a little more hunched than when she'd seen him last on the Fourth of July. More silver gleamed in his sideburns, too, and his belly pressed against his shirt.

But when he stepped forward and hugged her, Glenda's feet left the ground. As always, he held her as if she were light as a feather.

"There's my Baby Buffalo," he said.

Her father smelled smoky from the charcoal grill— ironic, since his nickname had been Coal.

"Hey, Daddy," Glenda said. "You look fine."

"Thank you." He put her down and drew back. Coleman Reginald Birdsong wasn't a man to linger with his affections. Sometimes he seemed aloof even to his own family. Glenda knew he wasn't unloving; his ever-present sense of dignity kept him from fawning. Her father cherished dignity above everything because he'd had none growing up. He'd fought for it, and she knew he found it hard to let down that barrier.

Glenda's mother came out holding an enormous bowl of potato salad and glanced critically at her husband and elder daughter. Seeing no claws out, she pushed forward. She put the bowl on a table, wiped her hands on her apron and reached to smother Glenda.

Glenda smelled sweat and paprika.

Where Glenda's father was frugal with his affections, Mom was exuberant. She gave attack hugs and took no prisoners. Glenda marveled again at her parents' differences. Sophie Lieberman Birdsong was as short and plump as her husband was tall and lanky. She was Brooklyn-born and a committed socialist. It was only natural that she would shock her neighborhood and bring her fight against oppression into the marriage bed by wedding an African-American. Glenda's mother didn't stand on dignity. She said what she thought and didn't give, as she put it, "a good goddamn" whom she offended. Glenda's mother had political opinions about everything. She even refused to stock Ted Nugent records in the store because he was a gun-toting Republican.

"Mom!" Glenda said. "You changed your hair."

"You like? Frosted with bangs. Your father says it makes me look like Meg Ryan."

"No, I didn't," her father said.

"And you look beautiful," her mother said. "You let your hair grow out." She explored it with her fingers.

"It just does that, Mom," Glenda said, trying to evade her mother's probing digits. "Sort of Janis Ian meets Michael Jackson."

"I was thinking Chaka Khan," her mother said. "That *Destiny* album is doing pretty well at the shop."

"I wish I had her career, too," Glenda said. "But I'll settle for her hair."

Her mother laughed. "I want to hear all about what you've been up to, but first I've got to get ready for the horde."

"I'll help," Glenda volunteered.

"No," her mother said, scoffing. "You just talk to your dad." She leaned in and added, "And play nice this time. I mean it." She pecked Glenda on the cheek and vanished into the kitchen.

Glenda's father finished tying off the tarp, stepped back, inspected his work critically, squinted at the sky and nodded to himself. He gave Glenda a careful grin then said, "Well, guess I'll take ten." He gestured to the sliding glass door. "Join me in the living room?"

"Sure," Glenda said. They strolled amiably but warily into the room. Her father walked to the stereo and picked up a record album from a large pile. He showed her the cover. It was *Destiny*. He smiled and put it on. Glenda admired the elegant way his long, slender musician's fingers handled the disc, with a kind of reverence. "Love of a Lifetime" bounced out of the speakers. Glenda dipped her head in time, admiring the cheery buoyancy of the song despite its overproduced glibness.

Her father folded his length into his old leather armchair and stretched his legs out on an ottoman. Glenda took the sofa.

They listened together for a moment.

"Mom says this is selling pretty well," Glenda said.

"Yeah," her father said. "Ever since the summer single. Thank God for the video. I hate having to listen to MTV in the shop all day, but it does sell records."

"What else is big these days?" Glenda asked.

"*Thriller*," her father said. "It's Halloween." He quirked an eyebrow at Glenda. "And you. Still sellin' your stuff."

"Don't I wish," Glenda said wryly.

"It'll happen," her father said. "Lightning strikes twice. Just keep pushin'."
"I am pushing, Dad."
Her father held up his hands soothingly. "I know you are, baby."
There was an awkward silence, broken by the militarized funk of "Earth to Mickey."
Her father changed the subject.
"So, guess what? Your sister wants to change her name."
"She wants to change her name? To what?"
"Crystal."
"Crystal?"
"Yeah."
"Crystal Birdsong?"
"Um-hmmm."
They both shook their heads.
"Jesus, Dad!"
He shrugged. "I guess Abigail is too unhip for a fashion model."
"Oh, don't tell me you're gonna let her model. Dad, she's fifteen."
"Uh-huh," Her father said. "And how old were you when we were driving you around to auditions?"
"I was *not* fifteen," Glenda insisted. "And I was a lot more mature."
Her father leaned back in his chair and steepled his fingers over his stomach. "Uh-huh."
Glenda bridled. "What does that mean?"
Her father shook his head. "All I'm saying is that Abby has found something she loves. She designs her own outfits; she can wear anything. She's got the looks. What's wrong with that?"
Glenda made a disparaging noise. "Do I have to tell you?"
"You don't think your mother and I would let anything happen to her?"
Glenda thought she heard him add mentally: *after what happened to you.* "Stuff happens," Glenda muttered. Chaka Khan began to sing "Watching the World."
"Baby," her father said. "She's gonna do what she's gonna do. Maybe it's a kid thing she'll grow out of. Either way, it's better if your mother and me are there. You know we'd do anything for you girls."

"All I'm saying, Dad, is that sometimes you let her get away with too much."

Her father crossed his arms. "Uh-huh," he said.

"Uh-huh," Glenda retorted.

Her father frowned. "Girl, I am your father. You do *not* uh-huh me." He added, "You know what I think this is? You're jealous."

Glenda snorted. "Are you kidding me?"

Glenda's father nodded vigorously. "Yes, you are. A little bit."

"That is ridiculous!" Glenda got to her feet.

"You don't need to be jealous," her father continued soothingly. "Baby, everybody's got different talents. You know, you can sing. Your sister sounds like a walrus."

"And I guess I look like one," Glenda said, her voice rising.

"I did not say that!" her father said, his voice also rising. "We love both of you…"

"No matter what I look like," Glenda cut in angrily.

"That is not—" her father began.

"Ten minutes!" Glenda's mother stalked into the room from the kitchen, her glasses steamed. "I leave you two alone for ten minutes, and it's World War Three!" She glowered at Glenda. "You! What did I tell you? For God's sake, you're not six years old, you're thirty!"

"Twenty-nine!"

Her mom glared and for a moment, Glenda felt six again.

"This family's *meshuga*," Mom said with exasperation. "That Reagan is talking about tearing down the Berlin wall. Maybe they should put it up between you two. Except it wouldn't be high enough!"

Her mother tossed her head in disgust and stomped out of the room. From the kitchen she shouted, "And you could do some work. We've got guests coming!"

Glenda and her dad shared an uncomfortable glance.

"Well," her father said. He pushed himself up from the chair, lifted the needle from the record and turned off the stereo. "Guess I'll go grill something." He hitched up his pants and his dignity and went out to the patio.

Glenda stared at his empty chair.

A knock sounded at the front door. Everybody else was busy, so Glenda answered.

Standing on the stoop was a man in his late fifties. He had a soft, pleasant face. He wore a nondescript hat and an open beige trench coat. He had a disturbing amount of hair in his ears but immaculate eyebrows. They were his best feature. Glenda wondered if he combed them. He was holding a big white box stamped with a cartoon picture of a baker and the name Martino's.

"Uncle Marcus!" Glenda's foul mood fizzed away. She gave him a hug.

"Hey, don't crush the tea cakes," Marcus said in a soft drawl. "I went all the way to Burbank for these, darlin'."

"I'm so glad you're here," Glenda said as Marcus wiped his feet on the doormat and entered. "But you didn't have to knock."

Marcus Reid shrugged. "Never take your family for granted. Especially your adopted one."

"Blood ain't everything," Glenda muttered as she took her godfather's hat and coat. Marcus had a cheap haircut and wore a sweater and slacks. Glenda thought his clothes always looked a little unpressed. Marcus never wore a tie, but if he had, Glenda thought he'd probably have chosen something with comic strip characters on it. Yet Marcus was one of the most powerful music producers in Hollywood.

"Yeah, I heard you and your dad. Same old duet." Marcus pursed his lips in disapproval.

"He just gets to me," Glenda said.

"Yeah," Marcus said wryly. "Why couldn't he be more like you?"

Glenda laughed in spite of herself.

"Where is he?" Marcus asked.

"Out back. Burning something."

"I'll go say hello."

Glenda put a hand on his arm. "Listen. Um, I wanted to ask you something."

"Sure. Anything."

Glenda hesitated. "You heard about Bernie?"

"Yes. A tragedy but not surprising. Still, I'm sorry. Are you going to be all right?"

"I'm not sure," Glenda said truthfully. She thought of the missing tape and the mystery visitor to Bernie's house. She wasn't sure her godfather could fix things, and anyway, all she had were vague suspicions. She decided to stick to real issues. "I don't know what'll happen now." Glenda said, blushing. "To me, I mean. I hate to ask you for advice..."

"As always," Marcus said with a grin.

"I just don't know anybody else I can trust," Glenda admitted. "It's music business stuff."

"Go on," Marcus said.

Glenda sighed. "It's all a mess. Bernie stole one of my songs, and God knows what else he did."

"I'm not even sure God knows," Marcus said. "What's your question?"

"What happens with my song rights and my album? Who owns my contract now that Bernie's gone?"

"Good questions," Marcus agreed.

"I'm going to see Bernie's accountant. If Bernie cut some sleazy deals for my music, he might be able to find the paperwork."

"You trust him?"

"I don't think I'm important enough to be worth screwing," Glenda said. "He's got Bernie's whole operation to loot." Glenda thought about helping the accountant haul paintings out of the house and rubbed a sore shoulder. "But I'd really appreciate you helping me go through the papers when I get them. I'd like to know where I stand."

"Of course," Marcus agreed. "It could be complicated. Probate and all that." He ran a hand through his thinning hair. "Okay. Let me see what I can do."

The conversation was interrupted as the door banged open. Glenda's sister and a gaggle of chattering teenagers burst inside. Glenda grudgingly noted that her sister was blossoming. Unconsciously elegant, she had her father's clear-cut features and her mother's gold-flecked green eyes. Her once coltish figure had become graceful. Glenda thought she could see what her sister might become: someone who could make a potato sack look like a Chanel suit. At the moment, Glenda's sister and her friends were wearing fuzzy sweaters and white sneakers with their hair fluffed out or gathered into side ponytails. It seemed to be some kind of uniform. The room filled with giggles and swirling colors. It was like being swarmed by canaries.

Marcus raised his voice over the din.

"We'll talk later," he told Glenda. "Here, hide these in the kitchen. You might need them."

He handed Glenda the box of tea cakes.

"Thanks."

"It's just backup," Marcus said. "In case your mother is planning something flamboyant for the birthday cake."

Glenda nodded. "Amaretto Cloud Surprise. She told me on the phone."

Marcus winced. "What is that?"

"No idea. She got the recipe from her book group."

"At least it's not rhubarb éclairs."

"No, with luck she'll never try those again."

"Well, warn me if she has a relapse." Marcus winked and strolled to the patio.

"Sis!" There was a peck on Glenda's cheek and then Abby— no, "Crystal" —and her crew surged past like a wave flowing around a pier. For an instant, Glenda was inundated with teens, and then they vanished. She looked down at the box Marcus had handed her and lifted the lid. The angelic smell of pastry filled her emptiness. Glenda looked around to make sure she was alone. She reached in and snagged a moist square of heaven, roofed with translucent yellow icing.

"Hello, my little friend," Glenda said, licking her lips, and sank her teeth into it. Sweetness exploded in her mouth.

Two bites later, the tea cake was gone and Glenda returned to Earth. She went into the kitchen with the box.

Her mother was dumping trays of ice cubes into two big pitchers of fruit punch.

"Take these outside," she ordered without looking up.

Glenda opened a cupboard above the sink, stashed the box of tea cakes— minus a casualty —and then carried the pitchers outside. She passed Marcus coming back in. He gave her a wink.

Rain had begun drumming on the tarpaulin with a dull, booming sound. Glenda's father had rolled the grill under the covering and was cooking heaps of hamburgers and hot dogs, stacking them on large serving plates. A picnic table had been married to a couple of card tables and covered with pink vinyl tablecloths. Glenda's sister and the other teens had come to roost there, apparently impervious to cold. Glenda set the pitchers down and went over to her father. She watched him for a moment. He was intensely focused on the grill. Everything he did, she thought, he did with passion. But he could be frustratingly opaque with emotions.

"Dad," Glenda began. "Sorry."

"Hey," he said. "Grab some of those plates and take 'em to the table, will you?" Glenda knew this was her father's way of saying everything was right between them. He never directly acknowledged confrontations. He forgave and forgot easily. Glenda kissed him on the cheek and grabbed a heaping platter.

Crystal and her Crystalettes— as Glenda dubbed them —managed to keep up an unending flow of chatter while somehow devouring impossible amounts of food. They even managed a slice each of Mom's cake, which she brought out proudly on a silver platter. It was mottled and grainy and had a cloying taste of almond liqueur. When Mom returned to the kitchen briefly, Glenda slid most of the remaining cake into the trash can and rearranged soggy, used paper plates to hide it.

Mom returned, beamed and offered second helpings.

"Can't, Mom!" Crystal said. "The movie! We're gonna be late!"

"Patrick Swayze can wait ten minutes," Her mother said. "Oh, all right. Open your presents."

The party ended in the living room, with Crystal surrounded by a massive pile of shredded wrapping paper, like a contented hamster. Glenda was surprised and touched that Abby— *Crystal,* damn it! —loved her gift: white clip-on suspenders and a matching purse.

When their ride arrived, the girls raced into the pouring rain, shrieking and giggling. Glenda felt sorry for the mother who had volunteered to drive them. Being in a minivan full of chattering teens was like being stuck inside a box of caffeinated squirrels.

"Phew!" Glenda's mother said, closing the door and wiping her hands on her apron. "Everybody all right? Did we lose anyone in that typhoon?"

"You mean the rain or the kids?" Glenda's father said. "Glad I put that tarp up."

"Let's clean up," Glenda said.

"No, no leave it. That's why we used paper plates," her mother said. "Your father and I will throw it all in the trash. Now we can eat like adults. Glenda, can you get the cake?"

Glenda went outside, looked at the remaining wedge of cake, pitied her family and decided to make a sacrifice. She took the platter and went back inside.

"Gee, Mom," Glenda said, holding out the tray. "This is all that's left. And, well, I kind of wanted to take some home."

"Really?" Mom looked skeptical, and for a moment Glenda thought she'd overplayed her hand. Then her mother beamed.

"Oh, I didn't think it would be such a hit. It's so sophisticated. Well, well." She looked at her husband and Marcus. "Now I wish I'd made two."

"One is fine," Marcus said quickly. "Let Glenda have it." He couldn't quite hide the relief on his face.

"Yeah," Glenda's father chimed in. "Our daughter deserves the best."

"Oh, but that's not fair to you two," Glenda's mother said. "All the grownups should have some."

"We'll live," the men said simultaneously.

Glenda's mother squinted at the cake dubiously. "Maybe I can get a slice each out of this..."

There were swift, pained glances around the room.

Glenda gritted her teeth.

"I really want the cake, Mom," she said. "And Uncle Marcus brought tea cakes from Martino's. You can have those."

"Well, if you're sure..."

"I'm fine," Glenda's father said quickly.

"Well, in that case, all right. Thanks, Marcus."

"Yes. Thanks to you, dessert is saved," Glenda's father said in a dramatic voice.

"All in a day's work, citizen," Marcus replied in a superhero tone.

Glenda's mother actually giggled. "Marcus, you take such good care of us."

"Marky Sharky is the man," Glenda's father agreed. "Without him, I'd be another broke-down sax player collecting nickels on street corners."

"Oh come on, Coal," Marcus said. "You were the first artist I ever signed. Without your genius, I'd be nobody. Just another soulless millionaire." He put his palms together in a prayerful gesture and added: "I was just the stork. You were the baby."

"Stork?" Coal raised an eyebrow. "You were a vulture."

They both laughed.

"Well, if you two birdbrains don't mind, go to the living room," Glenda's mother said. "I'll take this into the kitchen and go make coffee."

"I'll make it, Mom," Glenda said. "You sit down. You've done everything."

"Do you know how to make coffee?" her mother asked.

"Yeah, Mom. You scoop it out of the Nescafé jar."

Her mother gave Glenda a look of horror. "Just go sit down, please." She turned on her heel and headed for the kitchen.

A few minutes later, they were all munching tea cakes and sipping coffee from a French press.

"Great coffee," Marcus lied. He did it smoothly, Glenda noticed. Probably from long practice.

The entire extended family was used to concealing its views on Sophie's culinary pursuits. Sophie had grown up in a household where everything was either bland or burnt and, unfortunately, her growing-up years reflected in her cooking despite her best efforts.

"Enjoy it while you can," her mother told Marcus. "We might not be able to afford coffee next time we see you."

"Why not?" Glenda asked, shocked. "Is the store in trouble?"

"No," Marcus and Glenda's father replied together.

"Your mother's overreacting," her father said.

"I'm overreacting? The stock market drops twenty-two percent in a day, and *you* think I'm overreacting."

"Honey, you'll frighten the child," Marcus said.

"She should be frightened. Reagan's let the fox in the henhouse and feathers are flying! Glenda, how much do you have in stocks?"

"I don't have any stocks, Mom."

"Well, thank God for that," her mother declared.

Glenda decided not to mention her bank account, which had stalled in the double digits.

"Sophie," Marcus said soothingly. "Don't worry. I already told you. You're not gambling in the market, your bank deposits are insured by the feds and your store is paid off. You'll be fine."

He took a deliberate sip of his coffee. Glenda felt for him.

"Poor people won't buy records," Glenda's mother said. "They'll be too busy trying not to starve."

"Things won't get that bad," her father said. "And even if they do, people will just buy more records to cheer themselves up."

"'Happy Days Are Here Again,'" Marcus said. "That was a hit during the Depression."

"Speaking of hits," Glenda's father broke in. "How's the album coming?"

Glenda felt her shoulders tense. Her mother gave him a warning look. Her father had asked the same thing on the Fourth of July, and the day had ended in an epic shouting match.

Marcus's eyebrows rose.

"Good," Glenda replied carefully. "We've got a few more tracks to work out, but I think it'll be done by the end of the year."

"Oh, that's wonderful!" Glenda's mother said and clapped her hands.

"I look forward to hearing it," Marcus said in a neutral tone.

"Is that a commitment?" Glenda's father asked.

"Coal..." Marcus warned.

"No offense, honey. I know you're doing your best."

Before she could stop herself, Glenda blurted, "When *don't* I do my best?"

"You always do," her father said placatingly.

"Yes, I do!" Glenda said. "Maybe that's my fucking problem!"

The words seemed to freeze in the air and shatter like icicles. An embarrassed silence ensued.

Glenda was abashed and ashamed at her outburst.

"Excuse me," Glenda said. She stood and made for the door without another word.

Her mother gave Glenda's father a look.

"Go," she said.

Her father took a deep breath, stood, straightened his shoulders and followed Glenda to the door.

As she walked out, Glenda heard her mother ask Marcus calmly: "More coffee?"

HER FATHER FOLLOWED Glenda into her old bedroom, which was now the music and storage room. Her bed had been shoved against one wall. Glenda sat on the edge and aimlessly shuffled through a stack of compact discs.

"Hey," he said.

Without looking at him, Glenda held up a disc. "Pink Floyd?"

"It's the promo copy," he said. "I listen to everything we get before we stock it."

"The plastic's still on it," Glenda said.

"Yeah, well," her father said. "You okay?"

Glenda put the disc down and looked around. Against one wall stood her old bookshelf, now stuffed with her mother's cookbooks. Above it were framed Glenda's Glitter Lizard albums, and fifteen-year-old photographs of her teenage performances. She stood and walked to the bookshelf. A battered saxophone lay on top of it.

"Josephine," Glenda addressed the instrument. "How are you, old lady?" She ran her fingers over the brass. It warmed to her touch.

"She's looking good," Glenda told her father, avoiding his eyes.

"Yeah," he said. "Took her out on the town last weekend."

"Oh, yeah?"

He shrugged. "You know, I jam with some old friends here and there."

"A gig?"

"Yeah, I guess. The Ice House on jazz night. Guess we still sell a few drinks."

Glenda patted the sax and moved on. She returned to the bed and sat, her hands between her knees.

"I'm sorry," she said. "That one was my fault."

"Mine, too," her father said. "I didn't mean to poke at you."

"No, I overreacted." Glenda laughed mirthlessly. "Like always."

Her father said nothing. She raised her head and peered at him. "Dad, did you ever worry about it not being the same?"

"About what not being the same?"

"Playing with your old friends, I mean."

"Well, some nights it's good, and some nights it's shaky. No different than it ever was."

"What do you do on the shaky nights?"

"Wish I was still drinking." He laughed, but then saw Glenda was serious. "Honey, Josephine's in charge, not me." He nodded at the sax. "And she's got her moods." He saw Glenda's expression and paused thoughtfully.

"You don't feel that way," he said.

Glenda shook her head.

"Ah," he said. "You and that album."

"I put my soul into it, Dad. What if everybody hates it?" Glenda dropped her head again.

He sighed and stepped to the bed.

"Mind if I sit?" he asked. "I'm a little creaky these days."

Glenda nodded, and he sat down next to her. She glanced at him. He still had a strong profile, long-jawed and lean as an ebony carving.

"When I was young," he said, "I thought I was hot stuff. I couldn't wait to get up on that stage and blow 'em all away. And sometimes I did."

"You did," she agreed.

"But sometimes I didn't," he added. "One time in Baltimore, somebody threw fruit. Honest-to-God fruit. I got smacked in the face with a tomato. After that, the boys called me 'Reggie the Veggie.'"

Glenda turned to him in surprise.

"I thought that was because you ate carrot sticks when you stopped drinking."

"That's what I told your mother." He gave her a sly grin. "Sometimes she's not as clever as she thinks she is."

Glenda grinned back.

"Anyway, after I got turned into salad, you know what I did?"

She shook her head.

"I got up the next night and played. That's it."

"I don't understand..." Glenda said.

Her father rubbed his head.

"Look," he continued. "Some of the guys I played with, they would fluff a note and it would eat at them for days. I mean, they would get *sick*. And I know the great men, the so-called geniuses, some of 'em felt like that. But so did a whole lot of guys nobody remembers."

"But this might be my last chance," Glenda said, almost plaintively.

"For what?" her father asked with a flash of anger. "You want to worry about whether people like you? Damn, honey, just worry about the music. You remember when you were six and we got you a tambourine— which your mother still calls a big mistake —and you banged on it for hours? Well, that music mattered just as much as what you're doing today."

"No it doesn't," Glenda said. "Because, Dad, I hadn't—"

"What? Messed your life up?" he frowned. "Well, join the club. Ten years as a functioning alcoholic, right here." He tapped his chest. "I got back on the horse. And I'm telling you, sweetheart, that horse ain't strong enough to carry you and your baggage."

"You're saying I should let go," Glenda said. "But I don't know how."

"It's not the way you're built, I know," her father said. "I know you always got to ride that horse. But maybe you should hold the reins a little looser— and trust the horse."

Glenda made a wry face. "I just don't want to, you know, fall *off* the horse. Again."

"You fall, you get back on. Album fails, you make another one. I can't give you better advice."

Glenda heard a cough. She and her father looked up.

Marcus stood in the doorway.

"You know," Marcus said. "I had that same conversation twenty years ago. With your father."

GLENDA TOOK HER CUE to leave when she heard her sister returning. The pack of teens converged on the doorstep, then burst into the entry in a cacophony of chatter and giggles. They shed umbrellas and coats. Her sister gave Glenda a perfunctory wave and patently ignored her mother before the entire crowd swept into a bedroom.

Her mother's pursed lips told Glenda there was unfinished business—and Glenda refused to be drafted into another family battle. So she put down her coffee cup, glanced out the window and exclaimed, "Looks like there's a break in the rain." She stood. "I'd better get a move on before it gets dark. The streets will be safer, too."

Glenda's mother seemed about to argue, but Glenda knew she had a full-proof exit strategy. Her mother couldn't complain about Glenda wanting to drive safely; Sophie was always carping about the dangerous lunacy of Southern California drivers.

But Mrs. Birdsong was not entirely thwarted. She stood, too.

"I'll pack you some leftovers," she told Glenda and bustled off to the kitchen.

Glenda's father and Marcus also stood. Glenda went to the entry and took her coat from a peg. Her godfather and father shook hands. Her mother returned with a bulging shopping bag.

Glenda took it.

"Okay," her mother said. "That should hold you for a while."

"Probably for a month, Mom."

They hugged, and her mother whispered in her ear, "You need to talk to your sister."

Glenda pulled back.

"Mom..." she began.

"Please," her mother said. "She'll listen to you."

In your dreams, Glenda thought, but said simply, "I'll do what I can."

"Bye, bye baby. Be safe," her father said. He gave her a quick kiss and a brief, enveloping hug.

Marcus laid a hand on her arm. "About that other thing," he said. "Let me know when you're ready."

"I will," she promised.

"Call me at home or the office. I'll buy lunch."

"Deal," she said. "Thanks, Unc."

Glenda dragged the big bag of food out to her car. The seats were squelchy with rain. Cursing, Glenda slid onto the damp leather. Then a thought hit her. She got out, went to the back of the car and pulled on the stuck roof. Now that the rain had stopped, the canvas slid easily into position, protecting the already-soaked interior.

Of course, Glenda thought.

She took the 210 West, managing to devour a cold hot dog and its bun by the time she crossed into Glendale.

Her mother's cake made it home untouched.

CHAPTER ELEVEN

Glenda arrived at work refreshed and bearing gifts. She'd spent most of Sunday sleeping.

She found Trina already at her desk. Glenda was supposed to be the office manager but she couldn't type, so Troutman had hired Trina to come in twice a week to handle correspondence. With Troutman away, Glenda had asked Trina to work full-time, and the temp agency had agreed.

Sorting through letters, Trina looked up greedily when she saw Glenda come in. She was a tiny woman with the appetite of a boa constrictor. She would eat anything. She never gained a pound. Glenda hated her.

"Morning," Trina said brightly. Then she frowned in confusion. "No donuts today?"

"Nope. Something special."

Glenda put the box she was carrying on Trina's desk. It was the Martino's box, minus the tea cakes. With a flourish, she opened the lid.

Trina's eyes went wide.

Inside were the remains of her mother's Amaretto Cloud Surprise. The cake looked like a bad avalanche, which her mother insisted was the meringue topping. Splattered over that was something drippy that was supposed to be caramel but, to Glenda, resembled congealed motor oil. There were three other layers, each oozing stuff of a different color. The kiwi layer was particularly disgusting. Its green reminded Glenda of the slime in the *Ghostbusters* movie.

"All yours," Glenda said. "My mom made it."

"You don't want any?" Trina asked.

"I'm dieting," Glenda lied.

"Glenda, you are just too sweet," Trina said, reaching into her drawer for a fork.

During the morning, Glenda made three calls to Fink. The phone rang unanswered. At lunchtime, Glenda went to his office.

The Creque was a four-story Art Deco building. The second floor had offices with wide hallways, old-fashioned lighting sconces and tiled floors.

The accountant's wooden door sported a full-length glass insert. It was locked and the lights were off. Through the glass, Glenda saw a reception area. What appeared to be several days' worth of mail— letters, circulars and bills —littered the carpet under the mail slot.

Glenda rapped on the glass. As she expected, nobody appeared. She pulled a notepad and pen from her purse, scribbled "Call me. Glenda," added her phone number, folded the note and slipped it through the mail slot.

She walked down the hall to another office. This one had "Scott Insurance Agency" in pretentious gold script on pebbled glass.

A secretary sat behind a small, cluttered desk. She wore cat's-eye glasses, and her hair resembled a Pomeranian squatting on her head. She had a watch on each plump wrist. A brass nameplate on the desk read: "Mrs. Priscilla Barnes."

"Hello," the secretary said brightly as Glenda entered. "May I help you?"

"Maybe," Glenda said. "Do you know the accountant, Mr. Fink, next door?"

Mrs. Barnes giggled.

"You know, I've been working here for five years, and I've never met him. Can you believe it?"

"You've never seen him come into work?"

"No, I mean he never leaves. When I get here at eight-thirty, the light's on in his office and his inner door is closed. And when I leave at five-thirty, the light's still on."

Glenda frowned.

"Then how do you know he's there?"

"Well, I've heard him." Mrs. Barnes glanced at one watch, then the other and shook her head.

"My husband gave me this one," she told Glenda. "It's a Longines. But it doesn't keep time. I don't have the heart to tell him, so I wear this old Timex." She raised the other hand. "Takes a lickin' and keeps on tickin', right? I take it off before I get home. I really must get this other one repaired. But on my salary—"

"You were saying you heard the accountant," Glenda said.

"Oh, yes, I did. It was so strange. He's normally such a quiet man. Soft-spoken, I mean. Never raises his voice. Very hard to make out what he's saying."

"That's a shame," Glenda said before she could stop herself.

"Well, the walls are very thin," Mrs. Barnes said a bit huffily. "Sound travels."

"What was strange, then?"

"Well, twice last week, I heard him shouting. On the phone."

"Shouting? Really?"

"Bellowing!"

"What did he say?" Glenda asked.

"Oh, I didn't eavesdrop!" Mrs. Barnes protested, straightening her glasses. "But it was so loud, everyone in the building could hear him."

"What did he say?" Glenda repeated.

"Well, I'm no accountant, so I didn't understand most of it. But Mr. Fink did keep shouting, 'The blankety-blank numbers don't add up!' And then he said the next straw would be the last or something like that."

"Did he say anything else?" Glenda asked.

"He said: 'my blank is on the line, too.' And then he slammed the phone down. I could hear it from here. Practically shook the building." She made a clucking noise.

"My goodness," Glenda said. "Do you know who he was talking to?"

"I don't recall a name," the secretary said.

But Glenda had her suspicions. "Well, I wonder why he's not here today," she ventured.

"Yes," Mrs. Barnes said. "Come to think of it, the lights haven't been on since, maybe, Wednesday."

"Wednesday? Are you sure?" Glenda thought about it. She had seen Fink last Thursday night at Bernie's house, and he'd been sick. Maybe he'd spent the rest of the week in bed. That would explain his absence.

Maybe.

"Well, thank you for your time," Glenda said.

"My pleasure." Mrs. Barnes held up both hands to display the watches. "I've got plenty of it!"

Glenda left the building. There was a hole-in-the-wall Chinese takeout place nearby. She bought a couple of egg rolls and ate them while walking back to work. She pulled a ball of Kleenex from her handbag and wiped her greasy hands before sitting at her desk. She worked into the afternoon, handling calls from clown pimps who knew they had a hot item for Halloween and were asking far too much for it. In between there were the usual party setups, from kid-friendly magicians to a lone cake stripper.

At three o'clock, just as Trina was finishing the last of the cake— which she downed after consuming a take-out lunch that consisted of a log-like burrito —the phone rang again. Trina's cheeks bulged with cake, so Glenda picked up the receiver. "Gould and Troutman Talent Agency," she said.

Nobody answered for a moment, then there was click and a voice came on the line.

"I am going to kill you," it shrieked. The line went dead.

Glenda sat, stunned. She hung up the receiver.

Trina looked up, wiping meringue from her mouth.

"Who was it?" Trina asked.

Me, Glenda thought.

The call had been her own voice, part of her rant to Bernie about the MTV commercial on the missing answering machine cassette.

"Just a prank call," Glenda said hastily. "Heavy breather."

Trina nodded and went back to munching.

"Say, Trina, could you do me a favor?"

"Sure," Trina said. "Name it."

"I'm kind of in the mood for a... for a snack."

"Didn't you have lunch?"

"Not much of one," Glenda said. She lowered her tone to a confidential wheedle. "To tell the truth, I would kill for a jelly donut!"

"Oh, Glenda, you are so bad!" Trina said, pretending shock. "I thought you were on a diet."

"It's been a long day," Glenda said. "I just need a pick-me-up."

"Well..."

"Just one," Glenda said. "And get a couple for yourself." She watched a greedy look blossom in Trina's eyes.

"Okay," Trina said.

"Great!" Glenda pulled some crumpled bills from her purse. Trina took them with a wink and skipped out of the office.

As soon as Trina left, Glenda picked up the telephone receiver and dialed the operator.

"I just lost a call," she told the woman. "Could you give me the number?"

"No, I'm sorry," the operator said. "But I can reconnect you."

"Yes, thanks," Glenda said.

A series of clicks, beeps and thunks smote her ear, and then Glenda heard the familiar Morse code of the phone ringing. After several seconds, someone picked up.

"Hello?" The voice didn't sound familiar. It was high, male and slurred. "Who is this?"

"You know who," Glenda said coldly.

"No, I don't."

"You just called me."

"I didn't call you, man," the voice protested. "You called me."

"Enough games," Glenda said. "I get it. You have the tape. What do you want?"

There was a confused pause.

"Look, I picked up the phone, all right?" the man said. "I was just cruisin' by and I heard it ringing. I don't want no trouble. So... bye."

"Wait, wait," Glenda said. "Don't hang up. Where are you?"

"Why?"

"Just please, tell me."

The man grunted.

"The Boulevard, lady."

"Sunset or Hollywood?"

"Uh... Sunset. I think."

"You're on a pay phone?"

"Yeah. Whadya think? I was checking for dimes."

"Somebody just used that phone before you. Did you see anyone leave the booth?"

"It's not a booth."

A pedestal phone, Glenda thought.

"You didn't see anybody leave the phone?"

"It's Sunset," the man said. "There's a lot of people."

True, Glenda thought. Someone could have been standing there for minutes, then simply hung up and merged with the crowd.

Then a thought hit her. It made her stomach knot.

"One more question," Glenda said. "What's the cross-street?"

There was a pause broken only by the hum of passing traffic.

The man came back on the line.

"Formosa," he said.

"Thank you," Glenda said dully and placed the receiver back in its cradle.

Formosa Avenue and Sunset Boulevard. Four blocks from her apartment.

She left the office, manufacturing a bad case of menstrual cramps and leaving a commiserating Trina to close up all alone with the donuts. Glenda glanced nervously around as she walked home, feeling eyes like knives between her shoulder blades.

At Formosa and Sunset, she found the pay phone on a pedestal, protected by a head-high steel box open at the front. The enclosure was scratched and disfigured by graffiti and band labels. It was just a phone, but to Glenda it seemed sinister; the metal loops of the handset looked like a coiled cobra.

She walked home quickly.

As she crossed the street to her apartment, Glenda saw Mrs. Patakian walking her children. The late middle-aged woman pushed a huge double baby carriage with the hood raised. She wore a big woolen scarf and a tam o'shanter.

Mrs. Patakian was the neighborhood gossip. She waved as Glenda approached.

"Glenda, darling, how are you?" she asked.

"Doing well," Glenda said. "And how are the girls?" Glenda glanced in the carriage. Two long, pointed noses and two pairs of glittering eyes peered back at her. The dachshunds wore little knit sweaters.

Mrs. Patakian pulled a face.

"Cookie's fine, but Claudette's been scratching."

"Maybe it's the sweater," Glenda suggested.

"Oh, no, I knitted it just for her," Mrs. Patakian said. "She'd tell me if she didn't like it." Mrs. Patakian thought for a moment and then said urgently,

"She just had a play-date. I hope she didn't catch anything. I heard of a schnauzer that had dendritic mites—"

"I'm so sorry," Glenda cut in. "I hope she feels better. So, tell me, Alice, did you see anybody go into my building today?"

"Well, there was the postman, of course. He was wearing bright green socks. With his blue trousers!" Mrs. Patakian shook her head. The dachshunds whined. "I know," Mrs. Patakian cooed at them. "It was horrible!"

"Nobody else?" Glenda asked.

"I don't think so, although I did hear the rooster squawking at around two-thirty. But I was getting the babies dressed, so by the time I got to the window, nobody was there."

Two-thirty, Glenda thought. Plenty of time for someone to slip into the building and out again. Leaving something? Hoping to confront her? She didn't know. She would only find out by going home.

"Thanks," she said. "Well, I'd better get going."

"You're welcome," Mrs. Patakian said. "Say goodbye, darlings." She clucked at the dachshunds, and they poked their noses over the carriage, their tongues lolling and their beady, bulging eyes fixed on Glenda.

She didn't like their stare, which spoke of too much knowledge, as if they were reading her future with dark eagerness.

"Bye," Glenda said uncomfortably and crossed the street.

She climbed the stairs as quietly as she could. The landing was empty, but she stood a moment in front of her door, then gently turned the knob. The door was locked, just as she'd left it.

As she attempted to slip the key into the lock, her jittery fingers missed a couple of times before it went home. She went inside, closed and relocked the door and attached the security chain, which she rarely used.

She darted into the other rooms casting anxious glances. No one was there. She returned to the living room. On the table near the door, the light on her answering machine flashed red.

Holding her breath, she pushed the playback button.

"Two thirty-nine," the voice stamp announced tonelessly. There was no message; someone had called and hung up.

Shakily, Glenda pulled her Silva Thins from her handbag and lit one, calming herself with a deep lungful of smoke. She was too anxious to feel guilty about smoking. She put the cigarette pack down next to the answering machine and began to pace the small living room.

She shivered, laying out a scenario in her mind.

A stranger— Glenda's brain conjured up a shadowy figure in a trench coat and Bogart hat —had knocked, realized Glenda wasn't home, and rattled the doorknob.

That alerted the rooster, who had crowed.

Startled, the stranger had slipped out of the building. He'd walked four blocks to the pay phone and called just to make sure Glenda wasn't there. Then he'd called her work and played a snatch from the tape, using a portable tape player.

Glenda took two quick puffs on the cigarette and crushed it out with a nervous effort.

Somebody knew where she lived and where she worked. Glenda knew *nothing* about that person. The caller was a murky presence, a blurred outline of fear, who could stalk her relentlessly, and there was nothing she could do about it.

Her overactive imagination called up images from old black-and-white movies: sinister silhouettes bleeding smoke from their nostrils in dingy alleys, or hunched under streetlights, or gliding noiselessly along wet streets. Glenda pictured a hand rising up from the shadows, a sudden flash from a gun barrel...

She caught herself. She was turning a simple phone call into a full-fledged panic attack.

Glenda put her hand to her lips and realized she wasn't holding anything. She picked up the cigarette pack, shook loose another smoke and lit up. She went through that coffin nail in a matter of minutes, lit a third from the stub and forced herself to stop pacing. She sat on the couch and considered what she knew.

Her mystery caller had the answering machine tape. That meant they must have been connected to Bernie and probably had taken the tape from his house. If so, there were only two possible reasons: because there was something on the tape they wanted, or there was something on the tape they *didn't* want discovered. If they'd wanted to hide something, they could simply have destroyed the tape, but they hadn't done that.

So they wanted something on the tape. What was it?

Glenda inhaled another lungful of nicotine.

She was on the tape.

But why play the tape for her? Was it a threat? A warning? Did someone think she knew something she didn't? *What did they want?* The whole thing made no sense.

The only conclusion Glenda reached was that whoever had the tape would probably call again. She would just have to wait.

And watch her back.

Thank God for cigarettes, she thought, reaching for another. She'd have to lay in another carton at this rate.

She would have to calm down, if only to spare herself from incipient lung cancer. She needed advice. But who could she call? Not the cops, for sure. Not her parents; Glenda could imagine setting her mother off. Mom was a worrier, usually at the top of her lungs. Marcus? He'd want to protect her. Probably hire a bodyguard. And that might get back to her parents.

But when she thought logically about her situation, Glenda doubted she was in physical danger. Playing the tape signaled more mystery than menace.

A fragment of the Talking Heads song "Life in Wartime"—- that ode to paranoia —flashed through her mind. Would she be driven from her home? Hiding by day, skulking by night.

She needed to talk to *somebody* about what had happened, just to get out of her own head.

By her fifth cigarette, she realized that she had only one choice. With a sigh, she stubbed out the cigarette and picked up the phone.

"Talk to me."

"Hi, Larry."

"Glenda."

"Yeah. Hey, I…" Glenda stopped for a moment, unsure how to proceed. "Did you get a phone call recently?"

"Yeah. From you."

"Yeah, no, I meant before me."

"Like who?"

"I don't know. A man?"

"Pizza guy? He calls all the time. He keeps trying to order pizza. I think he's high or something. Keeps mixing up the number. He always wants the Hawaiian Special and I'm like, 'man, pineapple on pizza is an offense against nature.'"

Glenda sighed again. "Okay," she said. "Forget that. I have another question."

"Shoot."

"What do you remember about the night you found Bernie?"

"Lots of things. You don't forget shit like that. Trust me."

"I don't mean the body, Larry. I mean anything I didn't see."

"Oh, you mean suspicious."

Glenda wondered why Larry didn't think a body in a bathtub was suspicious but decided not to press the issue.

"Yeah," she said. "Anything unusual?"

"Nope," Larry replied. "Pretty normal, just your crazy calls. They were pretty entertaining."

Glenda ground her teeth. "So, nothing else?"

"Nope, it was pretty boring after that. He was still alive. We were gonna watch a movie, but I decided to leave. He got hung up on some stupid phone call."

Glenda felt a chill. "He got another call? Who was it?"

"Who was who?"

"Who was Bernie talking to when you left?"

Larry hesitated. "Maybe somebody who was angry with him?" He paused. "He started using the weasel voice..."

"I know the weasel voice," Glenda said. "But you couldn't hear who it was or what they were talking about?"

"No," Larry said. "And then I left."

"Larry, listen. Somebody was in that house *after* you left. Maybe it was whoever called Bernie."

"Why do you think that?"

She took a breath. "Because somebody just called my work and played a tape of me threatening to kill Bernie. From the answering machine. And they couldn't have gotten that tape unless—"

"Unless they were in the house," Larry said. "Well, I didn't see anybody. Maybe you should call the cops."

"What would I say?"

"You could say you have a stalker."

"A stalker who has a tape of me threatening to kill Bernie."

"Yeah."

"Because that would go over so well with law enforcement."

"You could say you're being framed."

"But I'm not. That really is my voice, and I really was threatening Bernie."

"Well, plausible deniability worked for Nixon…"

"No it didn't, Larry. And it can't be plausible because it's *me* on the tape!"

"Jeez, you don't have to be so negative. And so loud."

"So you don't have any idea who it could have been?"

"Not really."

"Well," Glenda said. "Whoever it was must have seen the body. I mean, if they took the tape, they were near the bed, and that's near the bathroom, and the water was running…" Glenda stopped.

"What?" Larry asked.

"The water was *running*," Glenda said. "If you walk into a house and you hear running water, maybe even see it all over the house, what do you do?"

"Get my bathing suit? "Larry suggested.

"No, Larry, you shut it off. But this guy didn't."

"We didn't either," Larry noted.

"All that says is that the guy didn't want anyone to know he'd been there," Glenda replied. "That's why he took the tape. That's probably why he didn't call the police when he saw the body. Just like us."

"No," Larry said haltingly. "Not just like us."

"What do you mean?"

Larry didn't answer.

"Larry?" Glenda asked.

There was an uncomfortable silence on the line.

"Larry!"

"Glenda," Larry's voice was uncharacteristically hesitant. "What if he didn't find the body?"

"What do you mean?"

"What if he didn't *find* the body?"

Glenda suddenly realized where the conversation was going.

"Larry, calm down…"

"What if he turned Bernie *into* a body?"

Glenda laughed uncertainly.

"Come on, Larry," she said. "We saw him. No bullet holes, no stab wounds, no sign of a struggle. He hit his head, fell in the tub and drowned."

"Oh, yeah, right," Larry said. "Come on, does that seem believable?"

"Yes," Glenda said. "It does."

"Or," Larry countered, "he forced Bernie to kill himself. And now he's trying to make you crazy so you'll kill *yourself.* Like in that old movie."

"Why would he do that?" Glenda asked.

"Tying up loose ends, man," Larry said. "He goes over, maybe Bernie owes him money for drugs—"

"Drugs, Larry?"

"—Or something else. Anyway, say it's somebody Bernie cheated or owed money to."

"That I buy," Glenda said.

"So then he gets Bernie to kill himself. Maybe he chases Bernie, and Bernie slips and falls."

"Naked?" Glenda asked. "Bernie's naked, right?"

"Why naked?"

"Because he wasn't wearing anything in the tub."

"So," Larry said slowly. "He was gonna take a bath."

"With the guy chasing him?"

"No. Let's be *serious*, Glenda."

"Where is this going?" she asked.

"Getting there, if you let me," Larry said, his voice rising. "So Bernie's dead. Now the guy panics, takes the tape and gets out. Just like you did. But he beat you to it."

"But why call me?"

"Because the bad guy doesn't know *you* weren't there before *he* got there," Larry said. "Maybe Bernie told you about him. Named names. Or, *you* played the tape with both your conversations on it but left without taking it."

"That makes no sense," Glenda said.

"It does," Larry insisted. "You *were* going to take the tape, but you got interrupted. Maybe *you* panicked. The thing is, if he's the guy who called Bernie, he can't take the risk that you heard his name. He has to eliminate you as a threat. He has to make sure."

Larry was being disturbingly logical. For Larry, Glenda meant. She did not like it.

"But why call me?" Glenda asked again.

"That's the genius part," Larry said. "He has the tape, right?"

"Obviously."

"So if you talk to the cops, it's your word against his. That's why he has to make sure nobody believes what you say."

"And how is he going to do that?"

"He's gonna drive you crazy, and maybe even get you to kill yourself, see?"

"I don't think…" Glenda began slowly but Larry charged ahead.

"It's perfect!" he said. "Oh, my God! No, it isn't!"

"What now?" Glenda asked.

"He takes care of you, right? You know what that means."

"No witnesses," Glenda said. "For the sake of argument."

"No," Larry said. "That leaves one witness. Somebody who might have heard Bernie talking to him…" Larry paused and then said dramatically: "Me."

Glenda stopped, dumbfounded.

"You?"

"Me! Hell, I may even have seen him!"

Glenda's pulse quickened. "You saw him? Where? What does he look like? You said nobody came to the house."

"Yeah, but when I was driving *back* to the house, some jerk in this big Cadillac was coming downhill and almost ran me off the road."

"It could have been anyone," Glenda said.

"Doing fifty in a fifteen mile-per-hour zone? That guy was in a hurry!"

"Did you get the license plate?"

"I was too busy trying not to die. The Cadillac was a light color and maybe ten years old. That's all I know."

Glenda shook her head. This wasn't getting her anywhere.

"Well, thanks Larry," Glenda said. "If you think of anything else, call me, okay?"

"I have thought of something else," Larry said.

"What?"

"You need to find him. He's gonna come after me." He added in a hoarse whisper: "I know too much!"

"You don't actually know anything," Glenda said.

"He thinks I know too much." Larry made a strange, strangled sound. "You got me into this. You have to help me!"

"I got you into this? Into what?"

"Oh, don't play dumb. We have to find him before his nefarious plan is complete."

"Nefarious?"

"Nefarious. Look, if you want to find this guy, I may have an idea."

"I think I've heard enough of your ideas."

"No, listen. What do we know about this guy?"

"Nothing except he knew Bernie and maybe Bernie owed him money."

"For drugs. And he might drive a Cadillac. And he's going to kill us—"

"We don't know that!"

"But he knew Bernie, probably. So, if you want to find him, go where he might show up."

"Where?"

"The funeral!"

"Why would the killer go to the funeral?"

"Because," Larry said, "if he knew Bernie and everybody *knew* he knew Bernie, it would be suspicious if he *didn't* go."

Larry's unusual flash of insight startled Glenda. "Larry," she said uncomfortably. "You're actually making sense."

The funeral was set for tomorrow, Tuesday.

"We'll go," Glenda declared.

"You go," Larry said. "If we both go, we're both targets. It's too dangerous. He could hurt me! You can't let him do that!"

"You're all heart, Larry."

"Hey, you got the phone call. So he already knows you, obviously. That means you're the one he's looking for."

Glenda sighed. "I'll go."
"And look for the Cadillac."

CHAPTER TWELVE

Bernie's funeral was held at Mount Zion Memorial Park. The Jewish cemetery perched on a hilltop whose irrigated lawn was usually the only greenery amid the parched brown of the western San Fernando Valley. But recent rains had turned the whole valley to emerald.

Bernie's will specified an outdoor ceremony and folding chairs had been set up amid the grave markers lying flush on the hillside in long lines. The guests were forced to tread carefully to avoid stepping on the dead.

They wore raincoats and carried umbrellas but with well-timed irony, the weather had turned dry, although the sky was cloudy. Thunderheads brooded over mountains to the northeast. Bernie's coffin rested on trestles on a raised stage. Its gold handles gleamed every time a sunbeam broke through the clouds.

Glenda almost wondered if Bernie had ordered the heavenly shafts of light.

Two extremely large men who'd been poured into dark suits stood on either side of the funeral bier and eyed the crowd. They wore skullcaps.

"What's with the Jewish Marines?" someone asked.

"Guards," somebody replied. "I hear the body's supposed to be shipped back east, and the family didn't want a Gram Parsons."

Glenda remembered the overdose death of the twenty-six-year-old rocker in 1973. His body vanished from the airport en route to Louisiana. His friend, producer Phil Kaufman, had stolen it and, honoring a pact they'd made, cremated the body in the rocky desert of Joshua Tree.

In front of Bernie's casket stood a row of microphones on stands. The space was bookended by large speakers. Thick electrical cables snaked away over the grass.

Huge displays of lilies sat in waist-high vases next to overblown photos of Bernie. Here he was beaming in a Boy Scout uniform. Over there, he was a young man in a black turtleneck and Beatles mop-top hairdo. In two other shots, a slightly older Bernie hugged Janis Joplin and draped arms around the shoulders of Country Joe and one of the Fish.

Glenda was glad there weren't any more recent photos. She didn't think the mourners would appreciate how the sad progression of Bernie's coke addiction had altered him.

The folding seats were filling rapidly.

Glenda had hoped to see Fink but didn't spot him. She also didn't see anybody suspicious among the many freaks and eccentrics. Her mysterious caller could be right in front of her and she wouldn't know it. She glanced up at a line of cars parked on a lane just above the funeral site. There were a few Cadillacs, but they were newer models in black, red and gold. None fit Larry's description. She was surprised by the size of the crowd. Several hundred people had come to pay their respects. She recognized a one-time member of Rare Earth, two ex-disco queens and a handful of people who must have been famous, because paparazzi were snapping away at them from a safe distance.

She also spotted three of her old bandmates. Nancy, Mimi and Lou huddled together, all in black, like Macbeth's witches. Nicole, the bassist, wasn't with them. Nancy glanced at Glenda, seemed to rivet her with a gaze, then leaned over and said something to the others. They gave Glenda sour looks, then deliberately turned away. Glenda ducked her head and chose a seat to the left of the stage, as far from them as possible.

She looked at the program. It seemed to include everything but actual angels with trumpets.

"So, you come to mourn Caesar or bury him?"

Glenda looked up at the woman who dropped into the seat next to her. "Nicole!"

"Hi, y'all." Nicole wore a Cossack hat, a coat with a fur collar, a bright red scarf and a miniskirt. She sat, crossed her booted legs, fished in her coat pocket and drew out a small packet.

"Well, look at that. Must be from the last time I wore this, last winter." Nicole offered the pack to Glenda. "Gum?"

Glenda shook her head, too embarrassed to say anything.

Nicole opened the pack, took a stick, unwrapped it from the bright aluminum and popped the gum in her mouth.

"Mourning makes my mouth dry," Nicole said. "No disrespect intended. Well, maybe a bit." She glanced at her program. "Hey! A monkey with a tambourine!"

"What?" Glenda said. "It doesn't..."

Nicole gave her a puckish grin. "Made you look," she said. "How've you been, Glenda?"

Glenda looked at her, surprised. She'd never managed to ask her bandmates for forgiveness— hell, she was still working on forgiving herself.

But Nicole acted as if nothing had happened. Her attitude confused Glenda.

"Busy," Glenda answered lamely. "Uh, you?"

"Oh, you know. Still in this crusty town, doing crusty stuff. I didn't know you'd be here. You look uncomfortable. Sure you don't want the gum? It's Juicy Fruit." Nicole cocked her head thoughtfully. "At least, it was a year ago."

"I'm just a little amazed that you don't want to, well, punch me or something," Glenda said.

"No, I got over that pretty quick," Nicole said breezily. "Lou, though, she really hates you. She's a high school music teacher now. Loathes kids. Probably wishes you were in that coffin with Bernie."

Glenda laughed, causing a few heads to turn. "I guess I can't blame them for feeling that way."

"Actually, I understand what *you're* feeling." Nicole nodded at the band members. "They hate me, too."

"Really? Why?"

"I kind of crashed and burned after you did. Nothing to do with you. I'm gonna try to talk to 'em later, bury the hatchet."

"I'm really sorry," Glenda said.

"Don't be," Nicole said. "It's the biz. Look around. Half the people here are feuding with the other half. Artistic differences, drugs, whatever. They're like street gangs, only with lawyers instead of switchblades."

Glenda laughed again in spite of herself. She'd forgotten how much she loved Nicole's irreverent, take-no-prisoners style.

"And then there's the two sides of the aisle," Nicole added. "Like at a wedding."

"Which sides?"

"Love Bernie, hate Bernie," Nicole said. "Bernie helped some of them, but he screwed a lot more. A lot of them showed up just to make sure he's dead. Some of them are probably sorry they didn't get to kill him first."

Glenda compulsively jerked her head around to eye the crowd, but felt no joy. She had no idea whom she should be looking. Somebody evilly twirling a mustache? A guy leering from under a lowered fedora? Glenda cursed Larry for putting the idea in her head without giving her more information to go on.

She turned back to Nicole. "So," she asked. "Which side are we on?"

"You tell me," Nicole said.

But Glenda couldn't, because just then the service began.

A man wearing a skullcap and a trim goatee walked onstage and took a microphone. He reached into the breast pocket of his suit, pulled out a sheaf of index cards, cleared his throat and began the eulogy.

"Hello," he said in a smooth, calm clergyman's voice. "I'm Rabbi Nathan Weiss of Shalom Temple. We're here today to honor the life of Myron Feinholtz, better known to most of you as Bernie Sherman. Now, I wasn't privileged to know Bernie, but I recognize many of you folks. Yes, the rabbi watches MTV." There was a small ripple of laughter. "And from what I read in the tabloids, some of you could benefit from my pastoral services. Our doors are open." This time the chuckling was merely polite.

The rabbi pressed on. "From his earliest days, Bernie had a passion for music and the people who make it. True, Bernie could be hard-nosed. He was a tough man in a tough business. He learned the art of survival as a skinny little kid on the gritty streets of Philadelphia. And it was in Philly that Bernie fell in love."

The rabbi paused meaningfully.

"First it was Tommy Dorsey, then Chuck Berry and rock and roll. Bernie decided he wanted to "Rock Around the Clock," too. So at the tender age of seventeen, he quit school to manage a local band called the Grasshoppers. From there, you might say his career grew— by leaps and bounds."

The rabbi waited for laughter. Hearing none, he rushed on.

"Seeing so many famous faces here today is a tribute to what Bernie accomplished in his all-too-brief forty-seven years. Bernie fought hard for what he loved. And what he loved was *you*." The rabbi spread his hands toward the audience.

"And money," Nicole stage-whispered. Someone shushed her.

"And coke," Glenda added, earning a louder shush but also some murmured agreement.

The guards onstage caught the murmurs. Their casual glances at the crowd became sharper, and the muscles in their huge necks tensed. Glenda almost thought she could hear them growl.

The rabbi made a placating gesture. "There'll be time for you to share your memories in a moment. But first, let's move to Bernie's later years."

He nodded to the front row. Six teenage boys stood up, threw off their coats and strode quickly to the stage. Skinny kids with glossy black hair, they wore Elvis-style shirts with rhinestones and black, glittery hot pants—except for the lead singer, who had pink shorts. Their go-go boots clattered on the stage as they took positions.

The rabbi joined the lead singer at the mic.

"In the past few years, Bernie discovered a love of Eastern culture," he said. "In 1982, he was awarded a Golden Buddha for his support of Asian music. During his frequent trips to Thailand, he sought out and encouraged many gifted local musicians, like these young men."

Glenda glanced at Nicole and rolled her eyes. Nicole sniggered and snapped her gum.

"Ladies and gentlemen," the rabbi continued, "today one of Bernie's most promising groups is here to honor his memory. Incidentally, they'll also be performing at the Queen Mary in Studio City on Thursday night."

"Been there," Nicole whispered. "Transvestite bar. Fun. Guy there did a great Judy Garland."

She was shushed again.

"Please," the rabbi continued, raising his voice. "Join us now in remembrance as the Bangkok Boppers offer a medley of Bernie's favorite songs."

The rabbi backed away and the lead singer leaned forward into the mic.

"Thank you," he said in heavily accented English. "And hello, Los Angeles. Bernie was a good guy. Let's rock."

He put a finger on the mic and tapped out a four-beat intro.

The sextet swung into an a cappella version of "Rock Around the Clock." Glenda and Nicole listened with mouths agape as the group merged into "In-A-Gadda-Da-Vida," then the Rolling Stones' "Brown Sugar" and an old Glitter Lizards tune, "Shook-Ah Bye-Bye."

"They sing it better than we did," Glenda whispered.

"That pretty boy has a higher range," Nicole said. "And better legs."

The music was accompanied by choreography. The singers, aping Sixties Motown groups, threw out their hands, rocked their shoulders and swiveled their hips in syncopation. During the finale, which was a rendering of Judas Priest's "Breaking the Law," the performers imitated drums and guitars while the singer did the splits.

The audience sat stunned, unsure how to take the twinkly bubble gum performance in the midst of a funeral. Someone gave a lone shout of "Yeah!" and a wolf whistle. It set off a brief but fierce chorus of cheers, hoots and catcalls. The rabbi seemed confused, but the Boppers beamed coquettishly.

The rest of the service went quickly. The rabbi called on people to share their memories of the deceased. A handful of people stepped up to remember Bernie Sherman, without an ounce of irony, as a cross between Albert Einstein and Mother Teresa.

"Why do people always lie at funerals?" Glenda whispered to Nicole. "Why not say someone was a jerk?"

"Old superstition," Nicole said. "Speak ill of the dead, and their ghost might decide to haunt you."

"Well, I'll haunt the shit out of somebody if they don't tell the truth about me when I die."

"What'll they say?" Nicole asked.

"That I was a genius and a wonderful human being."

They erupted in giggles. For once, nobody shushed them.

The service ended with the release of a flock of white doves, although the birds didn't want to fly in the chilly air and had to be flung, complaining, into the sky. The Bangkok Boppers acted as pallbearers. They carried Bernie's coffin slowly offstage to a waiting limousine while singing a slow, solemn dirge. It took a moment for Glenda to identify the song as "Baby Love" by The Supremes.

"So, that was interesting," Glenda said as the crowd streamed away. "Everybody was amazingly well-behaved. I thought it was gonna be another Altamont."

"Where are the Hell's Angels when you need 'em?" Nicole said.

A line of vans waited on the curve of the main road near the parking area to shuttle guests to the reception. Bernie had no close relations in town, so it had been arranged at the local Double Tree hotel.

The clouds began to thicken as guests trudged toward the shuttles.

"Should we take the vans or get our cars?" Glenda asked.

"Shuttle," Nicole said. "I parked way over there." She pointed uphill to the left.

Glenda glanced casually in that direction and felt a chill. A solitary figure in an overcoat stood silhouetted against the hilltop.

She blinked, and the figure was gone.

Cursing under her breath, she decided she was spooking herself.

She hoped.

THE RECEPTION ROOM was a functional space with innocuous wallpaper Glenda thought would work with everything from weddings to insurance conferences. Round tables were scattered around the room, but most of the action seemed to be at the buffet table laid with cold cuts, cheese, rye bread and heaps of potato, bean and coleslaw salad. Slices of marble cake and cheesecake were flanked by coffee urns and bottles of beer. The beer was cold and going fast.

Mourners streamed in, shed their coats and clustered at the tables in cliques. Glenda noticed scowls and fabricated smiles. Most of the celebrities she recognized at the funeral had passed on the reception, which made sense. Their time was money, she thought with a trace of envy.

Nicole reached the buffet first, cutting off a long-haired young man without apology.

By the time Glenda had stocked up, she found Nicole at a table. He ex-bandmate was halfway through a piled plate.

"Is that all you got?" Nicole asked.

"Where are you putting all that?" Glenda retorted.

"I'm eating for two," Nicole said.

"You're pregnant?"

"No, my sister. She lives in Biloxi. She couldn't be here," Nicole added. "She's usually pregnant, though. So I guess I'm eating for three. I just bumped into Eddie Van Halen."

"Really?" Glenda looked over at the buffet table. "What's he like?"

"No. I literally bumped into him. He's short. I didn't see him. Almost knocked him over."

"Big talent, though. I didn't know Bernie represented him."

"Naw," Nicole said, "Eddie Van Halen couldn't have been stupid enough to sign with Bernie."

"We were," Glenda reminded her. "Young and hungry."

"Well," Nicole said, "Bernie did troll Pasadena. And look at that ass. It's possible."

"Brrr," Glenda said. Her shoulders quivered in mock revulsion. "Gay's okay, but with Bernie?" She shook her head.

"He was a butt vampire," Nicole said.

Glenda had a sudden vision of Bernie's chalky moons cresting the bathtub. She shook it off and watched Nicole spear a pickle with a long varnished fingernail.

"Like your nails," Glenda said. "But isn't it hard to play?"

Nicole held up her right hand. "These are real." She waved her left hand. "These are fake. I can take 'em off. But I don't play all that much." She shrugged. "Doesn't pay the bills."

Glenda looked uncomfortable, so Nicole added: "Like I said, I don't blame you. I blame Bernie. He pushed you into leaving."

"No, I blame myself," Glenda said.

"That, too," Nicole agreed. "No doubt. And I heard you landed hard. No parachute."

"Yeah," Glenda said. "I lost some teeth." She thought about her probation.

They both smiled ruefully. Glenda took a thoughtful bite of her sandwich. It was delicious.

"So," Nicole asked. "What do you do now?"

"I work for a booking agency," Glenda said around a mouthful of roast beef. "Mostly I book clowns for kids' parties. You?"

"I take my clothes off for pervs and drunks."

"Ewww."

"Pays the rent. Besides, dudes are dudes. The only difference from the old days is now I show a little more skin. So they don't have to undress me with their eyes."

Glenda found herself nodding. "We didn't get much respect from those asshole rockers when we were performing," she said. "Remember that scumbucket in Tampa who asked if we had real musicians behind the curtain?"

"God," Nicole said. "I'd forgotten that guy. We should have been punkers. Punk guys take women musicians seriously."

"I know," Glenda said and blushed as she thought of Nelson.

"So," Nicole said. "You hustle clowns."

"And I'm working on an album."

Nicole snorted around a bite of cheesecake.

"No offense, but everybody in town knows about your album."

"Hey!" Glenda said defensively. "It's got to be right. Perfect."

Nicole sighed. "Not perfect," she said. "No offense, but that was your problem, all right? Perfect wasn't perfect *enough*." She gave Glenda an arch look and smiled. "You never settled for just brilliant."

"I know." Glenda had to agree. She sighed, too. "At this stage, I'd settle for finished."

"No," Nicole said. "Just settle for great."

"Yeah," Glenda said dismissively. "Like I can do great."

"Lover, you always had the chops," Nicole said. "Just dump the ego and the annoying, anal retentive, ant-fucker attitude. No offense."

Nicole's words touched Glenda's rawest nerve. She blurted, "That's the third time in thirty seconds you've said 'no offense.' You don't need to put me down. I already do that!"

She stopped speaking suddenly, aware that she'd shown her vulnerability. She made a big display of examining her food, hoping Nicole's eyes weren't on her.

Nicole put a hand on Glenda's wrist.

"Hey, I'm sorry. I was just joking. I do respect you. You know that, right?"

Glenda looked up, embarrassed about exploding. "Don't worry about it," she said. "It's just… well, it's everything that's going on." She thought about finding Bernie's body, the phone call she'd received, Larry's warning and that glimpse— *maybe* —of a figure on the hill just after the funeral.

Larry's ravings suddenly didn't seem so far-fetched.

"Nicole," Glenda said. "What were you saying about Bernie… about people wanting to kill him?"

"A lot of people," Nicole said as she demolished a heap of potato salad.

"Well," Glenda said tentatively. "What if someone did? What would you do?"

"Applaud?" Nicole said but then she saw Glenda's face. "Wait, are you serious?"

"I'm just saying," Glenda began.

"No, you're not," Nicole said. "Do you know something?"

"No!" Glenda said hastily. "It's just so weird, isn't it?"

"What's weird about a drug overdose and a fall?"

"Nothing, I guess," Glenda said. "But still, if it turned out he'd had a little help, and you knew it…" Her words trailed off and then she added, "What would you do?"

Nicole's eyes widened suddenly. She dropped the fork and put her hands over her mouth.

"You did it!" she said in a stage whisper.

"No! *No!*"

"Joking," Nicole said, rolling her eyes. "But I think *you* were being serious. Do you want to talk about it?"

"I really don't know anything," Glenda said. "I think the whole thing has kind of freaked me out. I mean, there are these big contract issues I have to sort out… it's just kind of weird."

"I get that," Nicole said, then added shrewdly, "But there is something worrying you, isn't there?"

"I don't know," Glenda said uncertainly. "Maybe. Theoretically."

"Well, theoretically, then, if I knew Bernie had been murdered, I'd go to the police."

"And if you couldn't?"

"Theoretically?"

"Yes."

Nicole sighed. "Then, *theoretically*, I'd keep my big, fat theoretical nose out of theoretical things where it didn't belong. *Theoretically*. It's not your job to play detective."

"But then someone could get away with murder."

"Theoretically?"

Glenda said nothing.

Nicole sighed again. "Look, Glenda, you're not a guilt hog. You can't even apologize to those gals." Nicole nodded at their former bandmates who had taken an entire table for themselves. "How do you think you could live with the guilt of concealing a murder?"

Glenda nodded.

"If you're asking me for moral guidance, girl, well, I haven't cracked a Bible since I was fifteen. But we have a saying in the South: 'What would Jesus do?'"

"I'm Jewish," Glenda said.

"Yeah. So say to yourself: "What would Bernie do?"

"What would Bernie do?"

"Yep. Then do the opposite."

Glenda laughed.

"I'm serious," Nicole said, lowering her voice. "And listen. Whatever you know, or think you know, be careful. Things can get too real, real fast. You may not be able to handle it alone." Nicole raised her fork and pointed it at Glenda and then at herself. "If that looks like the case, you call me, okay?"

Glenda looked at her in surprise. Nicole tended to do things on the spur of the moment. She was instinctive. But she'd never flaked on a promise. Nicole meant her offer of help.

Glenda had an ally.

"Thank you," she said, touched.

"No problem," Nicole said. "We outcasts got to stick together."

"Outcasts don't stick together. That's why they're outcasts," Glenda pointed out.

"See, that's your problem again," Nicole said. "Carnal relations with ants."

"No offense," Glenda said.

"Oh, no, big offense," Nicole said, smiling.

Glenda snorted. "Thank you for busting my balls."

"Figuratively," Nicole said. "You only have figurative balls."

"Now who's being anal retentive?"

"You're anal retentive. I'm a nitpicker. The difference is, people need their nits picked."

"Man, I've been missing you," Glenda said. "Hey, I'm going to be in the studio tonight. Wanna swing by and pick my nits?"

"Well," Nicole said in a cutie-pie voice, "how often does a girl get an offer like that? Blush, blush."

"No, seriously," Glenda said. "You might be... you might have a tiny point about my, um, attention to detail. You can let me know if I overdo it."

"You're saying I get to kick your ass!" Nicole said delightedly.

"I'm not saying that!" Glenda protested.

"I'll think about it," Nicole said. "I might like to hear your dinner set."

"Oh, shut up."

"Easy listening covers are always fun," Nicole said.

"I'm withdrawing the offer."

"I knew you didn't really want my advice," Nicole said in mock stuffiness.

"Fine," Glenda said. "You can kick my ass. A little."

"I will think about it," Nicole repeated.

"Nine o'clock, Bronson Studios. And you can bring your long-necked boyfriend."

Glenda and Nicole had always joked about the myth that bass guitar vibrations caused orgasms in women. Nicole suddenly looked hesitant.

"You know, I really haven't played that much lately," she said.

Glenda caught a glimpse of concealed insecurity. Nicole might be flippant about her change of careers, but the musician in her clearly was hurting.

"Hey, no pressure," Glenda added quickly.

Nicole looked down at her plate, stabbed another pickle and chewed.

"Maybe," Nicole said. She dabbed pickle juice from her lower lip and pushed back her plate. She forced a smile. "Now if you'll excuse me, I have some apologies to make."

Glenda watched her rise and walk over to the Witches Three. They gave her the same sour looks they had given to Glenda. Nicole said something. The women looked grim. Then Nicole said something else, and there were curt replies. Then Nicole said something insistently, moving her arms with fluid emphasis and, miraculously, the women burst into laughter. A few more words and they were all looking at Glenda, who put her head down and pretended to be busy with her food. When she looked up again, everyone was hugging. Then Nicole beamed, kissed everyone on the cheek and strolled back to Glenda.

"All done," Nicole said. "We're good. We won't be having any potlucks anytime soon, but we're back on speaking terms. They may drop me a phone call from time to time."

"You're amazing!" Glenda said. "You were only gone five minutes!"

"I work fast," Nicole said. "I take my clothes off for a living, remember? I know how to read people and give 'em what they want. Oh, and I apologized for you, too."

"You did what?" Glenda blushed. "You didn't have to… you shouldn't have…"

"No thanks necessary," Nicole said airily. "I told them you were really sorry and they could take your apology to the bank."

"And what did they say?"

Nicole shrugged. "They're deciding whether to cash it." She looked down at her plate then up at Glenda. "Seconds?"

THE SHUTTLE DROPPED Glenda back at the cemetery. It had finally begun to rain, and Glenda hurried to her parked Porsche, glad she'd left the top up. Then she swore. There was a long, thin rip in the ragtop just over the driver's seat. She was furious. How had that happened? She opened the door and found out. An envelope lay on the driver's seat. Somebody must have slashed the canvas and dropped it in. Glenda jerked her head around but saw nobody suspicious. She thought again about the strange silhouette on the hill. She shivered.

She slipped into the car, slammed the door and tore open the envelope. A folded letter dropped into her lap. She unfolded it. Inside was a slender, passport-sized booklet. The letters SWM were stamped in gold leaf on the front. Glenda opened the book and was taken aback. It was a savings account passbook for the Songwriters and Musicians Credit Union. Typed on the inside cover was Glenda's name in capital letters. The other pages contained a long list of deposits and withdrawals. None of which she'd ever made. The numbers were very large. Glenda flipped to the last entry and did a double-take at the balance. *Fifty thousand dollars.* She took a deep breath and shook her head to clear it. She rechecked the book. The numbers hadn't changed. And the name still read GLENDA BIRDSONG.

She picked up the letter. Typed on cheap paper with no letterhead, it read: "You have twenty-four hours to withdraw the money or the tape goes to the police. Get cash. Delivery instructions will follow." There was no signature.

A finicky part of Glenda's mind was irked. Twenty-four hours from when? From the start of the funeral? From the time the envelope had been left in the car? And how was she supposed to know that, anyway? Why couldn't the blackmailer just write a time, like, say "a quarter to twelve?" And if the creep was going to send new instructions, wouldn't she have to wait for them? So how would she even know when the time was up? It was amateur hour, Glenda decided grumpily. Then she realized she was doing her mind-blabbing thing again, which she did when she was nervous.

Glenda had never banked at that credit union. She'd never even been there. She checked her watch. The credit union probably closed at three o'clock. Banker's hours. She had just enough time.

She turned the key and shifted the car into gear. As she drove, rain began coming down in buckets. Water dripped onto her head all the way back to Hollywood.

CHAPTER THIRTEEN

Glenda broke every speed law and managed to pull into the credit union parking lot with ten minutes to spare. She hurried inside, where she was greeted by a big handmade sign on the back wall that proclaimed in rainbow colors: "New! Extended hours: 9 to 6!!!!!!"

Swearing, Glenda shook her soaking hair like a wet poodle and then stood impatiently in line at the teller's window, dripping water on the marble floor. When she finally reached the counter, the chirpy teller beamed.

"Miss Birdsong, good to see you again. Did you have a nice vacation?"

"Two weeks of bliss," a confused Glenda improvised, remembering the last withdrawal date.

"I bet you ate tons of lobster," the teller said, her eyes darting over Glenda's ample proportions.

"You have no idea," Glenda said, a bit testily. The woman didn't seem to notice.

"Well," the teller said, "what can we do for you today?"

"I want to make a withdrawal," Glenda said.

"How much?"

Glenda passed over the bank book. "All of it, please."

The teller, oddly, blushed and looked happy.

"Does this mean you're going to finish the album?"

"Um," Glenda said, nonplussed. "Getting really close."

"Well, congratulations!" the teller said. "I'll just need to get the manager's signature." She passed Glenda a withdrawal slip. "Go ahead and fill this out."

The teller reappeared as Glenda signed the slip, accompanied by a man with half-moon glasses and a protruding Adam's apple who had probably been born to be a bank manager.

"Miss Birdsong, how nice to see you again," he said, taking the teller's place at the counter. Glenda smiled. The manager nodded and held out a hand.

"May I?" he said, indicating the slip. Glenda slid it across the counter. The manager peered at it, then looked up at her.

"If I may ask, is there a problem with our service?"

"No," she said. "Not at all."

"But by taking out the entire balance, you'll be closing the account," the manager said.

The teller leaned in and whispered something.

"Oh," the manager said. "It's for the album! Congratulations. It has certainly been a journey for you, I'm sure."

"Thank you," Glenda said. "You know what? Maybe I should keep the account open." She wasn't sure if the blackmailer wanted her to close it. "What's the minimum balance?"

The manager chuckled. "Well, five dollars would do it."

"Make it ten."

Glenda left the bank with forty-nine thousand, nine hundred and ninety dollars. The envelope, choked with bills of large denominations, bulged in her purse. The money seemed to weigh as much as one of Mrs. Patakian's dachshunds.

Driving home, she sat with the brick of cash stuffed between her rump and the seat. She was literally sitting on a pile of money. Her gaze darting everywhere, she drove slowly and carefully, watching for shadowy criminals. The sky was dull yellowish-gray as she pulled into the carport. The light was dim and she peered around for several seconds, scanning every corner before finally getting out. Moving furtively, she went through the back entrance and upstairs to her apartment.

After shooting the deadbolt, Glenda slid the security chain on the door and took the money from her purse. She breathed a little heavily. She was holding almost fifty thousand dollars! It was like holding a live rattlesnake. She didn't want it anywhere near her. She thought hard for an instant, glancing around the living room, then strode into the kitchen. Walking to the oven, she bent down, opened it and put the stack of cash in a chipped casserole dish her mother had loaned her years ago. She pushed the dish to the back of a lower shelf and closed the oven door. It would be safe. She never cooked, so the only way the oven would get hot was if the entire apartment caught fire.

Glenda had just returned to the living room when a knock came at the door. A voice called "Miss Birdsong?" Glenda peeked through the spy hole and saw a woman in a blue post office jacket. She held a letter and a clipboard.

Glenda waited.

"Miss Birdsong, are you there?" the woman said. "I have a special delivery letter."

The woman waited another minute as Glenda held her breath. The woman shrugged and bent down. Glenda saw the back of her head disappear and then the corner of an envelope emerged from under the door. The woman straightened up, made a note on her clipboard and moved out of sight. Glenda heard her footsteps as the woman descended the stairs, but waited until she heard the front door open and shut before reaching down and pulling on the envelope.

It was stuck. Glenda tugged but the letter wouldn't move. The corner started to tear. Cursing, Glenda straightened and unlocked the door.

She'd opened it only a few inches when it slammed against her, knocking her back. A woman was doubled over on the doorstep with one foot on the letter. In one hand, she held an ice pick. In a fluid movement, the woman uncurled and stepped through the door. She had the pick pressed to Glenda's heart before Glenda could move.

"Don't," the woman said. "Just step back. That's a good girl." Keeping her focus on Glenda, the woman called out, "Baby, come on up."

The woman with the post office jacket came back upstairs and strolled into the apartment. She gave Glenda a dirty grin.

The woman with the ice pick closed the door and locked it, her gaze never straying from Glenda.

Glenda stared at the invaders. The woman in the jacket was blond. She was about Glenda's height and build, although twenty pounds skinnier. She had long fingernails that reminded Glenda of Nicole's. The woman with the ice pick was half a head shorter, thin and sour but tough-looking. She wore a T-shirt and motorcycle jacket. Her chopped hair looked as if she'd shampooed it with axle grease. She had reptilian eyes and a spider web tattooed across her throat.

"Sit down," the blonde said. Glenda sat on the couch, sinking into it, her knees up.

The tough woman took the chair across from Glenda. She held the ice pick confidently, as if it seldom left her hand. The word SLASH was tattooed on the back of that hand.

"You like Guns N' Roses?" Glenda asked.

"What?" the woman said.

"Slash. The guitarist."

"I had it first," Slash snarled.

"Because you slash things?"

"When I have to."

"But you don't have a blade. You have an ice pick."

Slash looked puzzled. "So?"

"Well, shouldn't you be called Prick?"

"Don't be a smartass," the woman said in a flat voice. "You'll live longer."

Blondie bent down and asked Glenda, "Where's the money, honey?"

"My purse is in the bedroom," Glenda said. "It's got about twenty dollars in it. Take it, please."

Blondie laughed. "You're funny. Where's the money?"

"I don't—" Glenda began.

"Oh, you do, sugar," Blondie said. "I was just down at the credit union to make a little withdrawal, the way I always do, and surprise, they told me I'd already been there— and I'd cleaned out the account. I was embarrassed."

The blood in Glenda's veins turned to ice.

"Now I haven't been able to reach Fink," the woman continued. "I figured with Bernie dead, whatever tax scam or embezzlement scheme that accountant had going is over, and he's going to split with the money. Which is good in a way, because now I don't have to wear that stupid wig anymore when I make deposits. But it's bad because for some idiotic reason, that asshole decided to cut me out instead of paying me off." She shook her head. "But why use you? Did you get wise? Threaten him, maybe?"

"No," Glenda said. She saw no point in lying. "I never saw him. Somebody left an envelope in my car today with the bank book and told me to get the money or I'd be in bad trouble."

"Huh," Blondie said and turned to the other woman. "You believe that?"

The other woman shrugged.

Blondie shook her head. "I don't really care. The money is real enough. So hand it over, and we'll part friends."

"If I do that, I'm in trouble," Glenda said.

"We all have our problems," Blondie said. "Get it."

"It's not here." Glenda's jaw tightened. "I took it right to my bank. I can't get it until tomorrow."

"Uh-huh," Blondie said. She looked at Slash, who gave a little shake of her head.

Blondie grinned, straightened up and tapped a finger against her temple and frowned, like the Scarecrow cogitating in *The Wizard of Oz*.

"Hmmmm," Blondie said. "I. Don't. Think. So." She began walking slowly around the room, talking to herself. "Let's see. Couch? No. Too obvious. Behind the TV? Nope. Ooh, guitar case."

Blondie went to Banshee's case leaning against one wall, opened it, saw nothing and sighed dramatically.

"You're gonna make me look around, aren't you?"

Glenda resisted the urge to protest as the woman strolled to the back of the apartment.

Slash kept her cold, emotionless stare on Glenda.

Glenda heard Blondie throwing things around, opening and slamming closet doors and drawers as she moved through the house. It took only moments before Blondie reappeared. The pocket of her jacket boasted a thick bulge.

Blondie patted the pocket gleefully and told Slash: "Got it. Let's go."

Slash stood in one swift motion. Blondie opened the front door and went through. Slash paused and told Glenda, "Don't call the cops and you'll never see us again." She left and closed the door.

Glenda waited until she heard the two women's footsteps vanish and the building's front door close with a bang. She took a couple of deep breaths and then jumped up from the couch, ran into the kitchen, opened the oven door, reached inside and grabbed the baking dish. Relief flooded her, followed instantly by confusion. The money was still there. Glenda picked up the stack of bills and held it. It was real.

She was still holding the cash when the front door opened. Slash and Blondie walked into the kitchen.

"Everybody falls for that," Blondie said and snatched the cash. With her other hand, Blondie reached into her jacket pocket and pulled out Glenda's bath sponge. She flipped it at Glenda. It hit her shoulder and bounced to the floor. Slash's tongue darted out and flicked her upper lip. Then the women turned and were gone. Glenda stood motionless in the kitchen. She heard the building's front door shut, more softly this time. This time, the women didn't care if Glenda heard it.

She stood for a moment, then dashed into the living room. She went to the front door, tore it open, looked outside at the empty stairwell, then closed the door and shot the deadbolt, bitterly aware that she was far too late. Clenching her fists, she breathed thickly and fought down a scream. She shook with anger and humiliation. *Stupid, stupid, stupid!* she thought.

After a long minute, some small part of her mind sneered and said: *this is not helping.*

But what could she do? The money was gone.

No, Glenda thoughrt suddenly. It wasn't gone. Those assholes had it.

All she had to do was find them.

And take it back, the voice in her head jeered. Glenda ignored it. One step at a time.

She needed to find them. But how? She replayed the entire episode in her head. What had Blondie said? Fink had hired her to impersonate Glenda. Everything made sense, now: why the credit union teller had seemed to recognize Glenda— and had implied she'd gained weight.

Glenda grabbed the phone and called the accountant. She knew now that Fink had set up the bank scheme, which made him the only link she had to the women. As expected, there was no answer.

She checked her watch. It was six o'clock. Most of the people in Fink's office building probably had left work for the day. With luck, she'd have a clear shot at his office door.

Shaking her head ruefully, she realized burglary was becoming a habit.

IT WAS SIX-THIRTY WHEN Glenda reached Fink's office, and the floor seemed deserted. None of the people in nearby offices apparently wanted to put in overtime. She still glanced both ways and peered through the glass before trying the door. It was locked. But she had come prepared. Trying not to think of her probation, Glenda pulled a screwdriver from her raincoat and attacked the quarter-inch of deadbolt she could see through the gap between the door and the frame, trying to force it backwards. The blade slid on the metal and did nothing but leave brassy scratches. She looked around again, then pulled a hammer from her other pocket. She wedged the claw end into the gap and pulled. Nothing happened. Glenda threw her weight into it. It was hard work, but the wooden door gave an alarming crack. Glenda stopped, frightened.

The edge of the door now bore claw marks but the gap between it and the frame had widened. *Progress!* Glenda exalted. Puffing, she put down the hammer and pulled a coat hanger from her inside pocket. Feeling like MacGyver, she bent it and fed it through the gap, trying to reach the deadbolt turn piece.

She was no MacGyver. Glenda managed to catch the piece, but every time she tried to turn it, the wire bent or slipped. No matter how she contorted her makeshift burglary tool, she couldn't get any leverage. Feeling the sweat under her arms, she cursed silently and grappled with the lock.

After five long minutes, Glenda pulled out the wire and threw it down. In frustration, she slammed a palm on the edge of the lock— then gaped as the entire glass insert of the door fell inward in slow motion, hit the hardwood floor of the office and, with an unholy noise, exploded into thousands of tiny chunks.

That's an A-sharp, Glenda thought dazedly. She realized the dried-out, ancient putty that held the glass had given up the ghost, thanks to her pounding and prying. She was sure the noise must have awakened the dead, but her frightened glance showed the hallway still deserted. There was no sound of running feet, no shouts or alarms. The dead still slept soundly, apparently, along with the security guard, if there was one. No burglar would bother hitting the building, she realized. None of the shabby little businesses inhabiting it had anything worth stealing.

But the accountant did.

Fink had banked somebody else's money, maybe Glenda's. And someone had stolen it from Glenda— which really meant from Fink. And Glenda was going to get it back, damn it.

She hoped.

Glenda stepped through the smashed door.

She flipped the light switch, went to the reception desk and rifled the drawers. She found an appointment calendar, but there was nothing important written in it. She went into the main office and checked Fink's desk, a glass-topped piece of abused mahogany. Several business cards had been stuck under the glass, and a ring-bound desk calendar sat on top of it. Glenda flipped the calendar pages. Again, nothing struck her. She tried the desk drawers, but they were locked. Leaning over, she was about to use the screwdriver on them when her eye caught a splotch of color on the desk. She took a closer look. One of the business cards stuck under the glass had a colorful cartoon of a leering clown's face. The card read: *The Big Top*. It also bore a hand-written phone number in pink ink. Glenda couldn't see Fink using pink ink.

She picked up the desk phone. It had a dial tone. She dialed the number from the card.

On the other end of the wire, the phone rang three times and then a voice cooed: "Hi, lover. I'm missing you. If you miss me, too, leave your number." The message ended with a giggle.

Glenda hung up, fuming. She'd heard that giggle quite recently. *Blondie*.

She looked at the card again. Fink must have met Blondie at The Big Top. She phoned the business number.

"Big Top, where all your fantasies come true," a bored male voice said.

"Is Blondie there?" Glenda asked.

"Which one?"

"The one with the butch girlfriend."

"She's on stage."

"Thanks," Glenda said and hung up.

After wiping the phone clean of fingerprints with the sleeve of her coat, Glenda marched out of the office and through the shattered door. She wondered idly how many weeks it would take before somebody noticed the damage.

CHAPTER FOURTEEN

The Big Top was a dark, red pit with chrome highlights. The walls bore fat red and white stripes like a circus tent. Carousel horses, impaled on poles, hung from the ceiling. Glenda wondered if those horses were used in the more bizarre acts.

The room smelled of stale cigarette smoke and musk— apparently management's idea of a sexy aroma. She walked in without a second glance from the doorman and took a seat at a booth in a corner. The hammer and screwdriver rode bulkily in her raincoat pockets.

Gyrating on a raised stage, Blondie made circular love to a pole. Her hair fell to the small of her back, and shiny red boots rose to her thighs.

George Michael's "I Want Your Sex" blared from the speakers. Glenda groaned. She'd been hearing the song for the past three months from every record shop, supermarket and car window in Hollywood.

With a leer, Blondie turned her rear to the audience and bent over.

Glenda winced and turned her head away. She'd already seen more of that woman than she'd ever wanted.

Blondie spread her legs and peered between them. Her hair swept the stage. A dozen men seated around the stage whooped.

Glenda looked around the room. A few other men sat at nearby tables. A curved bar faced the stage a few feet away across a checkered floor.

The only person at the bar was Slash. She had swiveled the stool around and lounged back with her elbows on the bar. Her lizard-like gaze never left Blondie. A big pink purse sat on the floor beneath her boots.

A waitress came up to Glenda. She held a tray of beers and looked at Glenda quizzically.

"Are you waiting for somebody?" the waitress asked.

"No," Glenda said, realizing it must be rare to see an unescorted woman in the place.

"Oh." The waitress frowned. "Well, what can I get you?"

"Nothing, thanks."

The waitress gave her a sharp look. "Um, if you're waiting to go up there, you're a day early. Amateur night is tomorrow."

"No, no, I'm not—" Glenda began, shaking her head emphatically.

"Well," the waitress cut in. "If you're gonna sit, there's a two-drink minimum."

"Okay," Glenda said. "I'll have a—"

A beer bottle thunked down on the table. The waitress strode off.

Glenda nervously took a swig without tasting it. Blondie strolled across the stage, pausing as men reached up to stuff dollar bills into the top of her boots. Slash watched expressionlessly. Her eyes didn't blink.

Glenda, unnerved, took another sip of beer and wondered what her next move should be.

Slash and Blondie decided the matter for her. Blondie, her boots sprouting bills, disappeared behind a velvet curtain to one side of the stage. Slash, panther-like, glided up from the bar, took the purse and followed.

Glenda looked around and saw that the waitress had gone down to the stage and was taking orders before the next performer came on. Glenda got up, wrapped her raincoat around her and crossed swiftly to the velvet curtain. Behind her, she heard a Gloria Gaynor song begin to blare.

Parting the curtains, Glenda found herself in a short, dim corridor with rooms on either side. Raised voices issued from one of the rooms down the hall. A door on her left was ajar and she ducked inside. It was an empty dressing room. She closed the door and waited with her ear pressed against it. The music thumped dully through the walls.

The voices from down the hall seemed to rise in pitch, and then Glenda heard two sudden flat snapping sounds, like muffled drum raps. She waited, but heard no more voices. After counting the beats of her racing heart, she chanced a peek through the door into the corridor. Seeing nothing, she slipped into the hall. As she did so, she pulled the screwdriver from her pocket and walked as quietly as she could down the hall, checking doors. Another door on her left was open. That room, too, was empty. Two doors on the right were locked. The handle turned on the third. Cautiously, Glenda opened it a crack, keeping most of her body away from the opening in case Slash came at her with the ice pick. A wedge of fluorescent light, the color of a bleached corpse, spilled from the opening, and Glenda caught a whiff of acrid smoke.

With her screwdriver raised, Glenda pushed into the room.

Blondie lay on the floor in front of a makeup table, her white terrycloth robe soaked with blood. Her open eyes were empty as glass marbles— a doll's eyes. Glenda shivered. Blondie had worn white slippers. One had come off and lay beside her foot. Glenda noticed she wore Band-Aids on several toes.

From the stage Gloria Gaynor, with unintended irony, belted the last verse of "I Will Survive."

Glenda was losing time. At any time the stripper could end her stage set. With luck, the girl might head into the audience for lap dances. Glenda might get another song or two before she came back through the velvet curtain. Glenda did not intend to be there.

Through the curtain came the sound of Jermaine Stewart's "We Don't Have To Take Our Clothes Off."

Tearing her gaze from Blondie's body, Glenda surveyed the makeup table, cluttered with bottles, brushes and powders, tubes of lipstick, eyelash crimpers, eyebrow pencils and nail polishes in a half-dozen shades. The table held more makeup than Glenda had owned in her entire life. Perching on the edge of the table like a contented cat sat the big pink purse.

Glenda wondered if the money was in it. Only one way to find out, she told herself. She stepped into the room and stopped.

Black cowboy boots jutted out from behind the door, the toes pointing at the ceiling.

Glenda caught her breath sharply.

Careful to avoid stepping in blood, she entered the room and eased the door toward herself.

Behind the door, Slash sat propped in the corner, her back to a wall. There was a bloody wound in her temple and a gun at her side. Blood and wads of greasy hair splattered the corner. Slash's reptilian eyes seemed just as cold and lifeless as always.

Glenda gagged and swallowed hot bile. She breathed heavily through her nose and avoided looking at the bodies until she felt her nausea pass, aware all the time of how it would look if she were caught in that room. With an effort, she shut down the shocked and horrified part of her mind. Shock and horror would just have to wait until later. It appeared that Slash had shot Blondie and then herself. Maybe they'd argued over the money. That would be ironic.

Glenda suppressed the thought and focused. She had come for the money; that was all.

Jermaine Stewart finished his song.

In the brief silence, Glenda stepped to the makeup table and opened the purse. The envelope with the money was stuffed inside. She grabbed it.

Glenda hadn't heard any footsteps, but suddenly a voice at the door called out: "Blondie, somebody wants a lap dance." It sounded like the waitress.

Casting a frantic glance at the door, Glenda saw it was ajar. All the waitress had to do was push it open, and she would see the carnage and Glenda with her arm in the purse. She held her breath, hoping the woman wasn't waiting for an answer.

The door didn't move.

Time seemed to stop, and then the waitress walked away. This time, Glenda heard the footsteps.

She hauled the packet of cash out of the purse. With it came a small amber pill bottle that clattered onto the table. Without thinking, Glenda snatched it and slipped it into her jeans. She stuffed the envelope of cash inside her coat then grabbed a clump of tissues from a box on the table and wiped the clasp of the purse. Stuffing the tissues in another pocket, she carefully navigated to the door, glanced out, saw the corridor was empty and made for the fire exit.

IT WAS DARK AND COLD and approaching eight when Glenda pulled into her carport in the alley. She was exhausted and jangled. That's why— she told herself later — she didn't see the robber.

The man came up behind her and something hard prodded her back.

"Don't turn around!" a raspy voice ordered. "Hands up!"

Terrified, flashing on the carnage she'd just left, Glenda blurted out: "I gotta pee."

"Oh, Jesus," the voice said with disgust.

"Look, I don't have anything," Glenda said.

"You better have my money!" the voice said testily.

Suddenly, Glenda realized who was behind her. The man who had given her the bank book. Fink? Her fear eased incrementally.

"You had all day to get it," the man complained.

"You gave me twenty-four hours," Glenda protested.

"No, I gave you a day," the man said. "Day's over. Where's my money?" He prodded her even harder in the back.

Glenda flinched. "Here," she said. "It's here. In my pocket." She started to reach a hand into her raincoat.

"Don't!" the man warned.

Glenda put her hands back up and felt him pat her pockets. He pulled out the screwdriver. She heard it clink on the pavement. Then he grabbed the hammer, which she heard thunk against her car. Next came the wad of tissues and, finally, he groped inside the coat and grabbed the cash.

She heard him fumbling open the envelope.

The pressure against Glenda's back eased, but she was afraid to move. She didn't hear him walk away. Her arms began to ache, and slowly she lowered her hands. Nobody shot her. When her arms were at her side, she turned around.

The alley was empty. Glenda looked at her car and saw a new dent in it. The hammer lay on the ground. She bent, picked it up along with the screwdriver, and for a second fantasized about finding the accountant and putting a dent in him. Then suddenly she was all out of everything. She felt drained as she trudged into the building. Staggering up the stairs, she clutched the banister as if she would tumble without its support. Her hands felt nerveless as she struggled with the key. She barely made it inside before she slumped onto the couch. She felt as if her bones had melted. The day had been too much.

She wanted to curse, but fell asleep before the words left her mouth.

CHAPTER FIFTEEN

Glenda awoke feeling as if someone had flattened her with a steamroller, backed over her and did it again. And then *again*.

For a moment, she didn't know what time it was or even what day. But something nagged at her. There was something she was supposed to do. Needed to do, although her exhausted and shell-shocked body told her what she *really* needed to do was go back to sleep. She glanced at her watch. Nine o'clock. She'd been asleep for less than half an hour.

Glenda suddenly remembered. She had a rehearsal. She had never missed a rehearsal, even when she was stoned.

But she stayed glued to the couch. Her eyes felt raw, as if they'd been sandpapered. With a grunt, she forced herself up, which was almost too much effort. Dragging herself to the bathroom, she splashed water on her face and looked in horror at the mirror, seeing matted hair and ashy skin.

As she leaned closer to the mirror, she pushed against the edge of the sink. Something dug into her hip. She reached into the pocket of her jeans and pulled out the pill bottle. It had no label.

She peered at it, confused. For a moment she couldn't remember where she'd gotten it. Then the bloody scene at the strip club flashed into her mind. Glenda swallowed hard, uncapped the bottle and poured pills into her hand.

There were two kinds: round white ones stamped with crosses, and shiny red capsules. Glenda recognized them. White crosses were the amphetamines she'd used to diet. The capsules were Seconals.

Uppers and downers.

She shuddered but couldn't look away. Intending to flush the pills, she staggered toward the toilet. But she was so tired, so beat up, and she had a whole night to get through.

She had never missed a rehearsal, even when she was stoned.

Besides, she'd invited Nelson. She refused to explain to herself why Nelson mattered.

She watched herself pick out two white crosses. She swallowed them dry, recognizing the familiar bitter taste. She looked at the remaining pills in her hand. She made a fist, held it out over the toilet, hovered a moment. Then she returned to the sink, poured the pills back into the bottle and capped it. Holding up the bottle between her finger and thumb, she stared at it; noticed its tawny goldness in the light. She blew out a long breath, opened the mirrored front of the medicine cabinet and put the vial on the top shelf behind a bottle of cough syrup.

Running a brush through her hair, she rinsed her mouth under the tap, walked to the living room, picked up Banshee and left the apartment, repeating to herself: *Just this once.*

She was halfway to the studio when the pills kicked in. She began to sweat and her blood felt fizzy. Her left knee jittered up and down on the Porsche's floorboard. She cursed. The dose wouldn't have fazed her three years ago, but now drugs shot through her unprepared body like a skyrocket. Her mind was getting sharper, but so were her nerves. Right about then, it began to rain. Cold drops trickled through the rip in the car top and dropped onto her forehead like Chinese water torture, making her feel homicidal. She couldn't risk being out of control in the studio. She had to focus. She needed to even out. She thought longingly of the blood-red Seconals in the bottle and regretted that it was too late to turn back and get them.

But she needed a downer, something to take the edge off.

Glenda jerked the car to a stop at an Osco Sav-on. She bought a fifth of something that claimed to be Kentucky whiskey and a roll of duct tape. She taped up the torn car canopy, got behind the wheel, opened the bottle, took three fiery gulps, then stashed the bottle behind the seat and drove on. Having an open container of alcohol in the car was just one more thing she wouldn't share with her probation officer.

By the time Glenda got to the studio, she was steady and alert. The blood and fear and nightmares of the past few hours had faded into the background like grisly wallpaper.

Bronson Studios was, as the name implied, located on Bronson Avenue. Although Glenda's clothes were damp from her brief sprint from the parking lot, she strode into the studio with calm confidence to find, for a change, everyone waiting for her. From behind the mixing boards in his glass-fronted room, Eddie the sound engineer gave her a thumbs-up.

The stale studio air smelled of damp socks, since everybody had tossed their wet boots in the corner. The drummer, J.B., kept swearing about the humidity and tightening the drumheads, lamenting that he couldn't afford the new Remos.

Noodling on a Fender bass, Nicole sat hunched on a metal folding chair. The bass was white, scraped and worn, with wood showing through its veneer; a real musician's instrument, not the shiny toy Nicole had used onstage. Glenda approved.

Nelson sat across from Nicole watching her fingering intently. He held his own guitar. So engrossed were the two, they didn't register Glenda's entrance. She felt a twinge of jealousy but quickly buried it.

"Hi, guys," she said. Nelson jumped to his feet as if he planned to salute. His enthusiasm made her smile. Everyone else glanced up and murmured greetings or waved, except for a lanky stranger behind the studio keyboards.

Glenda eyed him narrowly. Her godfather had mentioned he was sending a keyboardist, but she had forgotten his name.

"Hi," Glenda said, smiling at him. He didn't react, but simply stared at her. She wondered, absurdly, if he was deaf.

"That's Keith," Nicole said. "He told us his name when he got here. Said he doesn't like to repeat himself."

"Wow," Glenda muttered. "Where's Rick?" The bulky lead guitarist was nowhere in sight.

"He got a studio gig," J.B. said, still fiddling with his drumheads. "It's for some cartoon show called 'Fraggle Rock.' Pretty good money. It's a union deal." J.B. rapped a cymbal, and a ringing metallic tone filled the room.

"Brought my shredder," Nelson said, holding out his guitar by the neck. It was an Ibanez Destroyer, black with jagged scary angles, "Just in case," he added, almost shyly.

Glenda repressed another smile. "Okay," she said. "Great. This will work out. You and Nicole don't need to catch up, because I've been working on something new."

The drummer groaned.

"Again?" J.B. said and did a rim-shot.

"I was told we were doing *Snakes in the Grass*, Keith blurted.

Glenda had to bite her tongue to keep from replying, "Oh, it speaks."

"Let's try this first," Glenda said.

The keyboardist looked sullen but sat up straighter, flipping his greasy bangs out of his eyes.

Glenda took Banshee out of her case, plugged in and ran the band through the chord progressions of a song she tentatively called *Winter Fever*.

Nicole got it in one. Nelson flubbed it twice, apologizing profusely each time.

Keith didn't speak, but he unerringly hit the chords.

At last, Glenda felt comfortable enough to try a take.

It was rough, but she liked what she heard— especially from Keith.

Her godfather had warned her the keyboardist might be temperamental. Marcus had explained that Keith only did studio work. He was barred from touring, Marcus had said, because he had a tendency to blow up at other musicians onstage. But, Marcus had added, Keith was also a genius.

"He'll turn anything into gold, if you can stand him," Marcus had told her.

Glenda reluctantly had to agree as Keith attacked the synthesizer and proceeded to weave a spell.

On the first take, Keith played a series of church-organ chords for an almost Deep Purple vibe. The second time, he made the melody ethereal, but punctuated it with staccato accidentals. Two more takes followed. On one of them, Keith overrode the drummer and doubled the tempo, dragging everyone into a frenetic but exhilarating take that left them laughing and sweating.

The fifth time, Keith's variations were so complex, Glenda didn't even know what to call them. Awed silence filled the room as the last note died away, followed by whistles and clapping.

Keith, his hair matted to his forehead, threw up his hands and banged them together in triumph like a boxer. "That's it! That's it!" he crowed.

J.B. and Nicole looked at Glenda, waiting.

"That was great, guys," Glenda agreed, nodding.

A round of laughter.

"But..." Glenda added.

A collective groan.

"But," Glenda continued. "Let's try this: J.B., for the second chorus, what if you just use the bass pedal and a cymbal for shimmer?"

"Can do," J.B. said with a shrug.

She turned to the keyboardist. "Keith, I loved it, but you need to slow it down just a smidge." Glenda hummed the melody, moving her hands in rhythm.

Keith look perplexed. "Why?" he asked.

"I just want to try a little variation," Glenda said.

"But it's done," Keith said. "I did it. It's finished."

"And it sounded great," Glenda said. "But I just want to change it up a little, put a little more soul into it."

Keith shook his head. "No."

"No?" Glenda repeated.

"No."

The studio went quiet. All eyes swiveled to Glenda.

"You can't change it," Keith said.

Glenda smiled, but there was far too much canine showing for it to be a happy expression. "This is my song," she said quietly. "And I want to try it this way."

Keith flushed. "I'm not changing a note," He said. "You're just stuck in the Seventies."

Glenda said nothing. Pointedly. Heads craned first at her, then at Keith, as if the singer and keyboardist were locked in an invisible tennis match. "Fine," she said with deathly calm. "Then you're done here. Get out."

Keith glared, stood up and took a step from behind the synthesizer.

"I'll just remix it," she added.

Keith erupted. "Don't you dare! Don't you touch it. It's right! It's perfect!"

"I say when it's perfect," Glenda said, her voice rising.

"Don't fucking mess with my work!" Keith said.

"Don't fucking tell me what to do with my song!"

"Fuck you!" Keith screamed. A vein stood out in his forehead.

"No, fuck you!" Glenda shouted back.

"Everybody stop saying fuck!" Nicole said.

Glenda and Keith turned to her.

"Fuck you!" they both yelled.

Keith hurled himself against the synthesizer keyboards and knocked them over, then stalked toward the studio door. He kicked the drum set on the way out.

"Hey!" J.B. said, jerking back.

Keith, his face scarlet, paused and turned at the door. He pointed a finger at Glenda.

"Touch my work and I'll end you!" Keith said. "You're on the list!"

The door slammed and left a jarring echo.

"Holy shit," Nelson said. "Is it always like this?"

"Well," J.B. said. "Usually I make the death threats. From the top, Glenda?"

Without the keyboardist, Glenda concentrated on older material. It was nearly two in the morning when she called it. J.B., as usual, went outside for his last joint before going home. Nelson and Nicole packed their instruments, retrieved their boots, and accompanied Glenda to the studio door.

Nelson seemed both exhausted and flushed. "That was... really incredible," he said. His eyes were red-rimmed but bright.

"Thanks," Glenda said. "You were really good, Nelson."

"Hey," Nelson said. "Are you doing anything tomorrow night?"

"Well..." Glenda began, suddenly cautious. Would he ask for a date or something?

But Nelson seemed to understand and quickly added: "We've got a gig at Gazzarri's. You should come."

"I'd like to hear you," Glenda said.

"No," Nelson replied, a little embarrassed. "To sing. Just a song or two. We'll back you."

Trying to figure out if he was tempting her with a pickup line, offering her a pity gig or genuinely wanted to hear her, Glenda stared at him hard. Then she decided to go with the least humiliating choice. Besides, here was a chance to be onstage for the first time in three years. She felt a little of the old thrill, maybe mixed with a dash or two of fear.

Nicole nudged her, and Glenda realized she had been standing in silence.

"Do it," Nicole said quietly.

"Really?"

Nicole nodded.

"Okay," Glenda said. "Sure. Thanks."

Nelson looked absurdly pleased.

"Okay" he said. "I'll call you. We're gonna bring it!"

Nicole looked at Glenda and raised an eyebrow. Glenda ignored her.

Nelson put down his guitar case, reached out and gave Glenda a clumsy hug. She felt his rough cheek and smelled tobacco and sweat. The combination made her tingle.

"Thanks," Nelson said.

"You, too," Glenda said.

Nelson picked up his guitar and left. Glenda watched his back appraisingly.

"Not bad from the front, either," Nicole said.

"It's not like that!" Glenda said.

"Not for you," Nicole said.

"He's a friend."

"Yep."

"And he's young," Glenda said.

"Oh, yeah," Nicole said. "But they grow up so fast."

"Shut up," Glenda said, but she grinned. "Hey, Nicole, I'm really glad you came tonight. Look, let's not make it a one-time thing, okay?"

Nicole frowned. "We'll see," she said.

"Oh," Glenda said, a little crestfallen. She thought about her blowup with the keyboardist and was mindful she'd promised Nicole she wouldn't be a tyrannical jerk.

"Listen," Glenda asked, worried." How was I tonight?"

"Better," Nicole said. "On the bitch scale, you were only a six."

"Thanks," Glenda said, and meant it.

Nicole gave her an impish smile.

"I'm starving," Nicole said. "Wanna get a bite?"

Glenda thought about it for two full seconds. "Hell, yes."

CHAPTER SIXTEEN

Glenda and Nicole wound up at Canter's Delicatessen, which was packed. Canter's and Union Station hit about the same noise level. Every booth was full of people, a lot of them rockers out for late-night pastrami and beer. Giant hairdos in every color rose from the seats, like a field of Martian haystacks. Waitresses with thick waists and support hose navigated between the seats with trays and order pads. The place smelled of potato salad, cold cuts and steam— a nostalgic funk Glenda recognized because her mom's brother ran a deli. Nicole and Glenda were waiting in line for a seat when they heard a shout.

"Glitter Lizards! Glits! Over here!"

Glenda looked up. A tall, busty woman with pale skin topped by a volcanic explosion of black hair waved to them from a booth. Glenda recognized her and waved back.

"Who's that?" Nicole asked.

"It's Dot. From Catwitch," Glenda said. "Remember? We shared a gig in Seattle."

Nicole squinted, then beamed. "Dot!" she shrieked.

Dot waved again and motioned for Nicole and Glenda to join her.

The two threaded their way to the booth. Four other women were sitting there. They cheerfully moved aside so Glenda and Nicole could squeeze in. Beer bottles crowded the table and a cloud of cigarette smoke hung overhead.

"Ladies," Dot said to her crew. "This is Glenda and Nicole. And this is the new Catwitch: Susie, Cath, Deb and Kimberly."

"Hi," Glenda said.

"We just ordered," Dot said.

A busboy came up and scooped a few empties into a rubber bin, followed by a waitress with a tray who added more beers to the table. She was a big, sagging woman in her mid-fifties. Glenda reflected that all the waitresses at

Canter's seemed to be in their fifties and always had been. Maybe it had been that way since the place opened in 1931.

Glenda ordered a Reuben sandwich and a chocolate egg cream. Nicole had blintzes and a Michelob with lime.

"So," Dot said. "How are you? What's it been, four years?"

"Almost," Glenda said. "You look great." She glanced at the others. "You all look great."

"It's that wholesome rock 'n' roll lifestyle," Dot said, sipping her beer. "Early to bed."

"Depends with who," Susie said.

"That one," Kimberly said loudly, eyeing one of the interchangeable leather-clad boys in a booth across the way. He looked over. Kimberly made grunting pig noises. The leather boy looked scared. His buddies guffawed.

"I'll take any of 'em," Kimberly said, loudly.

"Oh, Judas Priest," Dot said. "Who has Kimberly's leash?" Everybody laughed.

"So," Dot said when the laughter faded. "How about you, Glenda? How's it going?"

"Fine," Glenda lied, unwilling to recount anything about her past few days. "We were just working on some new stuff tonight."

"For the album," Nicole said with a teasing smile.

"Aaaah," Dot said. Everybody at the table nodded knowingly.

Glenda felt a bit defensive. "It's coming together," she insisted. "I think it'll be done by the end of the year."

Dot gave Nicole a questioning glance. Nicole gave a nearly imperceptible shrug.

"You on it, Nicole?" Dot asked.

"Maybe," Nicole said. "We'll see. It's sort of all pick-up right now."

"Well, anyway, the end is near. Congratulations," Dot said, and everybody clinked their beer bottles.

Feeling absurdly touched, Glenda said, "Thanks. Oh, and congratulations to you, too. You charted!"

"Really?" Nicole said.

"Yeah," Glenda said. "Hyena & Butterfly. Billboard last week."

"Yup," Dot said. "Lucky number fifty-three."

There was a general chorus of affirmation of the rodeo kind, with "yee-haws" prominent.

"Of course," Dot said. "If I had a cock, we'd be top five."

That got hoots of agreement. The rockers at the next booth glanced up, then returned to their beers with sniggers.

"Look at those guys," Deb said. "They think we're talking about them."

Cath put her hands to either side of her face and said in a breathy, cooing voice, "'Cause that's all girls think about."

With a snort of disgust, Deb said, "What is it with these guys? Every time you open your mouth, some jerk wants to stick his tongue in it."

"Or worse," Susie said. She waved a hand around the room. "They don't see us as musicians or artists. We're just..."

"Chicks," Cath said. Everybody nodded.

As if on cue, there was a raucous sound from the adjacent booth. Glenda glanced over. One of the rocker boys was standing up and shouldering his buddies aside. He approached the Catwitch table with half-lidded eyes, an expression that he probably thought was smoldering. To Glenda, it simply looked like he was suppressing a sneeze.

He sleazed up — there was no other word for it — and said in a beery voice: "Hey, ladies."

"Hey yourself," Kimberly replied before anyone could stop her.

Glenda clocked him from top to toe. He was lean and lanky and reminded her faintly of Nelson — if Nelson had favored fuschia shirts open to the naval and was allergic to showers. Predictably, a massive silver-skull belt buckle was mounted above his crotch.

He gave the women a smile that he doubtless thought was irresistible; to Glenda, it was just a cut-rate Billy Idol sneer. He didn't offer his name. Apparently, he assumed everyone knew it.

"Were you at the show tonight?" he said. "Cause if I'd seen you there, I would have brought you backstage. You are fine."

A look passed between Nicole, Glenda and the Catwitch crew.

"Oh, gosh," Cath said in exaggerated awe. "How did you know? That's my dream!"

"Well, dreams come true," he said, putting his hand on his chest and weaving it south until he hooked a thumb in his belt. Then, he tossed his stringy hair as if he were in a shampoo commercial.

Dot and the others looked on, barely managing to keep from cracking up. Then, as one, they all flipped their hair.

The dude failed to catch the mockery. He smiled a thousand-watt grin — made somewhat dimmer by his dingy teeth — and said: "So what do you say, ladies? Ready to party?"

Deb said brightly: "Let me guess: hotel room? Booze? 'Ludes?"

"Whatever you want," the dude said. He was practically licking his chops.

"Tasty offer," Dot said. "But how about this: Instead, you come to our show."

Glenda and the others could practically hear the gears turning in his head until something finally clicked. Glenda fancied she could hear a ding like a cash register drawer opening but it was the dude's mouth that formed the words: "Show? Oh, cool! Where do you dance? Seventh Veil?"

Glenda cast a quick glance at Nicole, who was smirking.

Dot slowly sipped her beer, wiped her lips with the back of her hand and said: "Perkins Palace."

Still the dude didn't get it.

"Perkins? Like in Pasadena?"

"Yup."

He gave a puzzled frown. "That's not a strip club..."

"Good boy," Deb said. "Yes, Perkins. The place where every huge rock band plays."

"We're billed next week with Vixen and Klymaxx," Dot said.

Glenda thought she saw his eyes cross with concentration. She thought his simian brain might explode with the thought that women were actual musicians.

She decided to turn the thumbscrews of education.

She held up a hand, turned to Dot and said: "May I?"

"He's all yours," Dot replied.

"They're not strippers, doofus," she said. "This is Catwitch. They're opening at Perkins."

"That's cool," the dude said uncertainly.

Glenda honed in. "I'm guessing you never got a gig at Perkins."

He said nothing.

"And guess what?" Glenda added, with more than a hint of gleeful malice. "They charted."

"What?" the dude said. "Charted?"

"You know, had one of their songs on the Billboard charts. Look it up. You ever charted?"

"Not yet," he said. He thumbs jerked out of his belt and he crossed his arms defensively.

"Not yet?" Glenda's voice dripped with sarcasm. "Well, I'll tell you what, little boy. When you do, come back and see us. And hey, why don't you come to the show? We'll get you some passes. Maybe, if you're lucky, we'll bring you backstage."

Glenda said it so loudly that the nearby tables — including the one with the rocker's buddies — detonated with laughter.

The dude turned bright red, spat and said: "You bitches can go to hell."

Then he slunk back to the table. A few seconds later, an argument broke out and the rocker got up and pushed his way past his buddies and out the door.

Kimberly leaned over and hugged Glenda and said: "I am so hot right now!"

Dot said: "You totally shut him down."

"Well, I've had a little experience," Glenda said.

Nicole said: "'Backstage!' That was your best line. You gotta put that in a song."

"Three cheers for Glenda!" Dot said, holding up her beer. Glenda blushed when everyone clinked their bottles.

The food arrived. Dot and the others ordered another round of beers. Glenda passed. The waitress, who up to then had expressed no more interest in the proceedings than one of the chairs, leaned over as she put the Reuben sandwich in front of Glenda and said in a smoker's rasp: "Atta girl."

The sandwich was delicious but Glenda was smiling too hard to scarf it down. She had to work hard to chew slowly and carefully, leaving the food no chance to fall out of the corners of her mouth.

Everybody else plowed into their food and the next few minutes were messy and clamorous as they replayed the conversation amidst gales of laughter.

Glenda felt exhilarated and almost drunk, even though she'd stuck to her chocolate egg cream.

When the laughter died down, Glenda saw a look pass between the Catwitch crew.

"Hey, Glenda," Dot said. "I got a question."

"Shoot," Glenda said.

"You doing anything special next week?"

Glenda shrugged. "I honestly don't know. Why do you ask?"

Dot paused dramatically and then said: "Because, if you can swing it, I might be able to get you a gig."

"Oh, shit," Nicole said in amazement.

"Really?" Glenda asked.

Dot nodded enthusiastically, her crested hair making her look like an over-caffeinated cockatoo. She said: "If you'd like to sing a number or two with us at Perkins, I think that'd be great." The others nodded.

"Really?" Glenda asked again. "I'm not sure any of my stuff is ready to perform yet, and I don't know yours."

"Then do your old stuff," Dot said. "We'll back you."

Glenda made a face. "That wasn't my stuff. That stuff was crap."

"Whoa!" a couple of voices said.

"It was fun!" Dot protested. "Everything doesn't have to be a masterpiece."

"Glenda doesn't do fun," Nicole said, archly.

"Well, whatever. Just think about it," Dot said. "I always thought you had pipes, Glenda. And Nicole, you had chops."

"Mmmm," Kimberly broke in, licking her lips. "Pipes and chops. Now I'm kinda sorry we sent that dude away."

"Shut up, Kimberly." It was a general chorus.

CHAPTER SEVENTEEN

Glenda got home at four in the morning but couldn't get to sleep. Her mind jumped around like a chimp on a jungle gym, and her nerves buzzed with the perverse energy of extreme exhaustion. Thrashing in her bed, she cursed. She couldn't miss work; nobody else could do bookings, and she had to get more clowns. Besides, Troutman might call from Canada and wonder why she wasn't at the office. If she could get three or four hours of sleep, she'd be able to prop herself up enough at work to use a telephone.

After twenty minutes of staring at the lightless corners of her room, Glenda got up, went to the bathroom and took a Seconal. She went back to bed and was asleep almost before her head hit the pillow.

The alarm clock shouted her awake at eight-thirty. If the rooster had crowed, she'd never heard it. Rising, she felt as if she'd been sandbagged. She washed her face and brushed her teeth and hair. Then she opened the medicine cabinet and got the pill bottle, looked at it, put it back and took it out again. She uncapped it, got a Kleenex and tipped out two white crosses and a Seconal. She wrapped up the Kleenex and stuffed it into the pocket of her jeans. Unless an emergency happened, she wouldn't take anything, she told herself. But she avoided looking at the mirror as she left the bathroom.

By lunchtime, Glenda had managed to sign up three more clowns, although she'd had to promise them double the usual rate to lure them away from children's Halloween parties. She'd even had to hire a clown she hadn't used for years. He called himself Bon Bon and had an unnatural attachment to balloon animals. When Glenda arrived, she'd gulped down two cups of coffee, and they seemed to have worked, because she felt completely normal until just after noon. Then the energy seemed to flow out of her like water down a bathtub drain. She figured she had done enough work and could leave early. She had Nelson's gig tonight, after all— the thought made her stomach flutter —and she could catch up on the work Thursday.

Besides, Glenda had promised to stop by and ask her godfather about her contract. That sort of qualified as an emergency, she told herself. She fished in her pocket, unwrapped the Kleenex. It held only one white cross and one red capsule.

She didn't recall taking the other upper. With a worried frown, she popped the remaining white cross, promising herself she would nap later.

THE FIRST THING GLENDA heard when she entered Marcus's office was screaming. Two voices boomed through the closed door. She couldn't hear the muffled words, but the tone was obvious.

Ellie, her godfather's longtime assistant, who dressed like an aging hippie, sat at the reception desk. She brushed a lock of graying hair off her face and looked apologetic.

"It'll just be a minute," Ellie said. "He's in a meeting."

"So I hear," Glenda said cheerfully. Although she hadn't heard her godfather shout much, she knew Marcus could verbally rip the skin off people who ticked him off. Glenda took a seat on the dilapidated sofa that Marcus refused to replace. It was surprisingly comfortable. She sank into the cushions and glanced at the gold records on the walls.

The office door opened.

Keith the keyboardist stomped out, his face pinched and flushed, as if he had tried to swallow something bitter and it wasn't going down. He had almost made it to the door before he suddenly swiveled around and glared at Glenda. "You cunt!" he said in a tight, venomous voice, taking a step toward her.

The secretary picked up the telephone and said: "Security."

Although Keith stopped, he continued to glare at Glenda, breathing heavily and nearly vibrating with rage. He stabbed out a finger. It shook. "You... *suck*," he said, and turned and left.

Glenda sat stunned.

Ellie shook her head. "All kinds," she said and put down the phone.

Marcus poked his head out of the office doorway and saw Glenda.

"Hey, darlin', how long have you been here?"

"I just got here," she said.

"Where's my hug?" Marcus asked.

Glenda rose from the couch and hugged him.

Marcus stepped back and appeared embarrassed. "I hope you didn't have to hear that ruckus."

"Just the tail end."

"He had a word with Glenda," Ellie said, pursing her lips. "I won't repeat it."

"Cunt," Glenda said. "He called me a cunt."

Marcus punched a fist into his cupped hand. "That son of a... " He frowned. "Well, that's it. I told him to watch his mouth, and he just waltzes out here and insults you. He's done in this business. I will personally make sure of that!"

"Oh, I don't know," Glenda said generously. "We had our differences, but that's music. It happens. Just so's I don't have to work with him again."

"Sweetheart, I do appreciate your tolerance, but that boy crossed the line. He insulted you last night—"

"I held my own," Glenda said defensively.

"—and he doubled down just now. After I warned him. I said, 'You do not mess with my family.'" Marcus sighed. "I should have realized. You can't fix stupid."

"He does have problems," Glenda agreed.

Marcus laughed. "Problems? He's like something out of *Apocalypse Now*. I swear, he's gonna kill somebody someday."

Glenda had a thought. "Did he ever work with Bernie?"

"Probably," Marcus said. "He's burned through just about every producer and musician in town. Why?"

"Just curious," Glenda said quickly. "He's really brilliant but he's also really an asshole."

"Ah," Marcus said. "Kind of like Bernie."

Glenda was surprised at the comment, coming from a man who placed such high store on Southern gentility. Marcus caught her expression and dipped his head.

"Sorry. Didn't mean to speak ill of the dead. But Bernie did leave your career up in the air."

"Literally," Glenda agreed, thinking of her collapse while dangling over the audience.

"Well, we can talk about it over lunch," Marcus said, but Glenda shook her head.

"Can't today," she said ruefully.

"Still on the clown hunt?" Marcus asked.

She nodded and sighed.

"Well, I've got clowns to deal with, too. Don't suppose you're free for dinner?"

Glenda shook her head. "I've got plans."

"Oh, a hot date?"

"He's just a friend!"

Marcus nodded his head slowly. "Sure. Friends are good."

"He's got a band. They've got a gig tonight at Gazzarri's, and he asked me to sing!" Glenda couldn't keep a note of breathlessness out of her voice.

"Really? That's terrific."

"It is, and I'm not even nervous," she said nervously.

"Well," Marcus said. "As your mother would say, mazel tov. And as your Daddy would say, 'Light that fuse!'"

CHAPTER EIGHTEEN

The first thing Glenda noticed was the smell of smoke and cheap wine. It felt like home. Nelson's band was roaring onstage. He was bare-chested, hair pomaded into a rooster crest. He really was a good-looking dude, she thought, then added to herself: *Boy. He's a boy.*

The music was so loud it made her teeth vibrate. Gazzarri's was one of two Meccas for glam rockers, the other being the Whiskey. Glenda had played many grimy, over-packed nightclubs before the Glitter Lizards had made it. She remembered the feverish excitement and passion of applause—her first taste of the drug that eventually would nearly kill her. So to her, the dim, grungy, smelly venues packed with faces would always be romantic. She tugged down her black leather jacket and fluffed nervously at her hair, which had reached Himalayan heights through frantic teasing and a fire-hose application of Rave hairspray.

On the stage, only feet from the audience, the band reached a crescendo. Cymbals crashed, and the guitar razored through the vocals. The song ended with a hammer blow of noise and left a silence so rich it throbbed. Then the audience caught its breath and erupted in shouts and screams. Glenda felt a little intimidated.

Nelson dropped his guitar to his hip and took the mic. Breathing hard, he thrust it high in the air. Glenda was uncomfortably aware that his lean chest gleamed with sweat.

After waiting for the noise to subside, Nelson spoke softly into the mic. "All right! All right, all right."

Whoops answered him. A smile flickered on his lips.

"I know you liked that," Nelson said, sparking another round of energetic yells. "Well, you're gonna like this better." He paused and looked over at Glenda, who stood on the dance floor at the left edge of the stage. He winked. "A friend of mine's gonna take the next number," Nelson said. "And ladies, you better grab your man by the balls— because that's where they're gonna feel it!"

A new roar erupted. "She was the bomb before I was the fuse!" Nelson said, his voice rising. "And she *will* bring it. People, give it up for Glenda Birdsong!"

Glenda winced. That was way too much of a buildup, considering she hadn't been on a stage for three years. Feeling queasy but also determined, she reminded herself she had been a pro— and she still had it.

She hoped.

"Yeah!" Nelson turned toward Glenda and gestured.

She took a breath, held it, lifted her head and stepped forward. She climbed the short flight of steps, and there she was in front of the audience. Overhead lights beat on her face and blinded her. She took a step forward and tripped, one boot heel catching on a cable. Blindly, she threw out her hands. She was going flat on her face in front of all those people before she could sing a note!

But Nelson dashed forward. Before Glenda had a chance to topple, his sturdy hand held her upper arm, giving her balance. Nobody laughed. Nelson had made it seem inconsequential. He handed her the mic with an acknowledging glance and backed up.

The crowd cheered. Glenda let the approval fill her. She felt like Dorothy, clicking her ruby slippers together and thinking: *there's no place like home.*

This *was* home, she thought. Then she got down to business.

"Thank you," Glenda said. "This is a new one. You might have heard it already but you ain't heard it right. It's called 'In the Flow.'" She turned to the drummer, who nodded and gave her the four-beat intro. The band had graciously rehearsed her song for a good hour before the gig.

Glenda turned back to the audience. She'd practiced this song a hundred times. Now, she simply let it free. Singing, she felt herself disappear. Moving with the music, she felt right, as if she'd never left the stage.

She felt *fine.*

For thirty seconds, Glenda was divine.

But as she got to the chorus, something went wrong. Not in her singing and not with the band. But something was off. Glenda felt it the way a sea creature can feel a changing tide. She couldn't identify it at first.

Then she got it.

She was losing the audience.

She stumbled over her words.

What was happening?

And then she looked down at the faces in the front row and saw what she had feared most, ever since she had slumped in that harness three years ago.

Laughter.

They were laughing at her. She couldn't hear the laughter over the music, but she could see it. People were telling each other something, passing it from ear to ear. Mouths gaped, heads bobbed, shoulders heaved in amusement. It was like an infection, moving with the speed of a wildfire.

Then Glenda heard someone shout at the very edge of the stage.

"Hey! Help! I've got the *shits!*"

Glenda gamely tried to continue the chorus. But the band was now ahead of her.

The crowd followed the rhythm but began to chant a single word to it:

"Diarrhea! Diarrhea!"

She stopped singing as if someone had grabbed her by the throat. She couldn't breathe. The microphone dropped from her nerveless hand. The band ground to a halt, the drummer letting out a last forlorn thump.

And Glenda stood there feeling the exuberant crowd destroy her with casual and joyous cruelty.

She felt faint. She swallowed bile. She stumbled off the stage.

She fought her way to the dressing room at the back of the club. The security man let her through without a word.

Mercifully, the room was empty. Glenda threw herself onto the ratty couch.

Through the door, Glenda heard Nelson announce: "We're gonna take a break. Be right back!" Canned music instantly took over.

Glenda buried her head in the corner of the couch. She wanted to disappear, but she was too big. She wanted to die and be buried in that stupid corner of that sickly green room, with the cushions over her head. She shook with sobs.

"I am so sorry."

Glenda looked up through a glaze of tears. Nelson stared at her in pale shock, as if he'd just witnessed a road accident.

And that's exactly what he was seeing, Glenda thought. She'd been mangled. He should just leave the broken body in the road and walk away.

"Go away," she said, and pressed her face back to the cushions.

Nelson didn't say goodbye.

After a time, Glenda raised her head to take a breath.

He was still there.

Slowly, she pulled herself up to a sitting position and wiped her tears. Her fingers came away black. Her mascara had run.

I probably look like a raccoon, she thought.

Nelson's gaze bored into hers.

"What?" she asked angrily.

He shook his head.

"Look," she said. "You can't help, okay? Just leave me alone."

"You were good," he said quietly.

Glenda laughed bitterly. "I was garbage."

"No," he said calmly. "You were amazing. They were idiots."

"No, I was shit. I am shit. The audience was right. It's always right. The song is a joke, and I'm a joke." She hung her head. "I just wanted to do my song right. I'm such an idiot. I didn't belong up there. I was a moron. I was a joke."

"No!" Nelson said sharply. "They weren't laughing at you."

"Who were they laughing at then?"

"They were laughing at the TV commercial. They didn't hear *you*." he looked at her. "*I* heard you. You kicked butt."

Glenda put her hands in front of her face. "I should have known when to quit." She pressed her palms hard against her eyes.

Nelson crouched down. Glenda felt his heat. He took one of her hands and gently pulled it away from her face.

"You are so great," he said urgently. "You've gotta believe me on this." He looked earnest and sincere.

"I'm not. I'm not," Glenda moaned.

"You are, Glenda," Nelson protested. "They just didn't listen. They got sidetracked. You gotta make 'em listen. Get their attention. Grab 'em by the throat."

"No," she said, her face crumpling. "They saw everything I had. They saw. And they fucking laughed."

"Don't think like that. You'll kill 'em next time. You can go out there and grab 'em by the balls! Take no prisoners!" Nelson paused, then said almost pleadingly, "You're the music! I believe in you."

Glenda pulled her hand away sharply and balled it into a fist. She glared at him.

"You believe in me?" she said. "Who the hell do you think you are? You don't know me. You've got this stupid kid fantasy that I'm a genius instead of a fat old has-been."

Nelson recoiled as if she had slapped him. He opened his mouth to protest, but Glenda cut him off.

"I'm a loser!" she screamed. "Do you get that? Why won't you leave?"

Nelson gave her a long stare and then slowly rose from his crouch. He walked to the door with rigid dignity. He turned back to look at her. "This was my fault," he said. "I talked you into this. I thought you were..." He shook his head and walked out.

Glenda heard him stalking down the short corridor to the stage until the sound of boots vanished into the general welter of noise.

Choked with despair, she looked around the room blankly. She was alone with scuffed walls, torn posters, ashtrays overflowing with butts. The only thing half-alive in the room, she thought, was an open bottle of Jack Daniel's, which sat on a chair like a forlorn party guest. It held four inches of glowing amber. She decided to make friends with the wallflower. They could commiserate. She hefted herself off the couch and took the lonely bottle by the neck. "Screw it," she said, and made its acquaintance.

Her throat caught fire. The Jack burned all the way down to her soul. Her eyes and nose watered and she coughed and spat.

"Some outlaw you are," she said bitterly, wiping her nose with the back of her hand. "I can't even handle a drink." She glared at the bottle. "Don't you laugh at me, too!" she shouted, and hurled it against a wall. The bottle exploded against the cinderblock.

The security goon poked his bullet head around the door frame, saw no blood and ducked back.

Breathing heavily, Glenda looked at the glass shards of the bottle and thought: *Did I do that?* Her heart was jumping. She relived the last moment, felt again her arm hurling the bottle like a thunderbolt. Something had surged through her like an electrical charge as the bottle smashed with a musical sound. It felt... well hell, it felt *great*.

She wanted to smash something else, which was kind of scary.

For an instant, she felt barely in control. She thought to tamp down the feeling and force it back. But then she'd be back on the couch with her self-pity. *And* without the bottle.

Instead, she let her body lead her to the doorway. Glass crunched under her boots. Aflame, she approached the stage. She shoved through the crowd, which parted for her as if she really were on fire, perhaps because of the furious look on her face or the fact that she kept mumbling to herself, "By the balls!"

The canned music was still blaring. Glenda saw Nelson smoking a cigarette by the side of the stage. He ignored the crowd and looked dejected. Even his hairdo was wilted.

Glenda brushed past him and took the stairs two at a time. She snatched the microphone from its stand and closed her eyes.

The watcher in the back of her head— the scared one —howled at her: *What the hell are we doing?*

She opened her mouth and screamed at the watcher's voice, *"Shut up!"*

The audience went silent. The canned music kept on for a second or two until somebody stopped it.

Glenda took a deep breath, gathering it inside herself.

And then, she let it out.

At first it was just a baby's wail— a tiny, lost thing. But just as babies grow, Glenda's voice grew. She got louder and louder, and then she was screaming an eagle shriek of hunger and rage, and finally she howled like a wolf.

The howl became a note. The note became a song.

Alone on the stage, she began singing Janis Joplin's "Cry Baby," her voice like a spike through the head.

Out of the corner of her eye, Glenda saw Nelson gape, drop the cigarette, crush it under his boot heel and sprint to the stage. After a second, the rest of the band followed. They grabbed guitars, hastily slung straps over their shoulders. The drummer threw himself onto the stool and snatched up his sticks. Frantically, Nelson's band jumped in.

The crowd roared.

Glenda roared back. Something had torn loose inside her— something feral —and she struggled to ride it, claws and all. It was her rage, her yearning, everything she'd kept behind one dam or another for three years. It swept her away.

As she sang, Glenda wanted nothing between her and those feelings— not insipid lyrics, not careful staging or elegant song phrasing. Even her clothing. She tore off her leather jacket, tossed it, then stripped off her T-shirt and threw it to the crowd. She stalked the stage in her bra.

She felt raw. A force of nature.

Strutting around the stage, she let her voice carry her where it would. The audience vanished. The club didn't exist.

Glenda herself finally disappeared. Something savage and menacing and completely free finished the song. That creature— that panther? —stood glaring. Then Glenda threw down the microphone, gave the crowd the finger and marched offstage.

Nelson found her back in the dressing room. She was sitting on the couch, her arms hugging her body. She was shivering.

"I'm cold," she said.

Nelson held her jacket. He placed it carefully around her shoulders. He stepped back as if afraid to touch her further, as if he might burn his hands.

"That was…" Nelson said. "You were…." He stopped, his mouth hanging open. "Wow."

Glenda felt exhausted. Her teeth chattered in delayed reaction. Adrenaline overdose, she thought.

Nelson screwed up his courage and took a seat next to her on the couch. He shook his head. "I have never…" he began. "I didn't even know…"

Glenda looked at him. There was an awed look on his face. His eyes shone. She shivered again.

"I'm cold," Glenda repeated. "Take me home."

CHAPTER NINETEEN

Larry had forgotten to bring his Goo Goo Dolls T-shirt, so he had to sacrifice the ZZ Top one he always kept in the trunk for emergency changes of clothing. But nothing was too good for his Thunderbaby. He slipped another quarter into the slot of the self-serve wash, picked up the long wand and lovingly applied a third coat of wax, then got to work buffing and glossing with the T-shirt.

Probably because of the rain, he was the only customer at the car wash on Santa Monica Boulevard. That suited Larry; he didn't like waiting in line. The car wash had little stalls covered by awnings, so it wasn't like the car would get wet while he was washing it. Larry didn't like natural water on his car; natural water left spots. With a twenty-five cent uber wax, his baby would shed the rain like a greased seal. If he remembered to put the top up.

He finally ran out of quarters. He gave the Thunderbird a final swipe and then took off. His chore day frequently started at noon and ended at midnight, but his customers seemed to have taken a powder— *no pun intended,* he thought —and so he was quickly burning through the his need-to-do list.

The list included one extra item, marked in red felt pen at the bottom: *Ask Glenda about mad killer.* Larry hoped he had time to get to that.

Rain drummed on the ragtop as Larry pulled up in front of Gepardo's barbershop. Forty minutes later, he exited with a shaggy new haircut and a plastic bag over his head to protect it.

He stopped at The Burger That Ate L.A. for lunch, as always awed by the building in the shape of an enormous golden, seeded bun. Then he finished off by doing his shopping at the 7-Eleven. Larry liked to patronize local shops, and this one was just around the corner. He arrived back at his apartment clutching a Slurpee and a plastic bag full of necessities that he tossed on the kitchen counter.

Grabbing a handful of leftover paper napkins from last night's dinner, he carefully wiped dry his zebra cowboy boots. Then he checked his list.

It was time to call Glenda. He sighed. He hadn't heard from her since telling her to go to Bernie's funeral and try to find the Cadillac-driving killer. It was selfish of her not to call him when his life might be in danger.

Remembering their conversation made Larry shudder, but then he got hold of himself.

After all, if there really was a killer, he'd be after Glenda first. So Larry really didn't need to panic. He just needed to check to make sure she was still alive. He went back into the living room, patted the statue of Ganesha on the head, picked up the phone and dialed her house but only got the answering machine.

He didn't leave a message.

Checklist completed, Larry decided to reward himself. He got his stash, made himself a joint the size of a scuba tank, plopped down on the couch and stared absently at his zebra boots as he released skunky clouds at the ceiling. He felt himself relax, then, inevitably, he got hungry. He ambled into the kitchen and unpacked his groceries: toilet paper, three bags of nachos, six frozen Swanson dinners he shoved into the small freezer, and a cellophane package of Oreos. Larry couldn't figure out why he'd bought the Oreos. There had been a reason, he was sure...

Oh well, he thought. He snagged the package, returned to the living room and the sofa, which had an enticingly Larry-shaped dip in one corner. Glancing at his Rolex, he saw he was just in time for the After-School Special on TV. He liked to stay educated. One show had been about surfing, which Larry had tried once and never again. He didn't see the point of going through all the trouble of getting out into the ocean, then just turning around and coming back again, over and over. People needed goals, in his view.

His last big goal had been to get religion. The Hari Krishnas down at the auditorium in Culver City had put on a big feast every weekend. And they gave away really colorful books full of bright blue gods, which made Larry think he might want to learn more about the Hindu religion. He'd even planned to go to India but never did because, well, it meant going to India.

He switched on the television and settled in for some after-schooling. He ripped open the Oreo package and stuffed one in his mouth. The chocolaty crumbly outside and the creamy center were like some perfect, divine food, he thought. He approved of cross-breeding food: chocolate-dipped strawberries, s'mores, and especially Korean burritos.

The After-School Special this time was a nature show on Africa. Lions and cheetahs stalked and wandered, or sometimes just lay around looking lazy, which Larry appreciated. Then he sat up straight, a grin on his face.

The screen showed a parade of elephants, slowly and majestically trooping through the brush.

"Hey!" Larry shouted. He turned and looked at Ganesha. "It's your people!"

Then his jaw dropped and his eyes went wide. Sitting in front of the Ganesha statue was a little table where Larry placed offerings to the god. And on that table was an empty package of Oreos.

Suddenly, Larry knew why he'd bought the new package. The old ones had gone stale. Ganesha had been out of treats. In dawning horror, Larry stared at the package in his lap.

There was nothing left but crumbs.

Larry had eaten Ganesha's cookies. He glanced again at the god, who seemed to pierce him with a furious glare. He trembled.

Ganesha was a pretty friendly god, but he was also an elephant. And Larry knew elephants never forgot. Anything.

There was going to be some karmic hell to pay.

CHAPTER TWENTY

Aching all over and famished, Glenda woke in bed. She could hear the heater going full blast. The sheets were rucked up and she was naked—except for a strange arm that seemed to have attached itself to her stomach. She was almost sure she hadn't grown it. She followed the arm to Nelson. He lay on his stomach, his long legs stretching off the bed. A bunched blanket barely concealed his lower body. His cockatoo hair had collapsed in a tangle over his forehead. He snored gently.

Dark and exotic images crowded in Glenda's head, each attached to a sore body part. The night flooded back in a series of impossibly passionate and potentially fatal maneuvers.

She looked at Nelson's young, trusting face, full of peace and innocence. "Oh God," she said, and then thought: this is going to be complicated.

She managed to extract herself, dress and slip out to work without waking him. She hoped he wouldn't be there when she got home. On the way in, she bought an extra box of donuts.

Instead of eating out, Glenda came home for lunch, telling herself she wanted to save money. Quietly, she opened the door and stepped softly across the living room. She opened the bedroom door, hoping and yet not hoping that Nelson was gone.

He wasn't.

In fact, he was still lying on the bed. He didn't appear to have moved at all. The light through the window was full in his face. He snored peacefully, oblivious.

Glenda was about to back out of the room when Nelson opened one eye. Then, as she watched enthralled, he slowly came awake. He rolled over, stretched with the grace of a cat and sat up.

"Oh, hi," Nelson said. "What time is it?"

"I came home for lunch," Glenda said lamely, too aware of his bare torso.

"Oh. Well, I could use some breakfast." He looked questioningly at her.

She heard herself agreeing and then wanted to slap the schoolgirl smile off her face.

They walked to the Formosa Cafe across from the Warner Brothers Hollywood studio. A smell of garlic and grease clung to the old place like wallpaper.

Nelson looked around with interest. "I've never been here," he said as they slid into a booth. "Isn't it kind of famous?"

"Yeah, the stars used to come here."

"Like who?"

"Clark Gable, Jimmy Stewart, Ava Gardner." Glenda pictured them slurping noodles and Scotch.

Nelson looked unimpressed.

"Bono," Glenda said. "Guns N' Roses. INXS."

"Oh, wow. What did they order?"

"I don't know if they ate food here," Glenda said, gesturing at the wall-to-wall bar.

The waiter, a white-haired Chinese man with a wrinkled vest, plunked down two menus and a pot of tea. Nelson poured for Glenda and then himself.

"Thanks," she said, surprised at his courtesy. She compared it to her last date with Harold, he of the burning chest hair.

Wait, Glenda caught herself. *Was this a date?* She stared uncertainly at her cup. Tea leaves swayed at the bottom of the clear brown liquid like ocean life. She looked at Nelson, whose hair was still mussed. She focused on his pursed lips as he blew steam from his cup, and felt a surge of heat in her stomach— or possibly lower down. She squelched the thought.

"So," Nelson said. "What's good here?"

"Nothing," Glenda said. "But it's cheap and close by and sticks to your ribs."

"Well, what are you having?"

"I always have the vegetable chow mein."

Nelson looked skeptical. "For breakfast?"

"No, lunch."

The waiter returned. Glenda ordered her usual. The waiter turned to Nelson.

"I'll have the deep fried prawns and, ah, the sweet-and-sour chicken," he said. "Glenda, you want to split some egg rolls?"

"Not for me," she said.

"Okay, just one order for me."

The waiter scribbled on his pad and moved off.

They drank their tea. Nelson picked up the pot, refilled the cups, then leaned toward Glenda. "Listen, about last night." He shook his head. "You were unbelievable." He raised his cup in a toast.

Glenda felt embarrassed and flattered at the same time.

"Thanks," she said.

"No, I mean you were *amazing*. I couldn't keep up with you. You almost killed me."

Glenda got a wicked grin. "I was trying."

Nelson smiled. "Let's do it again!"

"Now?" she asked.

He laughed. "Whenever you want."

"I'm flattered," Glenda said. "But look, Nelson, I wasn't planning any of this. It just sort of ... happened, you know? Maybe we should just take it slow and see where it goes." She wanted to add *and what about your girlfriend?* but it wasn't the time and besides, she didn't like the slut.

"Sure, no pressure," Nelson said. "But just so's you know, I talked to the guys and they were blown away. They all want you, too."

Glenda's cup hit the table with a thunk, sloshing tea over the tablecloth. Her voice was icy. "The guys? What do you think I am?"

Nelson looked surprised. "Do I have to tell you?"

Anger and shame burned in her chest but before she could speak, Nelson added: "The best damned singer in the universe!"

"What?"

"I never heard anyone sing like that," he said.

"Oh. The singing," she said dumbly. "You were talking about my *singing*."

"Yeah! I never heard anything like it," Nelson repeated enthusiastically. "The guys want you to front for us." He paused. "I mean, if you're interested?"

Before Glenda could reply, the food arrived. Grateful for the interruption, she grabbed an egg roll and stuffed it into her mouth.

Nelson eyed her.

"You can sure sing," he said. "The only thing you do better is screw." He guffawed as Glenda started, spitting half-chewed egg roll onto the table.

"You okay?" he asked, handing her a napkin.

"Not funny," she said, wiping her chin.

"A little bit."

"You set me up!"

"Well, I really was thinking about your singing. Then you got this look on your face and I realized *you* weren't. So, I couldn't resist."

"Fair enough," she said. "But now can we talk about something else? I'd like to eat the rest of my lunch, not spray it."

"Sure."

Then Glenda simply watched in jealous awe as Nelson shoveled immense quantities of food into his mouth. She glared at his slender frame and wondered where it all was going. She picked at her vegetable chow mein resentfully. It seemed everyone she knew was able to gorge without gaining a pound.

Nelson stopped with an enormous forkful of food halfway to his mouth. "So," he said. "Tell me about you."

"You know a lot about me," Glenda countered. "Tell me about you."

"What do you want to know?"

"Well, you're from Nebraska, right?"

He nodded.

"Any brothers or sisters?"

He shook his head.

"Well, what got you into music?"

"Oh, the usual: chicks, money, fame." Nelson grinned.

"Really? How's that working out for you?"

"Well," he said around a mouthful of chicken. "The chick part is great!" He waggled his eyebrows suggestively.

"Don't gloat." .

"Sorry."

"Seriously. I've seen you play punk, heavy metal, some of my stuff. You're just really versatile. Did your parents teach you?"

"I mostly grew up with my grandparents," he said. "They weren't musical."

Glenda realized he was being intentionally vague. She switched gears. "Well, you're really good, Nelson."

"Shucks, thanks, ma'am," he said in a comic Western twang. He leered at her.

"I meant your guitar playing," she said snappishly. "Do you read music?"

"No."

"Well, if you learned, you could score some studio gigs. It's good money."

"Do you read music?" Nelson asked.

"Yeah. My dad taught me when I was six."

"You could teach me," he suggested. "If you join the band, we'd have more time together."

A neon sign blinked to life in Glenda's head. It flashed the warning: *Watch it.*

Unfortunately, Nelson chose that moment to pick up the last egg roll and gently move it to her lips. She bit before she could stop herself.

"Look," she said when she could talk again. "I can't really make any commitments right now. I've got to sort out my contract. It's all a big mess."

Nelson looked intrigued. "What's the problem?"

She sighed. "It's complicated, with my manager dead."

"Yeah, Bernie, stupid way to die."

"Yeah," Glenda said, unnerved by his apparent indifference. "Anyway, I owed him the album."

"He stole your diarrhea song," Nelson reminded her.

"It's not a diarrhea song," Glenda snapped. "But yeah, he took it."

"He was a creep," Nelson said.

"Well I should have expected it. I mean, he screwed me over three years ago when he promised I'd have a solo career. You've heard about that?"

"Something," Nelson said. "You got sick."

"I got stupid," she said. "Stars in my eyes. I let him convince me I needed to lose weight. I got hooked on diet pills and bulimia." She flashed uncomfortably on the purloined pill bottle in her medicine chest but brusquely pushed the thought aside. "Anyway, I still owe the album, but I don't know who to."

"Well, that's bullshit. But that was Bernie, right?"

"That was Bernie," she agreed. "You're lucky you never met him."

He gave her a strange look. He opened his mouth as if to speak but then closed it.

"Nelson?" she asked.

He was suddenly distant. Glenda was a little bit frightened at how swiftly his mood had shifted.

"Have you got a cigarette?" he asked.

Glenda fished the pack of Silva Thins from her purse. Nelson didn't seem to notice the brand. He lipped a cigarette from the pack, pulled a lighter and lit up. As he smoked, he slouched in the chair and his chin went up arrogantly. She was reminded of his pose when she'd first seen him at the Cripple Cafe. He was playing tough. He had retreated into himself. It was a type of armor, she realized. She wondered what he was protecting himself against, so it was a shock when he spoke again.

"I never met that fucker," he said, breathing smoke. "But my mom hooked up with him."

"Bernie?" Glenda said. "I thought he was—"

"He was," Nelson said. "He used her as his beard. Paid her in coke. Then he passed her around to clients. Anybody he wanted a favor from." His voice went flat. "I'm not sorry he's dead. I could have killed him myself." With a savage jab, he snuffed the cigarette on his plate.

"I've been hearing that a lot," Glenda said. "I'm sorry about your mom."

Nelson shrugged. "She was a junkie and a whore."

"But she was still your mom," she said. "We went through some bad times with my dad, but he was still my dad."

"Your dad was a junkie?"

"Alcoholic. Ten years, almost. He's sober now."

"Good."

There was an awkward silence. She wanted to ask Nelson more about his mother, but decided to do so would be breaching some kind of wall. She looked at him. He was so hard and yet so fragile. Both older and younger than he looked. "They fuck you up," she said at last.

"What?"

"Your parents," she said. "It's from a poem."

Nelson looked thoughtful. "So how's it end?"

"The poem?"

"Yeah."

"Basically, die early and don't have kids."

Nelson snorted. "Poets are assholes."

She laughed. Nelson smiled. It was like watching the sun emerge from clouds. He straightened in the chair, glanced down at his plate and looked surprised that it was empty.

"Wow," he said. "That was great." He paused. "Dessert?"

CHAPTER TWENTY-ONE

Walking back to Glenda's office, they strolled side by side down Sunset Boulevard. Occasionally Nelson moved out of the way of passersby and his body brushed hers. Each time, Glenda felt a tiny electric charge. She found herself wishing there were more people on the street.

"So," he said as they neared her building. "What are you doing for Halloween?"

"I'm working. Catering a big party up in the hills. You?"

"Got a gig in Brentwood," he said. "A fan set it up. Somebody's got rich parents. Hey, you want to meet up after?"

He spoke the words casually, but Glenda was under no illusions. The question wasn't whether she wanted to get together again. Her desire was obvious, she thought with a shudder.

The real question was, should she?

This time, her cautious angel won. "Thanks, but I think we'll finish late and I'm gonna be dead." Her angel smiled approvingly.

"Oh," Nelson said. "That's okay."

"But," she blurted, "some other time when we're both not so busy would be nice." Somewhere in her head, an angelic palm smacked an angelic forehead.

Nelson's face brightened. "So, there'll be another time?"

"I'm not—" she began.

"How about tomorrow? We can hit the Roxy."

Glenda flushed. "Look, Nelson," she said. "Maybe we should slow things down a little bit..."

"Oh." he stopped short. He looked embarrassed. "No pressure, okay?" He thrust his hands in his jacket pockets.

Glenda thought he looked like a schoolboy— one who was about to get a whack from his teacher's ruler.

"I just don't want to give you the wrong impression," she said earnestly. "I've got a lot going on, and it's been a while since I've had a relationship. I'm not really ready to jump into anything."

Nelson frowned but then nodded slowly. "I get it," he said. "But for the record, I like you. I like being with you. And I respect you. So whatever you decide, it's good. When or if."

Glenda stopped abruptly. She looked him up and down, marveling. That didn't sound like a kid's words— or a rocker's for that matter. "Wow," she said. "Are you sure you're only twenty-one?"

"I was twenty-one when I was eleven," he said.

She gave him a puzzled look.

He sighed. They began walking again. "I had to grow up," he said. "I knew a lot of musicians. My mom shacked up with tons of them. They were all jerks. They taught me to play, but they smacked me around when they were drunk. They all thought they were gonna be rock stars, so we traveled around living in cheap motels, until they finally decided to dump my mom and she'd dump me back with my grandparents."

"Shit," Glenda said. She wanted to take him in her arms but he kept his hands in his pockets.

"I'm sorry," he said. "I didn't mean to say that. All I meant is that I can handle it."

Glenda didn't know what to say but they had reached her office building. "This is my stop," she said lamely.

Nelson gave her a clumsy hug and walked away without a goodbye.

Glenda paused, her hand on the cold brass handle of the door. Above her, a telephone began to ring in one of the upstairs offices. No one answered.

CHAPTER TWENTY-TWO

By late afternoon, the rain returned. By nightfall, it was a deluge that turned gutters into rivers. People holding newspapers and purses over their heads scampered for the shelter of doorways. Nobody in Los Angeles owned an umbrella.

The downpour gave Glenda an unexpected opportunity for studio time. Another band had cancelled because of the weather. Word from the sound engineer was that their bald-tired Econoline van had skidded into someone's living room coming down Laurel Canyon.

Unwilling to trust the makeshift patch in its slashed top, Glenda left her Porsche in the carport. She'd planned to spring for a taxi but, with impeccable timing, there was a break in the rain. She wrapped Banshee's case with plastic trash bags and sprinted to the studio.

GLENDA AND THE BAND were putting the finishing touches on *The Chinese Donut Blues*. She had sworn to the musicians that she wouldn't nitpick, vacillate or throw tantrums. Tuesday's midnight meltdown still throbbed like a sore tooth, and Glenda had to pinky-swear to Nicole that she would use the words "let's try it again" and "one more time" sparingly. There had been a few nasty looks when she had substituted the phrase, "It's not the vibe I was looking for."

J. B. had threatened to bounce a drumstick off her head.

The session guitarist, Clifton, a bald, ponytailed Alabaman, kept a pack of what he called his "Willie Nelson Specials"— marijuana cigarettes in a Camel pack —rolled up in his T-shirt sleeve.

Without a keyboardist, they were working with the tracks laid down by Keith. Glenda had changed her mind a half-dozen times about which one to use before admitting, much to her chagrin, that Keith had been right all along.

So, for a change, the work was moving briskly when the sound engineer flicked the lights off and on and said over the intercom: "You're going to need to wrap up."

"What the hell?" Glenda yelled, then put up her hands in apology to the band. "What's the problem, Eddie?" she asked.

"I just got a call from Mr. Ross. I'm off the clock. Your producer hasn't paid in over a month."

"He's dead," Glenda explained.

"He's dead?" Clifton said. "Oh."

Eddie didn't miss a beat.

"Yeah," Eddie said. "And I'm sorry, but the boss said until we're paid up, he won't cough up. His exact words were: 'No moolah, no music.'"

"Those were his exact words?" Glenda asked skeptically. She knew the studio owner.

"Well, I paraphrase. I left out a few adjectives."

"Oh, come on, Eddie, be a sport," Nicole said. "One more take."

"Sorry," Eddie said.

"But we were really cranking for a change."

"Yeah," Eddie said. "That keyboard really brought it all together. But no."

Glenda remembered her promise to Nicole and fought an urge to toss the microphone stand through the window of the sound booth. She turned to the band. "It's cool, guys," she said. "We'll be back in a few days when this all gets ironed out."

"And," Eddie said, "don't forget to take your tapes."

"Really, Eddie?" Glenda said, starting to simmer despite her best efforts at self-control. "It's pouring out there. Can't you just hold onto 'em for a day or two?"

"Again," Eddie replied, "to paraphrase my boss: 'Their crap goes with them or it goes to the curb.' Okay, actually, those were his exact words."

"You're all heart, Eddie."

"Sorry for your loss."

Nobody seemed to have a spare bag and Glenda— unwilling to risk Banshee's health —refused to use the trash bags she'd brought. Instead, she used her coat to cover the box containing two dozen bulky tapes and lugged it out the door. Nicole offered her a lift, so Glenda waited outside under the front awning as Eddie locked the door and strolled off in the rain. She hoped his earring rusted.

A throaty roar sounded, and a black-and-yellow Chevy Nova with enormous back tires and an aggressive forward slouch lurched up.

She dumped the box and Banshee in the back seat before piling in. Standing even so short a time coatless in the cold had raised goose flesh on her arms. Luckily, Nicole cranked up the heater, gunned the engine and rumbled away, gripping a steering wheel made out of chrome chain.

"My last boyfriend was a drag racer," Nicole explained. "He sort of gave me this when he went to prison."

"What did he do?"

"The shorter question is what didn't he do?" Nicole said. "But he never did it to me. We broke up, but we're still pen pals. Of course, his are in crayon."

"I'm not even asking," Glenda said.

"See?" Nicole said, taking a corner and glancing at Glenda ruefully. "You're not the only one with poor judgment."

"Bernie," Glenda said, shaking her head ruefully. "I can't believe he didn't pay the bills. He's dead, and he's still screwing me." She gave a small, embarrassed laugh. "Sorry, I shouldn't have said that."

"No," Nicole said. "This all blows."

"Seriously does," Glenda agreed. She stared out the window at the rain-starred red, yellow and silver of traffic lights and street lamps. The Nova purred.

"Well," Nicole said, "I've got the evening free."

"Yeah. You hungry?"

Nicole laughed.

"When am I not? I'm a dancer."

THIS TIME, THEY WOUND up at Roscoe's House of Chicken 'n Waffles.

Glenda eyed the menu dubiously.

"You never had soul food?" Nicole asked with surprise.

"Daddy never shared his Southern roots," Glenda said. "He said he hated grits. His idea of perfection was steak and onions, medium rare, and a martini."

"Well, allow me to introduce you to a little slice of heaven."

"I was going to watch my weight," Glenda protested.

"You can't watch what you ain't got, girl," Nicole said reasonably. "Besides, you need some comfort food."

Glenda's stomach chose that moment to agree, loudly, with a rumble like the Nova's engine. It was hitting ten o'clock and she had last eaten at lunch.

That thought brought back images of Nelson, which Glenda briefly savored. Her lips quirked.

"Oh, well," she said and ordered the house special.

The chicken arrived tawny and bubbling with fat. The waffle was a perfect disc about the size of the moon. Butter pooled in latticework like liquid gold. The smell of syrup hovered over the plate like a benediction.

"No donuts for me tomorrow," Glenda swore.

Nicole had some kind of gravy-smothered French fries with greens, cornbread and Sweet Netta Ta Ta Pie.

They both drank lemonade ice tea.

There was a significant pause as forks met food. When the two women came up for air, Nicole took a gulp of her tea and regarded Glenda.

"Well," she asked. "Feeling better?"

"Feel like I swallowed the *Titanic*," Glenda said. "You're the Devil. In a good way. Thank you."

"Well, when life gives you lemons…" Nicole raised her glass. "You make this stuff. Remember those ribs in, where was it, Lubbock? That was the only good part of that damned tour."

Glenda looked uncomfortable. "I wasn't on that tour."

Now Nicole looked embarrassed. "Oh, right. That was our last tour. I was a little hazy on that one."

Glenda swallowed and said quietly: "Because of me."

Nicole gave her an arch look. "You blaming yourself for what happened to the band?"

"Well...." Glenda paused. "I was the one who bailed on you."

Nicole looked at her sharply. "So we were nothing without you?"

"I wasn't saying that!" Glenda said, stumbling over the words and blushing.

"Well, you should," Nicole said. "'Cause it's true."

"No, it's not! You guys were great musicians."

"We were *good* musicians, Glenda," Nicole said. "Not great. You, though. You were going places."

"Yeah, hanging myself in front of an audience."

"Over an audience," Nicole corrected. "Lou and Mimi kind of felt that was karma."

"I deserved it. I let Bernie fill my head with bullshit. I was a stupid, selfish baby."

"Hmmmm," Nicole said, and Glenda couldn't tell whether she was agreeing or simply wondering. "Bernie told us it was your idea to go solo."

"What? No!" Glenda protested. "Yeah, I finally agreed, but he spent weeks talking me into it. I mean, I wanted to do my own songs but I never would have..." She didn't finish the sentence.

Nicole laughed. "You can't say it, can you? 'Cause you would have, at some point."

Glenda looked down at the remains of her syrup-stained plate. "How can you sit here with me?"

"Like I told you at the funeral, I don't hate you," Nicole said. "Look, I knew you were what made us. I was having fun, but you were the gen-u-wine article."

"I just wanted to do my own songs."

"I know. I won't lie. The way you ditched us was pretty shitty," Nicole said. "But I've got no claim to perfection myself. It was a bad year after you left, but I didn't do myself any favors. I chose the wrong guy, as usual. Like they say, my heart follows my cunt. I'm always confusing sex and love." She finished the ice tea and thumped the glass on the table. "My only flaw!"

Glenda laughed. "You seem tough to me. Pragmatic."

"I am, mostly. You grow up on a Mississippi tenant farm, and you learn real quick the difference between dreams and dirt. That's why I can admit

I wasn't in your league, Glenda. But, honey, that don't mean I don't occasionally want to reach for the brass ring."

"Shouldn't that be a gold ring?"

"Should be," Nicole said. "Never is, though. Anyway, what are you gonna do now?" She gestured at the last slice of sweet potato pie and then at Glenda.

Glenda forced herself to refuse. "Well, I guess I'll lug the session tapes over to my parents' garage and set up there. My dad has an old four-track mixer. It's a long way to Altadena, though."

"Are you thinking of getting together a band, is what I meant."

"I hadn't thought that far ahead," Glenda admitted. Then she remembered Nelson's offer. "I did get an offer to sing with a band."

"Oh, your gig at Gazzarri's. That the band?"

"Yeah," Glenda said, surprised. "How did you…?"

"Word gets around," Nicole said. "I heard you wailed."

"Yeah," Glenda admitted. "It really was working for me."

"I heard you did the whole set naked."

"No! It was hot. It was one song, and I took my top off. That's all."

Nicole chuckled. "Anyway, you're not gonna take that offer, are you?"

"I hadn't thought about it that much," Glenda lied.

"You won't," Nicole insisted. "You won't front for any band unless it's yours."

Glenda laughed. "Am I that much of a power freak?"

Nicole toyed with her fork, making circles in the syrup. "How can I put this?" she said. "Yes. Yes, you are."

"That's insulting."

"No, it isn't," Nicole said. "Why are you in this business?"

"Because I love to write songs, and I love to sing."

Nicole shrugged. "You could do that at home. Why do you need an audience?"

"I don't," Glenda said.

"So Gazzarri's was nothing? Just singing in the shower?"

"I never thought about it."

"You didn't need to. It's an obvious truth. Expressing yourself is great. But performing is real power. When you sing or play, it's like casting a magic spell. You make those people laugh or cry or dance."

"It's not about power," Glenda protested. "It's about joining your soul with the audience."

"Maybe, but you're the one arrogant enough to think those folks need to hear you. And you wouldn't ever give up that magic wand."

Glenda quirked her lips. "Except sometimes the magic doesn't work. Then you're just a sad little witch with a broken broomstick."

"Glenda, the Good Witch," Nicole said. "Anyway, if you ever do put a band together, I'm available for weddings, birthdays and bar mitzvahs."

"That is a very gracious offer, considering," Glenda said.

"Not really. Since I started playing with you again, I realize how much I missed it. Everything I do, I do to please somebody else. But this... it's just for me."

"I know what you mean," Glenda said. "Dancing naked can't be what you want to do with your life. I can't see you doing it when you're sixty."

Nicole made a dismissive gesture. "Can't see being a rocker then, either. But you never know. Anyway, it beats working cotton ten hours a day."

"I guess," Glenda said. "And you do play a mean wand!"

They laughed.

"So," Glenda asked. "Do you miss the star trip?"

"I tell you what I don't miss," Nicole said firmly. "I don't miss all those creepy, grabby producers, agents and club owners. At least dancing at The Playground, I only have to *shake* my ass. And if somebody tries to grab it, the bouncer will kick theirs."

Glenda nodded. "And you get to eat what you want," she added ruefully as Nicole flagged down a waitress for a second slice of pie.

"Oh, you don't need to look like a supermodel," Nicole said. "One of the girls, Lana, she has huge stretch marks and a waffle butt. But boy, does she rake in the dollar bills."

"Huh," Glenda said. "I should think you'd need... well, certain assets. I mean, look at you!"

"What you need," Nicole said, ignoring the compliment and rapping the table with her fork, "Is a pair of stiletto heels and an attitude. And nothing in between."

"Really? What attitude?"

"Ah, that's a professional secret," Nicole said with a wicked smile. "I take it you've never been to an adult entertainment venue?"

"Just once," Glenda said, remembering the bloody back room of the Big Top. "I wasn't there long." For now, she didn't feel like sharing the recent madness in her life. In fact, she desperately wanted *not* to think about it.

"Well, a lot of the girls have problems," Nicole said. "Drug problems, self-esteem problems, obviously money problems. And a lot of 'em look on the clients with contempt."

"Understandable."

"Why?" Nicole said. "Those men need something— and God knows why. I don't judge. All I know is they want a little pleasure and a little fantasy, and we give it to them. You don't come out and look down at them. You look at them like they're scum, they'll know."

"Okay, what then?"

"You waltz out there and you put out. You show them you enjoy what you're doing. Some girls put their hands on their hips and come out on that stage like fashion models. They say 'I am incredible and you are lucky to look at me.' They demand you idolize them. They're like Marilyn Monroe!"

"So that's the attitude?"

"One of them. Then there're the bondage mommas. They bring a whip, they tease."

"What does the stretch-mark girl do?"

"Oh, they love her," Nicole said. "She bounces out there. She's so *happy* you invited her. She's loving it. And that girl has energy. She flashes, she jives. In a weirdly innocent way. She's like a cheerleader. A slutty one."

Glenda could picture stretch-mark girl doing her thing. She had to admit her thing wasn't so different from what rock and pop singers did; it was all stagecraft.

"What about you?"

"Me?" Nicole paused. "Well, I go out there and I look those guys in the eye. I look at each and every one of them and I move for them, and what I'm doing is telling them something, a secret message just for them."

"What's the message?"

Nicole leaned over, putting her lips close to Glenda's ear, and whispered breathily: *"I want you."* She leaned back and crossed her arms, smiling.

"I think I want some ice cream," Glenda said.

"So," Nicole said. "What's with this Nelson?"

"What about him?"

"I have eyes, Glenda."

Glenda blushed.

"Is he going to be in your band?"

"No, no," Glenda said, flustered. "And I don't have a band. And anyway, he was just helping out with the album. He has his own thing."

"Good," Nicole said. "Because if you were sleeping with him, that might be a problem."

Glenda coughed and reached for her ice tea. She took a gulp.

Nicole's eyes went comically wide. "You are!" she blurted out. "You big nympho!"

"It's complicated," Glenda said, her ears burning. She felt like she was back in high school, and she'd hated high school.

"Girl, the first rule of survival in this business is you don't sleep with band members," Nicole shaking her finger. "You can have lovers and you can have a band, but you can't combine the two."

"He's not in the band," Glenda repeated. "And I don't have a band!"

"Okay. Yoko Ono."

"Now that's unfair!"

"He's young," Nicole said, arching her eyebrows.

"Don't I know it."

"Yummy?"

"I really don't want to talk about this, if you don't mind."

Nicole shrugged. "He's not bad on the guitar. You might think about using him. Musically, I mean."

"After you just warned me about the unbreakable law?"

"Yeah, right," Nicole said. "Gets broken all the time. Besides, look at my track record. And incidentally, when did you ever listen to anybody?"

"I listened to Bernie."

"God rest his soul. In hell."

The second slice of pie arrived and Nicole dug in. "Speaking of which, if you don't mind my asking, how else did he screw you?"

Glenda sighed. "He sold one of my songs out from under me. I think he might have jimmied my contract, too. I was supposed to see his accountant, but I can't find him. I hope he hasn't skipped town. Went back to Peoria or something."

"Peoria?" Nicole said. "Why Peoria?"

"I dunno. Doesn't everybody have a relative in Peoria?"

"What's his name?"

"Kirby Fink."

"Oh, that guy."

"You know him?" Glenda's eyes widened in surprise.

"He's a regular. Look." Nicole fished in her purse and drew out a business card. She handed it to Glenda. It was the accountant's. "He said he'd do my taxes for free."

"Do you know how I can get hold of him?"

"I haven't seen him at The Playground lately. But I know he has a place out in Palm Springs. This summer, he hired six of us to go out there."

Glenda looked scandalized. "Nicole, you didn't!"

"No, no, not for sex. He's got a thing. He's addicted to strippers in a sort of weird romantic way. He kind of puts us on pedestals. I don't think he has great social skills. He hired a limousine to take us out there. We danced and then we had a pool party, and that was it. It was a great day except for the sunburn." She paused to stab at the pie. "Let me see if I can remember where it is."

Nicole closed her eyes and thought about it, chewing thoughtfully. "Okay, we went past all those new stores and past Mrs. Ford's drug treatment place... hmmmm... past that home where the Queen visited a couple of years ago."

"I've never been to Palm Springs," Glenda said.

"Shhhh," Nicole said. "I'm trying to remember landmarks." She opened her eyes. "Okay, so it's off Palm Canyon on Indian land. Go about five miles past the tennis club and you'll hit it. There's a dirt road that goes back into the desert. His home is at the end. It's the only one. Fifties-style, lots of glass windows and a pointy roof like a diner. Lot of Italian-looking trees all around."

"Got it," Glenda said.

"So, you're gonna go out and see him?" Nicole asked.

"Yeah. I might."

"To talk about your contract?"

"Hopefully."

"But," Nicole said, "what if he won't see you?"

"He will," Glenda said. "I'll pretend I'm a stripper." She winked.

CHAPTER TWENTY-THREE

"Yes!" Glenda pumped her fist in the air.

She had her thirteen clowns, and it was still only ten in the morning. She had done it! True, one of those clowns was Larry. Glenda had not quite blackmailed him into helping, but she had casually mentioned that he had absconded with Bernie's statue of Ganesha and how that might play out legally and karmically.

"It's the elephant in the room," she had joked.

Larry had mumbled something about karma coming home to roost and Oreos, which made no sense to Glenda. But then, she thought, Larry seldom did.

She glanced gratefully over at Trina. The assistant had done her part, too. Trina had convinced her ex-husband, a part-time movie stuntman, to take a clown gig by promising he might make some good contacts at the party. Trina had sealed the deal by plaintively asking if her ex was still living with the young lady who'd broken up their marriage.

Guilt was really rocking the house today, Glenda thought. She was weirdly proud of Trina. Lately, she was discovering that she knew a lot of kick-ass women. It was a heartening discovery.

On a Friday the day before Halloween, there really wasn't much other work to be done. Since Glenda was temporarily in charge of the office, she felt no guilt in deciding to cut the day short, close the office and allow Trina to go home with a full day's pay.

One problem down, Glenda thought. She was exuberantly grateful. After all, in the past few days she had seen one corpse after another, been threatened, robbed, caught up in one mystery after another, got back her groove, got herself a lover— although she was in two minds about that —and still didn't know what was happening with her contract and career.

And she'd juggled all that while still keeping her day job. A simple, uncomplicated victory was just pure joy.

After locking up, Glenda took her time walking home. The weather had warmed a few degrees, and there was even some blue among the bovine herd of clouds. She strolled down Sunset Boulevard, idly glancing in the windows of clothing boutiques and debating what she'd wear for her next gig. She mused happily. Leather or tiger stripes? Tina Turner or Pat Benatar?

She made it home with barely enough time to drive to Marcus's office. They were going to lunch, and she decided she would eat whatever she damned well pleased.

But before she left, Glenda triumphantly took the bottle of pills from her medicine chest and ceremoniously committed the red and white occupants thereof to the depths of her toilet. She saluted them with a victory flush.

GLENDA AND MARCUS WOUND up at Cole's on Sixth Street in downtown Los Angeles. Marcus ordered a Beefeater martini. Glenda thought of ordering a mimosa, but she didn't need champagne; she already felt bubbly. Instead, she ordered a cosmo.

"So," her godfather asked, "how did your show go?" He looked both curious and concerned.

Glenda blushed. She seemed to be doing that a lot lately. Also shrieking and cringing. "It was a disaster. Then... it was incredible."

"Huh?"

Glenda described the diarrhea disaster and the aftermath when she returned and unleashed herself. She didn't mention the Jack Daniels, taking off her top or her private performance with Nelson. Thankfully— or tactfully —Marcus didn't ask.

"Well," he said. "I knew you'd come back. I couldn't be prouder. What did you think of the band?"

"You know, it was my first time in a long time. But I really liked playing with him... them," Glenda said. "They did ask me to front for them..."

"But you won't," Marcus said firmly.

"Why does everybody say that?"

Marcus just smiled and sipped his drink. "So. Back to business. What about your contract. Any word?"

"Um, I didn't find my copy," she said apologetically.

Marcus rolled his eyes. "Glenda, Glenda."

"But don't worry."

"Why shouldn't I worry?"

"Because," she said buoyantly, raising the almost-empty cosmo glass. "I've got the original. Bernie's original."

Her godfather looked stunned. "What?"

"Well, I don't have it yet but I will. I'm gonna get it from the accountant."

Marcus gave her a long, long look, and twirled his martini glass. "You told me you couldn't find the accountant."

Glenda snorted. Marcus winced.

"You remember Nicole?" she asked.

"Your bass player."

Glenda nodded. "She knows him."

"Is she with him?"

"No. She has a second job, kind of a revealing one, if you know what I mean."

"I don't," Marcus said, frowning.

"Stripper," Glenda said. "Day job. Except at night, obviously. Anyway, Fink invited her and some other ladies out to his place in Palm Springs for a hot tub party. Nothing happened. Just swimming."

Some part of her mind realized she was babbling.

"And you want to go out there?" Marcus asked.

"Yeah."

"What makes you think he'll give you the contract?"

"Why wouldn't he? He said he'd help me."

"Really, when?"

Glenda shook her head. The promise had been made while they were looting Bernie's house. "Doesn't matter," she said.

"But Fink disappeared," Marcus said. "You couldn't find him. I couldn't find him."

"Right, but Nicole knows how to get to his house. So I'm gonna go see him on Sunday."

"So you made an appointment?"

"No. I'm just gonna go out there. It's Sunday. He should be home."

"Unless he's been hiding— which he seems to have been doing."

"That's why I'm going," Glenda said. "It's all desert. He's got nowhere to run."

Marcus put up his hands. "Wait, wait. Give me a second to sort this out." He closed his eyes and pinched the bridge of his nose. His brow creased in concentration.

Glenda ran a finger around the inside of the cosmo glass and sucked it. It was a very strong drink. And delicious.

After almost a minute, Marcus sighed and opened his eyes. "Okay," he said. "Look. Why don't we go out together? I've got business with Fink, too. Besides, I know how to handle characters like him." He smiled. "It is my business, after all."

"Really? That would be great."

"My pleasure. I'll drive."

"Okay, Sunday it is." Glenda gazed longingly at her empty glass.

Marcus noticed. "Okay." He ostentatiously looked at his watch. "Oh, brother, look at the time. Sorry, sweetie, I have to get back to work."

"No problem," Glenda said. "I have stuff to do, too." Although actually, she didn't. She had the entire rest of the day to do whatever she pleased. After days crammed with obligations, having free time was exhilarating. She hadn't figured out yet what to do.

She rode with Marcus back to his office. He seemed distracted. She hoped he wasn't working too hard and then felt a little guilty about accepting his help with Fink. She added a kiss to her goodbye hug.

When she got home, Glenda decided to use her unexpected time wisely. She cleaned out the moldering junk food in her fridge and took her sheets, which carried the lingering scent of Nelson, down to the laundry room. She searched her house again for her contract, but came up empty-handed. She thought about calling her parents and asking them to look for her paperwork, which they'd already done, but decided she couldn't face having Mom drag her into a conversation about her sister. She picked up Banshee but wasn't feeling inspired and restored the guitar to it's stand.

Plopping down on the sofa, she thought about the various horrors visited upon her in the past week. Bloody deaths and attacks, all seemingly unconnected.

No, that wasn't true, she thought. There was one thread linking all of them.

Kirby Fink.

She couldn't quite make herself believe that Fink had robbed her or killed anyone. But he had evidently been stashing money away in a secret account. And he'd stolen a painting— with Glenda's help. He also had a weird thing for strippers. And Blondie's card had been on his desk.

But the reality was, it didn't matter what she thought of Fink. She had to confront him. She had to get her paperwork. Until she did, her career was in limbo. When Glenda thought about things that way, Sunday seemed a long time to wait. She checked her watch. It was a bit after three o'clock. She would have plenty of time to drive to Palm Springs before dark. And the day was a beauty.

She called her godfather's office to invite him along, but was told Marcus had gone out for a meeting.

"Oh," Glenda told Ellie. "Well, could you let him know that I decided to head out to Palm Springs today? He'll know what I mean. Tell him the weather's nice and it might rain on Sunday."

"I'll let him know, dear," Ellie promised.

It was a precaution. Glenda wanted somebody to know where she'd gone, just in case. She even thought of taking someone along for backup. Nicole came to mind because she already knew Fink. Glenda called Nicole's apartment, but she wasn't home. She didn't leave a message.

On the way out of her apartment, she slipped the big screwdriver into her jacket pocket. Just in case.

She tried not to think what that case might be.

CHAPTER TWENTY-FOUR

The sun was slipping behind the San Jacinto Mountains by the time Glenda reached the house, which stood in shadow. Her poor Porsche carried a coat of dust, and she'd had to virtually creep along the last quarter-mile of the dirt road to keep the low-slung sports car from bottoming out on the ruts. She'd felt every jolt in her coccyx, making this the only time she'd ever wished for more padding there.

Luckily, the driveway was paved. Glenda rolled to a stop and cut the engine. She tossed her sunglasses on the passenger seat, climbed stiffly out of the car and stood, rubbing her tailbone. A stand of towering cypress trees screened the house from the road. She smelled desert dust, sagebrush and spicy juniper. She heard only the ticking of her car's cooling engine and the power-line hum of insects.

No sound came from the house.

Dim and quiet didn't disturb Glenda; she'd had way too much sound and fury lately and she could appreciate the solitude.

Nicole had described the house well. It had a peaked roof and large windows that looked out onto a front yard of desert landscaping. A double carport sat to one side. Two cars were parked there, but Glenda couldn't tell the makes. She walked up to them.

One was the battered van she remembered from the nighttime foray to Bernie's mansion.

The other was a white Cadillac.

Glenda recalled what Larry had said and suddenly felt a chill. Retreating to her Porsche, she shrugged into her coat. Slipping a hand into the pocket, she gripped the screwdriver.

She walked to the front door and rang the bell and waited. No one answered. She tried again, giving a longer ring. Muffled chimes echoed inside the house, but no sound of footsteps. She stood nervously on the doorstep.

She was about to ring again when some insect brushed her ear with a high-pitched whine. She slapped at it, twisted and her shoulder bumped the door— which swung open.

She jumped back, then caught herself. The door hadn't been properly latched, she realized, and it now stood slightly ajar, revealing a two-inch strip of darkness inside.

Although she felt her heart trip-hammering, Glenda fought it down. This was the middle of nowhere, after all; Fink probably never locked his door. And it had rained recently. Maybe the door had warped a little, and the accountant hadn't realized the lock wasn't properly latched.

Maybe.

Rapping lightly on the door and calling through the gap, Glenda said, "Hello. Hello? Mr. Fink? Anybody home?"

Again, no answer.

Her moist hand gripped the screwdriver, and she backed away. If Fink was there and not answering, he might have a good reason. He might be napping or using the bathroom. She didn't want to barge in and give him a heart attack.

And then she remembered Nicole telling her about the pool. It was almost dusk, but despite Glenda's personal chill, the weather was warm enough that Fink might be out there. She walked to the side of the house and followed a concrete path around the corner, which ended in a wrought-iron gate. She opened it and walked into the backyard.

The pool was a slab of purple, reflecting the bruised dusk.

Glenda saw an unfinished drink on a table next to a lounger but no sign of Bernie. She crossed the patio and pressed her nose to a sliding glass door and saw the living room, sparsely furnished. The room was dimly lit by light spilling from some unseen adjoining room. In the middle of the room, an upholstered armchair lay toppled on its side. Nothing else seemed out of place.

She stepped back and saw a lighted window to her right. She went to it and peered in. The kitchen. It reminded her of her own. Pizza boxes and takeout cartons decorated the countertops along with empty soda cans. Apparently Fink shared her taste in cuisine. Or maybe, she thought, the accountant hadn't left the house for days.

Was he hiding? Or had he left?

But there were two cars in the carport.

Glenda paused, uncertain what to do next. She could try the sliding glass door, but decided instead to return to the front of the house. Whatever the situation here, she figured it was better to use the front door, making everything seem a little bit more normal, somehow. So she walked back around the house. The front door still stood slightly ajar in a way that Glenda firmly refused to call ominous.

Or spooky.

Or weird.

Or…

Before she could think of any more unsettling synonyms she pushed open the door and stepped inside.

"Hello," she called. "Mr. Fink? Kirby? It's me, Glenda."

No answer.

This is wrong, she thought. *Very, very wrong. I should leave now.*

But she had driven so far, and she still had unfinished business with the accountant. What if Fink was just passed out drunk? Then she would throw some water on him and have words.

But she knew she was whistling in the dark.

She found a light switch on the wall and clicked it on. A face leered at her from the far end of the room.

Startled, Glenda half-drew the screwdriver from her coat pocket before she realized she was alone. The face was her own, reflected in the sliding glass door. She saw the toppled chair. She was in the living room. It was high-ceilinged, deeply carpeted and painted a soft blue, as if the sky had leaked inside and stained the walls. The furniture was almost generic; the kind of tasteful yet characterless pieces you'd find in a model tract home. Two paintings on the wall appeared to have been chosen solely for their color palette.

Glenda saw no signs of Fink's actual personality here. The place was almost eerily featureless, surprising her mainly because the perceptive Nicole hadn't mentioned the fact.

It didn't seem to be the retreat of a man who had embezzled from his employer and invited a limousine full of strippers to party. Either Fink had hidden depths or a split personality. Maybe, Glenda thought, he only came to life in front of other people.

That was the creepiest thought of all, and she quickly suppressed it.

The living room was L-shaped. The sightline was partially blocked on her right by a wall with a closed door. She turned the corner and finally found a trace of Fink's personality. The back wall consisted of a fireplace built of cream brickwork rising right to the ceiling. In front of the fireplace, the carpet had been cut away and new stone flagging had taken its place. There was nothing else to see here. Glenda decided to try the other rooms.

She glanced into the kitchen, then tried the closed door leading off from the living room. Inside was a bathroom with just a toilet and a sink, tiled in a disturbing pink.

Crossing to the opposite wall, Glenda found a short hallway with doors on either side.

All the doors were open.

She looked into the first room on her left. It was a study or office with a large desk. All the drawers had been pulled out. She didn't go in. She turned to the door on her right. It was another bathroom, with a shower and tub this time, but still tiled with that unsettling pink, like well-scrubbed flesh.

The last door on the left was a guest bedroom, judging by the narrow and tightly made-up bed. A cheap dresser and a nightstand had both been ransacked.

The last room on the right must be the master bedroom, Glenda thought, approaching it warily. If Fink was home, here was the only place he could be.

She pulled the screwdriver from her pocket and walked in.

The room was very large, with another fireplace taking up a wall on her right. On the floor, partially finished new stonework had been laid, with tools scattered on it as if the workmen had been suddenly called away.

Maybe Fink had given them the weekend off for Halloween, Glenda thought.

The wall to her left held two windows on either side of a large, high bed. It jutted out to face the fireplace. The bed was neatly made.

The rest of the room, however, was a mess. Dresser drawers were pulled open and a closet door flung wide, clothing tossed on the floor. Then her eye caught an anomaly.

Above the bed between the windows hung a painting. It was the John Lennon tiger. Its psychedelic face leered garishly at her.

Fink had taken the painting from Bernie's house. The accountant had claimed he'd intended to sell it and, in fact, already had a buyer.

Fink had also said he hated the thing. So why hang it over his bed?

Glenda stepped to the bed and took a closer look at the painting. She noticed a small silvery-gray strip peeking from one corner. She touched it. It was sticky. Duct tape. It must have peeled away from the back of the painting.

Puzzled, she leaned over the bed and pulled the painting away from the wall. Taped to the back was a small rectangle. Gingerly, she pulled it free and examined it.

It was a cassette tape, the kind used in answering machines.

As she slipped the tape in the pocket of her jeans, she had an idea what was on it.

Fink must have been her blackmailer. That answered one question. But she wanted the accountant to answer some others. Where was he?

Suddenly she didn't like the room anymore. Among other things, its color scheme was just as unnerving as that in the bathrooms: Pastel walls, carpet and bedspread with an abstract design of dark spots and spatters.

Dark spots and spatters…

A sudden chill slid up her spine. She'd checked every room in the house. Fink wasn't there. If he was home, he had to be in the one place she hadn't looked.

Her feet felt like lead as she forced herself to walk around to the other side of the high bed.

The body on the floor wore plaid shorts and a once-white Izod shirt. The alligator logo on the shirt now lazed in a red swamp. The corpse had one bare foot, and a flip-flop dangled from the other. Somebody had smashed in one side of the man's head but Glenda recognized him anyway.

She gasped.

The face looking at her with staring eyes wasn't Fink.

It was Bernie Sherman.

CHAPTER TWENTY-FIVE

Glenda didn't remember the drive home. She was numb with shock. Using a gas station phone, she anonymously alerted the Palm Springs police about the body in Fink's bedroom, but everything after that was a blur. All she remembered were the headlights of passing cars illuminating the highway like shotgun blasts.

After parking the Porsche in her carport, Glenda staggered upstairs. She unlocked the door and practically fell into the living room. She slammed the door behind her, then locked it and re-locked it six times before she was satisfied.

She'd never so much as a seen a corpse in her life yet now she'd been up close with four in a week. Irrationally, she wondered if somebody was tracking her, leaving bodies for her to find like some sort of sick Easter egg hunt. Dead people just seemed to keep turning up wherever she went.

Images of Bernie's body and the bathtub corpse that no longer had a name flashed in her head. Glenda's gorge rose, but she fought it down. She had to *think*.

This whole thing made no sense. She'd believed Bernie had died in his house. Obviously, he hadn't. So who had mooned her in Bernie's bathtub and how had that man died? An accident?

No, she thought. Bernie had gone into hiding. He wanted everybody to think he was dead. Was that because he was the killer, or because someone was after him?

She had another thought: Could Fink have killed both men? The accountant didn't seem the type. Just a nerd with a stripper fetish. Besides, Fink had seemed convinced that Bernie was dead the night he went to Bernie's home. Otherwise, why would Fink have risked stealing Bernie's paintings?

And the person who had blackmailed and robbed Glenda: *was* that Fink? The tape had been hidden in his bedroom.

Unless Bernie had been hiding there and *he* was the blackmailer. But then what had happened to Fink?

Or maybe, she thought, Bernie had gone to the Palm Springs home to confront Fink about his stolen paintings, and Fink had killed him.

The possibilities made her head throb. But any way she looked at it, she seemed to be deeply involved in a mess she didn't understand. And she couldn't go to the police with the suspicious revelation that she was at the scene of, respectively, an accidental drowning, a murder-suicide, and the murder of her producer. That was a clear invitation to spend years in the California country club— the one with the iron bars.

Then a worse thought struck her. If she'd arrived only a short time earlier at Fink's Palm Springs hideaway, she might have been killed, too.

Still could be. Bernie's killer— whoever that was —was still out there.

That thought froze her blood. She needed a drink, so she got one. Unfortunately, the only thing she had in the house was a bottle with a few ounces of something called soju. Trina had brought it back from a trip to South Korea. It was overly sweet and barely alcoholic, but it was booze and it settled Glenda's mind, if not her stomach.

She emptied the bottle, chased it with a glass of cold water from the kitchen sink and walked back into the living room. Even if her body wanted to run away, her brain didn't. There was a mystery here. First question was not who had killed Bernie. It was *why*.

Putting her hands in her pockets, Glenda discovered the tape. She pulled it out and twirled it around in her fingers thoughtfully. She walked to her answering machine, inserted the tape and hit the play button.

Once again, Glenda heard herself ranting at Bernie. She let the tape run through a series of increasingly unhinged threats as she walked back into the bedroom to put on a fresh T-shirt.

Her voice ended with a click. A new message began, this one not in Glenda's voice.

"Bernie," Marcus said in a soft, menacing tone. "What have you done?"

Glenda whirled around and raced into the living room, but that was the last message. She rewound the tape and played it again and again until she was sure of what she'd heard.

Her godfather had called Bernie's house minutes after Glenda's last call. And there'd been a threat in his voice.

A knock came at her door. She jumped.

"Glenda!" The knocking resumed. "It's Nelson. Open up!"

Her thoughts scattered. She unlocked the door. Nelson struggled to hold up a young woman, who teetered despite his arm around her waist. Her hair fell in her face. Then the girl looked up at Glenda through bleary eyes smeared with blotchy mascara.

"Abby?"

"S'Crystal!" Glenda's sister slurred and then gagged.

CHAPTER TWENTY-SIX

"Bathroom, now!" Nelson said. "She already hurled once in my car."

Glenda rushed forward and took her boneless, reeking sister from Nelson's arms. They staggered to the bathroom. For a blessing, they made it to the toilet. Glenda held back her sister's hair as Abby lost what remained of her dinner and her dignity. It took her an uncomfortably long time.

Once Abby'd puked up everything and then some, Glenda cleaned her up, forced her to drink some water from a toothbrush glass, and helped Abby into her bed, where Abby collapsed like a sack of slightly green potatoes. Glenda removed Abby's shoes— *stilettos,* for God's sake! Abby seemed to be through vomiting, but just in case, Glenda turned her onto her side so she wouldn't asphyxiate if more stuff came up.

Glenda found Nelson in the kitchen, cleaning his hands with paper towels.

"I really hope that smell goes away," he said. "I left the car windows down."

Glenda's mind was whirling. Too much was happening, far too fast. But first things first.

"All right," she told Nelson. "What have you done to my sister?"

"She was at the Crip."

Glenda gaped. "The Cripple Cafe? Are you kidding me? My sister? She's sixteen years old!"

Nelson put up his hands defensively. "I guess she used a fake ID. With that makeup, she could have passed for eighteen, just."

"And what were you doing?"

"I was onstage. Can I sit?"

Glenda followed Nelson into the living room. She let him flop onto the couch and then asked, "What happened? What do you know?"

"The first I knew about her was when they asked over the PA if whoever had brought Abigail Birdsong would come and collect her from the bar. I heard the name and, since our set was over, I came down. Caesar— you know, the bouncer —told me she'd gotten seriously smashed and some troll was trying to pick her up. Apparently she made some noise when he—" He paused. "You want to hear this?"

"What did he do?" Glenda said through gritted teeth.

"He put a hand where it ... on her, um, upper ... leg."

"Goddammit!"

"But that's all," Nelson said quickly. "The bartender heard her squawk and gave Caesar the high sign. He came over, broke it up, and carded her for good measure. She opened her purse and took out her high school ID instead of the fake one. It had her real name. Then Caesar decided she should be eighty-sixed pronto or the place would get shut down. She said she had some friends with her, so they put out the call but nobody turned up. I thought she might be related to you."

"Yeah, not a common name," Glenda admitted.

"I said I'd bring her over to your place. I didn't want to pour her into a taxi. I figured she'd snuck out of the house, and your folks would not appreciate her showing up dead drunk at their door. So, here we are."

Glenda scrubbed her face with her hands. This was all she needed right now. But she still looked at Nelson with gratitude.

"Thanks, I mean it." She would have said more, but Nelson raised a hand carelessly.

"No problem. Look, I've got to get back. We've got another set soon." He rose and stood awkwardly. She realized he was waiting for something. A hug? Or maybe a kiss?

So she gave him both, but broke away before things got too intimate. "I'd better go check on Abby."

"Don't be too hard on her," Nelson said. "We all do stupid things when we're young."

"You are young."

"And I still do stupid things," he said with a grin.

"Me, too. I just want to make sure she skips a few of the worst mistakes." She watched Nelson go and thought with a pang how much nicer the night might have gone if he'd stayed.

When she looked at her watch, she realized it wasn't even ten o'clock. She sighed, picked up the phone and called her parents.

CHAPTER TWENTY-SEVEN

Abby's monumental hangover the next morning did not make her contrite.

"You called them!" she shouted, which made Glenda's head ache. She couldn't imagine what it did to Abby, who was nursing a glass of orange juice and some dry toast Glenda had scrounged in the kitchen.

"I had to," Glenda said. "They would have been frantic when you didn't come home."

"No, they wouldn't have," Abby said. "I told them I was sleeping over at Heather's, and she told her folks she was sleeping over with us."

"And then you both went club-hopping in Hollywood. How did you even get down here?"

"Gerald drove us. Heather's boyfriend. He's eighteen. He got us the phony IDs."

"Oh, great," Glenda said. "So what happened to Young Scarface? He and your girlfriend left you alone in that club."

"They might have been a little worried when I wouldn't go with them," Abby admitted.

"They wanted to leave and you wouldn't go?"

"I was having a good time."

"And they wanted to go off and have a good time, too," Glenda said. "Real piece of work, your friend, Heather."

"I told them I'd be okay," Abby insisted.

"I'll bet. How many vodka tonics had you slurped by then?"

Abby looked evasive. "I was fine!"

"You weren't fine," Glenda said waspishly. "You were shit-faced, and some jerk groped you. My friend managed to get you here, but you puked all over his car and then you puked here. What the hell were you thinking? You could have been raped or died of alcohol poisoning."

Abby rolled her eyes. "Overreacting, much? I just overdid it a little bit."

"Oh, bullshit, Abby. You're a teenager, for God's sake. What you did was stupid and dangerous."

"Well, you would know all about that. Hypocrite."

Glenda fought her temper. "Yes, I do know all about it. That's why I know how serious this is."

Abby gave a particularly derisive snort.

Glenda ground her teeth. "Finish your breakfast. I'll take you home."

"They'll ground me for life!" Abby wailed.

"I hope they do."

Abby gave her a somewhat bleary stink eye. "I will never forgive you."

CHAPTER TWENTY-EIGHT

Larry sat in a cheap chair across from a cheap detective. The detective's name was Bedell, and he was a robbery-homicide investigator. He wore a Miami Vice outfit: a white jacket with shoulders like a landing strip and sleeves pushed to the elbows. It made his head look like a gumball balanced on a ruler. Bedell's hair was an unnatural, greased slab that resembled newly laid tarmac. He was trying laughably hard to be a TV cop, Larry thought, although he liked his socks. They were a tasteful pastel.

Bedell sat behind a metal desk in an LAPD interview room that smelled of coffee, sweat and stale cigarettes. Moon and Moreno sat in chairs propped against one of the industrial beige walls.

Scraping his fingernails over the curated stubble on his jaw, Bedell said, "Thanks for coming, Mister Freckle."

"Freck-*hill*," Larry said. "It's pronounced Freck-*hill*. You say both parts of it."

"Right," the detective said.

"I want a lawyer."

The detective looked at Moon and Moreno.

"You're not under arrest, Larry," Moreno said. "We just want to ask you a few questions, as I explained to you when we stopped you."

"*Again*," Larry said. "You stopped me *again*. And you said you would stop me every day if I didn't come in."

The detective looked at Moon and Moreno. They shook their heads.

"You did so," Larry protested. He turned to the detective. "They harassed me. I was harassed." He repeated it again indignantly, stretching out the syllables: "Huh. Rass. Ed. " He crossed his arms, incidentally tucking the Rolex out of sight behind his right elbow.

"Mister Freckhill," the detective said, exaggerating the pronunciation.

"Call me Larry."

Bedell took a long, slow breath. "Larry," he said. "Let's move on."

"Where?" Larry asked.

"Where what?"

"Where are we moving?"

"I meant with the conversation."

"Oh. Sure."

"Thank you. Now, these officers stopped you in Hollywood on Wednesday night, and they questioned you about an item of jewelry you were wearing. Is that correct?"

Larry squeezed his elbows more tightly to his body. "Something like that," he muttered.

"And that item would be..." Bedell consulted a file on the desk. "A 1979 gold Rolex Submariner Model 5512."

Pointing at Larry's concealed wrist, Bedell asked, "Are you wearing the item?"

Larry reluctantly revealed the watch. "Yeah." He tucked it back out of sight.

"And you said it was a gift."

"It was."

The detective leaned back. "Could you give us a few specifics about the watch?"

"Like what?"

The detective leaned forward. Larry didn't like the look in his eyes.

"Like," Bedell said, and his voice was too casual. "Did you get it before or after Bernie Sherman turned up dead in a bathtub?"

Too stunned to speak, Larry sat mute.

"We traced the serial number," Bedell said. "It belonged to Mister Sherman. And you contend that he gave it to you."

"He did."

"When?"

"I don't remember the exact date."

"Before or after he died, Larry?"

"Well, he couldn't give it to me after he died."

"Precisely," the detective said. "Do you see where I'm going with this, Larry?"

"I don't think I like where this is going," Larry said. "I want a lawyer."

"Well, as we said, you're not under arrest," Bedell repeated. "If you don't want to talk to us, you can just get up and go. We're not forcing you to cooperate."

Larry stood. "Great," he said. "Thanks."

"I'll just have the officers escort you out," Bedell said, and nodded meaningfully at Moon and Moreno, who looked meaningfully at Larry.

Larry looked back, reconsidered, and sat down. "On second thought, I'm glad to help," he said nervously.

"Your help is much appreciated," Bedell said. "So, Mister Sherman gave you the watch."

"Yes."

"What for?"

"What for?"

"Yes, what was the occasion of his giving you the watch?"

Larry thought at top speed. "Birthday present," he said.

"Hmmm," Bedell said. He consulted the file. "So you've had this watch since July twenty-third?"

"No," Larry said quickly. "He just gave it to me a week ago. I hadn't seen him because... he was out of town. In Mexico. Somewhere."

Bedell shook his head. "Now you're telling a fib, Larry. We have phone records, and they show Mister Sherman made a number of calls, including several to you, from his house right up until the night he died."

"Not when I was there," Larry said firmly.

"Oh?" the detective said. "So you were there the night he died?"

"I didn't say that!"

"No you didn't," Bedell agreed. "What you did say is that at some point when Mister Sherman was in Mexico— *somewhere* in Mexico —you and he were in the house together. And at that point, he gave you the watch."

"You got it," Larry said.

"But you lied about his being in Mexico. Or you lied about getting the watch as a birthday present. Which is it?"

"You're just trying to trick me," Larry said. "You want me to say I stole it."

"Did you?"

"No!"

"Well," Bedell said reasonably. "You've got to understand how this looks, Larry. Mister Sherman turns up dead, and you turn up within hours of his death— that's based on the coroner's report — with his watch."

"I didn't steal it. I earned it." A second later, Larry realized what he'd said.

"For what, Larry?" Bedell asked calmly.

"For..." Larry said. "For..." He seemed flummoxed. "For services," he finished lamely.

"You're saying it was a payment of some kind. A watch like that?" Bedell asked.

"It was!"

"Um-hm." The detective looked at Larry, paused, appeared to think, and then asked quietly, "Was that for being his butt-boy or his drug dealer?"

"Hey!" Larry snapped. "I don't sell dope!"

Behind him, Moon and Moreno snickered.

"His butt-boy, then," Bedell said.

"I don't have to take this!" Larry said. "You can go smirk at people who... who deserve to be smirked at. And what I do with my body is nobody's business." He slammed a hand on the table and jumped to his feet.

"Sit down!" Bedell demanded.

Larry sat.

"I don't care if you're straight or gay, Larry," Bedell said.

"I'm not gay," Larry said. "But an orgasm's an orgasm..."

"Don't care, don't care, and for Jesus' sake, don't want to know," the detective said, covering his face with his hands. "What I want to know is that you had an intimate relationship with Sherman, which ended at some point with him dead and you with his watch. That tends to raise some red flags, you understand? So try to help me understand what happened." Bedell put both hands down flat on Larry's file and tapped it meaningfully. "And don't lie to me. At the very least, you might be facing a charge of possessing stolen property."

"Did he report it stolen?" Larry asked suddenly.

The detective stopped and looked momentarily uncomfortable. "No," he admitted.

"So it's not stolen, then," Larry said.

The detective looked surprised, as if confounded by Larry's sudden attack of cleverness, but then recovered. "Let's say burglary, then. And if it turns out Mister Sherman's death was suspicious..."

"It was an accident," Larry said.

"Was it?"

"That's what the news said."

"Well, thanks to you, we may take a second look at it. We might even have the body exhumed and reexamined." He eyed Larry. "Would that worry you?"

"It sure would, since he was cremated and the ashes scattered in Philadelphia. I don't want my taxpayer money going to finding bits of him. It would cost a lot."

Bedell gave Larry a fierce look. "Mister Freckhill, are you making fun of me?"

"No! Of course not! But the stock market just crashed."

The detective gave Moon and Moreno a look that asked, "Is he serious?" They shrugged.

"Mister Freckhill, I am getting very tired of this," Bedell said. "So let's be straight with each other, okay?"

"Okay."

The detective took a breath. "You've said Mister Sherman owed you the watch for unspecified services. Did you take the watch as payment? Remember, I'm not saying you stole it."

Larry thought. "As long as you don't say that, then, yeah."

"Was this around the time that Mister Sherman died?"

Larry flinched and seemed to consider.

"Don't lie to me," Bedell reminded him. "You already said you were in the home at some point. Were you there the night of his death?"

"No, he wasn't dead when I was there."

"When was that?"

"I went over for dinner," Larry said. "We had Chinese. You can ask the delivery guy. Fung Lum Restaurant."

"And then what happened?"

"Oh, you know. Stuff. We watched TV."

"Was anyone else there?"

"No, it was just us."

"And you left about what time?"

"I don't know. Late."

"You didn't look at your watch?" Bedell asked. Moon and Moreno chuckled. The detective gave them a sharp look, and they clammed up. Bedell returned his gaze to Larry.

"But would you guess before midnight?" Bedell asked.

"I don't know. Maybe."

"Okay," Bedell said. "Now I want you think carefully about this, Larry. Was there anything unusual about that evening? Was Mister Sherman acting oddly?"

"What do you mean?"

"Did he appear to be under the influence of, say, alcohol or possibly drugs?"

"I don't..." Larry began.

"Because," the detective continued. "It appears a large amount of cocaine was found in his bedroom. And probably in his system, if the deputy coroner had ordered an autopsy, which seemed unnecessary given the circumstances. Would you know anything about that?"

"You bet," Larry said quickly. "He tried to get me to take some. I said no way. That's why I left."

"So you left an intoxicated friend to fend for himself?"

"No, he kicked me out."

"You just said you left. Which is it?"

"I was leaving anyway."

"So why did he kick you out?"

"I don't know. He got a phone call. Something about business. He said he couldn't concentrate when I was there."

"I'm not surprised," Bedell said. "Any idea who he was talking to?"

"No. I left before he hung up."

"So the call came sometime before midnight, just before you left."

"Must have been," Larry said. "Because it was just after the diarrhea commercial."

"Excuse me?" the detective said.

"The commercial on MTV," Larry said. "We were laughing about it. Glenda was so pissed—"

Bedell held up a hand.

"Glenda?" he asked.

"Oh, shit," Larry said.

CHAPTER TWENTY-NINE

Palm Springs Detective Sam Klippinger wore a dark blue jacket, beige slacks and an ugly tie. Glenda wondered why all police detectives seemed to wear ugly ties. Maybe it was a way of softening up the suspect; they stare in fascinated horror, and then they crack. Also, Glenda thought it odd that Klippinger had a bristly ginger mustache and no tan. After all, he belonged to a desert police department. He sat straight-backed on the edge of Glenda's chair.

"So you did telephone Mister Sherman that night?" Klippinger asked.

"I did. I was righteously pissed, er, really upset with him."

"And what did you say?"

Glenda felt a wash of relief. This guy obviously hadn't heard the tape.

"I called him a few choice words," Glenda admitted, immensely understating her messages.

"Such as?" Klippinger asked, looking non-confrontational. *Just professional interest here*, his expression seemed to say.

"Well, I don't remember all of them," Glenda said. "Asshole figured prominently, though."

Klippinger nodded but didn't smile. He didn't take notes, either, which Glenda found worrisome. Maybe he had a photographic memory.

Without warning, Klippinger had knocked on her door Saturday afternoon, glanced with sharp and practiced eyes at her front room— the guitar, the tapes, the dusty carpet —and explained he was looking into the death of a man believed to be Kirby Fink.

"That's Bernie's accountant," Glenda said, after inviting him in.

"So we understand," Klippinger said. "There was no photo identification in the house, but Mister Fink was the listed property owner. We're waiting on the coroner to confirm his identity."

"How did he die?" she asked, repressing a shudder as she remembered the grisly scene.

"We think he surprised a burglar," the detective said. "Preliminary indications are that he was bludgeoned with some kind of blunt instrument, possibly a mason's hammer. Mister Fink was having some stonework done, and there were tools in the room. We haven't recovered the weapon, though."

"That's horrible," Glenda said and meant it. "But what's that got to do with Bernie and me?"

"Well," Klippinger said slowly, "their deaths were so close together, we can't rule out a tie-in to Mister Sherman's demise."

"That was an accident," she said. "Wasn't it?"

Silence.

"Oh, my God," she said, thinking about the corpse in the bathtub. "You mean someone killed... uh, Bernie?"

"Nobody has said that," Klippinger said. "We just have to cover all the bases."

And I'm first base, Glenda thought, sweat erupting from her armpits.

Eyeing her with blue, waterless eyes, Klippinger said, "When did you call Mr. Sherman?"

"I think around eleven o'clock, eleven-thirty."

"You can't narrow it down a little more?"

"I remember 'Headbanger's Ball' was on MTV," she said, "but I don't know. I just got back from a date. A really bad one. I needed a drink and to cool off."

"And you heard the commercial and decided to make a threatening call to Mister Sherman?"

Damn it, she thought. Where had they found this information, and how much did they really know?

"You called him a number of names and said you would go over there?" Klippinger asked.

"I called him a ... big jerk ... in so many words and said I would see him at the office tomorrow and have it out with him." That much was true, anyway.

"Um-hm. And you say he never picked up the phone?"

"He never answered. I don't know whether he was listening, I didn't know if he was even home. I just needed to vent."

"Um-hmmm." Shifting in his chair, Klippinger sat back. Beige slacks rode up a little on his slightly chubby legs, exposing white socks above thick loafers.

"And, Miss Birdsong, how many calls did you make?"

"Make? How many?" She felt prickles under her arms again. "I don't know, maybe a couple? Maybe three. No more."

"No more than three?"

"I don't think more than that."

"So you think three."

"More than one, anyway. Two or three." *Or ten,* she didn't say.

"Hmmmm. It was only two or three. Short, long?"

Shaking her head, Glenda feared the detective could actually smell her sweat. She wanted a cigarette; she'd even settle for another Silva Thin. "I honestly don't know," she said dishonestly. "I'd had a drink. Or two."

Nodding without comment, the detective hunched slightly forward, his hands clasped between his knees. "You realize, Miss Birdsong, that we can pull telephone records?"

"If it would help."

"What would help is if you could remember the specific time and duration of these calls."

"Why?"

"Because some time after you made them, someone might have come to Mister Sherman's house."

"Who?" she asked. "Someone who killed him?" She didn't have to fake her interest because she'd been having the same suspicion since Larry had described that mysterious Cadillac.

"We don't know who, and we don't know, as I've told you, whether your producer was killed," he said. "But if his death wasn't accidental, then clearly someone must have gained access to his home. It could have been anybody; I understand Mister Sherman had a number of musicians in his stable, and they generally keep late hours. As you know." It was the first time the detective had indicated he knew who Glenda was, she realized.

"I didn't associate with his other guys. I owed him a record. He paid for the studio time and that was it. Until he screwed me," she blurted out.

"Well, as I said, that isn't really why I'm here. Mister Sherman isn't my case, and this isn't my jurisdiction. I just thought it odd that there was a killing in Palm Springs that involved Mister Sherman's accountant a week after he died. By the way, how well did you know Mister Fink?"

"I never met him," Glenda lied. "That I remember, anyway. He was just an accountant."

"It turns out he also had power of attorney for Mister Sherman's estate. We found the document in his home."

"I didn't know that."

"It further turns out that he was the person who identified the body of Mister Sherman to police and the coroner's office. It's on record. I'm told that Mister Sherman had no close relatives to contact and his accountant's number was on his bedside table, so easy-peasy. Saves everybody time and effort for what clearly was an accidental slip-and-fall."

KLIPPINGER LOOKED AT Glenda without expression. "Incidentally, do you know how we learned about Fink's killing?"

Shaking her head, not trusting herself to speak, Glenda fought back an urge to swallow.

"Anonymous caller." Klippinger paused. "Female."

Glenda had nothing to say, but knew she was saying it too loudly.

Klippinger put his hands on his knees and pushed himself up, grunting slightly. Fishing a card from his wallet, he handed it to her. "Thanks for your time. If you think of anything else, give me a call."

The detective turned slightly toward the door, then turned back. "By the way," he said, and she noted it was the third time he'd used that phrase. Maybe it was a verbal tick. Whatever it was, it made her cringe.

"Yes?" she asked, not rising.

"I said this wasn't my case or my jurisdiction. Mister Sherman is the LAPD's investigation. I'm sure someone from the LAPD will be around to talk to you."

"Okay."

"When they interview you, you might want to be sure you tell them the same story you told me. It gets messy if we have different notes." He gave her an impenetrable look, and let himself out.

Glenda heard his rubber-soled loafers squish down the stairs. Then the front door of the apartment building opened and closed. Glenda felt hot and cold at once.

In the backyard, the rooster crowed.

CHAPTER THIRTY

Glenda arrived at the Hollywood Hills home at seven-thirty. The party was supposed to begin at nine. It was October 31st. The weather was dreary but dry at the moment, perfect for Halloween. The house was several miles from Bernie's home and only about twice as large, a soaring two-story with department store-sized windows.

Well, she thought, it was the eighties. Excess was success. At the driveway entrance, two bull-necked security guards wore fedoras. Each carried a Tommy gun in one hand and a plastic pumpkin full of Mars Bars in the other, which they passed out to the few hardy trick-or-treaters who made it up the corkscrewing street. The guns were clearly toys, but the bulges in the men's suits clearly weren't. Since the guards were supposed to be Prohibition-era gangsters, she'd say they were "packing heat." They checked Glenda's name off a list and let her through.

Larry followed. He'd parked down the hill and trudged up after refusing to park at the tradesman's entrance. As he gave the steering wheel a loving caress, he explained his refusal. "Somebody might scratch her."

"Well, let the valet park it," she'd said.

"No way! The temptation is just too great to keep driving. They'd take a cherry dream like this over the border in a split-second."

"Larry, look around," Glenda said, waving an arm. "They're parking Porsches and Rolls-Royces."

"Exactly!" he said. "They look at those tin cans, and then they'll see my Thunderbaby." He shook his head. "No contest."

So he'd dropped Glenda off. She made Larry carry everything all the way up the driveway by way of punishment. Also, because Larry had tipped off the police about her phone calls.

She'd grilled him on the way over. The only way Klippinger could have known about those calls was if somebody, probably an LAPD buddy, had tipped him off. But the police hadn't heard her rants because she had the tape. That meant someone had gabbed about her to the cops. And the list of snitches was short: Larry.

"They beat it out of me," Larry admitted at last. "They used rubber hoses. But all I said was that you called. And that somebody else called later. And that Bernie gave me this watch. For my birthday."

Glenda snorted. "So you didn't tell them we went to the house after Bernie died?"

"They never asked. I wasn't gonna share that bit. You don't tell the donut patrol anything. It's the code of the street."

The mansion's lawn was about the size of a football field and had been turned into a movie-set graveyard. Tombstones with funny sayings leaned like crooked teeth. Monstrous hands sprouted from fake graves. Fog machines pumped an eerie mist that rolled over the ground and through real, boxed weeping willows that had been trucked in and festooned with skeletons. Glenda prayed the skeletons weren't real, too. She'd seen enough bodies lately. At the moment, ghastly didn't seem playful, and deadly was no joke.

From hidden speakers, ghostly shrieks, groans and organ music blared.

The guards had pointed out the rear entrance for the servants, but Glenda wasn't about to walk all the way around the house. She pressed the front doorbell and a gong sounded.

"Whoa," Larry said. "Maybe there's a dungeon. Or a torture chamber. Sweet!"

She shook her head. "Act like a clown, not a ghoul."

The door was opened by a man in a black silk shirt, black slacks, black shoes and a black-stubbled jaw. Glenda guessed he used a dipstick to measure the oil content of his hair.

"Ooooh, welcome to Horror House," the man said in a spooky voice.

"Hi. I'm Glenda. I'm in charge of the clowns."

"I'm Sal," the man said, holding out a hairy hand. "Good to have you. Clowns are gonna make this party."

"Thanks," she said.

"Your makeup gals are here. We set up in the laundry room off the kitchen. Chairs, mirrors, the whole bit," Sal said. "Is there anything else you need right now?"

"Well, it's a big house," she said, looking around. "Maybe a quick tour so I know where to place my crew?"

"Good idea." You can leave your stuff here and I'll have it carried to the laundry room. Follow me."

Sal started off, leading Glenda and Larry through the cavernous living room and into the adjoining dining room, which was so large it echoed. It was decorated with skulls and flickering electric candles. Giant spiders with electric red eyes leered from fake cobwebs.

Glenda saw garish movie posters on the walls. One read "Tear 'er Island" and showed an enormous bloody shark mouth. Another proclaimed: "Rat Rage! When they squeak — you die!!!"

"Great posters," Larry said.

"They're my movies," Sal said proudly. "We kind of specialize in animal horror."

"Like 'Jaws,'" Larry said.

"No!" Sal said sharply. "That made the shark the bad guy. Shark's just gotta eat. Our animals are misunderstood. You take, say, a guinea pig who's tortured in a lab, and he gets mutated and escapes, he's gonna want some righteous revenge, am I right?"

"Damned straight," Larry agreed.

"Yeah. So that's the plot of our new one, 'Furball of Fury.' It's really an animal rights film. It's dedicated to Scarface."

"The Al Pacino movie?" Glenda asked.

"Nope," Sal said, knuckling a corner of his eye. "He was my pet hamster. I miss him"

"Awww," Larry said. "What happened to him?"

Sal looked down sorrowfully. "My brother got a python."

He took them through a dozen or so other rooms, including a movie theater in the basement with velvet seats and a popcorn machine in the corner.

"It's a beautiful place, Sal," Glenda said.

"Yeah," Sal said. "It's something, right? Jimmy Durante lived here, I heard. And Deano Martino went to parties. Paisanos." He grinned. "Pretty big stuff for me, a punk kid who sold hot watches on the Jersey boardwalk."

After leading them back upstairs, Sal paused at a glass door opening onto an outdoor patio/pool area. He slid open the door and Glenda glanced out. At one end of the Olympic-sized pool, a man tested a microphone. A shorter version of Sal, he sported a wild eruption of hair and was dressed glam-rock style.

Sal called out to him. "Hey, Joey, how's it going?"

"It's going," Joey called back. "But this weather. If it starts to rain, somebody's gonna get electrocuted on this thing."

"That's my little brother. He's in the band," Sal explained, then shouted, "Hey, Joey, what's the name of your band?"

"Coati Crawlers," Joey said. "Hey, you got any scarves I can wrap around this thing? I don't wanna get shocked."

"You already did, little bro. That hair! Jesus, you gotta slick down that haystack."

"We're glam, Sal. Jerry Lee Lewis isn't playing tonight."

"You wish you had his talent. And I wish you had his haircut."

"Ha ha," Joey said and went back to his mic checks.

Sal led them back to the kitchen where caterers were unwrapping enormous trays of canapés. Piles of pink shrimp on ice waited to become more snacks.

Glenda noticed a dozen cases of Dom Pérignon in one corner next to cartons of Gino's frozen pizza rolls.

"Hey, boys and girls," Sal said, clapping his hands. The caterers looked up. "This is Glenda. She's wrangling the clowns tonight. They're gonna be the waiters. But if you need an extra pair of hands, feel free to use 'em."

A fat man in a white chef's jacket gave a forced, toothy grin. "We sure will, Mister Ligotti." Glaring at Glenda, he added, "Nothing like having a bunch of clowns in a kitchen."

"Just remember to feed 'em," Sal said. "Glenda, the laundry room is over here. Call me if you need anything."

"Thanks, Sal."

"All right, I got party favors to arrange. See you later." Sal swept out.

The fat man watched him go, and then turned on Glenda. "We'll hand your people the serving trays at the door. It's gonna be crazy in here, and

I don't want waiters crowding me. If I see one pair of floppy shoes in this kitchen, that clown's going in the blender, okay?"

"Yeah. 'Cause defrosting pizza rolls is high culinary art." She and Larry brushed past the fat man as he began turning tomato red.

The clown crew was scattered around the industrial-sized laundry room. The scent of their talcum and grease paint mingled with those of ozone and flowery detergent. Half the clowns had their own costumes, and the makeup crew had brought outfits for the rest. Everybody was chattering but stopped and looked up as Glenda entered.

"Larry, why don't you suit up?" she said.

Someone handed him a costume, and he disappeared behind a screen in a corner. Standing at loose attention around the room, swathed in ruffles and with giant pom-poms down their chests, each clown wore an enormous pair of shoes.

"All right," Glenda said. "Listen up. We don't have much time, so if you've got to pee, do it now." Nobody moved. "Okay, we'll finish your makeup, and then I'll take you to your positions."

The makeup people had arranged chairs and card tables. Soon, a steady stream of horror clowns emerged, their faces blood-spattered and deathly white, with jagged teeth snarling from red lips.

For the sake of consistency, Glenda had brought rubber noses, fright wigs and fingerless white gloves. With a half-hour to go, she realized she had run out of clowns. Puzzled, she looked down at the orphan nose in her hand, then ran a quick eye around the room, counting.

"Where's my thirteenth clown?" she asked loudly.

Everybody appeared puzzled. She sighed and ran through the clowns' names in her head. Earl was missing. She'd half-expected it. Earl was great with kids, but adults scared him. Oh well. On with the show.

Then Larry spoiled it.

"Hey," he asked. "Aren't you getting dressed?"

"In a costume? No," she said. "I'm supervising."

"But you're gonna be out there with us," Larry said. "You gonna go naked? It's Halloween."

"Larry," she said tightly. "Just do your job and I'll do mine, okay?"

"I will, but I guess I'll be doing it alone, since we're short a clown," Larry huffed. He'd counted, too, she thought.

"You'll manage," she said, and looked pointedly at her watch. "Now, everybody—"

"Are you gonna refund that money?"

"What money?"

"For the thirteenth clown?"

"Larry—" Glenda began.

"Why don't you want to be a clown?" Larry asked.

"I don't *not* want to be a clown," Glenda said. "I just didn't plan on it."

"Well," Larry said, rubbing his big red nose thoughtfully. "You are short a clown and there's an extra costume."

"Larry, I really don't have time—"

"Oh, I get it," he said. He crossed his arms. "You're too good to be a clown."

At that moment, Glenda wished the nose in her hand was a grenade. All the clowns stared at her, and she thought she saw judgment in their eyes. Turning on her heel, she snatched the lone costume from a hanger and stalked off behind the screen, wondering how she could kill Larry and make it look like an accident.

CHAPTER THIRTY-ONE

For the next several hours, Glenda was never off her feet. She moved from room to crowded room, passing out hors d'oeuvres with Larry and keeping tabs on her crew, covering when they went on breaks. She had given the clowns their marching orders: they were not to sample anything set out for the guests; they were not to take a smoke or pee break without telling her; and they were not to bunch up, with no more than two in one room at any time.

As the night went on, the mansion filled with guests sporting wild hair, some in costume and some not. With the rockers, it was hard to tell. The guests drank beer and Jack Daniels, laughed, smoked cigarettes— some even made with tobacco— and shouted over the music of the Coati Crawlers. Everybody seemed to be into the music, she thought with a touch of envy. Sal's brother was onstage, and here she was: merely a clown handing out limp shrimp.

Passing a hallway, Glenda saw a drunk dolphin arguing with a winged fairy.

"If you talk to her again, I'll ram this magic wand in your blow-hole!" the fairy swore. They glared at Glenda as she moved on.

Near midnight, Glenda stepped into an empty upstairs room and saw the chubbiest of her clowns bent over a mountain of white powder in a bowl on a coffee table.

"Hey!" she hollered. The clown jerked up guiltily, shoving a straw behind her ear.

"What did I tell you," Glenda said angrily. "You don't eat, drink or snort anything that's for guests."

Hanging her head mournfully, the clowned whined, "I just wanted a pick-me-up."

"Get out of here," Glenda said with disgust.

The clown scooted past Glenda and out the door. Glenda called after her: "And that nose *never* comes off. Got it?"

Blowing out an exasperated breath, Glenda turned back to the room, suddenly exhausted. She hadn't eaten or drunk anything for hours, and she could use a smoke. Her glance fell on the unblemished powder in the bowl. Her attention focused on it. Her nostrils flared. The lizard part of her brain started to hum with the remembered rush. Just one little toot, she thought, and she could sail through the night. Licking her lips, she gently closed the door. She walked to the coffee table. The cocaine glowed with white radiance, like a snowy mountain in some fairy tale. Silver straws alternating with generous joints surrounded the bowl in a starburst pattern.

Her throat went dry. She looked down but she didn't reach out to the bowl. Hadn't she just chewed out somebody for wanting this stuff? She was not going to be *that* person. With a firmness she struggled to maintain, she went back and opened the door to the room.

Music blared up from below.

She shut the door again, muting the sound. Then, without apparent will, she was back at the coffee table, bending over it, the powder looming in her vision.

Suddenly, she could see the knitted eyebrows and disapproving lips of her probation officer as he signed her death warrant. Her spine crawled.

But she was *so* tired. Her nerves craved the jolt of electricity. Helplessly, she bent over and reached for a straw.

At that moment, the music downstairs stopped, and Glenda no longer heard the muted throb of bass and drums. That broke the spell. Once the band took a break, she knew, the guests would make a beeline for the drugs. Somehow, the fear of people discovering her was stronger than the coke appeal or the threat of prison.

Jerking up as if somebody had slapped her, she glanced quickly around the room as if to make sure no one had witnessed her moment of weakness. A little proud of herself for resisting temptation, Glenda told herself she *wasn't* an addict; she was simply overworked, hungry and stuck in a clown suit. She could sure use a smoke, though. After a moment's hesitation, she snatched a joint from the tray. She deserved a break.

The room opened onto a full balcony, so Glenda slid open the glass door and stepped out into the night. She took a deep lungful of the cold air that carried the scents of sage and wild jasmine. When she looked out over the waist-high railing, she saw mist-smudged lights in a house on a ridge across the canyon. A brushy slope under her retreated into darkness. She couldn't measure the drop.

Breathing deeply, she cleared her lungs, her head and her psyche. Only then did she return her attention to the joint in her hand. She held up the unlit twist of paper and frowned. She really didn't need it. Besides, it was a party favor. She should put it back.

As she began to turn away from the view, Glenda heard the room's inner door open and the sound of flapping feet. A clown was coming. She thrust the joint quickly behind her back and flicked it away.

"What do you need?" she began, and then watched in shock as the clown lowered its head and charged. It hit like a linebacker. She bounced hard against the railing, bruising her spine and barely managing not to plunge over the balcony.

She kicked out with her floppy shoes but didn't connect. She flailed at the clown's face. The clown slapped her back and punched her in the stomach. She gasped for air. White-gloved hands gripped her throat and squeezed. The clown's face, inches from hers, filled her vision. Its eyes bulged with hate. Its red gash of a mouth gaped with teeth. Its breath was surprisingly minty.

Glenda grabbed at the choking hands, but they were like steel claws. The clown forced her backwards and crushed her against the railing. Her back screamed. Glenda lost her balance. Her shoes skidded uselessly on the deck. Desperately, she clawed at her attacker's face and connected with clown flesh. Something squishy came away in her hand. The clown yowled and let her go but then kneed her. Glenda doubled over, retching, and the clown rammed its shoulder into her body.

Lights flashed and the air sang around her as, with surreal slowness, she toppled over the balcony into the void.

CHAPTER THIRTY-TWO

Larry was seriously miffed. He'd been lugging trays of food up and down the stairs for hours now, and Glenda wasn't helping. She kept disappearing, so he had to feed everybody on the upper floor by himself. He decided to demand more money. The downstairs clowns didn't have to climb stairs all night. Besides, people kept pinching his nose. And his ass. It was degrading. Climbing the stairs for about the hundredth time, balancing a tray of egg rolls and stepping around a dolphin humping a fairy, Larry fumed. Neither the dolphin nor the fairy appeared hungry, so he moved on.

No Glenda appeared when Larry opened the door to a small room. In fact, the room was empty, although it wouldn't be for long, he knew. The music had just stopped, and he noticed an inviting bowl on the table. After looking left and right, he closed the door. He walked over and put down the tray. Out of professional curiosity, Larry dipped his pinky in the coke and tasted.

The stuff was crap. Chalky and weak. Somebody hadn't just stepped on it; they'd jumped up and down on it and then run over it with a Jeep. Driven by a hippo. Shaking his head in disgust, he figured Sal had paid top dollar for this crud. He'd have to have a talk with the guy. People were always taking advantage of the rich. Larry thought of himself as an educator as well as a businessman. With Sal— very wealthy Sal —he might just combine the two enterprises...

But first, he had to finish his rounds. And that meant he had to find Glenda. The room had a balcony, the sliding glass door to which stood open. Maybe she was out there? He walked over, glanced out. No Glenda. He walked out on the deck. Still no Glenda.

His big shoes kicked something white, which flicked away and rolled to the edge of the railing. Following it, he bent down and picked it up. An unlit joint. As he inspected it with bemusement, he heard a ghostly moaning sound. Thin and weak, the moans seemed to come from down in the canyon.

Larry looked over the railing but saw only darkness.

The moan came again, spookily.

Good sound effect, he thought, but somebody should turn up the volume on the speaker, because he could barely hear it. He looked over the balcony again. As his eyes adjusted to the darkness, he caught a flash of something yellow far below. Somebody had tossed laundry into the bushes. That was weird. He wondered if somebody's coat had fallen and hit the speaker. That would be a good reason to speak to Sal, a conversation starter, and then he could mention the lousy coke, too.

Walking back into the room, Larry picked up his tray and headed downstairs. The dolphin and fairy were gone. One broken wing lay abandoned on the stair.

He found Sal at the pool, squatting by the edge and talking to a pair of topless mermaids whose elbows rested on the coping. Their hair streamed with water and their tails undulated. Mist rose from the water.

Larry cleared his throat noisily. Sal turned.

"Hey, Mister Ligotti," Larry said. The moment stretched.

"Yeah?" Sal said finally.

"Well, I thought you might want to know there's a problem with the speaker."

Giving him a puzzled look that made his thick eyebrows merge, Sal said, "What speaker?"

"The groany one. In the canyon. You can barely hear it now."

Because Sal didn't reply, Larry continued. "Somebody threw something over the rail, and I think it fell on the speaker. No biggie. Just thought you should know."

Sal turned to the mermaids and gestured, and they splashed away into the mist. He stood and turned to Larry. "There's no speaker in the canyon. What are you talking about?"

It was Larry's turn to be confused. No speaker? He thought maybe it would be a good time to back out gracefully. Clearly Sal was preoccupied. "Never mind. My mistake. Probably somebody just dumping a body." He chuckled at his joke. It was always good to leave them laughing.

Sal didn't laugh. He frowned, then grabbed Larry's arm and turned him roughly back to the house.

"Show me," he said.

CHAPTER THIRTY-THREE

Glenda awoke dangling from the harness. A blazing spotlight swept over her, penetrating her closed eyelids, then flicked away, making her flinch. This was a nightmare, but she wasn't asleep. She knew that, because she hurt like hell. Also, the crowd seemed to be above rather than below her. She heard shouting over her head.

Painfully, she opened her eyes. The darting spotlight picked out patches of a dark mass above her. Was she in a tree? No, she wasn't in it; she seemed to be growing out of it, her body entwined with leaves and broken branches. Her head hung below her feet, and her baggy clown clothing was pierced and snagged in a dozen places.

When she tried to move, something jabbed her painfully in the side. Her back ached and her face stung. People still shouted, but she couldn't make out what they were saying. Another beam joined the spotlight, and she heard something thrashing through bushes nearby. All of a sudden, she was surrounded, and hands reached for her, tearing her free of the tree and lowering her to the sloping ground.

The Devil loomed over her. He was scrawny and had a weedy mustache. "How do you feel?"

"Not ready to go yet," Glenda said groggily. "Get thee behind me."

Surprisingly gentle hands probed her arms, legs, back and stomach.

"Hey," Glenda said, and swatted at the hands.

"Does that hurt?" the Devil kept asking.

"Yes. And it's creepy."

"Does your head hurt? Any double vision?"

"No and no."

"Well," the Devil said, leaning back, "you seem to have abrasions, minor lacerations and contusions. But you were incredibly lucky."

"What happened?" she asked.

Larry's painted face joined the Devil's.

"You fell off the balcony," Larry said. "I found you."

"You hit a tree," the Devil said. "And you hit it just right. It broke your fall, but not you. You could have been impaled, or the impact could have lacerated your liver." He shook his horned head. "You'll live. I'd recommend rest and some strategic ice packs, but you should see your physician and get checked out."

Then the Devil spoke to someone behind her. "Do you have a first aid kit?"

"Somewhere," Sal said.

"Let's get her to the house. I'll clean those scratches on her face."

"Thanks, Doc," Sal said.

Glenda's head was clearing.

"I can walk," she said. "Help me up."

The Devil and Sal caught Glenda under her arms, and she grunted and staggered to her feet. When she looked up, she saw a little pane of light far above her. The balcony. She was on the side of a steep hill.

Larry retrieved something from where she had fallen and stuffed it into his pocket.

Sal and the Devil helped Glenda limp to a concrete drainage ditch, which curved around until they reached a row of steps leading to a gate and into the pool area. The ditch had an inch of mud in it and everybody got smudged as they crossed the pool patio, although Glenda noticed some very odd, large flat prints were already there.

"Look," she said, pointing at the muddy patio prints.

"Look at what?" Larry asked.

"Those!" she said. "The footprints! They're clown shoes." Putting one of her feet next to a print, she saw they were about the same size.

"Okay," Sal said. "So?"

"Who made them?"

"A clown," Larry interjected. "Glenda, are you sure you're okay?"

"Did you make them?" she asked Larry.

"No. We came up from the street side. We didn't come this way."

"Somebody came this way," Glenda said firmly. "Look at the prints. They lead to the house, not away. Somebody tracked mud from the ditch up to the house."

"Why would a clown climb up that hill?" Larry asked. "It's a pain in the ass."

Stricken by a flash of inspiration, Glenda said, "So he wouldn't be seen arriving by security. He wasn't on the guest list."

Larry, Sal and the Devil looked at each other.

"Let's get you inside," Sal said placatingly. "Clean you up. That was a hell of a fall you took."

Glenda didn't move. "I'm trying to *tell* you something!"

"Okay, all right," Larry said. "What?"

"I didn't fall," Glenda said. "I was pushed."

"Pushed?" the Devil asked.

"Yes," she said. "By a clown. A clown tried to kill me."

CHAPTER THIRTY-FOUR

The cab dropped Glenda in front of her apartment. She felt bruised and tired. Her bag, stuffed with her clown makeup and other odds and ends, dragged at her shoulder like an anchor.

Pushing through the door and up the stairs to the landing, she fumbled in her handbag for her keys and managed to spill its contents. Her mascara, her lighter and her clown nose tumbled out like a circus act. Then something hard and heavy fell onto her toes. It hurt like hell, which was saying something, considering the legion of aches she already harbored.

Cursing silently so as not to wake the rooster, Glenda bent and grabbed it and stared, stunned. It was a gun, black, snub-nosed and scary. She looked at it uncomprehendingly.

She'd never held a gun before, and this one weighed a ton. It surely must be loaded. She wondered how it had gotten into her purse. If someone had hidden it there, why? If someone wanted her to find it, to make her feel safe, they'd failed. The gun was just another scary thing in her life. She'd seen what guns could do to bodies at the strip club. She'd had one pushed into her ribs. A gun did *not* make her feel safe. Just the opposite. The gun was deadly and unpredictable as a rattlesnake.

Putting the gun and everything else but her keys back in her handbag, she unlocked her door and went inside.

Leaving the bag on the couch, she undressed and gratefully eased her aching body between the sheets of her bed. But she couldn't get to sleep. She lay there, bruised and worried. Fifteen minutes passed. At the half-hour mark— as observed by the luminous hands of the clock on the nightstand —she got up, went into the living room, took the gun from her bag, returned to her bedroom and shoved the weapon in the nightstand drawer. Then she got back into bed and finally got to sleep.

Her last thought was of the gun in the drawer, tensed like a sleepless jungle animal, its lone steel eye cold and unblinking.

CHAPTER THIRTY-FIVE

Larry woke up around noon with a runny nose and an attitude. He'd been dragooned into clown-wrangling after Glenda left Sal's party in a cab. He'd been forced to dip into his sample stash to keep himself and the other clowns going until four in the morning. Glenda definitely owed him for that. Plus, Larry hated being forced into management. He was an artist, not a bosshole. Now makeup and fright wigs cluttered up his apartment until they could be returned on Monday. Too much responsibility. Larry eyed Ganesha sourly.

"You let me down," he muttered.

On the other hand, he thought charitably, he had made a few contacts, and he'd even received a back-slap from Sal as he'd left. Plus, he'd handed out about a hundred business cards for his other profession and had left piles of them next to the coke bowls. People could use them to cut lines, he'd reasoned. Then they'd see the words LARRY and MASTER PERCUSSIONIST in raised crimson letters, along with his phone number and the bongos he'd lovingly drawn. He'd noticed the cards littering the mansion floor before he left. But if he got just one call, the six bucks he'd spent for them would pay off. Yes, he had splurged, but he knew marketing was crucial to his musical career. Especially now that Bernie's promised gig had died with him.

When he wiped his nose, the back of his hand came decorated with streaks of white. Only then did he realize he was still covered in greasepaint. He must have just collapsed when he came home. Grumbling, he staggered into the closet-sized bathroom and cleaned up with a towel marked "Holiday Inn" in festive green letters. He'd have to borrow another towel next time he went to the Laundromat.

Refreshed, Larry ambled back into the bedroom, pulled aside the sagging curtain and peered at the afternoon, which was still gray and looked cold.

Not a good day to be hustling up new business, he thought. Besides, he was out of merchandise and didn't feel like talking to his scary supplier right now.

On the other hand, he had a duty to his customers. He couldn't always be thinking of himself. That was bad karma. He'd have to page Pedro, and Pedro wouldn't like that. Pedro wasn't a morning person. Or a night person. Really, not much of a person at all, Larry thought. He often wondered about getting a better class of supplier.

So he went to the closet and took out what he thought of as his pimp suit. He believed in dressing for the part; the pimp suit gave him respect and helped his performance. The ice-cream white suit was freshly pressed, and his new boots gleamed. He took down the jacket and noticed it was unusually light. He checked the pockets and froze.

Now where, he thought, *did I put my gun?*

CHAPTER THIRTY-SIX

Glenda woke with a sore throat, which made swallowing difficult. For an instant, she wondered if she was getting sick. Then her sleep-fuzzed brain came awake and she remembered last night.

Terror kicked her in the pit of her stomach. Staggering to the bathroom, she retched, but nothing came up except glaring images of a distorted clown face and the ghostly feel of fingers tightening on her throat. In the mirror, she saw scratches where twigs had slapped her face when the tree broke her fall. A purplish chain of bruises adorned her neck. She tried to wash away the ghastly images with a shower, turning the faucet to extra hot.

Everything that had happened to her seemed to flash in her mind like frames from a movie beamed by a flickering projector. Far too many of the scenes were full of blood and bodies. She remembered what the Palm Springs detective had said about a possible connection between murders. And then she remembered the attack last night.

But that made no sense. If someone were trying to kill her, why not just shoot or stab her in the street, or even whack her with a hammer as someone had done to Bernie? Why dress up in a costume, find out her schedule, infiltrate a guarded mansion and then push her off a balcony? Those things took a whole lot of effort. Whoever had done them obviously liked to play sick games.

She prayed her attacker thought she'd died in the fall. If he didn't, she'd have to watch her back. Despite the heat of the shower, her flesh crawled.

As she got out of the shower and toweled herself off, the doorbell rang. She wrapped the towel around herself, went to the door and looked through the peephole.

Nelson. She felt a flood of relief.

She unlocked the door and dashed back to the bathroom, yelling, "Come on in! I'll be right out!" She didn't want Nelson to see her injuries, and she also wasn't sure how much she wanted to share with him.

Choosing an old black turtleneck to hide her bruises, she returned to the bathroom, brushed her hair and dabbed on makeup to cover the scratches on her face. Satisfied that she looked presentable, she walked back to the living room. Nelson wasn't there.

She found him in the kitchen, bent over, rummaging in the refrigerator.

"Find what you want?" she asked teasingly, then froze as Nelson stood and turned to face her.

His left cheek was marred by a bruise and four ragged scratches.

Without thinking, she took a step back.

"Got you some leftovers from the party," he said, grinning. "You wouldn't believe the spread they had."

"Your face," she said hoarsely.

Nelson lost his grin. "Oh, you noticed." He covered his cheek with his hand.

Glenda couldn't speak. Her throat tightened painfully.

Nelson gave an embarrassed laugh. "Yeah," he said. "Some drunk asshole was playing air guitar and decided he wanted a real one. Grabbed mine in the middle of my solo. We had a disagreement." He laughed again. "I was winning until his girlfriend jumped in. But I got the guitar." He shrugged. "Occupational hazard. It's not as bad as it looks."

He stopped talking and looked at Glenda, puzzled. "Hey, what's wrong?"

"Nothing," she said. But she couldn't take her attention from the fresh wounds on his cheek.

He took a step forward. Glenda backed away.

Puzzled, he asked, "Are you okay?"

Her mind whirled. *This is crazy,* she told herself. *This is Nelson. I know him. I like him. He's a good guy.*

Instantly another thought struck her. *Nobody really knows anybody.* And someone had attacked her. Someone who liked to play games. She put a trembling hand to her throat.

"Are you sick?" Nelson asked. "You don't look good. What can I do?" He took another step forward. She stepped back until she was in the archway that led to the living room.

"I'm ... I *am* sick," she said in a hoarse whisper. "Must have caught something last night. You better leave."

Nelson looked worried for a second, then his grin returned. "It's okay. I never get sick." He raised his hands. "Let me..."

"Don't touch me!" Glenda shrieked.

Nelson dropped his hands. "What the...?" he began, then his eyes went cold. "Oh. So, you know."

"I don't know anything," she said.

She slipped through the archway. He followed, his face pale and the scratches standing out like flaming claw marks.

"Go away," she said. "Please." She edged back until she came up against the arm of the living room couch, still several feet from the front door.

Nelson shook his head and looked disappointed. "We were having so much fun," he said. "And now, I guess, you just want it to be over, right?" He slapped his hands against his thighs in exasperation. "I thought you were different. I'm a fucking idiot."

Glenda scrambled back as Nelson stomped to the front door and stood in front of it with his hand on the knob, but he didn't leave. Was he playing with her?

He stood there for a long moment, head down, and then turned to face her. He smoothed his hair and looked her up and down. "I'd hoped..." he said. He touched his wounded cheek. "But I guess it ends with you, just like all the others."

Glenda let out a gasp, looked wildly around, then snatched a heavy glass ashtray from a table and hurled it. It struck Nelson in the head. It didn't break but exploded in a cloud of cigarette ash and flying butts. He coughed, staggered and clawed at his eyes, swearing. But he was still on his feet.

"What the hell!" he shouted.

Looking around desperately for something else to throw, Glenda suddenly remembered she had a weapon.

She raced into the bedroom, flung herself across the mattress to reach the nightstand, tore open the drawer and grabbed the gun. She gripped it with both hands as Nelson appeared in the doorway. She spun to face him. His eyes were red and furious in his ash-smeared face. Blood trickled down his neck. His hands balled into fists. He stepped through the door.

"Don't!" Glenda said, pointing the gun at Nelson's chest with shaking hands.

But he did.

So she pulled the trigger. The noise was deafening, making her ears ring. Nelson still stood in the doorway.

Panicking, Glenda fired again, then squeezed the trigger over and over until the hammer finally clicked impotently. Silence and acrid smoke filled the room. She looked at Nelson, who now crouched, his arms crossed protectively in front of his face.

He dropped them as the smoke cleared. Then he straightened up and looked wide-eyed at Glenda. "Jesus!" He patted his chest, feeling for wounds, found none and let out a deep breath of relief.

Glenda looked at the gun, then at the unmarked Nelson. She'd fired at point-blank range.

Out of options, she waited numbly for Nelson to kill her.

CHAPTER THIRTY-SEVEN

It took Larry nearly an hour of searching his pad before he remembered where he'd put the gun. First, he'd put it in the glove compartment. Then, because he hadn't wanted to leave it in the car at the Halloween party, he'd carried it inside with the clown costumes. Then he'd decided carrying a gun with all the security guys around was a bad idea, so he'd stashed it in Glenda's bag for safekeeping.

And then, of course, Glenda had fallen on her face and left early. With her bag. At least he now knew where the gun was. The gun was a crucial part of his image. He'd seen enough *Miami Vice* episodes to realize that. Still, he wasn't about to head round to Glenda's place to get it. He'd just have to postpone his shopping trip until Monday. Reluctantly, he put his white suit away in the closet.

Anyway, he remembered he wasn't hurting for cash. He'd earned from the party. *Earned the hard way,* he added mentally. In fact, he'd never worked so hard in his life. His legs ached from running up and down stairs, and his head ached when he remembered all the mental challenges he'd encountered. That hideous avocado dip! He shook his head. After the ordeal of last night's party, he decided he deserved to splurge on breakfast. Glancing at the gold Rolex, which never left his wrist, he gave a start.

He'd better hustle if he wanted to hit up Marie Callender's for their half-price pumpkin pies. He would take one home and sit on the carpet, crank up the reggae music and play his bongos. It would be a sweet afternoon. He was salivating and pulling on his leather jacket when the phone rang.

"Larry?"

"Maybe. Who's this?"

"This is Greg Lake." The voice sounded smooth and slightly foreign.

"Oh. Hi, Greg."

A slight spate of silence ensued.

"From Emerson, Lake and Palmer," the voice added.

"Oh," Larry said. "Huh. What Larry were you trying to reach?"

"The 'Master Percussionist,' it says on the card."

"Oh wow! Were you at the party?"

"I was."

"And you got my card?"

"You're a quick study, Larry. Yes, I was at the party, and I saw your card. And it just so happens, that we may need your services."

"One second, Greg," Larry said and covered the phone with his hand. Glancing at Ganesha, he beamed and said, "Yes! Thank you! You are getting some serious offerings, dude! Oreos *and* Cheetos, and I'm gonna score some major incense!" He made a quick half-bow and uncovered the phone.

"Okay, so what's the gig?" he asked.

"Well, it's a rush job," Greg said. "We'll need you this evening."

"Absolutely!" Larry blurted.

"For about four hours."

"You got it!" he said. "What should I bring? I have some righteous bongos—"

"No, thank you," the caller said.

"—And this enormous taiko drum, which makes an *awesome* sound, but it's kind of hard to move. You need, like, a dolly and a moving van—"

"No, thank you."

"—I bought this goat-skin drum from a guy in Norwalk, but it kind of smells—"

"Don't bring any drums, Larry!" Greg broke in. "We've got equipment. What we need is your professional skill."

"Right. See you, then." Larry hung up.

The phone rang.

"Hello?"

"It's Greg Lake."

"Yeah, I recognize the voice."

"I didn't tell you the time or the address."

Larry mulled this over. "Good point." Although he didn't know how it was possible, somehow he could hear Greg shaking his head through the phone.

Greg finally provided the necessary information, and the phone went dead.

Larry whooped jubilantly, threw two thumbs up at Ganesha, and decided to skip Marie Callender's. It had been weeks since he'd practiced, and he needed to sharpen up. He looked at the Rolex again. The gig was only five hours away! He went to the kitchen and, after a bit of scavenging, found half a Pop-Tart behind the toaster. Sticking it in his mouth, he headed back to the living room, where he suddenly felt Ganesha's eyes on him. Guiltily, he slowly took the Pop-Tart out of his mouth, bowed and placed it on Ganesha's lap.

"Thanks, dude," he said, reverently.

A short time later, he was engrossed in a tricky double-tap on the bongos. He kept getting thrown off by thumping and muffled curses coming up from the apartment below. He stopped, got up, walked over to the stereo. He stamped his feet in a hard little jig on the floor to further annoy the inconsiderate downstairs neighbors and turned the stereo up to maximum.

Then he went over and grabbed the taiko mallet.

CHAPTER THIRTY-EIGHT

Just before six o'clock, Larry pulled his Thunderbird up outside a warehouse on Vanowen Street in Burbank. A rambling industrial building next to a railroad track, the place looked dark except for a naked bulb over the door that picked out the street address and the words: "Wonderland Props." He shut off the engine, climbed out and went to the entrance. Although he knocked several times, there was no answer, so he tried the door. It was unlocked.

Opening the door, he stepped inside a shadowy room.

"Hello?" he called out tentatively, creating a flat echo that slowly died into darkness and silence.

"Hello," a voice replied softly from behind his left shoulder.

Larry jumped. "Uh, I'm here for the gig?"

"Right on time," the voice said.

There was a soft chuckle, and then Larry felt an arm around his throat.

He noticed polka dots, but before he could move, someone clamped a rag over his face. Larry smelled something sickly and sweet. He struggled and wrenched free. The next few moments were taken up with grunting, punching and grabbing at an enemy he could barely see in the dark warehouse. He kicked out and was rewarded with a yowl and a curse. Things toppled off of shelves as Larry and his attacker stumbled about. Then something sharp pricked his buttocks.

Punching wildly, Larry whirled around. He felt woozy, tried to stop moving but couldn't. He spun like a top, wobbling and staggering around in the darkness, lashing out again, until he was punched hard in the nose. Dizzily, he wondered if the blow might have been delivered by his own fist. Finally, he began to slow, swayed and toppled. The last thing he remembered was wondering vaguely how many miles he would fall before he hit the floor.

CHAPTER THIRTY-NINE

I'll never get to sing again, Glenda thought numbly. *At least I won't have to finish that damned album.*

She looked up at Nelson, dropped the gun and waited for him to kill her. She was done. She had no more will to fight. Feeling neither anger nor despair, what filled her was an overwhelming sense of futility.

Nelson stepped forward and loomed over the bed. She waited dully for the *coup de grace*, wondering briefly if the boy would strangle her or beat her to death.

Instead, Nelson laughed. And kept laughing. He roared, groaned and finally doubled over, clutching his hands to his stomach, laughing until he was gasping and his face was red.

It was hysterical laughter, Glenda realized.

At last he straightened up, wiping his streaming eyes. "This is insane. *You're* insane." Shaking his head, he turned to leave the room, muttering "Crazy-ass women!"

She watched him leave her room.

Then he stepped back inside. "And just so's you know, I don't have AIDS. So you don't need to worry."

Stupefied, she sputtered, "Wha...wha...what?"

He grimaced. "You and everybody else are so paranoid. I can't get it from my mother by touching her. So you didn't have to try to shoot me, you fruitcake."

"Your mother? "Glenda asked, stunned. This didn't make any sense.

"Yeah," he said. "Who I love despite all her shit. So I'm going to keep seeing her. And if anybody wants to run around behind my back spreading lies, then screw it. Maybe it's time everybody knew anyway. I'm not ashamed of her. Whatever she did, she didn't deserve this."

Glenda's fear-frozen mind lurched. It took a moment for her to piece together what he was saying. "Your mother has AIDS?"

Nelson nodded. "She's dying. I see her almost every night. I don't know how long she's got."

"You saw her last night?"

He nodded. "After the gig." He put his hand up to his scratched face. "I got this from her. She was a little bad. She has dementia. Thought I was one of her douche-bag exes."

"So *I* didn't do that?" Glenda said, staring at his face.

It was Nelson's turn to look confused.

"Someone tried to kill me last night," she explained. "I scratched him. Everybody thought I hallucinated. They almost had *me* convinced."

"Yeah. I can't see why they would think that. You being so sane and all." Nodding at the gun lying amid the bed sheets, he said, "I'm lucky you used blanks. You scared the crap out of me."

"Blanks?"

"You didn't know?"

"It's not my gun," she said apologetically.

"Jesus! You mean you really *did* try to kill me?"

"I thought you were the clown."

Nelson looked at her and slowly put out a calming hand— the way a trainer soothes a spooked horse. "It's okay. It's gonna be okay."

"Stop that!" she snapped. "I'm not crazy. There was a clown! Look!" She pulled down the neck of her turtleneck sweater to expose the bruises on her throat.

Nelson jumped. "Jesus!"

"No. Clown," Glenda said firmly. "At the Halloween party. Choked me. So when I saw you come in with your face all scratched up, I, um, overreacted?"

"I thought somebody had told you about my mother and you were freaking because of, you know. Us," he said. "That's what set me off."

"Oh, God, no! Although…"

"I've been tested," he said, his temper rising.

"I'm sorry," she said quickly. "I don't mean to sound like—"

"What's this about a clown?"

So she recounted the Halloween attack.

"Shit! Did you tell the cops?"

"I couldn't," she said, and then let go and explained everything: the stranger at the funeral, the attacks in her house, the blackmail, the money, the dead stripper, and finally finding Bernie dead.

Nelson looked stunned. "This all happened to you in one week? And I thought *I* lived in the fast lane."

"My life isn't always this complicated."

"God, I hope not. But wait. You said Bernie was in Palm Springs. I thought he died last week."

"He didn't."

"Then who was the dude in his bathtub?"

"I don't know."

"What was he doing in the bathtub?"

"Not breathing."

"How did he get there? Was Bernie there?"

"I don't know that, either."

"And was *that* guy murdered?"

"Dunno."

"Well, who did they bury?"

Glenda held up her hands and shrugged. "And before you ask, Nelson, I don't know who killed Bernie, either."

"I don't know who wouldn't," he replied. "Even I thought about it."

"Because of what he did to your mother," Glenda said.

Nelson looked away.

"Nelson," she said. "Maybe I shouldn't tell you all this. I don't want to drag you into it."

He gave her an arch look. "Are we friends again?"

"Are we?" she asked uncertainly.

"Well," he replied thoughtfully. "You did try to shoot me." He shrugged. "If that's all you got..." He smiled.

Suddenly, Glenda thought she'd like to get lost in that smile. Then she caught herself. "Listen, Nelson. I'm bad news. I'm dragging bodies behind me. Everywhere I go, somebody dies." She gave him a sudden piercing look.

"Naw," Nelson said. "You already tried to kill me, and it didn't work." He gave her a big grin. His eyes shone.

He's loving this, she realized. *It's an exciting adventure, a rush. He is* so *young. He still thinks he's immortal.*

"Just let me help," he said.

"Nelson, it's not your business."

"You are."

"Oh, *Jesus.*"

"Hey. You hungry? I'm hungry."

"Don't change the—"

"Bob's Big Boy? I am in such a pancake mood. We can talk there."

With a huge sigh, Glenda's resolve melted like butter on a hot stack of flapjacks. "Okay." *That smile...*

"Or," he added. "We don't have to go out. That's why I brought the leftovers."

Oh my, she thought, and then she thought, *Oh, hell, why not?*

"Well," she said, putting her hand to her chin in mock thought. "It is cold out. Maybe we should stay in. Watch TV or something."

"Whatever you want."

Still sitting on the bed, she leaned forward and tilted up her face, looking at Nelson through half-lidded eyes. "No TV."

As he leaned over the bed to kiss her, Glenda cupped his face in her hands until they finally broke apart. She felt slightly breathless. "Wow," she said and fell back dramatically on the bed. Something hard dug into her back. "Ouch!"

She reached under her hips and pulled out the gun, then held it by the barrel as if were a dead rat. Then she rolled over, opened the drawer to her night table, dropped in the weapon and firmly pushed the drawer closed.

She rolled back to face Nelson. "Where were we?"

CHAPTER FORTY

Glenda lolled in bed with one hand on Nelson and the other holding a slice of pizza.

This was wrong, she thought, and *delicious*.

They had made love for two hours and then they had eaten. Nelson had fallen asleep. Glenda envied him his ability to do that. Her mind still whirled. She knew that at some point, what they had wouldn't work. Nelson was simply too young and at a different stage of his life.

Oh, sure, she knew lots of older men who had young women as lovers, mistresses, and a few even married the youngsters. But that was men. Women, especially women of her age, were smarter and didn't have so much ego invested in a trophy. They looked to the future. And when Glenda looked down the line, she knew that her path and Nelson's would have to diverge.

But for now, she couldn't help but love it.

At some point, she would have to break Nelson's heart. Their age difference might cause it, her career might cause it— or even his, for that matter. She didn't know how much relief that sentiment gave to the part of her that feared emotional intimacy.

Besides, she told herself, Nelson was flexible; he'd get over it.

She also had to admit to herself that he was smart, maybe smarter than she was, in fact. Because he'd never actually used the word *love* with her, Glenda suspected Nelson knew the word would drive her away. But he wasn't experienced enough— not quite —to keep what he felt out of his eyes. Or the other parts of his body.

She sighed. It was always complicated.

Maybe it always would be.

She also felt a little guilty. Something she'd recently learned about herself was that guilt spiced things up. As a rocker, she liked being an outlaw, albeit on a fantasy basis.

And that made her think back to a few hours ago, when she'd fired the gun. God, she could have killed him. She'd *tried* to kill him, in fact. It was only a miracle that she had shot blanks.

Shuddering at the thought of Nelson lying dead on the floor from a bullet hole she had created made her angry; not at herself, but at whoever had forced her into a position where she was willing to take a human life.

Then and there, she determined she would get that clown-nosed bastard if it were the last thing that she ever did. She glanced at Nelson, who was snoring gently, his hair tangled over his face. He looked like an especially cute sheepdog. She brushed back a lock.

Opening one eye lazily, he said, "Hey."

"Hey."

The other eye opened, and Nelson looked at her without a trace of dreamy sleep. His gaze was unnervingly frank, as if he saw more than she wanted him to see.

"What are you thinking?" he asked.

"Nothing," She gave an artificial laugh. "I was thinking how much I love pineapple on pizza."

Nelson gave her a probing look, but let the comment pass. "Yeah," he said. "What time is it?"

"A little after seven," she said, glancing at her bedside clock.

She dangled her slice of pizza. "Want a piece?" she asked teasingly and was surprised to see Nelson's anatomical salute.

"Holy crap! You have got to be kidding me! You just woke up!"

"It's not every day I wake up with you," he said.

The phone rang.

"Saved by the bell," Glenda said with a laugh. She picked up the receiver.

CHAPTER FORTY-ONE

Larry awoke from a nightmare in which he'd been fighting with a clown. Then a buffalo charged him. Then he'd been caught by a giant spider. The whole thing was like a bad Halloween movie.

As he tried to stretch, he found he couldn't move. Then he discovered he'd been cocooned to the neck in some kind of netting. *No. Not a cocoon.* His wrapper was a spider web, one as big and tough as a volleyball net. And he lay spread-eagled, tied to the web.

So, he thought muzzily, *how big was the spider? And when did it last eat?*

Struggling, he discovered his bindings were too tight for him to escape. With superhuman effort, he managed to turn his head and look at his left arm. He heaved a sigh of relief.

The Rolex still adorned his wrist.

The effort left him nauseous, so he leaned back and dropped his gaze. On the floor in front of him lay a horned buffalo head, glaring at him with glassy eyes.

The only thing missing, he thought with a shiver, was the clown.

The clown stepped forward.

"Oh, crap," Larry said and retched.

"If you're gonna throw up, aim for the bucket," the clown said, nudging a tin pail between Larry's legs.

"No," Larry gasped at last as his retching subsided. "I'm good." After gulping a few deep breaths, he added warily, "Why is that buffalo looking at me?"

"Oh, you knocked it down while we were fighting," the clown said matter-of-factly. "After I chloroformed you."

"You what?" Larry asked, his brain still sputtering.

"It's not like on TV," the clown said convivially. "You didn't go down. You just thrashed around for, like, five minutes. You almost broke my nose." The clown squeezed the bulbous red appendage on his rubbery mask and said, "Honk honk."

"Oh."

"Yeah. I had to use Plan B. I gave you a knockout shot." Snapping his fingers, the clown added, "I should have used a tranquilizer gun like they do in those nature shows. Pow! You'd have gone down like a water buffalo."

"I thought a spider got me. So this isn't a spider web?"

"Halloween prop. You remember? We're in a prop warehouse."

Another rusty gear in Larry's brain began to turn. He remembered now. The call for a drummer audition in Burbank. Walking into the creepy, badly lit warehouse full of witches, shackled skeletons and other party gear waiting to be reshelved. And then the polka-dotted arm and all the rest.

"So," he said thoughtfully. "No audition?"

"You showed up. You passed. But it's a different kind of gig." The clown gave a sinister chuckle.

Larry looked around again and tested his bindings. "Is this a bondage video? 'Cause I'm not SAG. Is it a speaking part?"

The clown tilted his head and looked at Larry curiously.

"You think you were drugged and kidnapped for a video?"

"Could be MTV," Larry said reasonably.

The clown shook his head. "Sure," he said at last. "Let's call it a video. A music video. It's candid-camera stuff. That's why it had to look real."

"I get that. So what now? Can we take a break?"

"In a while. But first, we've got a problem."

"How can I help?" Larry asked.

"Well," the clown said, "we need a singer. Know any?"

CHAPTER FORTY-TWO

"Hello," Glenda said.

"Glenda. Glenda, it's Larry. Don't hang up."

"Larry. What do you want?"

"You're not gonna believe this, but I have a gig for you. Tonight!"

"Tonight?" Glenda glanced at the bedside clock again. It was still just after seven. Nelson leaned on an elbow, looking at her curiously. Glenda gave him an exaggerated eye roll and shrugged apologetically.

Stretching, displaying a lithe body, Nelson smiled, and Glenda momentarily lost her concentration. Then he rolled out of bed, grabbed his boxer shorts from the floor and strode into the living room.

"Yeah," Larry's voice was enthusiastic. "Look, I'm in a music video. And their singer didn't show. So I said I knew you, and the guy is like: 'Whoa! That's big time!' So if you can get down here fast and sing one song, they'll pay... how much?"

Glenda heard murmuring.

Larry answered, "Really?" Then he spoke to her. "Glenda, they'll pay two thousand dollars."

She sucked in a breath. That would buy a lot of studio time. But the offer sounded so screwy, it raised her bullshit antenna.

"Wait," she told Larry. "You're saying some people making a video somewhere just out of the blue needed a singer, and it has to be tonight? And you called me?"

"I thought I was doing you a favor," Larry said, huffily.

"Larry, doesn't this sound kind of fishy?"

"Well, it's a candid-camera thing. A lot of improv. And hey, if you don't like the setup, you can just split. Anyway, it's an easier gig than that damned party. You get to sing, and you don't fall off balconies."

"I was pushed," she said. "By a clown."

"Oh, sure," Larry said, then went silent. When he spoke again, his voice held an odd edge. "Glenda, you have *got* to come. It's a really great gig. Don't be a *Bozo*. I'm not *clowning* around!"

"Larry?" she asked. "What are you on?"

A rustle and a grunt came over the wire, and another voice spoke.

"Hello, bitch," it said in a raspy whisper. "If you want to see your buddy alive again, come to 3742 Victory Boulevard in Burbank in the next hour. Alone, and don't call the cops. Or your best friend dies." The phone went dead.

Glenda gripped the receiver, stunned. "He's not my best friend," she said blankly.

He's not clowning around, Larry had said. Glenda felt the prickle of cold sweat.

Shakily, she hung up the phone. Then she grabbed it again, convulsively, and began to dial the police before stopping herself. If that creepy voice came from the insane clown, Larry would be dead the instant the cops arrived. She guessed the lunatic had already killed at least once—maybe twice, if he'd murdered both Bernie and the man in the bathtub. And now Larry was in danger because of her. But she wasn't stupid enough to walk into a trap that would probably get them both killed. She glanced at the clock again. Ten minutes had already passed, and it would take twenty more to reach Burbank.

Staring around the room as if seeking help, she heard the television in the living room. Nelson was watching *Scooby Doo*.

She should call the cops.

She couldn't call the cops.

Sick with fear, she knew that, whatever she did, somebody was going to die. Even if the dead guy turned out to be Larry, she didn't want to be involved. But she didn't know what to do. As she saw things, she had nowhere to turn and no one to turn to.

In the living room, Scooby and the gang were running for their lives. She heard the comical skedaddling music and knew they'd be all right in the end. They always ended up safe and alive.

She heard Nelson humming along to the theme song.

A clear, cold thought hit her. Like Scooby, she had work to do now.

CHAPTER FORTY-THREE

Glenda stood at the warehouse door and shivered, whether from cold or fright, she couldn't tell. Hugging her coat tightly around her, she hummed tunelessly to keep her teeth from chattering. She peered through the glass of the front door but saw nothing. The interior was black— maybe as black as a nun's knickers, if not quite so black as her producer's heart. Her dead producer. Okay, so she was blathering to herself, a sure sign she was scared. Turning down the volume in her head, she focused.

She rapped her knuckles on the door and waited. Nobody answered so she tugged the handle, and the door swung open easily. Holding her breath, she stepped inside.

The darkness extended through a space she couldn't gauge, but it seemed vast, much larger than the building appeared from outside. Her breathing echoed harshly, and she fought to slow it. At the same time, the atmosphere seemed thick and oppressive. She inhaled unseen dust.

Then came several hard, echoing *thunks,* and she realized someone had thrown electrical switches. The warehouse erupted in pools of light, blinding her for a moment. When she could see again, she found herself in a nightmare. An army of demons, rotting corpses and ghouls confronted her, their clawed hands reaching. Tattered, bulging-eyed corpses, silent and sinister, bunched in grisly clusters. To her left, an entire platoon of killer clowns huddled. A scream nearly escaped her lips before she realized they were nothing more than Halloween props, gaudy and cartoonishly malignant. She didn't entirely suppress the scream, though; it came out as a mousy squeak.

Then one of the clowns stepped forward, and she fought a barely successful battle with her bladder. Advancing within a dozen feet of her, the masked clown halted, its rubbery face wearing an idiot grin from ear to ear.

"Halloween's over," she called with a bravado she didn't feel.

"Not for you." The clown clapped his hands and the lights went out. With another clap, a single spotlight blazed, throwing harsh light down on a solitary chair. The chair stood in front of the prop monsters as if before a ghastly audience.

Or a jury.

"Have a seat," the clown rasped.

"I don't think so."

With a sigh, the clown said, "Well, it was worth a try, and I had such a cool effect worked out." He reached up to a rope hanging above his head and tugged. A noose dropped down to dangle obscenely before the chair.

Glenda flinched, then caught herself and said sarcastically, "Ooooh. Scary."

With another clap from the clown, the lights went out again. Again, he slapped his hands together and the lights blazed. They extended down the warehouse in staggered rows leaving big pools of shadow. The illumination stopped just beyond the grim audience of the freakish, homicidal props. The entire back of the warehouse was in gloom.

The clown stepped into a shadow and vanished, but his voice didn't.

"It would have been perfect," he whined. "But you don't do perfect, do you?"

"Actually, people say perfect is my problem," Glenda replied. She wanted to keep him talking. She wondered how much time had passed. "What do you want?"

"You know that already," the clown replied testily. "You want to know *why*."

"I do."

This time his voice came from somewhere to her left. She couldn't pinpoint him, but she thought he was slowly circling her, moving from shadow to shadow. She suddenly realized she was in a patch of light, making her a target. Sidestepping into a shadow, she said loudly, "I guess being a crazy fucker is just your job."

"It's not crazy to get rid of people who trash beauty," the clown said testily. Had the voice come from behind her? Was it closer? She couldn't tell.

"I'm on the side of the angels," the clown said.

"And I'm not?"

The clown didn't reply, but Glenda heard footsteps— someone not trying too hard to be sneaky. A click sounded, and music boomed from what she guessed was a portable stereo.

She heard her own song, *Winter Fever*. Gasping in spite of herself, she realized the music came from last week's session.

"How in the hell did you get that?" Her hands felt slippery with sweat.

"You don't know?" The clown had moved again.

She slid away, avoiding another pool of light, hoping her movement would distract him. As long as they were both blundering in the dark, she was alive.

It was a desperate game of hide and seek. Her best hope was to keep him talking.

"I don't understand," she said.

"You don't understand anything," the clown said as he stepped from a shadow.

He was just out of arm's reach, so close she smelled the sour reek of his sweat. He fixed her with yellow-tinged eyes. They seemed to bore into hers, even though Glenda still stood in shadow.

He'd zeroed in on her. Hide and seek was over. Now Glenda deliberately edged into a pool of light a yard to her right. The clown watched with narrowed eyes.

"I understand you tried to kill me," she said. "But you messed it up."

Without warning, the clown lunged.

Taking a frantic step back, Glenda flung open her coat. "Stop! Stop!"

The clown stopped abruptly.

"You're joking." He glared at Glenda's waist, where a half-dozen long red tubes were duct-taped to her body. A conspicuous wire ran from the tubes up one sleeve. She plunged a hand into a coat pocket.

"Try me," she said, her voice trembling only slightly. "If I go, you go."

"Then I go," the clown said and looked about to spring again.

It took every ounce of her strength for Glenda to stand there and wait.

The clown backed off. "You suck. You're a big, fat train wreck."

Moving slowly, he circled, and Glenda pivoted to keep him in front of her. She realized with a tremor that he had moved between her and the front door.

"Where's Larry?" she asked.

"I spent hours wiring up all of this stuff. Clappers all over the place." The clown sounded angry.

"Yeah," she said, throwing a sneer into her voice. "Great job. Shadows and big lights and things jumping out at you, like a grade-school haunted house."

"Says the woman who does diarrhea commercials. You wouldn't know music if it was dry-humping you."

"Asshole."

"Bitch."

"Psycho," she said, and then shouted, "Larry? You back there? Are you okay?"

Crossing his arms, the clown deliberately took a slow step toward her.

Glenda edged back.

The clown nodded as if confirming something to himself. He reached into the pocket of his baggy pants and yanked out a revolver.

The barrel looked like a cannon. Glenda's mouth went dry.

Somehow she managed to blurt, "Does that thing shoot a flag that says 'bang?'"

"It shoots you," the clown said, almost conversationally. "It's messy, ugly, noisy. Just like you." He deliberately pointed the gun at her face.

Glenda had thought she couldn't be any more afraid. She'd been wrong. She felt faint with terror.

"I'll blow you to hell!" she warned, praying her knees didn't buckle.

"No, you won't." The clown had become preternaturally calm. "Because then your buddy Larry would die. So what would be the point?" He spoke in a reasonable tone, as if explaining a dry and obvious fact. "Last words? It's tradition."

Glenda opened her mouth for a quip, her last. She wanted to say, "Cram it, clowny!" but all that came out was a pathetic stutter. Her vision tunneled down to the barrel of the gun. At the edge of her sight, she was surprised to see her own hands. She had raised them without conscious thought. Why? Defiance? Surrender? Begging for mercy?

No.

Glenda clapped her hands.

All the lights vanished. With a scream, the clown fired, but Glenda had dropped and rolled to the side. Her ears rang from the shot.

She briefly saw the clown's face illuminated by the muzzle flash, which turned the mask's silly grin into a rictus of rage. A heartbeat later, the lights flashed on from the noise of the gunshot.

On the floor, Glenda desperately clapped her hands. The lights vanished once more, and she scrambled to her feet.

Screaming something unintelligible, the clown emptied the gun. The blasts echoed through the warehouse, and the lights strobed on and off with each shot.

Glenda and the clown wound up in darkness. The clown, breathing heavily through his mask, swore and threw the gun away. He clapped his hands.

The lights came on and he saw Glenda was running toward the back of the warehouse, clapping as she ran. The lights snapped off. Behind her, she heard the rhythmic flap of the clown's comically oversized shoes as he dashed after her. He clapped the lights back on as he ran.

They fought a running battle of Clappers. The lights flashed on and off in unpredictable patterns.

When Glenda reached the ring of monsters, she darted through them, knocking over some in hopes of slowing her pursuer. At the very back of the warehouse, shining like a beacon, she saw a green exit sign. The rear door! Risking a glance behind her, she saw the clown had closed most of the distance, even in his huge shoes. Now he stopped and ripped them off. He'd be faster now. Too fast. And quiet.

Glenda gauged the distance to the exit and figured he'd be on her before she could push through the back door. Evil figures surrounded her. She ran up to a zombie baseball player. It wore ragged pinstripes, one eyeball dangled on its cheek, and it clutched a bloodied Louisville Slugger. A weapon, Glenda thought. The statue gripped the bat firmly in both hands, and she couldn't pause to wrench it free. She passed a headsman, all in leather, leaning on an enormous plastic axe. When she slammed into a demon girl, all fangs and pigtails, the figure went flying. Behind the girl, another figure loomed: A gravedigger, leaning on a long shovel. And suddenly, Glenda had a plan.

CHAPTER FORTY-FOUR

The clown saw Glenda disappear into the crowd of horror figures, but he plunged furiously ahead, his gaily striped socks sagging at his ankles. As he bulled his way into the figures, he didn't see Glenda anymore, but he knew where she was going. His rage was the drug fueling him. He was moving so fast, he felt as if he were flying.

He would catch her. He would kill her. The clown gnashed his teeth under the mask.

And then something cracked across his ankles. His legs tangled. He tripped and threw out his arms, but it was too late. Hitting the floor full length, his face smacked the concrete, and his mouth exploded in pain. For a moment the fall knocked the breath out of him. When he caught it again, it sounded bubbly and fluid. Furiously, he tore off the mask, its huge red grin replaced by his own angry snarl. He touched his mouth. His glove came away streaked with blood and he realized he'd split his lip. His nose bled too.

Only seconds had passed. The clown got to his feet. Spitting blood, he dodged to his right and plunged into the intermittent darkness.

THE BACK OF THE WAREHOUSE was utterly dark, but it wasn't empty. Twice, Glenda smashed into metal shelves stacked high, forcing her to slow down. She clapped but nothing happened; apparently there were no gadgets here. She wished she had brought a flashlight or even her cigarette lighter.

Not smoking will kill you, she thought ruefully.

The farther back she went, the more stuff cluttered the way. She thought that she must be in some sort of corridor between shelves, but she couldn't determine the layout. Putting out her hands to feel her way, she moved cautiously forward. A few feet later, the corridor ended. After a moment of stumbling around, Glenda realized it wasn't a dead end. The corridor opened to the right. She followed, but in doing so lost sight of the exit sign.

Directions had always baffled her. She'd never received a Girl Scout badge for map-reading, and now that single turn had confused her. She was lost!

Where was the clown? Had he followed?

She stopped and tried to listen for his breathing. All she heard was her own ragged panting. Left with no choice, she continued following the corridor. But the damned thing was dark as a canyon.

But no, she thought, it wasn't entirely featureless. The rafter-high shelves blocked most of the light from the front of the warehouse, but not all of it. A faint glimmer turned the top shelves to her right into a dim silhouette, like a mountain range in moonlight, telling her how she was oriented. If she turned left somewhere, she should be heading toward the rear exit again or maybe a loading dock. But light didn't illuminate her path, and she couldn't risk winding up in a real dead end. Not with a psycho stalking her, who'd had hours to learn the building's layout.

Change of plans, she thought— if you called running in terror a plan.

Whirling around, she made her way back up the corridor until she reached the bend. There she stopped for just a second to listen, but again heard only her own labored breath.

She was backtracking, but she didn't have a choice. She couldn't wait for the cavalry. She would try for the front door and hope the clown wasn't waiting for her.

It almost worked.

CHAPTER FORTY-FIVE

The clown hadn't run blindly. He knew Glenda had a choice of four separate rows to the back, but some jinked and others were cluttered with unshelved Halloween items. So instead of rushing into a row, he'd climbed up one of the stacks. There he crouched on top of a crate, like a gargoyle drooling blood, and listened for her panicky footsteps.

GLENDA BURST OUT OF the dark corridor into a twilight in which the chase had toppled all the monster statues. A patch of floor reflected a dim apron of grey from one of the lights. She saw the gravedigger's shovel she'd used to trip the clown and also saw spatters of blood that seemed black in the dimness.

So she *had* hurt him, she thought with grim satisfaction.

Stumbling her way past the ring of fallen nightmares, she saw the front door. The way was clear. She plunged forward with a euphoric sense of relief and was mere strides from freedom when something struck her a terrific blow in her side. Grunting, she collapsed and rolled over.

The clown stepped out of a shadow just behind and to her left, holding the zombie ball player's bat.

She raised a hand, but the clown clubbed her arm and then stepped on her fingers, pinning them to the ground. She shrieked as she felt bones grind and looked up into his unmasked face.

"You!"

"Clap now, bitch!" the clown said, his voice stuffed up and flubbery.

His real nose was as swollen and pulpy as a fake one. Glenda hoped he'd broken it in his fall.

She tried to struggle, and the clown thumped her forehead with the bat, almost gently. The back of her head hit the floor. Her thoughts spun.

"Uh," the clown said in his adenoidal snuffle. He wiped away a stream of bloody mucus. Again he thumped her, this time in the stomach.

Glenda *whoofed* as her breath rushed out.

Slowly, the clown raised the bat over his head. His yellow eyes gleamed as he took several warm-up swings. "This is gonna be really, really ugly. You're gonna wish I shot you."

Glenda had no breath to reply. She watched him wind up.

Then behind the clown, a clap sounded.

The lights went out.

"Oh for fuck's sake!" the clown yelled in exasperation. "What the—*ooof!*"

Then there was a lot of yelling, a crash, and a sound like somebody slapping meat on a grill.

Glenda's fingers were suddenly free. She crossed her arms protectively in front of her face and rolled. Then she clapped her hands, although doing so cost her a jolt of pain.

The space burst into light, and she saw Nelson struggling with the clown on the ground. The bat had rolled away. Nelson gripped the clown's ruffles with one hand and punched him with the other wherever he could reach. The boy was strong and wiry, but the clown fought with crazed fury, twisting and thrusting his body as he gouged and bit, managing to plant a knee in Nelson's groin and scramble free. Nelson cursed and lashed out, grabbing the clown's ankle and trying to haul him off his feet.

Kicking out, the clown broke free and backpedaled.

Nelson leaped up, then put his head down like a linebacker and rammed the clown in the gut, wrapping his arms around him. They thrashed and grappled, the clown's eyes rolling madly as he spewed a pink spray of curses.

Glenda, still on the floor, scrambled for the bat.

She had just grabbed it when the struggling figures tripped over her prone body and went down in a heap on top of her. Again her breath was knocked out of her. Nelson's grip was broken. Managing to get up first, the clown aimed a sock-clad kick at Nelson's face, grazing him. Then he scrambled sideways like a crab and limped toward the front door, throwing them an evil leer and shouldering through the door into the night. Nelson aimed a volley of curses at his back, then looked at Glenda and rolled off her.

"You okay?" he asked.

"Fine!" she said. "Catch him! Don't let him get away!"

"I think it's too late. We lost him," Nelson said, panting.

Then they heard a car engine rev. Headlights pieced the door, blinding them. A second later, an immense crash and an explosion of glittering glass shocked them, and they saw the clown's splayed form hurtling backwards, hitting the floor with a flaccid thump. In place of the front door was the front end of Nicole's bumble bee-striped Chevy Nova.

"Or not," Nelson said.

But then, to their astonishment, the clown staggered to his feet and with surprising alacrity leaped onto the Nova's hood, clambered up the windshield, over its roof and disappeared into the night.

Glenda got to her feet, brushing small squares of safety glass from her hair. "I don't believe I just saw that." Realizing she still held the bat, she threw it away in disgust.

Nicole leaned her head out of the driver's window. "Everybody okay?"

Glenda and Nelson mumbled replies. Nelson got up, dusting himself off, his jeans torn at the knees.

"A little warning next time you make an entrance like that?" Nelson said.

"Just playing punchy clown," Nicole said. "I see an evil, bloody dude fleeing, I was afraid maybe you guys were toast. So, I decided to make him a hood ornament." She pointed at Glenda's midriff. "Those road flares look great by the way, really dynamitey. I really didn't think that would work."

"We had nothing to lose," Glenda said.

"Damn, almost had him," Nelson said. "At least you're safe."

"No, she isn't," Nicole said seriously. "He's hurt and he's mad, and he is just not gonna give up."

"If only we knew who he is," Nelson said. "Couldn't tell much in this weird light."

"I know who he is," Glenda said. "I saw his face. He played my song."

"Who?" Nelson asked at the same time Nicole blurted, "Keith. Shoulda known."

From the back of the warehouse, there came a muffled cry.

"Hey, Larry!" Glenda called.

"Oh, joy," Nicole said.

CHAPTER FORTY-SIX

They unwrapped Larry, who flopped like a rag doll until the circulation returned to his limbs.

"That was awesome!" he said. "You guys were great! You're like Charlie's Angels, except with a dude!"

"We're the Scooby Gang," Nicole said, grinning at Glenda.

"Really?" Larry said. "Where's your dog?"

"You're the dog, Larry," Nicole said.

Larry frowned, then smiled. "Yeah! I'm good with that!"

THE POLICE OFFICERS swarming the warehouse gaped at the monsters and shook their heads at the giant web. They declined Larry's offer to reenact his bondage.

Glenda told the detectives her attacker was the keyboardist. Paramedics were called and examined everybody. Glenda came in for the most intense examination. Her arm and fingers were badly bruised but not broken. The paramedic, unfortunately, put special emphasis on the scratches, bruises and chain of purpling fingerprints around Glenda's throat from the attack at the Halloween party.

"You didn't get those tonight, did you?" he asked.

"I had a fall," she said.

"Uh-huh." The paramedic went over to a detective and spoke softly. The detective, a man named Slovaski who looked barely old enough to shave, nodded and came back to Glenda. Politely, he asked to see her throat.

"The paramedic says some of these injuries are not from tonight."

"That's right," Glenda said. "He tried to kill me last night, too. Choked me and pushed me off a balcony."

"You're sure it was the same man?"

"Of course. Who else?"

Instead of answering immediately, the detective looked at Nelson, who was being interviewed by another investigator.

"I notice you've been looking at that man," Slovaski told her.

She flushed. "Nelson?"

"What's your relationship?"

"None of your business."

"Miss Birdsong, you don't need to be afraid. If he's been abusive—"

"He saved my life!" she almost shouted.

"Doesn't mean he's always a good guy," the detective said quietly.

"He is! The only thing he ever forced on me was a second slice of pizza. And it was really good pizza."

Slovaski held his hands up. "I had to ask."

"Well, how about asking me about that lunatic who just about killed me tonight?"

"We will," the detective said and walked away to confer with the other investigators.

Glenda declined to go to a hospital, and the paramedics packed up and left. Police photographers arrived and began to enthusiastically record the bizarre scene. Forensics people with big black cases showed up to fingerprint or whatever it was they did.

Larry sidled up to her; there was no other word for it. He sort of moved sideways, glancing over his shoulder at the police investigators. He might as well have tattooed the word "*shifty*" on his forehead.

"Glenda," he whispered.

"What?" she replied loudly.

"Shhhh!" Larry looked around nervously. "I left something with you, and I need it back."

"So? That's a secret?"

"Not my dick. My gun."

"The gun? That was yours?"

"Shhh!" Larry sounded like a tea kettle.

"You put that thing in my bag?" she demanded harshly.

"Well, I sort of accidentally left it in the car, and then I realized I had it when I picked you up. And I couldn't keep it in the car when we got to the house in case somebody stole the car, and I couldn't carry it, because Sal had goons all over and my pockets were full of clown stuff," he said reasonably. "Where else would I put it?"

"Anywhere else," she hissed. "Why do you even have a gun?"

"It's part of the deal," he said. "You know, I sort of... deal. And my suppliers, they have guns and they don't respect you if you don't have one. It's like not wearing a tie to a ball game."

"Nobody wears..." Glenda said, then shook her head. "I could have killed somebody!" She didn't mention she'd actually tried to do precisely that.

"Naw, you couldn't. It was loaded with blanks."

"Why would you carry a gun loaded with blanks?"

"So I don't hurt anybody. I got it from a prop guy I know. It's just for show. What do you think I am?"

Glenda was tempted to tell him, but she didn't have the energy.

"Go away, Larry. I'll get your gun later," she said as Detective Slovaski returned.

He took her into the warehouse office, where she sat on a folding chair and sipped horrible coffee from a Styrofoam cup. The detective spent about twenty minutes questioning her about the two attacks and the threats Keith the keyboardist had made at her godfather's office.

At last Slovaski nodded and flipped his notebook shut. "Thank you. You should know that we're already looking for him. Keith Hanley has a record with us for disturbing the peace. Yelling at neighbors, that sort of thing. Also, he used to be a security guard at this warehouse. Must have copied the key. We got a warrant and searched his apartment. He lives on Orchard, about a mile from here." Slovaski shook his head. "This man is certifiable. He had a list."

"A list?"

The detective nodded. "Of people he intended to kill. You were at the top."

"So I'm number one with a bullet." It was a bad joke and the detective didn't bother to laugh.

"Miss Birdsong," he said. "We'll catch this guy. He doesn't seem like a shrinking violet. But you might want to keep your head down for a few days. Do you have someone you can stay with?"

CHAPTER FORTY-SEVEN

Glenda's sister opened the door and glared at her.
"Hello, traitor!"
"Good to see you, too," Glenda said.
"Who is that?" Glenda's mother yelled from the kitchen.
"Nobody important!" Abby shouted back. She sneered at her sister.
"Is that Glenda?" her mother shouted. "Let her in!"
"Where's your teeny-bopper boyfriend?" Abby asked. "Got tired of grandma?"
Smothering a growl, Glenda said, "Let me in, or I swear I will hit you right in the face with this suitcase and ruin your modeling career. You disturbed little twerp." She hefted the big leather case and pushed her way inside as her sister grudgingly gave way.
It was going to be a long week.

GLENDA DIDN'T REALIZE precisely how long the week would be until the third day, when she couldn't decide whom she wanted to kill the most: her sister, her parents or herself. She had told her parents she was staying with them because her apartment building was being fumigated.

Her sister watched Glenda silently at breakfast, giving her evil looks, chewing noisily and obviously aiming to annoy her. Abby overheard a phone call from Nelson and announced during dinner that Glenda was cradle-robbing. After that, their mother made poorly concealed attempts to solicit information from her about her love life.

Her father came home from the record store with new albums he insisted Glenda hear. Inevitably listening led to arguments, especially because her father seemed to have fallen in love with sappy Latin music. He'd developed a troubling affection for the boy band Menudo. Then he went on to Hawaiian guitar music. Two days of "Sweet Leilani" made her feel as if she were trapped in the Disneyland Tiki Room. She wondered if Dad was smoking something.

Wednesday night, she missed dinner and came home late to find her mother, arms crossed, standing at the door.

"Where were you?" Sophie asked frostily, looking up at her.

"I told you I was eating out with my friends."

"With that Nelson boy?"

"With *friends*."

"It's almost eleven o'clock. You could have called."

"Sorry," Glenda mumbled, wondering how she'd regressed from thirty years old to sixteen.

The final straw broke when Glenda caught Abby using her makeup.

"You don't need it," she told Glenda with a sneer. "It doesn't hide anything."

"Mom!" Glenda had shouted. "Abby stole my makeup!" A second later she blushed bright red and wondered how she'd gone from sixteen all the way down to twelve.

It was then that she decided she needed a plan. Damned if she was going to wait for the police to find Keith, if they ever did. She aimed to get her life back.

CHAPTER FORTY-EIGHT

Glenda was at work when she called Dot from Catwitch and explained what she wanted to do. To Dot's credit, she was enthusiastic.

Around noon, Glenda's godfather arrived to take her to lunch.

"You okay?" Marcus asked.

"So far."

"Your mother called me. She says it's a pleasure to have both her daughters under her roof again."

"Oh, great."

"And your father... well, *Menudo*? Really?"

"Yeah. He wants my mom to learn salsa. I think he's having a breakdown. Or I am."

"Mid-life crisis?" Marcus suggested. "Having your adult daughter around kind of makes you realize your age."

"I'm getting out as soon as I can."

"Probably for the best," Marcus said. "I love your whole family. But you are all so intense."

"I think you mean disturbed."

"Well, not boring, anyway."

"Right now, I'd settle for boring."

"Ah, right," Marcus said. "By the way, the police finally got around to telling me there's a maniac loose. Nice of you to mention it."

"Oh," she said. "I didn't want to get you involved."

"Involved? Honey, I'm on a list. A murder list! That's pretty involved, wouldn't you agree?"

"But I didn't know you were in danger."

"I'm at the bottom of the list." He paused and gave her a stern look. "Guess who's at the top. You should have told me. I'm getting you 'round-the-clock protection until this lunatic is behind bars."

"No, don't," Glenda pleaded. "That would spoil it."

"Spoil what?"

"The plan."

"What plan?"

"To smoke him out."

Marcus sat back, flabbergasted. "Glenda," he said. "Are you seriously thinking of taking this man on?"

"Not alone," she said. "Unless I have to. But I'm tired of being a victim. I want to lure him out. I want him to come after me."

Shaking his head in disbelief, Marcus said, "You want to be bait?"

"Yep."

"Did the paramedics treat that brain injury?"

"I'm serious, Unc."

"Glenda, Glenda. That is a... a bad idea."

"The worst," she agreed. "But it beats not doing anything."

"It's stupid and dangerous!"

"No, it's not. Waiting around with a target on my back is dangerous. And who knows if or when the cops will get him. I want my life back— such as it is."

Marcus sighed. "I'm not going to talk you out of this, am I?"

"Nope."

"Christ."

It was the first time Glenda had ever heard her godfather swear.

"All right," Marcus said. "You've got this plan all worked out, I suppose?"

"Sort of." She briefly sketched out her idea.

Marcus nodded. "Bone-headed, idiotic, and possibly lethal."

"But you'll help?"

"You're my godchild," Marcus said. "You're family. And you do anything for your family." His gaze held hers. "Whatever it takes, I'm in. What do you need?"

Glenda's lips quirked. "Buzz."

CHAPTER FORTY-NINE

The hair boys must be furious, Glenda thought as the limousine rolled east on Sunset Boulevard. With a week's preparation, every building corner and power pole had been plastered with gaudy posters that crowed: "Catwitch with special guest Glenda from the Glitter Lizards. One night only." For a whole half-mile, flyers for every other band in town had been ripped down and replaced. Not to mention the billboard at Sunset and Vine or the radio commercials. She hadn't had the courage to ask her godfather what he'd spent. She'd only thought Marcus might pull some strings and get her mentioned by a few DJs.

This was publicity on the scale of the Normandy invasion, but it didn't help Glenda's nerves.

Neither did the nicely groomed and polite men in the car with her who were apparently built of cinderblock, to judge by their jaws alone. Marcus had insisted on the arrangement despite her argument that she could catch a ride with Dot's people.

"Are they armed?" Marcus had asked.

"God, I hope not."

"You're taking the limo," Marcus said and meant it.

Glenda made Pasadena two hours before show time. Through the rain-speckled window, she saw a line in front of the box office. People stared curiously as the limo glided past. The show would be packed.

Looking up past the brilliantly lit theater and the milling crowd to see her name on the marquee, Glenda felt high on the anticipation of performing.

Then the limo turned down a dark alley toward the stage door, and she became somber and remembered she wasn't just an entertainer tonight; she was a worm on a hook.

Her shoulders tightened with fear. If this went wrong, she could die. Images of the corpses she'd seen rotated in her mind like a grisly carousel, with one empty horse.

After the limo rolled to a stop, her guards stepped out with neat, alert movements. One took a stand in front of the stage door. The other opened the car door. He leaned over from the waist and extended a hand.

"Miss Birdsong," he said, then politely hauled Glenda out of the seat.

The man by the door knocked twice and someone who could have been his twin opened it.

"Miss Birdsong," the new man said.

She was led through the door, and her limo guards vanished. Without a beat, two other men appeared from shadows and stepped smoothly in behind her.

"Evening, Miss Birdsong," they said in unison.

The door opened directly onto the backstage. The curtain was up, and the stage was lit like a car showroom, full of people taping down cables, stacking speaker boxes, and fiddling with microphone stands. Tech people huddled in clusters, talking to each other in their impenetrable jargon. Somebody played a guitar riff that squealed through a speaker.

"No, nope," an amplified voice boomed. That would be the sound engineer high up at the rear of the theater, she thought.

"Take it down," somebody onstage shouted back. "That sounds like a dental drill!"

It was comforting chaos. Glenda wanted to stop and watch, but someone ushered her into the wings and escorted her to a dressing room. A police officer stood in front of the door with a German Shepherd. Looking busier than the man, the dog had its head down and was single-mindedly sniffing. Apparently satisfied, dog and handler moved off.

Glenda's escort opened the door and she walked in. Dot lounged in a chair with her feet propped on the dressing table. She saw Glenda in the mirror, beamed and rose to greet her with a crushing hug.

"I love the decor," Glenda joked. "Hot and cold running cops."

"Yeah. I think they got you covered."

"Too bad about the drug dog." Glenda jerked a thumb to the door where the German Shepherd had been. "I could use a hit."

"It's a bomb dog," Dot said.

"Oh, great. Now I could really use a hit."

"Your wish is my command." Producing a joint from her makeup bag, Dot lit it with a skull-embossed lighter.

Glenda took a couple of guilty puffs and handed back the joint apologetically. "I wasn't gonna toke up before the show."

"Nobody's judging," Dot said. "With all this crap hanging over your head, I'd be worried if you didn't."

With a laugh, Glenda said, "It seemed like a good idea at the time."

"It's all gonna go right," Dot said. "We'll get this asshole, you'll get a record contract and we'll move up to fifty-two in the charts."

"Are you scared?" Glenda asked seriously.

"Naw," Dot said. "I'm not the target. Plus, I can duck. Another hit?"

"You are a terrible person," Glenda said as she reached for the joint.

CHAPTER FIFTY

When Glenda and the band stepped onstage for the final sound check, things seemed unusually quiet. Crew members who had been bustling only a short while ago now stood around looking wary and downcast.

"This is ominous," Susie the drummer joked, then stopped short and gaped. "Hey! They moved my kit. The whole riser's moved!"

Glenda saw the drums, normally dead-center in the back, were now at stage right and forward in front of a towering speaker bank.

Susie stamped her foot. "I won't be able to see you, Dot. And I won't hear the monitors with these stacks blowing in my ears! What the hell!"

"Hey!" Dot echoed. "They moved my mic, too."

No center-stage microphone stood there, Glenda saw. Dot's stand had been moved to just eight feet from the wings.

"What the hell is going on?" Dot asked. She eyeballed a cringing roadie and raised her voice. "Sandy! Are you on crack? What is this shit? What are you thinking? Fix it!"

"It wasn't their idea. It was mine," someone said from down in front of the stage.

Sitting in the first row was a small man in a black leather jacket. He had a ferret face, the scrawny build of a heroin addict, and he looked pale as a corpse. Getting up, the man walked easily to the stage stairs and climbed them, ignoring scowls from Dot and the others. When he reached them, he nodded at Glenda.

She noticed he had a lip ring.

"Hello, Miss Birdsong," the man said. "Ladies."

"You better have a damn good—" Dot began.

"I do, believe me. I apologize for the last-second changes, but I was just called in. The detective who was supposed to cover the stage setup has the flu."

"You're a cop?" Dot asked dubiously, eyeing him up and down.

"Lieutenant Springer, LAPD. I'm a detective. I normally work undercover vice."

"So?" Susie said sharply. "That makes you a stage manager?"

"In this case, it does," Springer said calmly. "Your safety is our responsibility. The changes are for your protection."

"I don't get it," Glenda said.

"It's a failsafe," Springer said. "We need to plan for every eventuality."

"And that means screwing up our layout an hour before we go on?" Susie asked.

"Less," Springer replied. "Doors open in forty-eight minutes and we don't want you unprepared. And yes, it was necessary."

"Okay," Dot said, sounding disgusted. "Cut out the Yoda act and just tell us why you moved every single piece of equipment we have."

"Because," Springer said, "if something unforeseen happens, you are going to need to get off this stage."

"Explain that," Glenda blurted.

"All right," he said. "Look. I believe that we have this place secured. Pasadena police have officers stationed all around the building. Your friend, Mr. Marcus Reid, has supplied additional security for the backstage, the wings and all street approaches."

Glenda thought of the granite-jawed men who had melted away into the shadows. Apparently, they were still there.

Springer pointed at the seats. "When the show starts, I'll be down there in the audience along with a team of undercover officers. We know what the suspect looks like. We'll be scanning the crowd in case he shows up."

"He'll be here," Glenda said grimly.

"That is the plan," Springer agreed. "And we're more or less expecting him to try to blend with the audience. But just in case..." he stabbed a finger upwards. "We're even sweeping the catwalks."

"But," Dot said, crossing her arms.

"But," Springer said, "there is a small chance he may get past us. If that happens, you don't want any bottlenecks as you exit this stage."

"You mean if he jumps onstage?" Glenda asked.

"Or opens fire," Springer said.

Nobody spoke. Dot and Glenda shared a shocked glance.

"Shit," Dot said.

"We'll just run off," Susie said.

"Which way?" Springer asked. "Left or right?"

The drummer looked over at her drum set.

"Oh," Susie said. "Right?"

"Right," Springer agreed. "Or, if necessary, you can shelter behind the riser."

"And that's why you moved the center mic," Dot said.

"Yes," Springer said. "Remember, if there is gunfire, there will be chaos. Everyone will be dashing for the exits, and that includes the crew. A few feet could make the difference between life and death."

Dot frowned, then nodded. "I understand," she said. "Put it back."

"Excuse me?" Springer said.

"Put my microphone back center," Dot said. "This is the way we rehearsed it. We've got marks to hit. Glenda's gonna sing a duet. We planned out every step. You can't expect us to start over now."

"You can still sing together," Springer said. "Just at different microphones. Hers is over there." Springer waved an arm at the other end of the stage, where a timid crew member was setting up a second mic.

"Oh, hell no," Dot said. "Then there's no interaction! It's like we're on different planets."

"You cannot sing at the same microphone, and the microphones do not leave their stands while Glenda is on stage," Springer said, an edge creeping into his voice. "If the suspect shoots at Miss Birdsong, he might hit you."

"Put it back," Dot said. "I'll take my chances."

"And put my drums back, too," Susie demanded.

"That's not gonna happen," Springer said and glanced at his watch. "Now we're losing time. I'd like you all to run through your escape routes."

"We won't go on then," Dot said.

"That is your choice," Springer said.

"Neither will I," Glenda said.

Springer spread his arms. "Then all this will be for nothing. And I understand, Miss Birdsong, that this was your idea in the first place. Do you want this man caught or not?"

"Of course."

"So do we," Springer said. "More lives are at risk than yours. There are eight names below yours on that list of his. So I'm sorry if you are inconvenienced, but I have to keep you safe, and this is how it's going down." Springer stared at all of them, his lips tight.

Glenda looked at Dot, who was several shades redder than she had been. Dot tapped her claw ring angrily against her thigh. She looked at Glenda. They shook their heads.

"Cops are dicks," Dot said.

"You are entitled to your opinion," Springer said. "Now let's get to work."

The technical run-through was a joke. Glenda and the band barely had time to block out changes. Crew members followed the band around like Labradors, taping down new marks in their wake. The lighting crew swarmed up the racks and the catwalks, adjusting spots and fills.

Technicians filled the rafters with curses as they struggled to rearrange four dozen lights while trying to salvage their original choreography, rearranging on the fly. It was chaos, but not the good kind where things were coming together. The only thing keeping Glenda from exploding was the pot she'd toked.

Dot and Glenda worked out a bit where, during the bridge of Glenda's third and last number, they walked to center stage, slapped hands in a high-five and retreated to each other's stands. It was lame, but it was the only concession they could wring from Springer.

They finally finished and darted backstage to dress.

"This is insane," Cath said as they walked. "We've only got fifteen minutes."

"So we'll be late," Dot said, unfazed. "Builds the suspense."

Glenda thought more suspense was the last thing she needed.

The dressing room held the familiar bouquet of cigarettes and musky perfume, underlaid with the skunk smell of pot.

Dot and the band bounced off the walls with excitement as they squeezed into their performance leathers. With black humor, Glenda thought that whatever happened tonight, it would be good for everyone. After all, there was no such thing as bad publicity.

Holding up a biker jacket in each hand, Dot asked: "Hey, guys: spikes or rivets?"

The lead guitarist, Deb, rubbed her pants with liquid shoe polish on a rag. Then came clouds of hairspray, the glossy application of lipstick and the cruel and unnatural teasing of hair.

Glenda had wanted to wear her lucky dress, a spangly mini a little bit too Diana Ross for the gig and was way too tight in the wrong places these days. But she'd have needed to wear heels with it— and you couldn't run very fast in heels.

Dot had made some sartorial suggestions to help Glenda blend with the Catwitch style, so she settled for a gold lamé tank top under a motorcycle jacket and the leather pants she'd worn on the night she'd met Nelson, even though they'd be running with sweat and chafing her thighs by the end of the set. She tucked them into her favorite Doc Martens, put on flaming crimson eye shadow and then wiped it off; it looked too much like blood.

When they were ready, Dot called everyone together. "Ritual," she said, taking Glenda's hand. The other band members clasped hands in a circle. Then they dropped their heads. Glenda expected a prayer. Instead, the band members growled: a long, deep, throaty sound that actually raised the hairs on the back of her neck. She tried to growl with them, but only managed to sound like a squeaky kitten.

The band members stopped growling and dropped their hands. Glenda thought they were through, but Dot raised her head, looked at each of the band members and spoke.

"Are we a girl band?" Dot asked.

"Yes," everyone answered.

"Are we cute?" She batted her eyes.

"No," they growled.

"Are we...sweet?"

"No!" they said loudly.

"Are we... pretty?" Dot feathered the word with a girlish giggle.

"Hell, no!"

"Then what are we?" Dot yelled.

"Harpies!" the drummer shouted.

"Hell-hounds!" the bassist screamed.

"Headbangers!" the rhythm guitarist yowled.

"And," Dot finished, "after tonight, we won't be number fifty-three in the charts."

"No! No way!"

"After tonight, we will be... *fifty-two*!"

Everyone erupted in laughter and then spontaneously began chanting, "Fifty-two! Fifty-two! Fifty-two!"

In exactly fifteen minutes, a knock sounded on the door. A man with a skull earring poked his head inside.

"Ladies, are you ready, or you need more time?"

"We are ready," Dot said.

"We're always ready," purred Kimberly, eyeing him. "Are you?"

"Sorry," the man said, grinning. "I'm holding out for Klymaxx."

"Aren't we all," said Kimberly. "Lead on."

Dot, having chosen the spiked jacket, went first, avoiding the door frame. Glenda came next, followed by the others. Security men watched them, and Glenda suddenly became aware of the murmuring audience just beyond the lowered curtain.

The musicians moved to their positions onstage, except for Dot. She stopped and faced Glenda. "You okay?"

"Yeah," Glenda said. "I loved your pep talk."

"Well, tonight you're one of us," Dot said. "We've got your back."

"I know. Thanks."

"No, thank you. It's a blast. And I am going to love singing with you." Dot produced an impish smile. "Hey, as soon as you come out, let's move the mics center stage. Screw that cop!"

Glenda laughed. "Can't. The lighting guys changed everything. They'd have a fit."

After giving her a perceptive look, Dot then offered a genuine smile. "I know you're worried about this lunatic. But there are a hundred guys out there watching for him. That's their job. Yours is to get out there and make those people scream and love you. You're gonna do that, right?"

"Right."

"It's your chance, Glenda. Rock doesn't give you many of those. *Own it.*" Dot punched Glenda on the shoulder. "Remember, the only thing worse than dying is dying onstage."

"Ouch. But seriously, Dot, if anything happens..."

Dot shook her head so hard, her mane of hair waved. "I'm not worried."

"Why not? I am."

"Focus," Dot said. "Nicole and your boy Nelson are in the front row. Sing to them." She hugged Glenda, careful not to skewer her on her jacket. "Did your tits get bigger?"

"Shut up," Glenda said with a laugh.

"See you in a couple," Dot said and went to her place.

CHAPTER FIFTY-ONE

Things weren't good. The band started off briskly, but everything was just a little bit off. Susie, stuck off to one side and unable to see Dot's cues, started the second song too soon, and everybody scurried to catch up.

Playing ferociously, they were full of energy but sounded like a garage band. Cath, the bassist, flubbed two runs in a row. Dot, distracted, repeated the same verse twice in her signature song, *Nightshade*.

It felt like watching dancers at a high school prom, trying to avoid stepping on each other's toes.

Dot cursed and walked over to Glenda's mic, where the drummer could clearly see her. She tapped the mic and swore again. Glenda knew what had happened. Springer had made sure that mic was dead until Glenda came on. The detective was not going to allow any changes to his safety plan, thereby chaining Dot to her own mic.

By the time Catwitch swung into *Broken Focus*, ironically, they were in disarray.

Each mistake made Glenda's stomach churn. They didn't deserve this; they were better than this. It wasn't their fault that they didn't sound good. The fault lay with the stage changes.

And that, she thought guiltily, was all on her. If she hadn't asked to be part of this, Catwitch would have been pulling that whole crowd to its feet. Instead, the fans seemed grafted to their seats. They were tolerant and good-natured but not engaged. She felt them marking time, just waiting for the headliners.

This was supposed to be Catwitch's big break. Instead, they'd be just another forgotten warm-up band.

At the end of the third song, Dot glanced at Glenda. Dot's hair was plastered to her face. Her lips were twisted in frustration and disappointment. But her eyes gleamed. Glenda saw the will in those eyes, the determination. Dot was a pro.

Like the captain on the *Titanic*, she thought. It broke her heart.

Without thinking, she threw back her shoulders and strutted out onstage.

For a moment she wondered what the audience might be thinking, watching this big girl wander out with a brassy, curly mass of hair topping her head like a sea creature on a reef. But she moved purposely to Dot, who showed no surprise. Glenda saw no judgment in Dot's face, either; only strain and determination.

Dot covered the microphone with her hand as Glenda spoke into her ear. "We need to kick this," Glenda said. "Let's do *Screechers*. Right now."

"That's the finale," Dot said.

"Because it's awesome, and that's what we need," Glenda said. "I'm at the other end of the stage. The drummer can see me, and I'll follow you."

"Springer will choke."

"He won't turn off my mic, though." Glenda said with a smile. "Come on, everybody out there's wondering what the hell we're talking about. Make 'em scream and love you, remember? That's the job."

"That's the job," Dot said, her lips quirking for just an instant. She gave the smallest of nods. Glenda turned and walked back to her own microphone, putting more sway into her hips than was absolutely necessary.

Then she silently made a small prayer, telling the Universe that Dot and the others didn't deserve the ration of shit they were eating for helping her, and if the Universe didn't step up, then the Universe was just an ungrateful bitch. She reached down and tapped her microphone with a fingernail. The speakers gave corresponding little pops. The mic was hot. Springer was letting the show go on. He'd given in. It was a bitter little triumph.

Dot, meanwhile, grabbed her own mic. "Hey!" she said to the crowd. "You know who that is?" She pointed at Glenda.

"There were a few shouts of 'Diarrhea!" and a smattering of 'Glitter Lizards!'"

Dot let the scattered chuckles die. "That is Glenda Birdsong," she said at last. "Our special guest. And we were just talking about what we'd like to do for all of you." She gave an exaggerated hair flip, the tangled skeins gleaming, topping it with a sighing groan. Glenda had to admit the gesture was masterful: sexy and dangerous at the same time. It drew catcalls and hoots.

Now Dot had the crowd's attention.

"We're gonna do a song for you now that we call—" Dot paused, then said, stretching out the syllables, "*Scuh-reechers!*" She spoke loudly to make sure the band— especially Susie —caught the set change.

Glenda could almost hear the rustling of paper as the lighting crew frantically turned to the cues for the finale. She caught Susie's eye and pointed to herself and then to Dot. The drummer caught the message and gave an acknowledging rap on the snare.

Glenda held her breath. This felt like being poised at the top of the hill on a roller coaster ride, ready to plunge.

The stage lights dimmed. Two spotlights burst into brilliance, painting Dot and Glenda in ice and shadow. The singers stood poised in the cones of light like taut statues.

Glenda let out a silent breath, waiting. *Don't be a bitch,* she prayed to the Universe.

Drum taps and guitar chords as Susie and Deb began the intro. Together. Perfectly together. A staccato conversation, not a messy squabble.

Glenda blessed the miracle even as she counted off the beats in her head, felt their syncopation in her chest like a second heartbeat.

Susie caressed the drumheads rather than pounding them, adding the shimmer of cymbals.

Glenda let the music carry her. She wasn't fighting them— or anybody.

Her performance at Gazzarri's had been built of rage and frustration and a half-bottle of Jack. She'd been fighting free of darkness and had raged at the audience.

This would be an *offering*.

She bent to her microphone. Across the stage, Dot did the same.

"*I have never wanted you the way I want you today,*" Glenda crooned. Her voice was silky and dark.

"*I love the way you make me hate,*" Dot replied in her cigarettes-and-whiskey purr.

The duet was a honky-tonk tease, a mutual seduction.

Glenda sensed the audience responding. The restless flutter died. She and Dot drove on through the first verse. Building the pace, first Glenda and then Dot sang a line. They got faster and wilder until they were hurling lyrics back and forth with a clenched-fist intensity.

Susie struggled to keep up.

Glenda and Dot joined their voices for the bridge, but they barely slowed down. After the chorus, Glenda and Dot and all of Catwitch just let go. The song became a street riot.

Susie thundered on the drums while Kimberly and Deb made their guitars scream like dying souls. The crowd surged to its feet.

By the final chorus, all Glenda could see of the audience was a forest of pumping fists. The crowd's roar battered the auditorium.

As the song wound up, Susie was machine-gunning beats and hammering the cymbals. Deb's guitar screeched notes almost too high to be physically possible. The stage shook as the audience stomped to the beat.

When the song came to a blistering end, Glenda panted like a wounded buffalo. She was exhilarated.

As the crowd continued to roar, Glenda and Dot shared a look, and then they both laughed.

Together, silently agreeing, Glenda and Dot left their microphones, walked to the center of the stage and embraced. The audience erupted in cheers.

Nothing needed to be said after that except the name of the next song.

Glenda bowed, waved a hand to the audience and began walking offstage. Dot returned to her mic and shouted: "Thank you. Thanks! You rock, Pasadena!" She paused to let the resulting roar crest and subside. "Now," she went on. "Some of you may have heard this next song, but you ain't heard it done right. Glenda Birdsong!" Dot shouted at Glenda's retreating back. "Get your guitar, honey. Let's get *In the Flow*!"

Dot's words stunned Glenda. She'd meant to cut her set short now that Catwitch was back on track. But somebody thrust Banshee at her. Automatically, Glenda looped the strap over her head and felt the guitar's familiar weight on her shoulder.

Standing at her mic again, Glenda looked at Dot, who grinned wickedly. Glenda shook a finger at her. Dot gave an exaggerated shrug, then swept an arm out to the audience and back at Glenda. Dot stepped away from her mic and grabbed a tambourine, banging it against her thigh. Susie heard the tambourine and picked up the beat.

Glenda strummed the opening chord on Banshee, let it reverberate, and raised her hand high, ready to unleash her voice.

She was *back!*

But before she could sing a note, there came a ripping metallic squeal like the worst feedback she had ever heard. Her cone of light moved a foot and a half to her right, leaving her suddenly in the dark. Glancing up at the lights overhead, she thought she saw a shadow moving on the catwalk. She picked up the mic stand and took a couple of steps, following the wayward light. She cursed inwardly at the tech crew. Now, thanks to their screw up, the band was ahead of her. Glenda had missed the beat and would come in late.

Her annoyance was just turning volcanic when it was cut short by an immense crash.

The world fell on her.

CHAPTER FIFTY-TWO

Glenda opened her eyes.

"Where's the Devil?" Glenda asked.

The balding man with the stethoscope standing over her bed blinked.

"Did you see him just now?" he asked in a faint European accent, peering at Glenda seriously.

"No," Glenda said. "Last weekend."

"What happened last weekend?"

"That's the last time I got knocked out. I woke up, and the Devil helped me." Glenda noticed the doctor's expression and added, "It was Halloween."

"You were knocked out?" the doctor asked. He unclipped a penlight from his pocket.

"A fall," she said, deciding not to mention she'd been hurled off a balcony by an insane clown. "It wasn't serious. Mild concussion."

"Well," the doctor said as he shined the light into each eye. "Looks like now you've had two. But let's make sure this is a mild one, okay?"

"Okay."

"Your speech sounds fine. And you can hear me all right? Any ringing?"

"No."

"Blurred vision?"

"No."

"Do you have any nausea?"

"No."

"Count backwards for me please, from fifty."

Glenda got to thirty before the doctor stopped her.

"Now hold up two fingers, please."

That's when she noticed she couldn't move her left arm, which was wrapped in a big white plaster cast.

"What happened?"

"We'll get to that," the doctor said calmly. "Just use your right hand."

She moved her right hand.

The doctor nodded. "Now squeeze my hand."

Glenda gripped his fingers firmly.

"Good. How's your head?"

"Hurts. Like everything else."

"Hmmm. How badly, on a scale from one to ten?"

"Not as bad as my arm," she groused.

Her answer raised a smile from the doctor. He leaned back. "Well, it appears you do have a mild concussion. Surprisingly minor, considering. You struck the stage when you fell, and you've got a pretty big goose egg on your noggin. But I don't see any sign of cognitive deficit."

"What happened?"

"What do you remember?"

"I was playing and then I heard a noise. I blacked out, and here I am."

The doctor nodded as if her answer confirmed something. "There was an accident onstage. You were struck by some equipment, and it knocked you down. It dislocated your shoulder and caused a displaced fracture of your left radius and ulna. As I said, your head hit the stage. That was really my biggest concern, but I think you'll be fine."

"What fell on me?"

"I think I'll let the gentleman waiting outside go over that with you." The doctor put a hand on Glenda's shoulder— not the bandaged one. "I'll be back to check on you." He patted her and left the room.

Glenda heard him say to someone outside in the hall, "No more than five minutes and don't agitate her."

She recognized the voice that answered.

Springer walked into the room, wearing the same black leather jacket. Without asking, he took the chair, moved it to Glenda's bedside and sat. "How are you? Do you feel up to answering a few questions?"

"Yes," she said. "If you answer mine first. Did *he* do this?"

"We believe so."

"Well, did you get him?"

Springer blew out his cheeks, then said, "Yes. Yes we did."

She felt a gust of relief. "Sweet Jesus. What happened?"

"He was up on the catwalk," Springer said. "He used a power saw to cut the safety chains on a lighting rack."

"That's what I must have heard!" Glenda broke in. "A metal shriek. I thought it was feedback."

Springer nodded. "What else did you notice?"

"Nothing," Glenda said. "I looked up and saw a shadow, something moving up there. I thought it was a lighting tech."

"It was Keith Hanley. He cut the chains, and the whole lighting truss came down. About a quarter-ton of equipment. If you hadn't moved, you'd be dead."

"The light," Glena said. "My spotlight moved, and I had to follow it."

"I saw that," Springer said, with as much animation as Glenda had yet seen in him. "When he cut the chains, the last link must have stretched before it broke, so of course the lights would move out of position." He almost smiled. "So he didn't think of everything."

"But I thought you searched the whole place. How did he hide up there?"

Shaking his head, Springer said, "You won't believe this guy. He gutted one of the air conditioning units on the roof and hid inside the housing. We think he was up there for days, judging by the bottles and wrappers and whatnot. He didn't come down until just before you went on. So when we searched the catwalk, it was clear."

"So, how did you get him?"

"He went back to hide in the A/C housing. Like a rat in a hole. But he was moving in a hurry."

"And?"

Springer snorted. "He knocked over his slop bucket."

"His what?"

"He had a portable camping toilet. He knocked it over, and the smell led us straight to him."

Glenda had to laugh, and then winced. "So what happens now?"

"He's been booked for attempted murder. But you remember he had a list. We're checking to see if anyone on it has died under suspicious circumstances. If so, this guy may be facing a murder charge."

"Unless he's too crazy to stand trial," Glenda said.

"Then he goes to a mental hospital until he's fit to be tried. At any rate, you won't have to worry about him anymore." Springer made a show of looking at his wristwatch. "Well, that's five minutes." He stood. "Miss Birdsong, on behalf of the Los Angeles Police Department, thank you for your help. We wish you a speedy recovery." He walked to the door, put his hand on the handle, then stopped and faced her. "By the way, I think you were right about the microphone. You belong at center stage." Then he was gone.

A nurse came in sometime later and gave Glenda two pills. The next thing she knew, Glenda woke to morning light streaming through a window and to Nelson, collapsed in the chair like a gangly discarded puppet. He had a day's worth of fuzz on his chin, and the spikes in his hair drooped.

She yawned.

Nelson stirred and opened his eyes. "Hey. You're awake."

"I am. Were you here all night?"

Nelson echoed her yawn, throwing out his legs and arms in a massive stretch. "I've slept in worse." He uncoiled himself from the chair and went over to her. "How do you feel?"

"Achy and starving."

"Cool. There's a magic button right there. You press it, and a nice lady comes in with food and pharmaceuticals. And after you eat, we'll get you checked out."

"Don't use the words checked out. I nearly did that last night."

Looking solemn, Nelson said, "Oh shit, Glenda. When I saw those lights fall on you, and you hit that stage, I thought it was all over."

"Well, I don't remember it, so let's forget it. You heard they got him?"

"Yeah. That detective told me."

"So. Happy ending. I can get my life back."

"Well, in about six weeks. That's when you get your cast off."

"How do you know?"

"The doctor told me."

"Why would he tell you?"

Nelson smiled. "Because I'm your brother."

"Oh," she said archly. "You are?"

"Sure. Why else would they let me stay here all night?" He smiled.

Glenda thought he actually dimpled. "Oh, brother. Hey, you can't be my brother. That's against the law."

"Not in my state."

A nurse knocked on the door and came in, took Glenda's vitals and left her a couple of pills and a cup of water. Following the nurse came an orderly, who brought ham, eggs, bacon, oatmeal, coffee and orange juice. Nelson helped himself to the OJ and Glenda attacked the rest— clumsily, because of her cast.

"Did anyone call my parents?" she asked between mouthfuls.

"Oh, they were here," he said. "I think about two in the morning. You were asleep. I was worried."

"Why?"

"You didn't snore once. I kept thinking you'd died."

"I snore?"

"It's cute. Anyway, your mother cried and hugged me. Your dad shook my hand. Your sister cried and hugged me *and* shook my hand. She thinks you're a superhero, by the way."

"That's a change," Glenda said. "How could I have slept through all that drama?"

"And you didn't even snore," Nelson repeated. "You gonna finish that bacon?"

Glenda pushed the plate toward him.

"That wasn't all. Dot and Nicole were here for a while. Nicole had bad news."

Glenda's mouth went dry. "What? What bad news?"

He wiped his mouth and looked serious. "It's... it's Banshee. I'm afraid she didn't make it."

Glenda's heart sank. "Oh, no. I loved her." She made a dismal sound.

"I know. I'm sorry," Nelson said. "The neck just splintered. The pickups got smashed, and the body split. There was nothing anybody could do. They let Nicole take her. We're gonna have a funeral."

Glenda swallowed hard. "Damn it."

"But hey, you're alive," he said, taking her good hand. "And listen, we knew you'd take it hard, and maybe this is too soon, and Nicole wanted to wait to tell you—"

"You're babbling," she cut in. "Just tell me."

"We got you a replacement. You know, for when you get the cast off."

Stunned, Glenda murmured, "You mean you got me a guitar?"

"Yeah. A beauty, Glenda. I mean, I had a hard-on for this thing the moment I saw it. We couldn't find you a Flying V on short notice but we got you—" he paused dramatically. "We got you a PRS."

Her mouth went dry, again. "Are you kidding me?"

"No. Custom 24. Twin hums and everything. It's not red. It's magenta pearl!"

"Oh, my god. Guys, you can't! Those things run, like, two thousand dollars."

"We wanted to do this for you," he said. "Actually, it was Nicole's idea."

"I can't let you do this."

"You deserve it. You put your life on the line."

Glenda shook her head and held back tears. "I don't know what to say. When can I see it?"

"Nicole will bring it over."

Glenda laughed. "It's so funny. Backstage, I was ogling one just like that. You know, the one Laurie plays in Klymaxx."

"Yeah," Nelson said, looking distinctly uncomfortable. "Nicole thought you'd like it."

Something in the way he said it made Glenda put down her fork. "Wait. Nelson. You aren't telling me something."

"Like what?" he asked in a very poor imitation of innocence.

"Like where did you pick up a guitar like that in the middle of the night?"

"Friends in high places," he said. "Now if you're done, we've got to get you packed."

"Where," Glenda said firmly, "did you get the PRS, Nelson?"

"Nicole got it," he said defensively. "She sort of managed to get onstage in all the confusion after you were hurt."

Glenda looked at him with dawning horror. "You don't mean..."

"I wouldn't play it until Klymaxx has left town."

"You are taking it back!" she said. "A guitar is a baby. You stole Laurie's baby!"

"Not me. Nicole!"

"Well it's going back."

"Now?"

"No," Glenda said. "In six weeks. After I've had a chance to play it."

CHAPTER FIFTY-THREE

Three weeks later, Glenda went to her godfather's office for lunch. She decided to walk because she was taking a break from work and had the time. High clouds dotted the robin's-egg blue sky, and a crisp breeze wafted away the worst of the city smells. Since the concert, the gloomy weather had lifted. *A bit like my life,* she thought. The doctor had implied she might get her cast off early, since her arm was healing so nicely.

Larry had called to tell her he was going off to India because he'd received a call from Yanni. Larry had kept hanging up on him. But the new-age musician had finally convinced Larry he was legitimate and wanted him to drum on his world tour. The publicity from Larry's bizarre kidnapping had actually borne fruit.

"Speaking of which," he said. "I'm mailing you my key. Could you leave some fruit or Oreos or something for Ganesha every week or so? I owe him big-time."

"It's a statue, Larry," she'd said.

"Please. I don't want end up in an Indian jail."

"You're not gonna deal...?" she'd asked, aghast.

"No, I'm out of that business. I'm a paid musician, now."

"Oh, joy." Glenda felt sorry for Yanni and the audience. "Well, I'm glad you got religion."

"I didn't. I can't worship other gods. Ganesha might get jealous."

"They have a lot of Ganeshas in India," she reminded him. "You can worship him there."

"No way! That would be cheating."

"Larry, it's the same god everywhere. The statues are all of the same god." She heard him sigh over the phone.

"I don't think you get this, Glenda." Larry hung up.

Meanwhile, the chance of prison no longer hung over Glenda's head. Her probation officer had signed off without a qualm. Springer must have put in a good word for her, because the officer seemed to consider her a model of rehabilitation. He didn't even warn her to keep her nose clean. She almost expected him to hand her a lollipop, like a dentist rewarding a child who had no cavities.

Keith, she'd been told, had been charged with four murders: Bernie's, the accountant's— the body in the bathtub was presumed to be Fink's— and the stripper and her girlfriend. It turned out Keith had once dated the stripper whom Glenda thought of as Blondie, but whose real name was the prosaic Karen Davis. What Glenda had believed was a murder-suicide actually had been a disguised double killing. She had prudently decided not to tell the nice young officer who gave her the news that she'd been at the scene of every single death. Some things were better left unsaid.

The upside, as her godfather was fond of saying, was that publicity from her near-demise had won Glenda a slew of offers. She'd already done several interviews, and Marcus told her some of the less sleazy bids for her services were worth pursuing. As he was also working hard to iron out her contract details, their get-together was partly a working lunch and a partly celebration. Knowing she would order at least three mimosas gave her another reason to walk.

Strolling into Marcus's office, the sound of a ringing phone smote her ears. Nobody picked it up. Marcus's secretary had evidently vanished. Strange grunting noises came from behind the closed door of the inner office. For an instant, she wondered if Marcus was in there with Ellie. Maybe she didn't know her godfather as well as she thought. But then she heard a sharp cry behind her. She turned and saw Ellie, who had walked into the office, holding a paper bag from a Chinese restaurant.

"Glenda!" Ellie said. "What in the dickens is going on in there?"

After peering at Ellie, Glenda swiveled and rushed to the inner door, which wasn't locked. She threw the door open.

Keith had her godfather bent over the desk and was throttling him. Marcus, never a strong man, had turned purple as he pawed weakly at Keith's face.

Keith wore a canary-yellow jail jumpsuit and an ear-to-ear grin. His nose was covered in dirty white surgical tape. He looked up and saw Glenda's horrified face. His grin changed to a rictus of hate. Letting out a guttural yowl, he hurled Marcus off the desk and sprang over it like a panther.

Before Glenda could move, he was on her. She smelled his stinking breath as he punched the air out of her and slammed her against the office wall. He shrieked nonsense, spraying her with his spit. Possessing the strength of the maniacal, he delivered another blow that caught Glenda on her injured shoulder, which instantly exploded in pain. By a lucky blow, she lashed out her cast-wrapped arm and struck him squarely on his bandaged nose, which fountained blood. Keith screamed and stumbled, allowing her to duck and break his clinch. Raising her arm, she slammed his chin with her cast. She heard a crack and prayed it was the plaster and not her forearm.

Staggering, Keith kicked out, connecting with the side of Glenda's thigh, which hurt like hell. He grabbed her once more, and they crashed against a wall of shelves holding her godfather's trophies and awards. Plaques and statuettes toppled. Keith managed to pin her against the shelves with his body. Spitting blood and curses, he began choking her.

Her arms were pinned, and her vision began to dim as she twisted desperately. For an instant, her bulk countered his strength advantage, and a gap opened between them. She thrust up her arm, breaking his hold, then swung the cast with all her might against the side of his head.

Keith dropped like a stone. Glenda bent and hammered him a couple of times for good measure, his body flopping limply with each blow. Finally, when she was sure Keith was unconscious and pretty sure he wasn't dead, she rose and stood panting over the supine body like a prizefighter in a photo.

Only then did she look around. Her godfather was on his knees, one hand on the side of the desk, trying to rise. He levered himself into his chair and waved Glenda away with a weak smile when she approached.

Looking around at the carnage that had been Marcus's office, Glenda saw glass and broken bits of statuary littering the carpet. Mechanically, she bent down and picked up a Buddha that miraculously had survived the fall intact. She looked at it. The figure sat serenely on a stone base bearing a brass plaque. Dazedly, Glenda read the inscription: "To Bernie Sherman for humanitarian services to music and musicians worldwide, and for spreading brotherhood and harmony." She studied it for an instant, then put the Buddha carefully back on a shelf, turning it this way and that as if to make sure the little god was exactly back in his rightful place, serene and secure. She was still fiddling with the statue when the police arrived.

CHAPTER FIFTY-FOUR

The police took Glenda to an emergency room where she was probed, prodded, X-rayed, dosed with pain pills and given a new cast. Her arm, luckily, was only bruised. Still, the injury would add a couple of weeks to her recovery.

Marcus came by to thank Glenda for saving his life, to her stuttering embarrassment, but his voice was raspy and he stayed barely long enough to hold her hand and give her a kiss on the forehead. Still, it was long enough for her godfather to say everything that needed to be said.

Springer walked into the ward as she sat on the edge of the exam table and a nurse helped her on with her jacket. She decided it was lucky for the detective that she'd downed a couple of codeine pills before his arrival, or she would have torn his head off.

For once, however, Springer had an actual expression on his face, and it was not happy.

"As soon as that freak escaped, I tried to call you, but you weren't at work and you didn't pick up at home. I even sent a patrolman out to try to find you."

"I was on my way to lunch. How did he get away? I should have thought you'd have a serial killer chained to a wall somewhere."

"He was in solitary and on suicide watch," Springer said stiffly. "But he had court this morning, so we put him on the jail bus. The bus stopped at another jail to pick up some more inmates. That's when he got out." Springer laughed bitterly. "He'd been heading to a sanity hearing."

"And he walked all the way to my godfather's office? And nobody saw him? A guy in a yellow jail suit with a broken nose?"

"I'm sure lots of people saw him. But it's Hollywood Boulevard."

She couldn't argue with that. "So what happens the next time he gets out?"

"Well, first he has to get out of the medical ward. You did a number on him. He has a fractured skull. And anyway, he's a flight risk. When he can be moved, we're taking him to Castaic, which is maximum security. He'll be on lockdown. He won't be finding his way back here. The next time you see him, he'll be wearing a suit for court. Or a straitjacket."

GLENDA SLEPT WELL THAT night, thanks to medication and her own exhaustion. She dreamed she was picking up shards of the broken trophies in Marcus's office and piecing them together.

Around three in the morning, she bolted awake.

One piece wouldn't fit.

CHAPTER FIFTY-FIVE

Glenda walked into Marcus's office and palmed the door closed. Her godfather was on the phone at his desk. He glanced up as she came in and gave a little wave.

"Harry, my goddaughter just walked in. Let me call you back." He hung up. "Hey." He smiled at Glenda. "How are you? How's the arm?"

Glenda raised the cast slightly. "Fine," she said, tonelessly.

Marcus frowned. "Anything wrong?"

"You might say that."

Marcus motioned her to a chair, but she remained standing just inside the door. He frowned again and asked, "Are you in trouble? What can I do?"

Instead of answering, she walked stiffly to the wall shelves. The trophies— all that were undamaged or salvageable —had been restored to their places. She glanced over them, then turned to face her godfather. "You have a lot of awards, Uncle."

"Thanks, I think." He appeared confused by her remark.

She ran a hand along the shelf, stopped and let her finger rest on the Buddha. "This is my favorite."

"Yes, it's nice. Honey, are you all right? Maybe you should sit."

Continuing as if she hadn't heard him, Glenda hefted the Buddha in both hands. "It's heavier than it looks."

"Some kind of stone," Marcus said. "Glenda, baby, what is going on?"

After carefully replacing the statue, she turned her gaze on Marcus. "Do you think people who get these awards deserve them?"

Marcus gave her a sharp look. "You mean me? Well..."

"Not you. Bernie."

Marcus looked at her silently for a moment, then nodded. "He wasn't always a louse. I know he screwed you, but back in the day, Bernie did some good things. Sometimes this business brings out the worst in us." Her shook his head and added: "If you're thinking about the contract, I'm working on it." He pointed to a box full of papers that was perched on top of a filing cabinet. "Bernie's affairs were convoluted and tangled and Byzantine." He sighed. "I wish his accountant were alive."

Glenda gave a little humorless laugh. "But he's not. He died in Bernie's home. I saw the body."

"Oh, honey, I didn't mean to bring that up." Marcus's forehead creased in concern. He started to rise but something in her expression made him sit down again.

"When I was in Bernie's house that night, I noticed he had a shelf full of Buddhas in the living room," Glenda said, almost to herself. "I guess he collected them. But there was a space. One was missing."

"I don't understand."

"Imagine my surprise," Glenda said, staring at her godfather, "when I found it here."

After a moment of astonishment, Marcus chuckled. "Well. I hate to admit that Bernie beat me at anything, but the fact is I won mine the year after Bernie got his."

"This isn't yours," Glenda said, her eyes hard. "I read the inscription when I was here last time. I picked up the statue after the fight. This isn't your award. It's *Bernie's*."

"That's ridiculous—" Marcus began.

Snatching the statue off the shelf, Glenda strode over and thumped it on her godfather's desk. "Read it yourself."

Marcus picked up the statue, read the inscription and seemed puzzled. "What the hell. I don't understand."

"I think you do. Everybody thinks Keith killed the accountant and then Bernie."

"It does seem likely," Marcus said. "After all, he tried to kill you. Twice, or is it three times?"

"But there's a difference," Glenda said, eyeing Marcus sharply. "I was on the list. The accountant wasn't. The detective showed it to me." She leaned forward and said softly: "Why would Keith kill someone he hadn't marked for death?"

"Glenda, he's crazy."

"Crazy. But not inconsistent. He was systematic."

"We can't know," Marcus said, spreading his hands. "It could have been an impulse killing. Or maybe it was just what it looked like: an accident."

Glenda shook her head. "Then why make everybody believe Bernie was the body in the bathtub?"

"Well, then what are you saying?"

"You made an angry call to Bernie that night. Then you went over to his house. The accountant was there. You got into a fight with Fink, grabbed this Buddha statue and hit him. You didn't mean to kill him; you're not a killer by nature. Then you got scared and ran off. But you took the murder weapon and you put it here on the shelf. You hid it in plain sight."

Marcus laughed. "And where was Bernie when I was committing this murder?"

"He probably ran off. He was terrified that you'd kill him, too."

"It's a good scenario. Except that I never went to Bernie's house that night."

"Bullshit."

"I was furious with him," Marcus acknowledged. "Yes, I called but I never went over there. I was at the Blue Room in Pasadena. Your father was jamming there, and we had drinks after the set. I had a vodka martini. Your father had a virgin Bloody Mary with a celery stick." Marcus picked up the phone. "Here, call him yourself."

Glenda shook her head, knowing Marcus wouldn't lie about an alibi she could break with a single telephone call.

Marcus blew out his cheeks and raised his hands. "Here's what I think happened. I called Bernie and raised hell. Bernie swore he had nothing to do with stealing your song credit, but I know he did. He promised to call his accountant, and I think he did. He wanted Fink to hide his tracks. So Fink comes over, but maybe he tries to blackmail Bernie, or maybe he's just had enough of Bernie's bullshit. There's an argument and Bernie— who, let's not forget, was probably coked to the gills —goes into a rage and kills Fink. With that." He pointed to the Buddha on the desk. "Then *Bernie* drags the body upstairs and dumps it in the tub to make it look like an accident. And then, he has a bright idea. He's going broke. He owes everybody. Let's say the accountant was skimming off the top.

"Physically, there was a resemblance. So Bernie decides to *become* Fink. He gets to vanish and he gets Fink's money, or so he hopes. And from what you told me, Fink identified the body in the bathtub. Or I should say, Bernie *pretended* to be Fink and identified the body as his own. Simple identification for a simple accident. Case closed."

Glenda was about to challenge that scenario by saying she'd seen Fink alive *after* the body was found, the night she and Larry helped him remove paintings from the house. But really, in the dark all she'd seen was a man with dark glasses and a hat and a bad case of flu that made him whisper.

It *could* have been Bernie in disguise, she admitted to herself but then shook her head.

"No. That doesn't solve the problem. You're forgetting something: Somebody killed Bernie for real *after* the accountant was killed."

Marcus goggled at her. "You think I did it? Glenda!" He looked hurt. "*Keith* killed Bernie. The police said he made it look like a break-in gone bad."

Shaking her head, Glenda said, "But I found the answering machine tape hidden in Fink's home, the one where you and I both appear to threaten Bernie. Why hide that tape? What's on it only mattered to two people, Marcus: you and me. And I have no money. A blackmailer wouldn't look at me twice."

Marcus's face went blank and his shoulders rose slightly.

"Maybe Bernie did kill Fink," she continued. "But *you* killed *him*. He was blackmailing you with that tape, wasn't he?"

"Glenda, please sit down," Marcus said wearily.

Cautiously taking the chair in front of the desk, Glenda lifted her plaster-enveloped arm like a shield.

Marcus rubbed a hand over his face. "Look, honey. Yes, yes, Bernie blackmailed me. But you've blown it way out of proportion. I mean, murder? Come on. Glenda, you've known me as long as you've been alive."

"I'm not so sure of that anymore," she said quietly. "What happened?"

"All right. Bernie called me out of the blue. I almost had a heart attack. I thought I was talking to a ghost. Then he plays the tape, the same as he did with you."

"And then he asked you for money."

"Yep. I thought about refusing, but then I figured it was worth paying him a little to keep you and me out of trouble."

"How much is a little?"

"Twenty thousand." Her eyebrows shot up and Marcus shrugged. "That's small change to solve that problem."

"But he was a killer."

"Bernie swore it was an accident. And who am I to question that? I wasn't there. And even if he did kill Fink, I didn't have any proof."

"But you could have called the police and told them Bernie was alive."

"And then he would have given them the tape. It was a Mexican standoff, Glenda. It was just easier to pay Bernie so he could get out of town."

Nodding, Glenda decided his story made sense. "Except, blackmailers never stop."

"Maybe he wouldn't have, but he did. I went to Hollywood Park with a briefcase full of cash, gave it to Bernie, and that was the last I heard from him."

"But he didn't give you the tape."

"He gave me *a* tape," Marcus said bitterly. "I should have known it wasn't the only one."

"So when did you find out Bernie had a copy?"

"When you told me. After you got the phone call."

"And you never saw Bernie or heard from him until I told you about finding his body?"

"What is this, an interrogation? Am I on trial?" Marcus held up one hand as if taking an oath. "Ladies and gentlemen of the jury, I solemnly swear that I had nothing to do with Bernie Sherman's death. Can we adjourn now, Madame Prosecutor?" He shook his head in annoyance.

Glenda didn't move. "If I'm wrong, Uncle, I'm sorry. Just one last question."

"Shoot."

"Why did you ask Nicole how to get to Fink's house in Palm Springs?"

Marcus looked stunned. "I... Uh—" he stopped abruptly.

"You'd agreed to drive me to the house, so why would you need directions? I had them."

"My secretary said you'd left without me. I thought I'd better get out there."

Glenda gave him a level stare. "Nicole said you called her *before* I left. I called her and checked this morning."

Marcus said nothing.

"Here's what I think," she continued. "Bernie must have blackmailed you again. You figured out he was impersonating Fink and guessed he was lying low in Fink's house. You decided enough was enough, so you went out there and—" She couldn't finish because she'd suddenly flashed on Bernie's body on the bedroom floor. "Then you came home. You planned to drive back with me on Sunday. That way, you'd 'discover' the body and I'd be your alibi. But I screwed up your timetable. I went early. I went *Friday*."

Looking around as if seeking a place to hide, Marcus sighed. He stood, picked up the statue, read the inscription thoughtfully, then walked to the trophy shelf and placed it carefully back in its place. When he returned to his desk, he opened a drawer, rummaged inside and lifted something out, which he held out to Glenda.

It was another Buddha, in two pieces, the head broken off from the body. "You know. You think you've covered everything," Marcus said. "No loose ends, nothing to unravel. And then it all goes to hell because of some clumsy woman with a broom." He gave Glenda a look of disgust. "My cleaning lady. She must have knocked my Buddha award off the shelf some night when she was dusting. She got scared and switched them. I'd put Bernie's award in my desk drawer. She probably found it when she was looking for glue or something. And then you just happened to notice the inscription after the fight in my office." Marcus laughed mirthlessly.

"Where did you get Bernie's Buddha?"

"When I took that paperwork." Marcus pointed to the box atop the filing cabinet. "I found the Buddha at the bottom. God knows why Bernie kept it. I stashed it."

"Why didn't you get rid of it?"

"I was going to. It was the last detail."

"No, it wasn't. You didn't find the answering machine tape."

"Nobody's perfect. Bernie told me it was in a post office box. When I was in the Palm Springs home, I... *persuaded*... him to give me the key. At that point, he had no reason to lie. Or so I thought." Marcus laughed again. "When I opened the post office box, all I found was a stack of gay porn."

Still holding the pieces of the heavy statue, Marcus leaned over toward Glenda. She jumped up and backed away.

He looked stricken. "You don't need to be afraid of me, honey. I would never hurt you."

"I used to believe that."

"You know that!" He placed the pieces on the desk, took a breath and then slowly sat down, his focus still on Glenda. "Everything I did, I did for you."

"Oh, no!" Glenda said, shaking her head angrily. "Don't you put this on me."

"But it's true. It wouldn't have mattered if Bernie had just threatened me. But he was blackmailing me with *you*."

"What do you mean?" she asked.

"Your threats on the tape. Bernie knew he could threaten to send the tape to the police. And even without it, he could steal more of your songs, and he had your original contract. I would have fought him, but he could have tied me up in court for years and meanwhile, your career would be dead. Bernie held your future in his hands." Shaking his head, he said softly, "And it's like you said. Blackmailers never stop."

"I would have been all right. I can take care of myself."

"Oh, really? When have you ever done that?" He didn't give her time to reply. "How many times did I warn you not to sign with Bernie, not to put your money into a solo career, not to sign that contract?" he said, his voice rising angrily. "Your parents despair for you. They ask me when you're going to finish your album, when you're going to grow up. But you don't! You're like a child who sings nursery rhymes while wandering on a railroad track."

"You're rationalizing," Glenda's voice rose to match his. "You can't justify this!"

"And you can't be trusted! You almost died three years ago, and even *that* didn't wake you up. And you almost died *again* three weeks ago!" Giving her a pained look, he said, "You're all I have. I love you like my own daughter but *you keep screwing up!* You pretend you're in control; you might even believe it. But you control nothing. So I had to save you. Again." Marcus pulled a handkerchief from his breast pocket and mopped his face.

Glenda stood silently for a moment, then slowly approached the desk again and sat down. Her broken arm twinged. She'd been clenching her fist. "Nobody asked you to take charge of my life. It's my life to screw up. And I sure didn't ask you to murder anyone. You can't put that on me."

"What choice did you give me?"

They avoided each other's eyes for a moment, then Marcus said, "I'm sorry to cause you pain."

Glenda laughed joylessly.

Looking down at his desk, Marcus picked up the Buddha's head and tried to place it back on the body, twisting it this way and that. When he took his hand away, the head toppled.

"I can't fix it," he said at last. He glanced at Glenda. "Any ideas?"

She looked away. Then she rose and went to the door. Her hand was on the knob when Marcus called out behind her.

"Hey," he said. "You still believe in the Boo-Boo Fairy?"

She stopped with her back to him. When she was five or six years old, she'd been terminally clumsy. When she fell and scraped a knee or elbow, Marcus would tell her that the Boo-Boo Fairy would come and take away the pain. The fairy would lock up all that pain in a big vault in a castle across the sea so it could never return.

Turning on her heel, she faced her godfather. "No," she said firmly. "I don't believe anymore."

With a bittersweet smile, he said, "Me, neither. It's funny. She was so real once. I miss her." After staring at the phone on his desk, Marcus closed his eyes and took a slow breath. He opened his eyes and picked up the handset.

"Ellie," he told his secretary. "Get me the police."

Marcus put a hand over the mouthpiece. "You'd better go. I'd rather you weren't here when they come."

His attention went back to the phone, and he removed his hand from the mouthpiece. "Yes, I'd like to report a crime."

"Wait," Glenda blurted.

One of his eyebrows lifted. "One moment, please, officer," he said, and put a hand back over the mouthpiece.

"Don't," Glenda mouthed. She strode over, pushed the hang-up button and cut the call.

"What are you doing?"

"I can't let you do this."

His expression took on a thin edge of hope.

"No," she spat out. "It's not about you. It's for my mom and dad. It would destroy my father to learn what you did. What you are."

"Glenda—" he began, but she cut him short.

"I can't be near you anymore, though. I can't watch you smiling and laughing and joking with my family as if nothing had happened. You aren't innocent."

He hung up the phone and spread his hands. "What do you want from me?"

"Nothing. I only want what's mine." Her expression held no affection.

Marcus slumped in his chair. "You still owe an album under the contract."

"I think," she said slowly and distinctly, "I'm done owing anything to anybody. I paid those dues." She looked at her godfather, a man she had known all of her life and had never known at all.

There was an uncomfortable silence, then Marcus said, "No. I guess you don't. I'll release you from the contract."

Glenda nodded.

Marcus said, "I'll send you the masters for the album."

"No." she said. "Burn them."

"All right," Marcus said, resignedly. "So that's clear. Anything else?"

"No."

"We're done?" Marcus asked quietly. His shoulders were slumped and his eyes looked lost. He seemed shrunken and defeated.

"We're done," Glenda said.

EPILOGUE

"You look like shit," Nelson said.

"Sweet talker."

"Can I come in?"

Glenda opened the apartment door and let him in. Nelson sniffed. The room had the funk of burnt TV dinners and stale takeout. Glenda had been living on junk for the past week. She was suddenly aware of her own funk, which came from the oversized sweatshirt she'd been sleeping in for days.

"Are you sick?" he asked, worriedly. "Arm hurting?"

"Not really." She raised her cast. "It comes off in a week."

"I couldn't reach you and you didn't call. You didn't return my calls."

"I've been working out some... things."

With a nod, he said, "Well, after all the crap you've been through, you're probably not feeling very safe."

"It's not that. I just had some issues to work out." She thought of her godfather, who had left the country after telling her parents that he was going overseas indefinitely on business.

"You look like somebody died."

She swallowed hard and looked away. "Feels like that."

Nelson gave her a keen look. "This isn't something you want to talk about."

"Not right now," Glenda said.

"Well, you know, here I am. Whenever."

Glenda smiled for the first time in a week. "How do you do that?"

With a frown, Nelson asked, "Do what?"

She shook her head and her lips quirked. Even after what he had gone through in his own life, with his mother and everything else, here he was, willing to share her pain. And he said it so casually, so easily, without drama. She envied him his self-assurance. She wanted to be as grounded as he was.

All of a sudden, it seemed as if there were better things to do than to be despondent. *Black isn't always my color,* she thought.

"Hey," she said suddenly. "You hungry?"

After washing quickly with one hand— Glenda had perfected the skill since getting the cast —they headed to an El Pollo Loco where she had her first healthy meal in a week: citrus-marinated and fire-grilled chicken, according to the menu.

Nelson, who amazingly had never visited the chain, was fascinated by the long grill covered in dozens of chickens, their carcasses splayed out like headless sunbathers. The cooks used long tongs to flip them over, flames shooting up between the golden bodies. The smoky smell was mouth-watering.

Nelson wolfed down four pieces of chicken with black beans and rice, and followed them up with two churros. "I had my first churro when I got to L.A.," he said around a mouthful of fried dough. "I called 'em donut sticks."

Glenda passed on the grooved, sugar-and-cinnamon-crusted treat. She felt proud of herself. She and Nelson talked for an hour about absolutely nothing. She loved it.

Back at her apartment, she gave Nelson a goodbye kiss.

He didn't leave.

GLENDA JOLTED AWAKE and lurched up in bed. A noise had awakened her, and it took her a moment to interpret it.

Someone had opened her front door.

She reached out to wake Nelson.

The bed was empty.

The front door closed with a soft click.

She felt a surge of panic. Before she could do anything, however, Nelson walked into the room.

"Did I wake you? I tried to be quiet."

Glenda tried to slow her thumping heart. "It's all right."

He sat on the bed. "I went to visit Mom. You were sleeping, and I didn't want to disturb you. I borrowed your key."

"Oh. How is she?"

With a shrug, he said, "A little worse, a little better. It's hard to tell. For a moment, I think she recognized me. But she's thinner."

He accepted Glenda's embrace. His hair against her shoulder smelled of hospital disinfectant, tobacco and a trace of her own perfume.

"It's all right," she said soothingly.

Nelson sighed and lingered in her arms. Then he straightened up and peered at her. "I'm going to see her again tomorrow," he said, then paused and added shyly, "Do you want to come with me?"

Glenda swallowed. "You want me to meet your family?"

"Just my mom."

Glenda hesitated. He'd said the words casually, but there was tension in his face. This wasn't just meeting a relative. He was inviting her into the most private part of his life. She truly didn't know if she wanted that. She was rock n' roll. Intimacy wasn't bred in her bones.

And Nelson was so *young*.

If she went down this path, her brain warned, somebody could wind up being hurt.

So what, her heart replied. She'd been hurt before. The wound she sustained by the loss of her godfather gaped for an instant, but she tried to ignore it.

She'd survived pain. So had Nelson. Truckloads of it. They'd been hurt, and they would be again. But in the meantime, maybe there could be joy.

So *fuck* pain. For now.

Glenda took a deep breath and exhaled. She felt shaky. Her hand reached out tenderly to Nelson's face. "Yes. I'd like that." She clasped his nose between her knuckles and gave it a light tug.

"Got your nose!"

She *sucked* at intimacy.

THE END

Don't miss out!

Visit the website below and you can sign up to receive emails whenever J.R. Waterbear publishes a new book. There's no charge and no obligation.

https://books2read.com/r/B-A-ILVLB-WMRWD

BOOKS 2 READ

Connecting independent readers to independent writers.

Also by J.R. Waterbear

Killswitch
Hollywood Bodies

About the Author

J.R. Waterbear is the pen name of Southern California writers John Pulver and Robert Jablon.

Pulver's stories have appeared in various publications. He has won the Roselle Lewis Fiction Writing Award and co-hosts The Natural Muse, a group that connects authors with the joy and inspiration from writing in nature.

Pulver knows the 1980s Hollywood music scene well. As a young punk, he haunted the clubs where his musician friends played and moshed his way into near-infamy. The highlight of this dissolute existence was being kicked out of the famous Starwood for using drugs (he wasn't; it just looked that way).

Many years later, Pulver doesn't regret his wild youth and returns to it in spirit with "Hollywood Bodies."

Jablon is a former journalist who lived a block or two down from Sunset and Vine. He owns a Les Paul replica electric guitar and, through hard work and passionate devotion, he has now learned eight chords and hopes to double that number in the coming years. He once saw the Red Hot Chili Peppers in Hollywood before they got famous. They weren't wearing their dong-socks. He thought they were too noisy.

Milton Keynes UK
Ingram Content Group UK Ltd.
UKHW041918280824
447551UK00001B/85